Feeding the Beast

by

Richard Greene

-

Edited by Barbara Bowers

Editorial Review by Manybooks.com: Feeding the Beast by Richard Greene

A fast paced and brutal story, made complete by depth of character and excellent twists. Set in the 1950's, thirty years before the term 'serial killer' would exist, Richard J Greene's book is gripping in both its plot complexity and its investigatory thrill.

Detective Dan Morgan has plenty of internal demons to battle, but this particular demon is real and grows ever more demanding for its own battle. The teenage girls the killer slaughters are oddly treated -- staged, with a missing finger. The treatment of the bodies after death show an eerie tenderness, which is contrasted sharply by the immense violence during the murder itself. These things disturb our investigator, who has already suffered a lot in his life.

Still reeling from the tragic loss of his wife to cancer only two years before the first killing, the death of his daughter, and estrangement from his son, Dan Morgan doesn't have a lot to fill his spare time. However, when this particular criminal starts to correspond with Morgan, revealing a little more of their personality with each word, suddenly his time is not his own and his life is no longer the sad but safe routine he had retreated in to.

The book deals with historical policework quite well, as policing in the 1950's was very different from the way things are done today. This is more than the lack of certain technologies but a deeper attitude shift towards the job, the victims, and the world view of the character we follow through the story.

With a story so violent and brutal there needs to be a softer aspect, and although Greene achieves this through tragedy and relatability – Detective Dan Morgan is ultimately a sympathetic character despite his flaws. This book teeters on the brink between a modern murder mystery and noir, Greene has done well to weave them together because, without due attention, the two could easily have clashed.

Readers of historical fiction with a taste for murder as well as noir fans will find something to like in Feeding The Beast. Those more dedicated to modern true crime may find the characters' alarm at the violence and nature of the murder somewhat over the top. The way Greene's characters find the violence incomprehensible is almost naïve, and this genuinely adds to the atmosphere of ruined innocence that pervades the story.

Be prepared to want to read the whole book in one sitting, this page turning story and cast of well-developed characters is spellbinding.

This book is a work of fiction. Names, characters, places, and incidents are the product of the author's imagination or used fictitiously and are not to be construed as real. Any resemblance to actual events, locales, organizations, or persons, living or dead, is entirely coincidental.

Richard and his Lhasa Apso Jackson

About the Author

Richard Greene was born in Denver, Colorado, in 1939 and grew up in a small two-bedroom house in Englewood, a suburb of Denver. In 1954, his parents divorced, and his father moved to Houston, Texas. Soon after that, Richard dropped out of ninth grade, worked at various jobs, including sacking groceries at a local supermarket and as an electrician's apprentice for a neighbor. He spent his summers with his dad, who owned 'The Texan' bar on the outskirts of Houston, Texas, where he got an education in life unlike his friends back in Englewood, Colorado. In August 1956, at seventeen, Richard enlisted in the United States Navy. After boot camp and Yeoman School in March 1957, he was transferred to the USS Belle Grove LSD-2 (Landing Ship Dock), serving in the South Pacific and took part in the atomic testing at Eniwetok and Bikini Atolls in 1958.

Honorably discharged in 1960, he worked at Samsonite Luggage for a short spell and then went to work for Burlington Truck Lines as a billing clerk. The trucking industry fascinated Richard, so he attended Denver Traffic School to learn the trucking industry's ins and outs. He worked as a dock supervisor for United Buckingham in Denver and a sales representative for Californian Motor Express in Fresno and Los Angeles, California. Moving back to Denver, he went to work as Claims Prevention Manager for Consolidated Freightways, which included investigating road accidents of CF trucks within 100 miles of Denver. After a year with Consolidated, he was transferred from Denver to the General Claims Department in Portland, Oregon. In 1973, Richard left the Claims Department to become a supervisor in the Collection Department for Consolidated, where he remained until his retirement in December 1995 as Manager of Collections.

Still residing in Portland, Oregon, Richard, and his wife Cathy spend much of their time with their children and grandchildren. Richard's other interests are golf, long walks, reading, and oil painting.

Please visit my web page, www.richardjgreene.net, or visit me on Facebook at https://www.facebook.com/richardgreene.7393 or on Twitter at https://twitter.com/@dickiejoe All of my books are available on Amazon as ebook or paperback.

Contents

Prologue

1951

The Second World War has been over for six years, and the United States is now involved militarily in Korea, termed a Police Action rather than a war. On April 10, President Harry S. Truman fired General Douglas MacArthur as Commander of the United States Forces in Korea. This action resulted in the President's lowest approval rating of 23%, which remains the lowest of any serving president.

The Denver Police Department, protecting a population of fewer than 415,000 residents, was small compared to cities such as Chicago, New York, and Los Angeles.

The use of DNA by the judicial system is far in the future. Electrically powered streetcars are the primary transportation source and will soon be replaced by electric buses. Computers are in their infancy, and while most old newspapers and other public records are on microfilm, thousands of documents are not. Not every home can afford a television, so the radio remains the household's nightly entertainment. The closest thing to a cellular telephone is Dick Tracy's two-way wristwatch found in the comics, so the police must rely on rotary telephones and shortwave radios. Being Mirandized is not an option a criminal is given in 1951 and will not be available until 1966.

The term "serial killer" will not be coined by FBI Special Agent Robert Reesler until 1970.

*** One ***

Denver, Colorado

Monday - April 2, 1951

11:50 PM

Larimer Street, on the lower west side of Denver, Colorado, in 1951, was no longer a respectable street of businesses and homes as it once had been. Over the years, it had deteriorated into a place inhabited by addicts, drug dealers, alcoholics, and prostitutes. It was not uncommon to witness a fistfight, knifing, or shooting over something as simple as someone sneaking a drink from another's bottle or over the attention of a whore. It was a street lined with the bright, multi-colored neon lights of bars, small cafes, pawnshops, cheap hotels, and just a few honest businesses leftover from the old days. Although the lower west side streets were places that most decent people avoided, Friday nights often found cars of families parked along the street watching that night's entertainment.

A quick, light spring rain had fallen, and the wet street reflected the neon lights in a rainbow of colors as Homicide Detective Dan Morgan turned his black 1949 Ford off 15th Street onto Larimer Street. Turning off the radio playing a tune by Tommy Dorsey's band, he drove toward the corner of Larimer and 16th Street. Slowing as he approached the corner, he turned left onto 16th Street and drove toward the alley separating Larimer and Curtis Streets.

Three 1950 Ford black and white patrol cars with their parking lights on were parked facing the curb, their red taillights reflecting off the wet street. Just beyond the patrol cars, a white van with the word Coroner on its side with its parking lights on was parked across the sidewalk at the entrance to the alley. Its single rear door was open.

The headlights of Detective Morgan's black Ford lit up the small, curious crowd that had gathered along the sidewalk of the narrow cement alley that disappeared into the canyon of three and four-story dark brick buildings. As the front wheels of his Ford came to a rest against the curb, Dan turned off his headlights and engine. Sitting back in the seat, he took a deep drag from his cigarette while staring out the windshield at the curious, silent crowd.

A dark figure approachedand tapped on the car's window, saying, "You can't park here."

Ignoring the figure, Dan reached over to the passenger seat, picked up his brown fedora hat, slipped it on, and climbed out.

1

The officer grinned as he stepped back. "Sorry, Detective, I didn't know it was you."

Dan glanced around the scene as he greeted the young officer in a tired, raspy voice. "Sammy."

The young officer looked up at the night sky. "Looks like the rain stopped, Lieutenant."

Soft thunder echoed along 16th Street and down the alley between the buildings separating Larimer and Curtis Streets. Dan filled his lungs with smoke from his cigarette and then dropped it into a dark puddle that quickly swallowed up the bright red tip. Exhaling the smoke from his lungs, he looked up at the black, starless sky, smelling the fresh air that always follows a spring rain. Recalling his wife, Norma saying she loved the freshness the rain brought with it.

Shutting the car door, he turned his attention to the sidewalk and the curious faces reflecting the red, yellow, green, and orange colors of neon lights. He saw fear, worry, and even delight on their faces over the night's excitement that took them away from their monotonous life of booze and drugs.

Officer Sammy Price was twenty-four, husky with brown hair and eyes, new to the force, and like all rookies, was assigned traffic and crowd control. He leaned toward Detective Morgan, looking secretively, glanced around, and lowered his voice. "There's a body of a young girl up the alley."

Detective Morgan glanced at the faces in the crowd and then at two uniformed officers standing in the center of the alley's entrance, making sure no one, especially reporters, made their way into the alley. Another officer, standing next to the hotel, was talking to a well-endowed girl Dan recognized as a prostitute or a local, as some officers called the girls. The neon sign 'Rooms' with the second o burned out, colored their faces in a foggy red haze. Recalling a coffee shop around the corner on Larimer Street, he looked at Officer Sam Price. "Do me a favor, Sam," he said, reaching into his pocket. "I need a cup of coffee, and I'm sure my partner could use one. Would you mind --."

"Glad to," interrupted the eager young officer.

Dan pulled his hand out of his suit pants pocket and began sorting through the coins for fifteen cents. "Sue's Café is just around the corner on Larimer."

"Save your money, Lieutenant. It's on me. Anything in them?"

Dan smiled appreciatively but handed the coins to the officer anyway. "You have a wife and baby, Sam, and I make more than you. Take this and get two cups of black coffee for Jack and me and one for yourself."

2

Officer Price grinned as he stepped back. "I'll get them, Lieutenant." Then he turned and hurried toward the sidewalk.

Dan hollered after him. "I'll be in the alley." Then he stepped over the curb onto the sidewalk toward the buzzing, flickering red neon sign spelling out '*16th Street Bar*'. Pushing his way through the sea of endless questions that he had learned a long time ago to ignore, he walked toward the alley and the officer talking with one of the locals.

A woman's voice called out, "Hey, Lieutenant."

He stopped, turned, and let his eyes search the faces until they found a girl he knew only as Ruth Spencer by her rap sheet (police arrest report), or Ruthie, as her friends called her. He watched with curiosity as she pushed her way through the crowd wearing an unhappy expression.

Dan Morgan forced a small smile. "Hello Ruth, how's business?"

Ruth was a local who earned her money on her back, and her arms often carried the bruises of her pimp. She was a pretty girl, young, thin, small-breasted with dark brown hair, big brown eyes, and long legs. The type of girl you just knew was good at her profession. Over the months, Dan had arrested her for prostitution several times and had conducted a few discussions with her pimp Curley, whose real name was George Peterson, about how he treated his girls. Once Dan had tried to talk Ruth into leaving Curley, even offering to pay for her fare back home, wherever that may have been, but she just smiled, said no thanks, and walked away.

Ruth glanced around while eagerly chewing her gum and looked up into Dan's blue, tired eyes while gesturing with her hands. "Ain't making anything with all this going on."

He half grinned. "Well, I'm sure you'll make up for the inconvenience."

She didn't look convinced but did look worried. "Tell that to Curley."

Dan's hand disappeared under his topcoat, and when it reappeared, it was holding several business cards. He took one and returned the others to the pocket of his suit. "Take this, Ruthie, and tell Curley if he has any problems about tonight, he can give me a call."

She smiled as she took the card, slipping it into her small purse. "Thanks, Lieutenant."

Dan smiled. "Take care of yourself, Ruthie." Then he turned and pushed his way through the crowd toward the entrance to the alley, wondering why a girl like Ruthie stayed with an asshole like Curley. As he approached the officer standing at the alley entrance, the local saw him, turned, and hurried across the street, disappearing into the night.

The officer looked at Dan and nodded. "Evening, Lieutenant."

3

Dan reached into his topcoat pocket, pulling out an open pack of gum, and looked past the officer up the dark alley. A car he assumed was a police car was sitting in the middle with its headlights illuminating the scene. Several men were milling around in the bright lights and shadows, busy with flashlights and flashbulbs. "Hello, Charley." As he continued to stare up the alley, he noticed the figures of three men lit up by the car's headlights standing over two other men kneeling over something he knew was the body Officer Sam had referred to earlier. "That local you were talking to, did she have anything to say about what's in the alley?"

Officer Moore shook his head. "Nah, she was just wondering what happened. I told her I wasn't sure, and when she saw you, she took off."

Dan smiled. "I have that effect on women." Dan pulled out one stick of gum and put the small package back into his pocket. He peeled the wrapper off the single stick, shoved the gum into his mouth, and rolled the foil paper wrapper into a tiny ball as he began to work on the piece of gum. "Who found the body?"

Officer Moore gestured toward the window of a cheap hotel. "I believe it was the white trash inside the lobby talking to Bassich."

Dan flicked the tiny ball of foil into the darkness, turned, and looked past Officer Moore into the window of the cheap hotel. A skinny, balding man was sitting in a chair wearing a soiled, unbuttoned plaid shirt over a well-worn undershirt. He needed a shave and appeared nervous as he talked while staring at the notepad Officer Bassich was writing on. A fat, balding hotel clerk, also in need of a shave, was standing behind the counter watching the two. On the other side of the crowded lobby, two officers took notes while talking to a clean-shaven man and woman who looked like they didn't belong on the lower west side. He guessed they were gawkers out for a little excitement on Larimer Street. Returning to the crime scene, he asked who was in the alley.

"Your partner Jack Brolin, a couple of uniforms, the coroner, a couple of his men, and the crime lab."

Dan watched the flashlights in the alley as they leaped from this to that, occasional flashes from the cameras of the coroner and the crime lab. For some reason, he thought of Officer Moore's young daughter. "How's that little girl of yours?"

Charley smiled. Much better. Doc says the surgery on her leg was a success, and we can take her home next week."

Dan grinned as he patted Moore on the shoulder. "Glad to hear it." Then he stepped into the alley, and as he chewed his gum, he made his way around some small puddles left by the light rain that reflected the lights up ahead. Approaching the 1951 Ford, whose lights shone on the crime scene, he recognized the car as his partner's.

4

Dan Morgan was a little lean and in good shape at forty-one, standing five feet ten inches. He had graying thick brown hair, blue eyes, and a square jaw in need of a shave. The gray suit and topcoat he wore were a little wrinkled, and Dan still had not managed the haircut Captain Harold Foley had told him to get over a week ago. His curious, tired eyes went from the puddle he stepped over to the flashbulbs and flashlights lighting up the busy scene. Coming closer, he recognized his partner Jack Brolin's hatless head and Coroner Pete Lange kneeling over a body.

Dan knelt beside them, careful not to soil his topcoat, greetedLange, and asked his partner, "How long have you been here?"

Jack looked up. "Not long. Sorry about calling you at home this late, but I thought you'd want to see this one."

The body was that of a young girl dressed in a red skirt, white blouse, and a jacket with a big white E for East High School sewn on the right front chest.

"I had nothing else to do," said Dan Morgan. *It* was not sarcastic; he honestly had nothing else to do. His wife, Norma, the only woman he had ever loved, had died painfully two years ago from pancreatic cancer, and next month would have been their twenty-third wedding anniversary. Now, his life was a lonely existence of meals eaten out or takeout food partially eaten, and the rest tossed in the garbage. There were the occasional offers of dinner from Lori Brolin, his partner's wife, or an occasional neighbor, both of which he often politely refused. Eating with other families only intensified his loss and loneliness.

Dan and Norma's marriage had produced two children, a boy named Robert and a girl named Nancy. Sadly, five years ago, just two days after her eleventh birthday, Nancy had been killed by a hit-and-run driver while riding the bicycle Dan had given her for her birthday. Shortly after that, Dan and his son Robert became estranged, and a few months after Norma's death, Robert left Denver, taking up residence in Chicago, Illinois. In those last two years, Dan and his son had not spoken. The only communication Dan received was an occasional postcard from his son that never carried a return address and contained only two scribbled words: 'Doing fine.' Dan kept all nine cards in a neat stack in date order in the middle drawer of the living room desk.

Dan stared at the body lying on a piece of cardboard and asked Pete Lange, "What can you tell me, Doc?"

Coroner Pete Lange was a short, middle-aged, plump man with blonde balding hair that he kept in a crew cut. His face was round, his eyes brown and covered with round, wire-rimmed glasses that sat on the edge of a small nose. He turned his flashlight to the left side of the young girl's neck and pulled the hair away, exposing a small cut or puncture in the jugular vein. Pete softly said, "Exsanguination was most likely the cause of death. I'll know more after I perform the autopsy."

Dan looked at the pale white face of the victim. "How fast would she bleed out, Doc?"

Pete shrugged. "Small cut like that. I imagine it took a few minutes." He looked at Dan and then back to the girl. "It'd be like getting tired and going to sleep."

Dan Morgan stared at the pretty face. "Then she knew she was dying?"

"I'm sure she did," answered Pete as he lifted the girl's left hand. "Small finger is missing at the top knuckle. Whoever did this knew what he was doing."

"Shit," said Dan as he looked at the pale hand with the missing finger wondering what terrible things she could have gone through before she died. "Tell me that was post-mortem."

"Sorry, Dan," said Pete. "The hand has been cauterized. She felt it." He pointed to her head. "Strange that her hair is damp, but her clothes are dry."

Dan's eyes went from the girl's hair to her clothes. "That is strange."

"The girl's hair is neatly combed," said Pete. "My guess is whoever did this washed her hair and combed it."

Detective Brolin gestured to another piece of damp cardboard leaning against the brick wall of the building. "She had been covered with that piece."

Dan's eyes went from the body to the cardboard and back to the girl's pretty face. "Can you offer any theories, Pete?"

"I can't right now," said the coroner. "I'll know more after I get the body back to the morgue and onto one of my tables."

Dan's thoughts went to his daughter lying on such a table in Pete's morgue.

"Lieutenant Morgan!" called Officer Price.

Dan looked up at the young officer holding two paper cups of hot coffee. He stood and stepped away from the body, still considering the pieces of cardboard.

"Here's your coffee, Lieutenant."

Dan reached for the cups. "Thanks, Sam." Handing one cup to his partner he said, "Sammy bought."

Jack smiled at the young officer. "Thanks, Sammy."

"My pleasure," replied Sam while taking a quick look at the body. "She sure was a pretty girl."

Dan handed his coffee to his partner and took off his topcoat. "Put this on the front seat of my car if you would, Sam?"

Officer Price took the coat. "Sure thing."

"Keep an eye on the coat. I'd hate to think someone down here was wearing it while sleeping in one of these damn alleys or doorways."

"Don't worry, Lieutenant. I'll keep my eye on it." Officer Price turned and headed for the street toward Dan's car.

Dan took his coffee back and looked down at the body lit up by the headlights of Jack's car. Carefully peeling the thin cardboard lid off the paper cup, he put the cup to his lips, feeling the warm steam on his face, and took a quick sip, careful not to burn his mouth. Thinking it tasted good, he considered the cardboard again. "Our killer placed the cardboard under the blanket so it wouldn't get wet and then that piece over the victim so she wouldn't get wet."

A puzzled Jack Brolin looked down at the girl as he sipped his hot coffee. "Why take the time?"

Pete stood. "I'm about done here." He looked at Dan. "I'm not sure if Todd and his men are, so try not to move anything."

As Pete walked away, Dan glanced around, looking for Todd Anderson with the crime scene squad, and found him standing a few feet away, talking to one of his men. Glancing down at the girl as he walked past her, he said, "Hi, Todd."

Todd turned. "Don't have too much for you right now, Dan."

Dan gestured back toward the body. "Is it okay if Jack and I have a look around?"

"Go ahead, just don't move things around too much."

Dan started to turn away but stopped. "Did you find a purse or any identification?"

Anderson shook his head. "No. We're searching the area and trashcans for her purse or billfold." He gestured to the cardboard. "Don't touch the cardboard. We'll be checking it for prints."

Dan started to say he knew better but decided to let it go, turned, and walked back to his waiting partner, who was staring down at the body while drinking his coffee.

Detective Jack Brolin would soon turn forty-one and was looking forward to a long vacation in the sun in a few weeks. Standing five-eight, he prided himself on working out at the YMCA located a few short blocks from the police station. Jack was clean-shaven with brown eyes and graying black hair combed straight back. While he was not a big man, he was clever with a quick temper and unafraid to toss the first punch, having learned years ago the advantage of doing so. Since grade school, he and Dan had been friends, played football in high school, and served in the

7

army MP's together while attached to the Rangers in Europe. Both took part in Normandy's invasion and the infamous 90-foot climb up the cliffs at Pointe du Hoc. Jack and his wife Lori were high school sweethearts and had one son who was away at college. When Dan's wife died, it was Jack and Lori who helped him through the weeks and months that followed.

Careful not to block the headlights from Jack's car, Dan squatted down and looked into the open blue eyes of the young girl. She was lying on her back with her eyes staring up into the dark night sky of black clouds. As Jack knelt next to him, Dan silently agreed with Officer Price about her being pretty and guessed her age to be fifteen or sixteen. He leaned closer to look into her pale, white face and open blue eyes while he took a sip of coffee and thought of his identical twin brother murdered thirty-three years ago. The clanging bells of a trolley car passed the other end of the alley heading up 15th Street, and as the sound faded, his memory returned to that cold January afternoon in 1918.

Eight-year-old Daniel Charles Morgan was upstairs lying on his bed reading Tom Sawyer when he heard an automobile outside. He set the book down, slid off the bed, walked to the window, and looked down at a 1917 Model T Ford police car at the curb that had left a line of tire prints in the fresh, white snow. The door opened, and a police officer dressed in his blue uniform and blue hat climbed out and closed the door. Hesitating for a moment, he walked up the shoveled walk, disappearing under the snow-covered roof of the front porch. Charles Morgan, the boy's father, was a police officer, so Daniel thought nothing of it and returned to his bed and Tom Sawyer's adventures.

The sound of the front door closing made its way through the thin walls, followed by the sound of deep muffled voices, and then silence. Moments later came the sobbing screams of his mother yelling out, "Please, God, please," making their way up the stairs. More curious than afraid, Daniel set the book down, hurried off the bed, opened the door, and walked along the railing, stopping at the top of the stairs. With one hand on the top post of the railing, he looked down at the shadows on the foyer floor spilling from the doorway of the parlor. His father's angry voice cursing shocked young Daniel as his mother's loud, mournful sobbing escaped from the parlor and rushed up the stairstoward him. Having never heard his father curse in anger or his mother sobbing in such a manner, he took a step backward, bumping into the corner wall where the steps turned to the second floor, his eyes fixed on the doorway to the parlor.

The police officer he had earlier watched climb out of the car walked out of the parlor with hat in hand, head down, staring at the floor.

8

Reaching the front door, he stopped, looked back into the parlor, and then at Daniel standing at the top of the stairs. Their eyes met, but for a moment, and then the officer put on his hat, opened the door, and disappeared into the cold, snowy afternoon.

As his mother's sobbing filled the quiet house, Daniel cautiously walked down the stairs with one hand on the railing. Reaching the foyer's hardwood floor, he leaned forward and looked into the dimly lit room at his parents sitting on the sofa. His father was holding his mother in his arms as she sobbed. Mr. Morgan looked up at his son with red, welling eyes. "Go back upstairs, son. I'll be along in a minute."

"Dan?" said Jack Brolin.

Dan blinked back into the present.

"You alright?"

Pushing the memory from his mind, Dan stood. "I'm fine."

Jack looked concerned. "I asked if you knew about the homicides in Littleton and Englewood."

Dan thought for a moment. "Vaguely." Then he gestured to the girl. "Look at the way her arms are at her sides, legs straight." He paused in thought. "Her body is perfect. Everything about her is perfect. Even her wet, combed hair is perfect. She wasn't just dumped here, Jack. She was placed here." He glanced around. "This was staged."

"For who?" asked Jack as he looked around.

Dan sipped his coffee in thought. "Her maybe. Or us, no telling."

Jack took a drink of coffee. "Why go to all the trouble?"

"If this was staged," said Dan, "we need to figure out who for and why."

Jack moved the flashlight to the girl's wrists. "Rope Burns." Then to her ankles. "Same here."

Dan set his coffee down on the wet cement, took the flashlight, and carefully opened her East High School jacket, finding a name embroidered into the lining. "Looks like we've got ourselves a Barbara from East High School." He paused a moment. "Wonder how Crime Scene missed this?" Then he lifted the dress and saw she was not wearing panties and let the dress fall to cover the girl.

"Either she wasn't wearing any," offered Jack, "or he dumped them after he raped her."

"Or he kept them as a souvenir along with the finger." offered Dan.

Jack quickly considered that. "Sick bastard."

Dan thought about his brother's clothing that the police had never found as he looked at the girl's pale face and open eyes, thinking they looked rather eerie. Fighting the urge to reach down and close them, he

9

recalled Todd telling them not to move anything. In the quiet moments that followed, Dan thought about her parents, especially the mother wailing in sorrow as his wife and mother had done over their children's deaths. He took off his hat and scratched his head. "So, we have a victim named Barbara missing her panties, socks, and no billfold." He took a sip of the coffee that was getting colder with each passing minute. "We can pick out a picture that's not too gruesome tomorrow and visit the principal at East High. Maybe he or someone there can identify her."

Jack nodded in agreement as he took a drink of his coffee.

Dan put on his fedora and glanced back up the alley toward the hotel. "Maybe the drunk that found her also found her billfold, kept the money, and tossed it."

Jack shook his head. "I don't think so. He was pretty upset when I got here. I don't think he had the presence of mind to search for anything of value. I believe seeing her scared the shit out of him."

Dan smiled at that. "Was he sober enough to know what time he found the body?"

Jack thought a moment. "Probably not, but the call came in at nine twenty-two. I was leaving headquarters and decided to come and have a look. After I got here, I called you from the lobby of the hotel."

Dan looked at his partner. "What the hell were you doing at headquarters that late?"

Jack grinned. "After you left Micky's, I stayed and had a few drinks with Jeff and Harry. I left my revolver in the drawer of my desk and had to go back after it."

Dan looked at his wristwatch, thinking that almost two hours had passed. Then he glanced around the alley. "Someone had to have seen a car in the alley." He motioned to the dead girl. "She didn't fly in here."

Jack glanced toward the hotel. "I'll go see if Bassich and the others have learned anything new."

Dan stared after his partner as he walked toward the hotel, then turned, and watched two of Pete's assistants kneel next to the body and then cover it with a white sheet. Staring at the covered body, he asked Pete, "Any idea how long she's been dead?"

Pete thought a moment. "From the condition of the body and rigor, I'd say about four hours. No more than five for sure." He glanced around while gesturing at the body. "She couldn't have been in the alley long."

"Why's that?"

10

"If she had been in the night air for long, the body temperature would be much colder." He gestured toward the cardboard. "The cardboard would be soaked instead of just damp as it was when we arrived."

Dan thought the drunk hadn't missed the killer by much, and then he considered that the girl's blue eyes had last seen the killer at about seven or seven-thirty that evening while he was at home watching television. He watched two men lift the body, put it on a gurney, and then roll it toward the Coroner's van. "Let me know what you find out, Pete."

"It'll be sometime tomorrow," replied Lange with an annoyed tone as he walked away.

Dan stared after Pete thinking he must be in a bad mood, but then he figured he had put in a long day that was not yet over. He turned and looked at the pile of trash and an overturned garbage can, thinking this is a terrible place for such a young, pretty girl to end up. Hearing car engines starting, he turned from the scene in time to see the Coroner's van and Coroner Pete Lange's white Ford sedan drive out of the alley on their way to the morgue at Denver General Hospital.

Dan leaned against Jack's car and took a sip of cold coffee while watching the alley for his partner's return from the cheap hotel.

Jack rounded the corner of the building and stepped into the alley, and as he approached, he said, "No one saw anything."

Dan was disappointed but not surprised.

Jack looked at Dan. "My guess is no one was out walking around because of the rain."

Dan thought it hadn't rained that hard.

"Not much to go on," said Jack.

Morgan looked into his coffee cup, thinking that was true. "When is there?" He drank the last of his coffee, walked to a trashcan, crumpled the paper cup, and tossed it and his gum into it. Then he glanced around the scene in thought for a few moments before gesturing to where the body had been. "The killer placed the body on the blanket atop the cardboard and then covered it with another piece of cardboard at the high point of the alley, away from the drain."

Jack pondered that for a moment. "He didn't want her to get wet."

"Looks that way." Dan stared at the scene in silence for several moments. "When someone kills another person, they usually leave the body where they did the deed, or they dump it someplace and try and hide it." He looked at Jack. "But this guy," he paused. "This guy placed his victim where she would be found in such a manner that she wouldn't get wet. Why?"

"Maybe he felt sorry for her."

11

"Or loved her," offered Dan.

"Crime of passion?"

Dan considered that as they watched Todd Anderson and his men gathering up the pieces of cardboard, the blanket, and other objects as evidence. "If it was a crime of passion, why take the finger?"

Todd walked up to Dan and Jack. "When we're finished here, we'll head back to the lab and process everything." Then he gestured toward the trashcans. "We'll take those five garbage cans back with us and see if we can find the panties, socks, purse, or anything else that may be useful."

"Thanks, Todd," said Dan.

Jack Brolin looked at his partner. "You look tired, Dan. Go home and get some rest. I'll do the same, and we'll see what Pete and Todd have for us in the morning."

Todd Anderson walked away, talking over his shoulder. "Probably won't have much until afternoon."

Feeling tired, Dan thought about his sofa, told his partner he'd see him in the morning and walked up the dim alley between the canyons of dark buildings toward the street. Opening the door of his car, he shoved his coat over, got in, and started the engine while considering the two homicides his partner had mentioned.

*** Two ***

Jack Brolin looked as tired as he felt while climbing the stairs to the Denver Police Headquarters' second floor and the Denver Detective Squad. Telephones, typewriters, and muffled voices competed with one another as he walked across the floor. In his hand was a brown paper bag containing two glazed donuts from Grandma's Donuts. Finding his partner Dan sitting at his desk talking on the telephone, Jack set the bag down, placed his fedora on the corner of his desk, and pulled his Thirty-eight snub-nose revolver from the holster attached to his belt. Opening the top right drawer of his desk, he placed his pistol inside and closed the drawer.

Detective Dan Morgan looked as though he had been at work for a while, his white shirt sleeves rolled up to the elbow and his dark brown tie pulled away from the collar. His light brown suit coat was hanging over the back of his wooden swivel chair. He put his hand over the phone. "I'm on hold. What's in the sack?"

Jack opened the bag, took out a glazed donut, and reached across his desk, setting it down next to Dan's half cup of cold coffee.

Dan smiled and mouthed, thanks.

Curious who Dan was talking to, he removed the other donut, took a bite, then picked up his cup of yesterday's coffee, Dan's cup, and headed for the small kitchen in the back of the office. Returning several minutes later with two cups of fresh coffee, he set Dan's cup next to the untouched glazed donut and then sat down. While eyeing Dan, Jack started enthusiastically on his donut, washing down each bite with hot coffee he thought was too strong.

Dan took a bite of his donut, sat up, and swallowed. "I'm here, Sheriff."

Catching Jack Brolin's interest, Brolin paused eating his donut and wondered what Sheriff and what they were talking about.

Dan looked excited. "If it'd be alright, I'd like to come out and look at the file." He paused. "Thanks. I'll be there in about an hour." He leaned forward, hanging up the telephone while looking at Jack. "That was Sheriff Carl Brumwell in Littleton."

Curious, Jack took a drink of coffee and waited for Dan to explain.

Dan took a bite of donut. "You were right. They had a homicide involving a young girl on the sixth of March in a little park across the street from the Court House."

Jack was familiar with the park and watched Dan as he searched through the Rolodex on his desk. "Who are you calling now?"

Without looking up, Dan said, "Englewood Police Department. Maybe they'll let us look at their files."

Jack took a bite of his donut while Dan picked up the telephone and turned the rotary dialer with his index finger.

"Chief Travis, please," said Dan, and while waiting, he sipped his hot coffee, thinking it tasted like shit, and wondered who made it.

"This is Chief Travis," said a voice on the other end.

Dan set the cup down. "Chief Travis, this is Denver Homicide Detective Dan Morgan."

Wondering why a Denver police detective would be calling, Sheriff Travis asked, "What can I do for you, Detective?"

Dan glanced at his partner as he talked into the telephone. "We're investigating the death of a young girl from last night, and I'd like some information about the homicide of a young girl in your city not long ago."

Chief Travis thought for a moment. "Are you thinking these two may be connected?"

"We're not sure, Chief, that's why I would like to stop by today if that'd be okay and take a look at your file."

Chief Travis thought about that for a moment. "I see no problem with that. I'll have the file ready for you when you get here."

"Thank you very much, Chief Travis." Dan hung up the phone and looked at Jack. "Chief Travis said we could stop by anytime, and he'd have the file ready." He retrieved his Thirty-eight snub-nose revolver from the right top drawer of his desk and looked at his partner, enjoying the donut he held in one hand, his coffee in the other. "You coming?"

Jack glanced at the papers on his desk and the file folders in his inbox, needing his attention. "Guess this shit can wait."

Dan stood, lifted his coat from the back of his chair, and slipped into it. "I'll tell Captain Foley where we're going." Then he headed for the captain's office.

Detective Brolin shoved the last of his donut into his mouth, took a quick drink of coffee, retrieved his gun from the desk drawer, and holstered it. While he waited for his partner, he slipped into his suit coat and looked at the clock above the stairs, seeing it was only ten minutes to nine.

Moments later, Dan walked past Jack heading for the stairs. "Let's take a ride," he said as he reached across his desk and picked up his donut.

"I'll drive," said Jack.

14

As they walked down the stairs, Dan took a bite of the donut and asked Jack if he had checked for a missing person's report when he came in.

Jack nodded his head. "No one's filed a thing."

Jack Brolin turned his car off Littleton Boulevard onto the narrow street of Court Place between the railroad tracks and the big, three-story tan brick building of the Arapaho County Courthouse. Finding an empty parking place between two cars, he pulled head-on into the parking space, and after his front tires touched the curb, he shut the engine off. Jack and Dan climbed out of the car, walked across the wide sidewalk, and up the courthouse's concrete steps. Pushing the big glass doors open, they went inside and walked down the long, wide hall of marble floors, white walls, and high ceilings, passing several oak doors with frosted glass. Coming to a door with the words **County Sheriff, Carl 'Chip' Brumwell,** printed on the frosted glass, Dan turned the doorknob, pushed the door open, and then he and Jack stepped inside.

A woman in her early thirties with long, light brown hair that flowed over her left shoulder looked up from her desk with friendly brown eyes. "Good morning," she said, glancing from one to the other, and then she smiled at Detective Dan Morgan. "May I help you?"

Taking off their hats, Dan looked at the nameplate sitting on the front of the desk: **Cathy Holman.** "Good morning, Miss Holman. I'm Denver Detective Dan Morgan, and this gentleman is Detective Jack Brolin. I believe Sheriff Brumwell is expecting us."

"It's Mrs.," she said with a smile. "And yes, he is expecting you." She stood, ignoring Jack while giving Dan a friendly look. "Just a moment, please." Dressed in a plain, dark green dress that clung to all the right places of her slender body, she walked toward a closed door.

Jack noticed Dan was watching her, grinned, gently nudged him with his elbow, and whispered, "Wow."

Dan ignored his partner and his comment.

She opened the door and leaned inside. "Sheriff Brumwell, those Denver detectives are here."

A gruff voice from inside said, "Show them in, Cathy."

Holding the door open, Cathy turned and smiled at Dan. "The Sheriff will see you now." Then she stepped aside while Dan and Jack walked through the doorway.

Inside, they found a big man in his early sixties with a full head of white hair standing behind a big, dark wooden desk messy with papers. He was wearing western clothing with a sheriff's star pinned to the left side of his dark brown shirt. He stood six feet tall with broad shoulders, and his slightly tanned and wrinkled face was clean-shaven. His brown eyes

15

looked friendly as he smiled while holding out a large, calloused hand. "Sheriff Brumwell."

Dan shook the big hand, feeling its strength. "Detective Dan Morgan." Then he gestured to Jack. "This is my partner Detective Jack Brolin."

The two shook hands.

"Didn't expect two detectives," said Brumwell with a small curious smile. Then he gestured to a file on the edge of his desk. "I had the file pulled soon as I hung up." He looked at the two men standing in front of his desk. "Could I interest either of you in a cup of coffee?"

Both declined, and then Brumwell looked at Mrs. Holman waiting at the door. "Thank you, Cathy."

As Mrs. Holman closed the door, Sheriff Brumwell told them to have a seat, picked up a manila folder, and handed it to Dan Morgan. While the two detectives eyed the folder Dan held, Brumwell sat down in his black leather chair. "I expect you already know about another similar homicide in Englewood?"

"That's our next stop," said Jack eyeing the folder Dan was holding.

Dan placed his hat on the floor next to his chair as he read the name Diane Wagner on the tab of the folder aloud. Without looking up, he asked, "Her body was discovered in the park?"

Brumwell nodded. "In the park across Littleton Boulevard next to the railroad tracks. It ain't far from here."

"When was that?" asked Jack.

Sheriff Brumwell frowned. "It's in the report, but if memory serves me, it was early Tuesday morning on the sixth of March. Some kids found her on their way to school. The coroner said she'd probably been there most of the night."

Dan placed the folder on his lap, undid the small metal fasteners, lifted the tab, and peered inside. Reaching into the folder, he pulled several eight-by-ten black and white photographs, along with a coroner's report, some handwritten notes by the sheriff, from the file and placed them with the envelope on his lap.

Jack moved his chair closer to Dan's, so he could see the pictures as Dan slowly made his way through them. The first few were of the crime scene and a young girl dressed in blue jeans, a gray and white print shirt, and white tennis shoes. He noticed her long hair was in a ponytail, just like the girl in the alley. Her body was placed neatly on its back atop what appeared to be an old, brown army blanket, as had been their victim. Her right arm extended out to the side, her left was folded across her stomach,

16

and he noticed the missing little finger on the left hand. "She's missing a finger," he softly said as he handed the picture to his partner.

Jack took the picture, thinking of their victim.

Dan looked at the next picture of the left side of her neck, which bore a small puncture. "What was the cause of death?"

"Exsanguination, according to the coroner." replied the Sheriff.

Dan continued through the stack of pictures, and as he finished each one, he handed it to Jack. Then he came to one of a nude girl lying on a metal table in the Coroner's Office. "What the hell?"

Jack looked from his picture to the one Dan held. "Damn."

Sheriff Brumwell frowned. "I'd say we're dealing with a sick bastard."

Dan stared at the picture. "Must be a hundred," he said softly.

"She was stabbed seventy-nine times, according to the report," said Brumwell. "They're all post-mortem. According to the County Medical Examiner, they were not made by the same instrument that cut her neck. He thinks a small hunting knife may have been used to mutilate the body." He paused. "The Medical Examiner says the finger was taken and the wound cauterized while she was still alive."

Jack looked up from the photo. "Does your Medical Examiner have any suggestions as to what cut her neck?"

"You'll find that in the report also. A small, sharp penknife perhaps, but most likely, it was a scalpel." He paused in thought. "Nice little gal. She didn't deserve to be treated in such a manner. Even if she was dead."

Thinking the stabbing may have been in anger and realizing what the sheriff had just said, Dan looked up while handing the photos to Jack. Did you know the girl?"

The Sheriff nodded a few times. "I've known her family casually for years. They live on a small piece of land on the other side of Santa Fe Drive, beyond the Platte River and Centennial Horse Racing Track." He pursed his lips, looking sad. "Nice folks." He paused, adding, "Diane Wagner worked part-time at Hazel's Café on Main, just down the street. We'd talk a bit about school and other things when I stopped in for coffee or lunch."

Jack Brolin looked up from the photos. "Was she working the night she was murdered?"

Brumwell shook his head no. "Hazel Jenkins, the owner of the café, said she had not worked since Friday night."

Dan looked at Brumwell. "Had she been reported missing?"

"According to her mother, Diane never came home Sunday." He shrugged. "Her mother thought she had spent the night with a friend and went to school the next day. Apparently, that was not unusual."

Dan considered that as he looked at the Sheriff and thought parents these days don't keep track of their children as they should. Then he remembered his twin brother being gone most of the day he had been murdered.

Brumwell shifted in his chair. "My investigation showed that Sunday after church was the last time any of her friends saw her."

"Who ID'd the body?" asked Dan.

"I did at the scene." Sheriff Brumwell looked sad. "Then I took a ride to the Wagner home and gave the family the sad news about their daughter."

Dan imagined the scene as he started reading the coroner's report. "It was the sixth of March, Sheriff, just as you said. Time of death is estimated between six and seven p.m., Monday the fifth of March." Dan remembered that was close to the hour of death that Coroner Lange estimated on their victim. Looking at the girl's date of birth, he softly said, "She was only sixteen." Feeling sorry for the young girl and her parents, he continued reading the report. "Race: Caucasian. Height: 5'3'. Weight: 90 pounds. Hair: dark brown. Eyes: blue." Thinking of her parents, he quietly read on. "Mouth and mucous membranes were slightly burned." He read further and looked up at Jack. "The coroner thinks the killer used chloroform. I wonder if Lange will find the same thing on our victim."

Jack shrugged. "Maybe."

Dan looked back at the report. "I'll check with Pete when we get back."

"Maybe the killer works in a hospital," offered Jack.

Dan quickly considered that as he continued to read. "It says here that she wasn't sexually assaulted." Surprised by that, he looked up at Brumwell.

Jack looked up, surprised as well.

Sheriff Brumwell nodded. "That surprised me the same as it does you. If you notice a little further down the report, the coroner said the killer must have washed the body and fixed her hair in a ponytail after he washed it. He couldn't find any trace of blood anywhere on her, including her hair."

Dan thought about the wet ponytail on their victim and knew they were dealing with the same killer.

Brumwell shifted in his big leather chair, looking uncomfortable. "The only thing the coroner did find on her was semen in her pubic hair."

Dan looked up with a frown. "But none inside?"

18

The sheriff shook his head. "None."

Dan looked at Jack and then the sheriff. "So, he washes the body clean first, and then he masturbated into her pubic hair?"

"Sick bastard," said Jack, wondering if Pete would find the same thing on their victim.

"Won't argue that with you, detective," said the sheriff. "We never did find her panties." He looked sad and upset. "It wasn't an easy thing asking her mother if she wore panties. She got a little upset with me, but when I explained why I asked, she went into her daughter's bedroom and, after several minutes, returned saying that her daughter's yellow bra and yellow panties were missing." He paused. "We know where the yellow bra is."

Jack got to the picture with the stab wounds. "Mary, Mother of God," he softly uttered as he made the sign of the cross on his body. "Why would anyone do this to a young girl's body? You'd think killing her and taking a finger would be enough."

The room became silent as Brumwell and Dan considered Jack's statement. Then Dan turned his head and stared out the window past the one and two-story buildings along Littleton Boulevard running past the Rocky Mountains. Images of the pictures he found hidden away in his father's garage years after his brother was killed rushed through his mind. Turning from the window and Devil's Head Mountain in the distance, he looked at the sheriff. "Any suspects?"

The sheriff made a disappointed face. "None." He paused and then added, "Checked out everyone who ever knew the little gal." He shook his head slowly as he gestured with his open hands. "We checked out several boys that hung around the café that kept asking her out but came up with nothing." He smiled. "They were just horny boys, I guess." His face filled with sadness. "We may never know who did this terrible thing to such a nice little gal."

Dan considered that he would probably never know who the driver was that killed his daughter Nancy either, or the person that killed his identical twin brother. "Could we bother you for a copy of the file?"

Brumwell sat forward, reaching across his desk, and pushed a small white button.

Moments later, the door opened, and Cathy Holman stuck her head in, glanced at Dan, and then looked at Brumwell. "Yes, Sheriff."

"Darl'n," said the sheriff. "Do me a favor and see that these detectives get a copy of the coroner's report along with a set of photos."

While she walked across the room, Dan took the pictures Jack was holding, put them back in the folder, closed the tab, and smiled as he handed them to her.

19

She returned his smile as she took the file and looked at Brumwell. "It may take a few minutes."

Brumwell thanked her, and as she left, he looked at the two detectives. "Any similarities between our homicide and yours?"

"Some," replied Jack.

Dan took in a small breath letting out a soft sigh. "Jack's right, there are some, but we haven't received the coroner's, or the forensics reports yet."

"Well," said Brumwell. "If it turns out the same bastard killed both girls and maybe the young gal in Englewood, my feelings won't be hurt if you catch the son of a bitch before I do." Then he stood. "Cathy will have the files in a few minutes." With an open hand, he added, "You can wait in the outer office if you wouldn't mind, gentlemen. I have a couple of calls I have to make."

Dan picked up his fedora from the floor, stood, and shook the sheriff's hand. "Thanks, Sheriff."

"My pleasure, gentlemen," said Brumwell, then he shook Jack's hand. "If I come up with anything, I have your number, and I'd appreciate the same from you, boys."

"If we find anything new, Sheriff," said Dan. "We'll call you."

Brumwell grinned, looking happy. "Appreciate that."

Dan and Jack walked out of Chip Brumwell's office, finding two uncomfortable, straight-back wooden chairs against a wall and Cathy Holman's empty chair. They sat in silence for what seemed a long time.

The door opened, and Mrs. Holman stepped inside, carrying several pictures and the folder they had been looking through earlier. Her brown eyes glanced at Jack but looked at Dan as she shut the door, walked to her desk, and sat down. "Won't be but a moment." She opened a desk drawer and pulled out an ink pad and rubber stamp. "All I need to do is certify these, and you can be on your way."

Morgan noticed the wedding ring on her left hand as she went about the task of stamping the back of each picture and then the front of all the documents. When she finished, she put everything into a large ten-by-twelve manila envelope, closed the flap, bent the metal fasteners, and offered it to Dan.

Jack quickly took the envelope and teasingly slapped it against Dan's stomach. "Thank you, Mrs. Holman."

Dan took the envelope, thanked her as well, followed his partner into the hall, and closed the door. Followed by their footsteps echoing off the marble floors and walls, they walked toward the two heavy glass doors of the main entrance in silence.

Stepping outside, they paused in the warm spring sun and glanced at the few people walking up and down the steps of the courthouse. As the big door behind them closed, Jack turned his attention to the small town's main street of two, and three-story buildings set before the Rocky Mountains under a blue sky swept clean of clouds. The third range of mountains still held their winter snow that would soon melt, filling the streams with clear, cool water. "Too bad that Holman woman's married."

Dan was thinking of Diane Wagner and Barbara No Name instead of Mrs. Holman. As he watched the traffic along Littleton Boulevard, he reached inside his suit coat, pulled out a pack of cigarettes, took one, and offered the pack to his partner.

Jack took a cigarette, gave the pack back, and searched his pockets for matches. Finding a book with several missing, he tore off a match and lit Dan's cigarette.

Dan puffed his cigarette as he walked down the steps of the courthouse, leaving Jack to light his own, and upon reaching Jack's car, he climbed in and rolled the window down. While he waited for his partner to reach the car, he stuck his right elbow out the open window, staring at the courthouse landscape of brown grass. Soon the grass would turn green as summer approached, and the tall cottonwood trees would fill with buds that would soon become green leaves.

Jack settled into the driver's seat and closed the door as a distant train whistle broke the silence. Putting his keys in the ignition, he pushed the starter on the dash.

The blur of a freight train roared behind them, racing north toward Denver, while Dan Morgan stared out the window, thinking of Diane Wagner. The photographs of her body rode through his mind almost as fast as the train raced along the tracks behind them. As the noise followed the train north, Dan said, "It's after one. Let's pay a visit to Chief Travis."

Three

Detective Jack Brolin drove through the three blocks of downtown Englewood and turned his car off South Broadway into the long circular driveway of the Englewood Police Department. Dan recalled Christmases past when he would drive the family all the way to Englewood from their home in Denver to see the decorated fir trees in the center of the circular driveway. As Detective Brolin pulled into a small parking lot marked for visitors, Dan pushed those happy memories aside.

Jack parked the car, turned off the ignition, and the two climbed out and headed toward the front door of a large, two-story, gray cement building that brought the Alamo to mind. Pushing open one of the oak-framed glass doors, they stepped into a large open foyer containing several doors with small metal signs above each one and a set of wide staircases on either side of the lobby.

A heavyset, gray-haired woman sitting behind a marble counter, looking like she was in a lousy mood, glanced at them as they walked toward her. "May I help you?"

Jack read the nameplate sitting on top of the counter and smiled as he leaned on the counter. "Hello, Hazel. We're here to see Chief Travis."

She looked at him and then at Dan. "Is Chief Travis expecting you?"

"I believe he is, ma'am," replied Jack with another big smile. "I'm Detective Jack Brolin from Denver Homicide, and this is my partner Detective Dan Morgan."

She glanced from Jack to Dan, looking unimpressed as she picked up the receiver of the black telephone, put her chubby forefinger in the rotary dial, and dialed a number. "Sorry to bother you, Bernice, but there are two detectives from Denver down here to see the chief." She paused. "Yes, ma'am." She hung up the receiver and looked to her left, pointing to a wide staircase. "Just take those stairs to the second floor, turn right, and you'll come to a closed door with the chief's name on it." She looked at Jack Brolin. "Go inside, and Bernice, Chief Travis's secretary, will help you."

"Thank you," said Jack, and then he quickly added, "I like your dress."

She blushed and smiled, looking pleased. "Why, thank you."

After a few steps, Dan chuckled softly and whispered. "You sly, playful devil."

Jack grinned. "Up yours, Dan. She looked like she was having a bad day."

Dan grinned as he stepped onto the first step of the stairs. "And we're not?"

Reaching the second floor, they turned to the right as instructed and walked down the tiled hall of solid dark mahogany doors, each having a brass plate with a name and department hanging from a metal frame protruding from the wall. Moments later, they were at a dark mahogany door looking at the name 'Hugh R. Travis, Chief of Police.' They took off their hats, opened the door, and stepped inside.

A woman in her late twenties with short black hair and full red lips looked up as she stood with a smile. She walked around the desk to greet them, wearing a black short sleeve dress with a white lace collar. "Good afternoon, detectives. I'm Bernice Crenshaw."

Dan and Jack introduced themselves.

Still smiling, she gestured to a closed door. "This way, please. Chief Travis is expecting you."

She opened the door, leaned against the doorjamb, and poked her head inside. "Those two detectives are here."

"Send them in," said a voice from inside.

Bernice pushed the door open and stepped aside. "The Chief will see you now."

As they entered the office, Chief Travis stood and walked around his desk, looking glad to see them. Englewood Police Chief Hugh Travis was not a big man, standing five feet six, a little on the chubby side with black hair, brown eyes, and a thin mustache over a wide mouth. His uniform of black pants, dark gray shirt, and black tie fit a little snugly, and after they shook hands, Chief Travis gestured toward four dark brown straight-back chairs in front of his desk. "Have a seat."

They sat down, feeling uncomfortable as they glanced around the office looking at several pictures hanging on the walls. Most were of the Chief, with other police officers, scenes of the city, and most curious, a big picture of John Dillinger hanging behind his desk.

Chief Travis dropped into his chair behind the mahogany desk, noticing they were staring at the picture behind him. He smiled as he turned to look up at the picture and, as if admiring the man, said, "Don't see many men like that these days." He turned to the two detectives. "Just as well, I suppose. That was a rough time for law enforcement." Then as if in a hurry, he straightened up the papers on his desk, setting them to one side. "Terrible thing what happened to this young girl," he said while opening the bottom left drawer of his desk. He pulled out a ten by twelve manila envelope, placed it on the glass top of his desk, and looked at Dan.

"I've been chief for ten years, and I don't recall anything this terrible ever happening in our little town."

Dan Morgan considered that he should have been around when they discovered his brother's body in the park a few blocks west of here. Anxious to see what was in the envelope, Dan nervously fussed with the fedora he was holding while wishing Travis would slide the envelope across his desk.

Chief Travis looked at Dan. "You mentioned on the telephone that you have a homicide that may have something to do with ours?"

Dan nodded. "That's correct, Chief."

Travis frowned. "I read about the poor girl found in an alley downtown in this morning's paper. Larimer Street's full of thugs, dope heads, and prostitutes." He looked at Jack and then Dan. "But I guess I don't need to tell you two that." He leaned forward and slid the envelope across the glass desktop. "I had Bernice make you a complete set of the crime scene photos my men took, and the pictures sent over from the mortuary." He nodded at the envelope. "I included a copy of the coroner's report as well."

Dan leaned toward the desk, put his gray fedora on the edge of it, picked up the manila envelope, and silently read the penciled name: 'Gail Thomas.'

Jack Brolin smiled. "Thanks. Our investigation is just beginning, so we don't have anything to share yet." Then recalling that the chief had mentioned the mortuary asked, "You said mortuary?"

Travis nodded. "There's a mortuary a few blocks up East Hamden that serves as the coroner for the City of Englewood." Travis paused. "Has for years."

Dan opened the loose flap of the envelope and looked inside, seeing two smaller manila envelopes and some papers. He pulled the two envelopes out, set the bigger, empty envelope on the chief's desk, placed the envelope from the mortuary on top of it, and opened the one that said Crime Scene. Inside, he found several eight-by-ten black and white photographs.

Curious, Jack moved his chair closer as Dan started through them.

The first was in an alley with several fifty-gallon barrels used as trashcans and the body of a young girl dressed in jeans, a dark, short-sleeved shirt with white buttons, loafers, and her hair done up in a ponytail. Her right arm was stretched out from her body, while the left lay across her body, showing the left hand's missing small finger.

The body was lying between two of the trashcans on what appeared to be a brown army blanket similar to the ones found with the girl in Littleton and their Denver victim. It was the type of blanket anyone

24

could buy at any number of army surplus stores in the metro area. Dan handed the picture to Jack as he looked at the Chief. "Where were these taken?"

Chief Travis nodded toward the window. "In the alley behind the Pioneer Theater. It's about a block south of here on the east side of Broadway."

Familiar with the theater, Dan asked, "Who found the body?"

"Janitor by the name of Ira Tindle. He found the girl after he locked up and was on his way home."

"What time was that?" asked Jack.

"Around eleven." Chief Travis recognized Jack's suspicious look. "Ira Tindle may be a bit different, but he's harmless. He, his wife, and their daughter live in a small place on Dartmouth, just this side of Santa Fe Drive."

Dan's eyes narrowed. "What do you mean different?"

Travis shrugged. "Tindle was wounded on Iwo Jima." The chief paused. "He was awarded the Purple Heart and Silver Star. He never talks about the war and keeps to himself, mostly."

Dan and Jack were familiar with men like Ira.

Jack looked up from one of the pictures. "What day was she found?"

Chief Travis looked thoughtful. "If I remember, it was on the nineteenth of March." He gestured to the papers Dan was holding. "It's all in the coroner's report."

Dan went through the pictures until he found a photo with one of her wrists showing bruising and marks left by a rope and a close-up photo of the hand and the missing finger. He handed that along with the rest of the pictures to Jack, picked up the envelope with Mortuary written on it in ink, opened it, and took out another stack of eight-by-ten black and white photographs. The first was of the victim lying on a metal table, the second a close-up of Gail Thomas's head and face, and Dan thought she looked as if she were sleeping. Then he looked at the photo of the hand missing a finger, slid that picture under the others, and looked at the next picture showing a small puncture on the left side of her neck. He held the photo so Jack could see. "This girl has the same cut on her neck."

Chief Travis watched the two detectives with curiosity.

Dan slid that picture under the others and looked at a picture of a young girl's nude body bearing the familiar incisions of an autopsy. Relieved that there were no stab wounds, he slid that under the others and looked at Jack. "No stab wounds."

That puzzled Chief Travis. "Why would there be?"

25

Jack looked up, thinking Englewood and Littleton needed to talk to one another. "The girl in Littleton had numerous postmortem stab wounds."

Travis frowned. "Why would anyone do that?"

Jack shook his head. "Can't answer that, Chief." Then he looked at the next picture of the left hand and the missing finger.

Dan went through the remaining pictures rather quickly, put them back in the envelope, picked up the typed report from the mortuary, and read the date aloud. "Monday the nineteenth of March. Time of death was between six and seven p.m." His eyes met his partner's, and both thought the same thing: the killer likes that time of day and Mondays. He looked up from the report. "Did she have a billfold or any money on her?"

"According to her mother, the girl's black billfold is missing, but we found a student card in the back pocket of her jeans."

"That's how you identified her?" asked Jack.

"That's correct," answered Chief Travis. He looked down at his hands and softly said, "Gail Thomas was just sixteen years old." He paused. "I had the displeasure of driving to her home and telling Mrs. Thomas about her only child myself and then had to watch the poor soul as she identified her daughter's body." He looked up. "I hope I never have to do that again."

Dan imagined the scene. "What can you tell us about this Thomas girl?"

Travis shrugged. "Not much to tell. She lived with her mother in the thirty-eight hundred block of South Logan Street, attended Flood High School, and according to her mother, she was never in any trouble."

Jack wrote that in his notepad, then asked, "What about her father?"

"Her father was killed in an automobile accident three or four years back on Santa Fe Drive by the Overland Golf course. Some drunk pulled out of a side street, and Jack Thomas hit him. Both were pronounced dead at the scene."

Dan returned to the coroner's report from the mortuary and began reading aloud to Jack. "Race: Caucasian. Height: 5'2. Weight: 97 lbs. Hair: Dark Brown. Eyes: Blue." Then he stopped reading and scanned the document until he found what he was looking for. "Cause of death was exsanguination, and there was no sign of sexual assault." He looked at his partner. "Semen was found in her pubic hair."

Chief Travis recalled reading that in the report. "If you read further, it says the body was washed and cleaned, and her hair, which was in a ponytail, was still damp." He paused. "I thought that was a little strange, but then I realized the bastard masturbated on her after he washed

26

her." He paused as he looked at Dan. "Why do you suppose he would do that?"

Dan shook his head, looking uncertain. "I don't know, Chief. Maybe he's crazy."

Jack looked at Dan. "Anything in there about her panties?"

Dan shook his head. "There's no mention of them in the list of personal effects." He looked at Chief Travis. "Could you call the mortuary and see if anyone remembers whether or not she was wearing panties when they undressed her for the autopsy?"

Chief Travis picked up the telephone, and as his forefinger found the rotary dial and turned it, he gave both detectives a curious look. Moments later, he spoke into the telephone. "This is Chief Travis. When you undressed Gail Thomas for the autopsy, was she wearing panties?" He paused. "I see. Thank you." He hung up the phone and looked at Detective Morgan. "No panties. Just a white bra."

Dan began putting everything back into the big envelope. "We think that the girl in Littleton, your victim, and ours were all killed by the same individual."

Chief Travis sat back in his chair, looking troubled. "What you're telling me is that we have a repeat killer roaming around our three cities."

"For now," said Jack wondering if one would turn up in the city of Aurora, east of Denver.

Understanding what Jack meant, Travis asked. "What is the name of your victim?"

"We're still waiting for someone to file a missing person's report," replied Jack.

Chief Travis stared at the top of his desk for a moment and looked at Jack and then Dan. "The crime scene was full of things that should be there and clean of any evidence except for the body of Gail Thomas and the army blanket. That blanket had no blood on it, the same as the body and her clothes. We checked with the army surplus store on South Broadway, but they don't keep records of who buys anything. There were no fingerprints on anything and no tire marks or footprints we could use in the vacant lot."

"A vacant lot?" asked Dan with interest.

Travis nodded. "There's a gravel lot used for parking across the alley from the theater. The city had spread fresh gravel on the lot the week before the girl's body was found, so there are no footprints or tire marks that would serve any purpose. It's a public lot, and people park there all day, and there's always a few at night that frequent Andy's Bar two doors down from the theater."

Dan picked up the envelope. "So, that's how your investigation ended?"

"It is," said Travis looking regretful. "He didn't leave us anything."

Dan stood and held out an open hand. "Thanks for the file and your time, Chief Travis."

The chief stood and shook Dan's hand. "We better catch this son of a bitch and soon." Then he turned and shook Jack's hand. "Good day, gentlemen."

"We'll keep in touch," said Dan.

Jack shoved the key into the ignition of his car, but instead of starting the engine, he let go of the key and sat back in his seat, staring into the fir trees at the edge of the parking lot. "What would drive a man to kill three teenage girls by bleeding them out, cut off their little fingers, and then masturbate on them?"

Dan set the envelope on the seat between them, took off his hat, set it on the envelopes, and stared out the window. "I don't know, Jack."

Jack looked at Dan. "Our killer likes Mondays for some reason."

"And the hour," added Dan as he watched a big crow land on a limb of one of the trees. "We need to find a connection between these girls."

Jack considered that briefly. "They're all the same age. They all have dark brown or black hair, and all are about the same height and build." He looked at Dan. "He likes the same type of girl."

"Maybe," agreed Dan feeling there was more to it than that.

"But why these three particular girls?" asked Jack.

"Opportunity, maybe," suggested Dan.

Detective Brolin had no answers floating around in his mind, so he turned the key, pushed the ignition button on the dash to start the car, and backed out of the parking place. "Well," he said as he stopped and put the car in first gear. "We better damn well find a connection." He drove along the circled driveway and stopped at the exit onto South Broadway. After a streetcar passed on its way to the Loop, he looked at Dan as he drove north. "Want to get something to eat?"

Dan had other things on his mind as he shook his head no. "Let's head to Denver General and see what Lange has."

In the stillness of the car, Jack Brolin was thinking about food while eyeing every restaurant they passed. Dan Morgan was thinking about the pictures of the girls in the envelopes he was holding on his lap when his mind went to the two pictures of his brother's death that he had quickly looked at fifteen years ago. He was the only person who knew of their existence and how his brother had died now that his parents and his wife, Norma, were no longer alive. Jack Brolin, his best friend and partner never knew the truth about Dan's identical twin brother Donnie. Pushing those unpleasant memories from his mind, he returned to the three killings.

Dan and Jack walked along a quiet hall of black and white checkerboard tiles in Denver General Hospital's basement. Approaching Pete Lange's office, the quick cadence of typewriter keys flowed into the quiet hall from behind the closed door with the black letters *'Coroner's Office'* on the frosted glass. Dan thought about the night he and Norma had walked through it to identify their daughter.

Jack turned the knob, opened the door, and followed Dan inside, knowing he was thinking of his daughter.

Wearing a white smock over his street clothes, Pete Lange stopped typing, looked up from the bulky, black typewriter, and fussed with his glasses as he leaned back in his chair, looking tired. He ran his left hand over his crew cut and gestured to two uncomfortable metal chairs with gray padded seats in front of his gray metal desk. "Have a seat."

Dan took off his fedora, sat down with the hat on his lap, and glanced around the room with its bare, cold walls. Several gray five-drawer filing cabinets lined one wall, and an uncomfortable looking bench filled another, all looking impersonal as a coroner's office should.

Lange adjusted his glasses and then turned the roller of the typewriter, raising the set of duplicate forms separated by sheets of black carbon paper. "I've estimated the time of death between six and seven p.m. Monday night." Holding the paper forms, he gently shrugged. "That's about as close as I can come. The cause of death was exsanguination." Anticipating their next question, he said, "She had not been sexually assaulted, but I did find semen in her pubic area." Pete paused, looking troubled. "The killer took the time to wash the body clean before he masturbated there."

"Were there any burns in her nose and mouth?" asked Dan.

"Yes, there was," Pete said with a curious look. "How did you know?"

"Good guess," replied Dan.

Pete separated the carbon paper sheets from the forms. "I was just about to get to that. I'd say she had been subdued with chloroform. That certainly would account for the burning of the lips, nostrils, and membranes of the nose canal."

Dan and Jack remained silent about the other girls while Lange picked up a large ten-by-twelve manila envelope, set it on the top of his desk, slipped a set of the forms he had taken from the typewriter inside, and closed the tab.

Watching Pete, Jack asked, "Were there any marks on the body?"

29

Lange had a puzzled look as he handed the envelope to Dan. "What sort of marks?"

Figuring there were no stab wounds, or he would have known why he was asking, Jack said, "We were just curious if she was tortured."

Pete considered the question. "Well, she is missing her little finger, and what I find strange is whoever did that cauterized the wound so she wouldn't bleed." He looked puzzled. "Then he punctured her jugular in such a manner that her own heart would pump the blood out so she would slowly bleed to death. I guess you might call that torture." He nodded at the envelope Dan was opening. "You can have that."

Dan opened the envelope as he looked at Lange. "Any idea of what sort of weapon was used?"

"I'd say a scalpel. It's sharp, makes a clean-cut, and is easy to handle. I'm not sure about the finger. But whoever took it knew what he or she was doing. It wasn't sloppy."

Dan looked at Pete. "Could this guy be a doctor?"

Lang considered the question. "Possibly."

Thinking about that, Jack moved his chair closer to Dan and watched as he took out several eight-by-ten black and white photos and then placed the envelope on Pete's desk.

The first photo was of a young girl looking quite different from the girl in the alley the night before. A white sheet covered her body except for her head and neck, which showed the small cut. Her dark brown hair looked wet and had been combed straight back over the ears by Pete Lang after he washed the body.

Dan continued through the black and white photos that brought images rushing back to him of his daughter lying on a table in the same room. Feeling anxious, he fought the urge to leave as he looked at the next photo showing the surgical scars of Pete Lange's autopsy. He was thankful that there was no question as to how his daughter Nancy had died and that she had never needed an autopsy. Dan looked through the pictures rather hurriedly, to Jack's displeasure, until he found the photo of the girl's hand showing the missing finger. He stared at it a moment, picked up the empty envelope, and carefully placed everything back inside. As the memories of his daughter lying on the table crowded his mind, Dan felt sick and abruptly stood. Picking up his hat, he thanked Pete and turned toward the door.

Jack gave Dan a curious look, grabbed his fedora off Pete's desk, thanked him, and followed his partner out of the coroner's office, having a good idea of what was bothering him.

Four

Neither Dan nor Jack Brolin spoke as they walked up the steps to the second floor of police headquarters to the Denver detective squad. Walking through a maze of desks and noisy typewriters toward their desks, Dan placed the envelopes on his; and put his Thirty-eight Special in the drawer while noticing a folded note under his telephone. He unfolded the paper and looked at the scribbled note that had come from Irene at the switchboard. *'A man called at 1:15 and asked if you liked the package he left.'*

Jack looked at Dan, who was staring at the piece of paper he was holding. "What's that?"

Dan frowned, looking puzzled. "A note from Irene downstairs." He looked at Jack. "Someone called and wanted to know if I liked the package he left."

Jack looked confused. "What package?"

Dan didn't answer as he picked up the telephone and dialed the switchboard. "Irene, this is Dan Morgan. When you took the message about the package, did the caller leave a name?"

"No, sir, he didn't."

"And this is all he said?"

"Yes, it was."

"Thanks, Irene." Dan pushed the black button on the telephone base, removed his finger, and dialed the front desk. "Hi Joyce, this is Dan Morgan. Did anyone leave a package for me?" He listened, said thank you, hung up, and looked at Dan. "No package."

"Maybe it's waiting for you at home," offered Jack.

Dan considered that while looking at the note, wondering if it was something from his son in Chicago. "Maybe," he said thoughtfully, and then he looked at Jack. "Let's go see Captain Foley."

Dan knocked on the jamb of the open door to his captain's office. "Can we talk to you, Captain?"

Foley looked up from what he was doing, set his pencil down, and gestured to three straight-back, wooden chairs in front of his desk. "Close the door and have a seat."

Dan closed the door then he and Jack sat down, looking uncomfortable.

Foley looked from one to the other. "What's on your mind?"

Dan told the captain about their trips to Englewood and Littleton. "We just left Lange's office at the city morgue." He held up one of the three envelopes. "This is everything he has on our victim." He paused, looked at Jack, and then Foley. "We believe the same person or persons killed all three girls."

Foley looked from Dan to Jack and back to Dan. "You're telling me we have a multiple killer running loose?"

Jack quickly spoke. "Looks like it. The bodies of all three girls were lying on army blankets." He looked at Dan and then Foley. "All three had been killed by exsanguination." Jack paused. "They bled out."

Captain Foley gave Jack an irritated look. "I know what it means."

"All three girls," said Dan, "had the little fingers of their left hand surgically removed while they were still alive and, my guess is, awake."

Foley felt empathy for the girls and anger at the perpetrator. "Sick bastard."

Dan nodded in agreement. My guess is he takes them for souvenirs along with their panties since none had been raped."

Captain Foley looked curious. "Not one of these girls had been sexually assaulted?"

Jack sat forward in his chair. "Not unless you define it by leaving his semen in their pubic hair."

Foley looked from one to the other. "You shitting me?"

Dan looked from Jack to the Captain. "No, sir. All three girls had been washed clean, and then the killer masturbated into their pubic hair." He shrugged. "I guess that could count as being sexually assaulted."

"Sick bastard," repeated Foley.

Dan shifted in his chair. "One thing is different; the girl in Littleton had been stabbed over seventy times postmortem."

Foley frowned. "If it is the same guy, why just stab the girl in Littleton?"

"We may never know," said Dan with a troubled look. Then he shrugged. "She was the first, and maybe it was too much for him, and he couldn't do it again." He held up the envelope of Diane Wagner. "These are photos of Miss Wagner from the Arapahoe County Coroner. Want to take a look?"

Captain Foley looked at the envelope and gestured them off with his left hand. "Not at the moment." Silence filled the room, and then he looked at Dan. "Any closer to getting an ID on our victim?"

Dan shook his head. "No one's reported a missing girl yet." Dan fussed with the three envelopes sitting under his gray fedora on his lap. "Our victim was wearing an East High School jacket, so Jack and I are going to drive over to East High tomorrow morning and see if any of the staff recognizes her picture."

Captain Foley stood, took his sidearm out of his desk, and shoved it into the holster on his belt. "I promised my wife a movie after dinner tonight."

Dan and Jack stood.

Foley gave them a look. "Appetizing stuff to think about while you're trying to enjoy dinner and a movie with your wife." Then he grabbed his hat and headed for the door to his office, opened it, then paused in thought, looking from one detective to the other. "If this bastard is following a schedule, we have a couple of weeks before another girl turns up."

"If he has a schedule," offered Dan.

Captain Foley stepped out of his office and waited for the two to step out, and then he closed and locked the office door. "Looks to me like he has one, so let's catch him before he strikes again." He paused to look at Dan. "You still need a haircut. See you two in the morning."

Still hungry, Jack turned to Dan as they walked back to their desks. "Want to get something to eat?"

"Isn't Lori expecting you home for dinner?"

"She's playing canasta tonight. So, I guess I'm on my own. I know a nice little Mexican place on 38th Avenue over on the west side."

The restaurant Jack drove to was quiet and not very busy when they walked through the front door and found a table in the corner by the front window looking out upon a small park across the street. After ordering beers and enchiladas, they sat back, enjoying their beer in silence, each filled with their thoughts about the three murders. In the stillness at the table, they watched the young children in the park across the street playing on swings and slides or chasing one another as kids do, as if living in a perfect, safe world.

Dan was thinking about the note and package, hoping the caller had been his son Robert.

Jack turned from the scene across the street, took a drink of beer, and looked at his partner. "Thinking about the note?"

Dan nodded that he was, took a drink of beer, set the bottle down, and watched his thumb scrape at the frosted label. "We have three young, pretty teenage girls dead. All killed by the same person, or persons, all posed the same, and we don't have one damn thing other than the army blankets."

Jack returned his gaze out the window at the children playing across the street. "Most of our cases start that way. Don't worry, partner. They'll come."

33

Dan took another drink of beer. "They better come pretty damn quick."

Jack turned from the window, took a drink of beer, set the bottle down, and looked at his partner. "I can't get the semen out of my mind. What kind of a sick bastard would pleasure himself on someone after he killed them?"

Dan stared at the partially torn label on his bottle, raised his brow, and shrugged as he looked across the street at the children and thought of his dead daughter. "Can't answer that, Jack."

Then Jack asked, "Remember during the war when guys took souvenirs off dead Germans?"

"Yeah," replied Dan wondering what he was getting at.

"Think taking these girls' fingers is like that?"

"More or less," said Dan as he peeled the label away from the bottle just a little more, then pushed it back with his thumb, remembering the German Luger he had given his father that was now on the top shelf of his hall closet.

Jack's eyes returned to the window. "I wonder why he bleeds them out."

Dan thought about that as he took another drink of beer. "Some sort of ritual, maybe?"

Jack considered that while he drank his beer. "I wonder if he drinks their blood."

Thinking that was too sick to consider, Dan changed the subject. "We need to find a connection between these three girls."

"What if there isn't any?"

Dan considered that. "Then, we're going to have a hard time solving these killings." He looked at the playground across the street. "I'd like to know what's going on in this guy's mind. He mutilates the body of the first, does nothing to the second or third."

Jack took a drink of beer. "Maybe he's experimenting."

Thinking Jack might be right, Dan thought about the billfolds. "He keeps their billfolds, so they won't be identified right away but misses a student ID card in the back pocket of the second victim's jeans." He paused in thought. "He was either careless, or it was deliberate, and I have a feeling it was deliberate."

"But why?"

The heavyset Mexican waitress placed their plates of food on the table. "Plates are hot," she warned, adding with a big smile, "Enjoy, señors."

Disappointed at not finding a package on the front porch, Dan put his key in the lock of his front door, turned the key, and pushed the door open, stepping into the dark foyer. He reached for the light switch, and as the overhead light filled the room, he closed the door and locked it. Feeling something under his feet, he looked down at the mail lying on the floor beneath the mail slot at the bottom of the door. Thinking about the package, he bent down and picked up the mail, glancing through it as he walked to the small table in the foyer. Disappointed that there was nothing from his son, he tossed bills and advertisements onto the table and his keys into a glass bowl. Taking off his hat, he hung it on the crowded hat rack, and at seeing his image in the framed mirror above the table, he decided that Captain Foley was right. He did need a haircut.

Turning from the mirror, he looked up at the top of the stairs, and for a moment, he imagined Norma, dressed in her white silk robe, wearing a smile as she often had when he came home late. Feeling the loneliness of the empty house, he pushed the memory of her away and started down the dark, creaky hall toward the kitchen with the three envelopes under his left arm. Stepping into the kitchen, he turned the light on and tossed the envelopes onto the chromed framed red Formica table that Norma had picked out the year before she died. Taking off his topcoat, he placed it over the back of a matching kitchen chair, walked to the refrigerator, opened it, and pulled out a bottle of beer. Closing the door while thinking of the three girls, he turned to the opener attached to the side of the cabinet where the dishes were kept and slid the bottle cap under the opener. Pulling down on the bottle and popping the cap off, he managed to catch it before it fell to the floor and tossed it into the garbage can next to the sink. Taking a drink of beer, he turned and looked at the envelopes lying on the table and thought about the girls' families.

Taking another long drink, he let out a soft belch, pulled one of the chrome chairs with red padding away from the table, and sat down. After another quick drink, he set the bottle down, then pushed the manila envelopes of Diane Wagner and Gail Thomas to one side and picked up the one with the name Barbara Unknown written in Pete Lange's scribbled handwriting. Then he penciled the name on the envelope from Todd Anderson, opened it, pulled everything out, and looked at the first photo Todd Anderson's men had taken of the crime scene. The first photo was of the girl covered by cardboard in the alley. After examining it for several moments, he set it on the table, picked up the next one of her lying on the army blanket on top of the second piece of cardboard, posed the same as the girls in Littleton and Englewood, looking as if she were sleeping. He thought she was pretty and knew her parents were going crazy by now with worry. He stared at her for several seconds, then softly asked, "Why hasn't anyone come looking for you?" He sipped his beer and stared at the photograph, thinking that he didn't want her buried in the county cemetery

35

for the indigent to be lost forever. He set the picture down, shoved it and the others to one side, and picked up the coroner's report. His eyes settled on the word exsanguination, and he imagined how terrified she must have been while the blood slowly flowed from the wound in her neck, knowing she was going to die.

He started reading what Lange had typed. Name: Barbara Unknown. Race: Caucasian. Height: 5 feet 3 inches. Weight: 89 lbs. Hair: brown. Eyes: blue. He set Pete's report down, picked up the forensics report, and read that there were no fingerprints on the cardboard, which meant someone had taken the time to wipe it clean. The report also said there were none on the girl's shoes. Dan looked up from the paper and took a drink of beer as he stared out the kitchen window at the black night, considering that the killer had known it was going to rain and had brought the cardboard with him. Thinking the killer probably drove a van, his tired eyes returned to the report, where he found no mention of panties or purse found in the five trashcans Forensics had taken from the crime scene. Disappointed but not surprised, he tossed the report on the table and took another drink of beer.

Standing with the half-empty bottle of beer, he turned off the kitchen light and walked down the dim, creaky hall into the dark living room. He walked across the lighted replica of the doorway on the wooden living room floor, left by the lights from the foyer, and dropped into a stuffed chair surrounded by shadows. He took a drink of beer and glanced around the dimly lit room until his eyes found an eight-by-ten picture sitting on a nearby table, barely visible in the dim light from the foyer. Memory told him it was of the family taken the year before his daughter's death. In the stillness of the room, he stared at the picture, thinking of happier days and nights in this lonely, creaking old house. He looked away from that photo to the dark images of other framed pictures sitting on the shelves of the bookcase on the far wall. Although he could not see these pictures, he knew from memory there were several of his parents at different ages and a few of him and his identical twin brother. He recalled how Norma often commented on how he and his brother, Donnie, looked so much alike as children.

Turning from the bookcase, he stared into the darkness while his mind found the three murdered girls having the same marks on their ankles caused by a rope the killer used to hang them upside down so they would bleed out like animals. His tired eyes found the sofa thinking it looked inviting, so he drank the last of his beer, set the empty bottle on the floor next to his chair, stood, took off his gun, and set it down on the end table. Then he stepped out of his shoes, and as he lay down on the sofa with his clothes on, his hand found the wool afghan Norma had made several years ago lying on the back of the sofa. Pulling it down, he covered himself and closed his eyes.

Five

Dan opened his eyes, looking into the early morning sun that had found its way through the lace curtains of the living room window. Putting a hand up to shield the sun from his sleepy eyes, he looked at the grandfather clock sitting in the corner, showing it was almost a quarter to six. Feeling tired, he reached for the clock's alarm on the coffee table and pushed the button so it would not go off at six. Tossing the afghan aside, he sat up, placed his stocking feet on the area rug between the sofa and the coffee table, and stared out the window at the Martins' house across the street. He recalled that it had been a while since he talked to either Fred or Joyce, as he heard footsteps on the porch, followed by the sound of empty glass milk bottles being exchanged for full ones.

Slipping into his shoes and not bothering to tie them, he picked up the empty beer bottle from the floor, walked into the foyer, and paused at the front door. Pulling back the sheer curtain covering the window of the door to one side, he watched as the milk truck stopped at the house next door, and the driver, dressed in his white uniform and hat, stepped out, carrying a wire basket of milk bottles. Glancing across the street, Dan opened the door, bent down, lifted the lid to the white wooden box, and managed to pick up both the milk and butter without dropping the empty beer bottle. As the lid fell back onto the box, sounding loud in the quiet morning, he let the screen door slam, closed the front door, and headed for the kitchen.

After putting the milk and butter in the refrigerator, he set the empty beer bottle in the corner to keep the other empty beer bottles company. Then, standing at the stove, he took a match from the matchbox on top of the stove, struck it, turned the right front burner onto low, and put the match to the gas. Once there was a flame, he blew out the match, placed it in the tray on top of the stove with other dead matches, and then filled the coffee pot with water. He spooned four tablespoons of coffee grounds into the pot's basket, put on the lid, placed it over the low flame, and went upstairs.

Dressed in a dark blue suit, white shirt, and a dark red tie, he picked up the suit he had slept in from the end of the bed and went downstairs. Greeted by the aroma of percolating coffee, he dropped his suit on a chair in the foyer, rushed into the kitchen, and turned off the burner. As the coffee continued to bubble into the tiny glass coffeepot lid, he went about the task of preparing a breakfast of two pieces of buttered toast covered heavily

38

with grape jelly and coffee. Standing over the kitchen sink, eating in the silence of the house, he looked out the window into the backyard watching the birds dance from limb to limb and a lone squirrel as it scampered across the yard, disappearing into the shrubs in front of the neighbors' weathered fence.

Shoving the last of the toast into his mouth, he poured a second cup of coffee, sat down at the table, and picked up the photos of Diane Wagner. After studying them for several moments, he decided to visit Rio Grande Park, where the body of Diane Wagner had been discovered. Finishing the last of the coffee, he cleaned up his small mess, put the photos of Diane back into the envelope, and picked up the topcoat he had left on the chair the night before. Grabbing the three envelopes, he paused at the chair in the foyer and picked up his wrinkled suit. While taking one of his three fedoras from the hat rack next to the chair, his eyes stopped on the photo of his children, Robert and Nancy hanging on the wall. He looked at each child, wishing both were upstairs sleeping, and then opened the door and stepped onto the front porch. Locking the front door, he let the screen door slam, put on his dark blue fedora, and walked down the steps of the porch toward the driveway and his waiting car. Getting in, he thought about the girl with no name and wished again that someone would file a report.

Dan walked into the detective squad room past Jack Brolin hunched over his desk, looking secretive while talking on the telephone. Wondering who his partner was talking to, Dan tossed the three envelopes onto the top of his desk that faced Jack's desk. After putting his hat and topcoat on the coat rack, he slipped out of his blue suit coat and hung it over the back of his swivel chair, secured his pistol in the right top drawer of his desk, and sat down.

Jack looked up, put his hand over the mouthpiece of the phone, and lowered his voice. "Lori wants you to come over for dinner Saturday night."

Dan considered quickly, then silently mouthed the words, 'No, thank you.'

Jack took the phone away from his face holding his hand over the mouthpiece. "Come on, Dan, Lori asked you last week and the week before that. She wants to fix this pot roast she's been talking about for a while now, and if you don't come, I'll end up with goulash or chili."

Seeing the pitiful look on his partner's face, he surrendered. "Alright."

Jack grinned happily and turned away to tell Lori.

Dan moved the three envelopes to one side of his desk, picked up the papers in his inbox, and started sorting through them.

Captain Harold Foley stepped out of his office. "Dan, tell Jack to get off the phone with Lori, and then the two of you come in."

Knowing Jack had heard the captain, Dan grinned as he stood and walked toward the captain's office, leaving Jack to say a quick goodbye.

As the two entered the captain's office, he motioned to the three chairs in front of his desk. "Have a seat." Then he sat down and waited for Jack to close the door and sit in the chair next to Dan. Captain Harold Foley of Homicide and Robbery was a stocky man of fifty, with thinning, graying, light brown hair, and a long face that bore the scar of a Japanese bayonet he had received at Tarawa during the war. He had intense, brown eyes that always seemed to look angry. "Have either of you seen this morning's paper?"

Looking puzzled, Dan and Jack glanced at one another and said they had not.

Foley looked down at the Denver Daily News on his desk and read aloud. "Vampire Killer Stalks Young Women in Metropolitan Area."

"Crap," said Dan looking irritated. "What idiot wrote that?"

Foley looked at the paper. "Howard Trenton." Then he looked at Dan. "Crap isn't strong enough, Detective. I just hung up from getting my ass chewed by the chief, and he wants this guy caught." He looked at both detectives. "Give this case priority and run down any lead, no matter how small. It might be good to re-visit the people that the Littleton and Englewood law enforcement has questioned. A couple of fresh eyes and ears can't hurt."

Dan looked at Jack. "I'll pick out a picture we got from Lange that doesn't look too bad, and then we'll head over to East High to see if someone can identify the victim."

Jack nodded. "Right."

Foley picked up his phone. "I'll call Chief Travis and Sheriff Brumwell and clear this with them, so they don't think we're trying to take over their cases." As Foley put his finger in the first number of the rotary dial, he looked at both men. "And while you're at it, try and see if there is some connection between these three girls."

Dan stood, considering that he and his partner had already discussed that, and then he followed Jack out of the captain's office.

"And get that damn haircut Morgan," hollered Captain Foley.

Dan turned, and as he closed the door, he grinned at Foley, then walked back to his desk, thinking he would get a haircut in the next couple of days. He sat down and opened the manila envelope Lange had given him and gently dumped the pictures of Barbara Unknown on top of his desk.

Jack thought about the package they had talked about yesterday. "What was in the package?"

"There wasn't one," said Dan sounding disappointed.

"Maybe it'll be there when you get home today."

Hoping it would be, Dan started looking through the pictures looking for one he and Jack could take to East High School. The telephone rang, so he stopped, picked up the receiver, put it to his ear, and said, "Morgan."

A woman's soft, sexy voice said, "Good morning, Lieutenant."

Recognizing the voice, Dan smiled. "Hello, Joyce." Thinking how pretty she had looked sitting at the front desk when he walked into the building that morning, he asked, "What's on your mind?"

Joyce Moore was a busty, small-framed woman of twenty-three with platinum blond hair, blue eyes, and sultry red lips. She spoke in a whisper. "There is a Mr. and Mrs. Crowder here to report their daughter, Sally Ann Crowder, missing. I immediately thought of your case involving that girl in the alley."

The phone went silent for several seconds while Dan wished it was Barbara instead.

"Lieutenant," said Joyce. "Are you there? Shall I send them to the missing person's desk?"

"No," Dan said hesitantly while he considered the name in the coat lining. "No, don't send them anywhere. We'll be right down." He hung up the phone and looked at his partner. "There's a couple downstairs wanting to see someone about their missing daughter."

Not looking forward to telling them about their daughter, Jack looked a little upset as he whispered, "Shit."

Dan quickly found a photo of the victim, showing her covered with a sheet with only her head and neck showing, slipped into his coat, and then rolled the picture up and put it into an inside pocket of his coat. He shoved the other pictures back into the envelope, opened the center drawer of his desk, stuffed everything into it, and looked at Jack. "Let's go."

They hurried down the back stairs, stopping on the first floor at the stairwell door where Dan looked through the small window of the metal door toward the front desk and Joyce Moore. A nicely dressed couple in their early forties with worried faces was sitting on an oak bench holding hands. The man was wearing an expensive-looking tan suit, the woman a plain, dark brown dress with a small brown hat atop her short black hair.

Jack was standing behind Dan, looking over his shoulder through the small window. "Think that's them?"

"Don't see anyone else. Joyce said their daughter's name was Sally something."

Jack looked puzzled. "Then why not send them to the missing person's desk? Our girl's name is Barbara, so why are we messing with this?"

Dan stared through the window at the couple. "Maybe we're about to have a fourth victim."

Jack looked at the side of Dan's face hoping not, and as Dan pushed the door open, Jack whispered, "I hate this."

They stepped into the hallway, and as they approached the couple, the man saw them first, stood, and then helped the woman up from the bench, both looking nervous and afraid. The woman held a wrinkled hanky in her hands, and Dan could see that she had been crying. The man had a comforting arm around her and gently gripped her shoulder with his hand while holding his expensive hat in the other.

Dan looked at the woman and then the man. "You want to report a missing person?"

The man nodded and glanced around as if someone would overhear him. and lowered his voice. "This is my wife, Sylvia. My name is Leonard Crowder."

Dan smiled. "I'm Detective Dan Morgan." Then he gestured to Jack. "This is my partner, Jack Brolin." He turned to Joyce Moore, sitting behind the front desk, leaned toward her, and spoke above a whisper. "Is there an empty room we could use?"

Joyce glanced past Dan at the couple and then at the schedule on her desk, looked up, and pointed down the hall. "Room 104 is open."

Dan thanked her and then turned to the couple. "Let's step down the hall so we can talk without all this foot traffic."

Leonard Crowder looked relieved. "That would be much better, thank you."

Dan led them down the hall to room 104 while Jack Brolin winked at a smiling Joyce as he picked up a pad and pencil from her desk and then followed Dan and the couple into the room. Standing in the open doorway, Jack asked if they would like some water or maybe a cup of coffee.

Both said thank you but declined, and then Leonard Crowder glanced around the windowless room of empty white walls and pulled a chair out from under the long oak table surrounded by stiff back oak chairs. He waited for his wife to sit down, moved a chair closer to her, and sat down. Sylvia Crowder's eyes were red and puffy, and she looked worried as she took her husband's hand and clenched her handkerchief in the other hand.

Feeling uneasy, Dan and Jack sat down across from the couple. Then Dan leaned forward in his chair, placed his elbows on the table, and looked at Leonard Crowder. "Who is it you want to report missing, Mr. Crowder?"

Leonard looked worried as he put his right arm around his wife while holding her hand with his left. "It's our daughter."

Dan smiled, trying to make this easier for them. "And what is your daughter's name?"

"Sally Ann Crowder," replied Mr. Crowder.

Jack wrote down all their names on the piece of paper he had taken from Joyce's desk.

Dan asked, "Do you have a picture of your daughter?"

Mrs. Crowder looked up from the hanky. "Not a recent one." Then her eyes welled. "I just know something has happened to her."

Feeling sorry for her and knowing she was about to cry, Jack leaned forward and looked at her husband. "Can you describe your daughter to us?"

"Well," began Mr. Crowder. "Sally's around five feet three or four---"

"Three," interrupted his wife quietly, and then wiping her eyes, she took a quick breath. "Sally has shoulder-length brown hair and blue eyes." She paused to control her emotions. "She's slender." Then shaking her head and looking as if she was about to cry, she said, "She's not a very big girl."

The description fit the girl in the morgue at Denver General to a T, thought Dan, and then he asked, "How old is Sally, Mrs. Crowder?"

"Sixteen," she replied.

"Just turned sixteen on the third of March," added Mr. Crowder in a voice filled with emotion.

Dan looked at Mrs. Crowder and thought of Norma when he had told her a hit-and-run driver had killed their daughter. "When was the last time you saw your daughter?"

Leonard and Sylvia looked at one another, and then Mr. Crowder said, "It was Friday morning, just before she went to school. I gave her twenty dollars to see her through the weekend."

That's a lot of money, thought Dan. "You said through the weekend."

Jack frowned. "Today is Wednesday, Mr. Crowder. That was five days ago. Why did you wait so long to report her missing?"

Leonard looked embarrassed as he took his arm from around his wife. "She was staying with a girlfriend." Then, unable to go on, he turned his head and wiped his eyes and cheeks.

Mrs. Crowder put her hand on her husband's and affectionately squeezed it as she looked at Jack and then Dan. "Leonard and I went to

Colorado Springs to visit some friends for the weekend. Sally was to stay with her friend, Barbara Sutton, a girl from school."

Dan felt relieved, knowing that explained the name crocheted inside the jacket, and wondered where this Barbara Sutton was, hoping she would not turn up as their next victim.

"Where does your daughter go to school?" asked Jack.

"East High School," replied Mr. Crowder after composing himself.

Mrs. Crowder watched as Jack wrote on the pad, and then she looked at Dan. "It's not unusual for Sally to stay with one of her friends over a weekend and come home on Sunday night. She's a good girl, does her homework, gets good grades, and never gets into trouble."

"I'm sure she is," smiled Dan, who then asked, "How long were you gone?"

"What difference does that make?" asked Sylvia Crowder.

Jack leaned toward her. "We are just trying to get a timeline, Mrs. Crowder."

Leonard answered. "We left Friday afternoon and came back late Monday evening."

Mrs. Crowder looked at her husband and then at the two detectives. "There was no school on Monday, and it was after nine in the evening when we got home."

Leonard put his arm around his wife and looked at both men. "I called the Suttons, but the line was busy. Sylvia was tired and not feeling very well, so she went upstairs to bed. I read for a while, waiting to call the Sutton's again, and at some point, I fell asleep in the chair." He looked at his wife, filled with guilt. "I didn't wake up until early Tuesday morning." He looked down at the table and then at Dan with tearful eyes. "I went upstairs to Sally's room to see if she had come home, but her bed had not been slept in." He wiped his eyes as he looked at his wife. "I'm so sorry, Sylvia."

She gently put one hand on his cheek and whispered. "It's not your fault, dear."

Feeling sorry for the two, Dan and Jack sat in uncomfortable silence, letting them have their moment.

Mrs. Crowder looked at Jack and then Dan. "We thought Sally had decided to stay another night and go to school with her friend Barbara. She's done that before. We wanted to call the Suttons right away, but it was four-thirty Tuesday morning when Leonard woke up, so we waited until a more decent hour."

Leonard Crowder looked from Jack to Dan. "I couldn't wait any longer, and I called again at six." He took his arm from around his wife, folded his hands on the table, and wrung them while looking angry. "Mr.

Sutton was a little put out with us for calling so early." He looked up. "After he knew the situation, he calmed down and checked his daughter's room while I waited on the telephone. He told us that Barbara had said that our Sally had left for home Monday after lunch." Mr. Crowder looked at Jack. "That's when I called the police."

Dan was relieved about the other girl being safe at home.

"What did the police tell you?" asked Jack.

"The officer on the telephone said we had to wait forty-eight hours and then come down to the station and fill out a missing person's report. But before we did that, he suggested we check with her other friends and the school to make certain she was missing."

A heavy silence filled the room while Dan thought that was poor judgment on the officer's part. Then he tried thinking of a way to tell them their daughter may be lying dead in a cooler at Denver General. Deciding to go ahead, he reached into his suit coat pocket, pulled out the rolled-up picture he had brought with him, and held it at his side. "I have a picture I'd like to show you."

"A picture?" asked Mr. Crowder as he glanced at what Dan was holding. Fear filled his face as he looked at his wife and then into Dan's blue eyes. "What sort of picture?"

Dan wished he did not have to do this as he unrolled the eight-by-ten photograph and placed it face down on the table. "It's of a young girl."

Feeling sorry for the couple, Jack put the pencil on top of the pad and sat back in his chair, glad that his partner was handling this.

Leonard Crowder stared at the back of the picture for several moments, looking afraid.

"I have to warn you, Mr. Crowder," said Dan. "The girl in this picture is deceased."

A soft, mournful sound came from Mrs. Crowder as she buried her face in her hands and wept.

Feeling sorry for the couple, Dan slid the picture across the table toward Mr. Crowder and waited for him to pick it up.

Leonard slowly reached for the picture and pulled it across the top of the table face down while Mrs. Crowder sat up, slid her arm around her husband's, and stared at the back of the photo with fear on her face.

Mr. Crowder slowly turned the picture over.

Mrs. Crowder suddenly let go of her husband's arm and turned away, half crying and half screaming, "Oh my God!" Then she leaned down on the table, cradled her face in the elbow of her right arm, and sobbed.

Tears ran down Leonard's face as he stared at the picture for a long moment, listening to his wife crying before he looked at Dan. "This is our Sally," he said in a sobbing voice.

Feeling like shit, Dan stood. "We'll give you a few minutes." Then he turned to Jack and nodded toward the door.

After the door closed, Dan and Jack stood in the hall listening to the couple's muffled sobbing and Mr. Crowder asking God why He had let this happen. He recalled his mother's sobbing so many years ago and then Norma's over their daughter Nancy, both asking the same question of God that went unanswered.

Jack Brolin stepped away from the wall. "I'll call Pete Lange and have him get the body ready."

Dan stood in silence with his back against the wall, staring down at the floor, listening to the couple behind the door, remembering the day his dad had told him about his twin brother Donnie.

Six

January 14th, 1918

Daniel Morgan sat in the window seat of his bedroom, watching the soft snowflakes float past the window, getting lost in the white snow-covered yard and street. Staring at the tire tracks left by the police car, the sounds of his mother's muffled sobbing downstairs made their journey into his quiet bedroom. Wondering what terrible news the police officer had brought, he wished his brother was here with him while waiting for his father to come upstairs and tell him. The bedroom door opened, and he turned from the window.

Charles Morgan quietly closed the door, sat down on the edge of Daniel's bed, and motioned for Daniel to sit on the bed next to him.

Daniel slid off of the window seat and sat next to his father. As his father put his arm around him, Daniel looked up into his father's red puffy eyes and moved closer to him for comfort.

Charles Morgan looked at his son with welling eyes. "Donnie is gone, son."

Daniel stared into his father's tearing eyes, afraid of the answer to his question, but he had to ask. "What do you mean by gone, Father?"

Moments of silence passed while Charles fought the need to cry, and then he softly said, "The good Lord has taken Donnie, son."

Daniel's eyes welled, and tears ran down his cheeks. Standing, he stepped back and yelled, "You're lying to me! Donnie's not dead!"

Charles reached out and gently took his son by the shoulders. "I'm not lying to you, son, I would never be so cruel, but Donnie is dead." Then he slid from the bed to his knees and pulled Daniel into his arms.

As tears made their way down Daniel's face, he felt his father's wet cheeks on his. "How?"

Not wanting to tell his son the truth about Donnie being sexually assaulted and murdered, he said, "It was an accident."

His cheeks wet with tears, Daniel pushed away from his father's arms, ran out of his room and down the stairs. Grabbing his coat, hat, and scarf, he wrapped the scarf around his neck and looked into the parlor at his mother lying on the sofa, looking like she was sleeping. He wanted to go to her but instead reached for the doorknob.

His father was at the top of the stairs. "Where are you going, son?"

With tears in his eyes, Daniel looked up the stairs at his father, put on his hat, opened the door, ran outside, and closed the door behind him.

47

Pausing at the edge of the porch in the cold crisp air, he slipped into his coat and then hurried down the steps and ran across the snow-covered yard, chased by the sound of cold crunching snow under his feet.

It was late evening and getting dark when Daniel walked up the steps to the porch, paused at the door while wondering what he would find inside. Opening the door, he stepped inside, finding the house quiet and dark but for the light in the foyer. He quietly closed the door, locked it, took off his hat, coat, and scarf, hung them up next to the door, and started toward the stairs.

Charles was sitting in the darkness of the parlor. "Son," he said.

Daniel paused and then walked into the dim parlor, seeing his father sitting in a chair, staring out the window into the darkness. "Where's mother?" he asked with a child's soft voice.

"Upstairs. I hope she's sleeping, so be quiet." A long pause filled the quiet parlor. "Come sit next to me, son."

Daniel hesitated, then walked the short distance with slumped shoulders, sat down on the sofa across from his father, and stared at the dark floor.

"Are you alright, son?"

Daniel thought of life without his twin brother and began to cry. "I'll never be alright again."

Charles wanted to tell his son that one day he would be, but instead, he asked, "Where have you been?"

"Walking." Looking up from the floor, he saw his father's dim face reflecting what little light made its way from the foyer. "How did Donnie die?"

Charles lied. He must have slipped on the snow or ice and hit his head. Someone found him earlier today."

Daniel's eyes welled, and as the tears made their way down his cheeks, he stood. "May I be excused, Father?"

Charles managed a small smile. "Go on up, son, but be quiet."

Daniel walked up the stairs, paused at the top, looked at the closed door of his parent's room, and then at the closed door to his brother's room. He walked to the door, hesitated, then slowly opened it, and stepped inside. After quietly shutting the door and being engulfed in the darkness, he stood with his back against it and looked around at Donnie's room. The moonlight coming through the window left a perfect image of the window on the bed turning everything white, with black shadows. He walked to the bed his brother would never sleep in again, lay down on top of the covers, rested his head against Donnie's pillow, and stared out the window at the black sky and stars.

48

In the moonlit darkness of Donnie's room, Daniel Morgan knew life would never be as it had been or as it would have been. He and his twin had shared so many things that it seemed one always knew what the other was going to say, which caused them to giggle in secret. He felt different now as if he was incomplete and feeling very alone for the first time in his short life. Those feelings would stay with Daniel for the rest of his life, and as he wept for the loss of his brother, he remembered feeling anxious and fearful earlier that day. It was as if something was pulling at him, and he didn't know where to go or what to do, so he stayed in his bedroom and read. Now he knew it was because Donnie, lying hurt someplace, had reached out for him. As the guilt found him, he wondered if he had said something to his mother or father, maybe Donnie would still be alive. Fear of that settled within him, and he swore in silence that he would never speak of those feelings to anyone. Wanting sleep and hoping that this would be but a bad dream when he awoke, he closed his eyes.

"Lange said he'd have everything ready," said Jack Brolin.

Dan Morgan looked up from the floor, nodded as he stood away from the wall, turned, opened the door, and stepped into the room.

"Where's our daughter?" asked Leonard Crowder.

"A few blocks from here," replied Dan softly. "She's at Denver General over on 6th and Cherokee."

Mrs. Crowder wiped her red, swollen eyes with the wet hanky she held. "Can we see our daughter now?"

"The arrangements are made," said Jack. "We're sorry for your loss."

"One last question," said Dan. "Did Sally carry a billfold or purse?"

Sylvia Crowder looked at him with red, welling eyes and nodded. "A red billfold. Why?"

"It's missing," said Dan softly. He wanted to say something more than, *'Sorry for your loss,'* but words did not seem to be enough at this moment. "Maybe it would be best if the two of you ride over with us."

"That might be a good idea, Detective," said Mr. Crowder as he stood and helped his wife up from her chair.

Dan held the door open and waited for the Crowder's as they walked around the table holding onto one another, and as Sylvia Crowder passed, he said, "I'm very sorry."

She paused, looking sad, and softly asked, "Have you ever lost a child or loved one, Detective?"

Jack looked at his partner, thinking of Dan's daughter and wife.

Dan warmly smiled as he thought of his wife and daughter. "No, ma'am."

Sylvia Crowder touched Dan's arm gently. "Pray to God you never do."

The sound of leather soles on the checkered, black, and white tiled floor filled the empty basement hall of Denver General. Dan, Jack, and the Crowder's stopped at the door with the black words *'Coroner's Office'* painted on the frosted glass. Dan tapped the glass lightly and waited.

Pete Lange, dressed in his white smock, opened the door, looked at Dan, then Jack, and then at Mr. and Mrs. Crowder.

Dan gestured to the couple. "This is Mr. and Mrs. Crowder."

Pete stepped to one side. "Of course," he said softly with a small compassionate smile and gestured to the door leading into the morgue. "I have everything ready. This way, please."

Mr. and Mrs. Crowder hesitated, then looking fearful, they followed Pete into the other room. Just inside the door, Mrs. Crowder turned and looked back at Dan with a pleading face. "Would you mind coming with us?"

Not wanting to, Dan glanced at Jack but then stepped inside, closed the door, and waited in front of it while Mr. and Mrs. Crowder followed Pete to a high metal table on wheels where a body lay under a white sheet. The room was quiet and chilly, with every sound amplified off the tiled floor and bare white cement walls. He watched the Crowder's as Pete pulled the sheet back, exposing Nancy's innocent face. He remembered looking down at his daughter's face wanting to scream and tear the place apart. But all he could do was look down on his daughter's pale face, silently curse the driver of the car that killed her and hold Norma close.

Pete Lange had positioned the body so the Crowder's would look at the right side, away from the mark on the neck. "Ready?" he asked.

Both nodded their heads, and as Mrs. Crowder looked down at her daughter's pale face, she softly said her name mixed with sobs of sorrow. She leaned against the gurney that held her daughter and gently touched her hair and cold cheek. Suddenly her knees gave way, but Leonard and Pete grabbed her before she hit the floor. Dan rushed over to help while her husband and Lange slowly let her come to rest on her knees against the cold tile floor. Loud sobbing filled the impersonal room as she grabbed the sheet that covered her daughter in her hands and cried into it. Leonard looked at his daughter, then he knelt with his wife, and there they embraced and cried.

Several minutes passed before Pete Lange gave Dan a look he knew was one seeking his assistance.

Dan knelt beside them. "Please, Mr. Crowder, Mrs. Crowder. Let's go into the other room where you can make the necessary arrangements. There's nothing more you can do for your daughter here."

Moments passed before she looked up at Dan through red, watery eyes. "Why would someone want to hurt my baby?"

Not having the words that would comfort her, Dan said, "I don't know Mrs. Crowder."

Leonard Crowder looked at Pete Lange. "How did she die?"

Pete looked at Mr. Crowder and then Mrs. Crowder. "Loss of blood from a cut on the side of her throat." He paused a moment and then, hoping to ease their pain, added, "It would have been as if she went to sleep."

Mrs. Crowder continued to sob while Mr. Crowder asked, "Was our daughter…" then let the sentence trail off.

Knowing what he was trying to ask, Pete thought of the semen in her the girl's pubic hair and shook his head. "No, she was not."

Looking somewhat relieved, Mr. Crowder helped his wife up and watched as Pete pulled the sheet over the daughter he would never see again. Mrs. Crowder reached out and gently touched the sheet covering Sally's face, turned, and walked with her husband into the other room.

A heavy silence filled Dan Morgan's car as he and Jack Brolin drove the Crowder's back to the station, and their car parked on Champa Street in front of the police station. Dan parked his car, got out, and opened the back door while Jack climbed out of the passenger side.

Leonard helped his wife out of Dan's car and into theirs while Dan and Jack looked on, feeling sorry for the couple. As he closed the car door, he turned with a terrible sadness on his face and walked toward them. "My wife and I want to thank you both for being with us in that terrible place, Detectives. It meant a lot." He looked off into the distance of the warm afternoon for a moment while tears made their way down his unshaven cheeks. "I'm a deacon in our church," he said, turning to Dan. "And the Lord teaches forgiveness, but I have no forgiveness in my heart."

"We'll do our best to catch whoever did this," said Dan. "I promise."

"Yes, we will, Mr. Crowder," agreed Jack.

Crowder's face contorted with pain as he cried while looking at the car where his wife waited. "Death searches us all out, Detective, and God forgive me, but I hope it finds whoever did this and takes him in the worst and cruelest, painful of ways." He paused to wipe his face with both hands, and when composed, he looked at Dan and then Jack. "Thank you both for your kindnesses."

51

"One last thing," said Dan. "Did your daughter know or ever talk about a Diane Wagner or Gail Thomas?"

Leonard looked puzzled as he thought for a moment and then shook his head. "Never heard her mention either name. Is it important?"

"It could be," said Dan.

Mr. Crowder thought for a moment. "I don't recall the names. Maybe I'll ask Sylvia in a day or two when she feels better."

"Well," said Dan. "If you should run across the names, please call either my partner or me."

Leonard nodded. "I teach Bible school on Sunday mornings" He paused as if he wanted to say something more, but instead, he turned and walked around the car, getting into the driver's side.

Dan and Jack watched the car pull away from the curb while Dan Morgan wished today was Friday instead of Wednesday. Needing a distraction, he was looking forward to Saturday night and dinner with Jack and Lori. He put his hand on his partner's shoulder. "Guess we better tell the captain we've identified the girl."

Thursday afternoon, Detective Jack Brolin headed south to Littleton to talk with the parents of Diane Wagner and visit a couple of surplus stores to see if anyone had bought a supply of blankets. Both efforts were fruitless.

Dan drove to Sally Crowder's friend Barbara Sutton's house, who had probably been the last person to see her alive other than the killer. He parked in front of a beige brick home in an expensive east Denver neighborhood, got out of the car, and walked up the long sidewalk separating a well-manicured lawn to a small cement porch bordered in colorful flowers. He pushed the doorbell, hearing a muffled sound inside, and then pulled the leather wallet containing his badge from the inside pocket of his blue suit.

The door opened, and a woman in her late thirties stood in the doorway wearing black pedal pushers and a white silk blouse buttoned to the collar. She was pretty, with short black hair, brown eyes, and a friendly but cautious smile. "May I help you?"

He held his badge up so she could see it. "Sorry to bother you, ma'am. I'm Detective Dan Morgan of the Denver Police. Are you Mrs. Sutton?"

Her smile quickly faded. "Are you here about Sally?"

"Yes, ma'am."

"It's a terrible thing. Sally was such a sweet girl."

"I'm sure she was," said Dan. "I'd like to talk to Barbara for a few moments if that'd be alright."

Mrs. Sutton unlocked the screen door and stepped back, allowing Dan to step inside. "Of course. Forgive my rudeness. Please come in."

52

Taking off his fedora as he stepped inside, he folded the wallet with the badge and slipped it into the inside pocket of his suit coat.

Mrs. Sutton lowered her voice while glancing down the hall toward four closed doors. "I've been throwing away the newspaper so Barbara wouldn't see the headlines."

Knowing that neither the Littleton, Englewood nor the Denver Police Department had released all of the circumstances to the press, Dan lowered his voice. "The newspapers are just sensationalizing this to sell papers, Mrs. Sutton."

"I understand that, but I must ask why anyone would hurt a sweet girl like Sally?"

Dan shrugged, looking uncertain. "I'm afraid we won't know that until we catch him."

Mrs. Sutton considered that with a disappointed look. "Well, let's hope that's soon." Then she said, "Barbara is in her room. I'll get her."

Dan watched her walk down the long hall of closed doors to one where she softly knocked and then disappeared inside. He turned his attention to the large living room of expensive furniture, paintings, and a baby grand piano in the far corner by the window.

Mrs. Sutton cut his journey around the room short by saying, "This is my daughter Barbara."

He turned to a beautiful young girl with long, brown hair and red, puffy, brown eyes standing before him. "Hello, Barbara. I'm Detective Dan Morgan. I'm sorry about your friend."

"Thank you," she said, putting a wrinkled hanky to her eyes.

He smiled. "Are you up to a few questions?"

She sniffled and then nodded. "It's okay, I guess."

Mrs. Sutton put one arm around her daughter and gestured to the living room. "Perhaps we should all sit down." Then she looked at Dan. "Would you care for a cup of coffee?"

"No, thank you," replied Dan, and chose a comfortable overstuffed chair placing his hat on the floor next to it.

Mrs. Sutton and her daughter sat next to one another on the sofa, their backs to the large picture window framing a brick home and manicured lawn across the street behind them.

Dan reached into his suit coat and took out a small pad and a stubby pencil with a worn eraser. His face held a friendly smile as he looked at Barbara. "When was the last time you saw Sally?"

"Monday, just after lunch." She started to cry.

Her mother patted her on the shoulder. 'It's alright, dear."

Dan gave her a few moments. "Where was that?"

"We split a strawberry malt and some peanut butter crackers at a creamery on Capitol Hill."

"How did you get there?"

Barbara glanced at her mother and then looked at Dan with a small shrug. "Walked. It's only a few blocks. Then we walked to Chessman Park on 8th Ave."

Dan wrote that in his notepad, and being familiar with the park, he asked, "Why did you go to the park?"

She glanced at her mother and shrugged again. Something to do, I guess. We met some friends there."

"Guy friends?" he asked.

She glanced at her mother once again and then nodded with a shy yes.

Dan smiled at her. "Are you alright talking about this? If not, we can do this another time."

She shook her head, wiped her eyes and nose with the hanky. "I'm fine."

Mrs. Sutton looked worried. "Are you sure, sweetheart?"

She smiled at her mother and nodded. "I'm fine, mother. I want to do this."

Dan smiled at her. "Why was Sally wearing your jacket?"

She chuckled nervously. "I don't know. She didn't have one, I guess. We always borrow one another's clothes." Then she looked sad. "That is, we used to."

He smiled. "You're doing great. Just one or two more questions. Did Sally leave the park with anyone?"

"No. Sally said she had to get home before her mother and father got back from Colorado Springs."

Mrs. Sutton looked at Dan. "Are we about done, Detective? I think my daughter has answered enough questions for now." She smiled at him. "You're welcome back at another time."

Barbara looked at her mother. "It's alright, mother. I want to do this." She paused and looked at Dan. "I want to help."

Dan thought for a moment. "Where were you and Sally in the park at the last moment you saw her?"

She thought a moment. "I'm not sure."

He sat back, looking thoughtful, and then he looked at Mrs. Sutton. "I have a strange request, Mrs. Sutton."

"What is it?" she asked, looking worried.

"I'd like to take Barbara on a little ride if that would be okay?" He quickly added. "You're welcome to come along, of course."

Mrs. Sutton frowned and looked at her daughter with worry. "A ride? To where?"

"I want to go where the girls went on that day."

Mrs. Sutton thought for a moment. "I'm not sure that would be a good thing."

"It would help," said Dan putting his pad and stubby pencil away.

Barbara looked at her mother. "If it will help, I want to do this."

Dan helped Mrs. Sutton into his 1949 Ford's back seat while Barbara Sutton got into the passenger seat. He drove while she directed him to the creamery on Capitol Hill, where she and Sally had shared the malt and peanut butter crackers for lunch that day. He parked in the lot facing the windows of the creamery, seeing several young boys and girls inside at the counter or sitting in booths by the windows looking happy and having a good time while listening to the music coming from the jukebox. "Did you notice anyone strange or notice anyone following you?"

Barbara smiled. "All the boys are strange."

Dan grinned at that. "But you never saw anyone other than the usual strange boys hanging around?"

She smiled and shook her head. "Just the same strange boys that always hang out here."

He started the car and drove to Chessman Park, where she directed him to the parking area next to the giant sundial. After shutting the car engine off, he smiled at Barbara, opened his car door, and said, "Let's get out for a minute."

Mrs. Sutton waited in the car while Dan and Barbara walked to the sundial. Standing next to it, they looked out across the acres of green grass below a clear blue sky with the blue hazy Rocky Mountains in the distance behind the Denver skyline. She pointed to the south edge of the park. "Sally walked down the hill toward 8th Ave. She lives just a few blocks from here."

"Think for a moment," said Dan. "Did you see anyone suspicious hanging around?"

"I didn't pay any attention. There were a lot of people that day and lots of cars."

Thinking the park would be crowded, he asked, "Did you watch your friend for long?"

"No, we said goodbye and that we'd talk the next day at school." She pointed in the other direction. "I turned and walked home that way."

"Did you walk alone?"

She shook her head. "Steve and Billy walked with me." She smiled. "Steve was sweet on Sally. He lives just a few houses from mine." She paused, looking sad. "I think he'll miss her."

Dan quickly considered that. "One last question. Do you recognize the names Diane Wagner or Gail Thomas?"

She thought for a moment and then shook her head. "No, I don't think so. Why?"

"Just a couple of names I came across." Disappointed, he took Barbara back to the car and drove her and her mother home. After seeing them to the door, he thanked Barbara, shook Mrs. Sutton's hand, got into his car, and drove back to Chessman Park. He pulled into a parking space in front of the sundial, shut off the car, and wrote everything that Barbara had told him into his notepad. Then he put it into his suit coat pocket, took off his hat, tossed it on the passenger seat, got out. He glanced round as he walked to the sundial, where several people were walking around, talking, and laughing. Another man took a picture of his wife standing next to the sundial using the mountains and Denver skyline as a backdrop.

Dan lit a cigarette and looked in the direction Barbara and her friends had walked while taking a long drag from his cigarette, wondering if she would be the one missing if Sally had been with the two boys. Blowing smoke from the cigarette into the air, he turned and looked in the direction that Sally Crowder had gone and then at the winding street snaking its way through the park with several cars parked on the grass alongside the paved road. He took another drag from his cigarette as he looked at the parking lot. "You were here, weren't you, you bastard? You were hunting."

He dropped the cigarette on the cement, stepped on it, and started walking down the hill, tracing Sally's steps. Reaching the bottom and the sidewalk along 8th Ave., he paused to take the small notepad out of his coat pocket. Opening it, he flipped through the pages until he found the Crowder address. Memorizing it, he put the notepad back into the inside pocket of his suit, hurried across 8th Ave., and stepped up onto the sidewalk. He turned and walked toward Sally Crowder's home at the next corner, looking for a place where someone could abduct her without anyone seeing. He walked to within a few houses of the Crowder residence. Having found no such place, he turned and walked back toward 8th Avenue., wondering where Sally had gone after she left her friend Barbara.

Leaving Chessman Park, Dan drove west on 8th Avenue toward downtown and Police Headquarters, filled with the mystery of Sally Crowder. The light changed to red, and as he stopped, he noticed a young girl on the

56

corner leaning into the window of an older 1940 Ford, talking to a couple of young boys. The door opened, one of the boys got out, and the girl climbed into the front seat, sitting between the two boys. He watched as they drove away and wondered if Sally Crowder had gotten into a car with someone. A car horn behind him sounded, and as he looked in the rearview mirror at the impatient driver, he drove across the intersection, thinking Sally may have gotten into a car, believing she was getting a ride home. Maybe they were dealing with an older boy at East High or a college student from the university.

Arriving back at headquarters, Dan and Jack compared notes and then met with Captain Foley. Jack did not have a lot to show for his visit with the Wagner's, and the names of the other victims were not familiar to any of the family. The two surplus stores he visited had said they sold many army blankets, but they didn't keep track of who bought them.

Captain Foley was interested in what Dan had to say about the park and Sally's walk home and agreed that she might have taken a ride from someone. He particularly liked Dan's idea about a college student. He sat back in his chair, looking concerned. "I'd hate to think we have a repeat killer at our college. A lot of girls these days get into cars they have no business getting into." He looked at his two detectives. "This may be a new student at the college. It might be a good idea to visit there and see who's new, then canvas the school and see if anyone remembers seeing her that day in the park or getting into a car." He paused, then asked, "What's next?"

"Well," said Dan. "We need to pay a visit to Gail Thomas's home tomorrow." Dan paused and looked at Jack. "When we're done there, we'll go to the college and then talk with some of the neighbors living between the Crowder's and the park."

On Friday, the visit to Gail Thomas's mother provided no new evidence or theories of the three murders. She had never heard of the other two girls, and it was looking more and more like there was no connection between the three high school girls except for their similarity in age and looks. After leaving the Thomas residence, they stopped at two army surplus stores and got the same story Jack had gotten from the other two. Both sold lots of army blankets and other surplus items, but neither kept records of who bought what, and neither could recall anyone buying a large number of blankets. They drove to the college from the last surplus store and found several new students from out of state. After getting a list of those students, they drove to the Crowder neighborhood. They talked to several neighbors, but no one remembered seeing or hearing anything the day Sally disappeared.

Returning to headquarters, Dan sat down, took the list of students out, and started going over it.

Jack pushed his chair away from his desk and stood. "It's almost six," he said, slipping into his coat.

Dan looked at his wristwatch as he leaned back in his chair and stretched while looking into the captain's empty office. Then, he looked at Jack. "I'll see you tomorrow afternoon."

"You staying?" asked Jack as he pulled his Thirty-eight out of his desk and slid it into its holster.

Dan stood. "No." He stood up, retrieved his gun from his desk drawer, shoved it into his holster, pushed his chair under his desk, and slipped into his blue suit coat. Taking his topcoat from the coat rack, he put on his fedora and picked up the three large manila envelopes. "There's a couple of army surplus stores I pass on my way home. I think I'll stop in and see what they have to say."

They walked down the stairs together and out the front door to the parking lot. Dan drove east on Colfax, stopping at the two surplus stores, but neither kept records as to who purchased what from their stores, and both had sold army blankets in the past month. He walked out of the last store, feeling the failure of his quest, got into his car, and drove home.

Seven

The Saturday afternoon sun was all but gone when Dan Morgan turned north off East 6th Avenue into Jack and Lori Brolin's quiet neighborhood. He was still thinking of the murdered teenage girls and was sure there was a connection, but none of the families were familiar with the other girl's names. He recalled how bitter Mrs. Thomas was over her only daughter's death when he and Jack had visited her on Friday. Knowing how it felt to lose a child, he felt sorry for her and remembered his bitterness.

Stopping in front of a modest, single-story, brick home with manicured lawn and colorful flowers lining the front of the house and big cement covered porch, Dan noticed Jack's new, gray 1951 Ford. Looking like it had just been washed and polished in the driveway, Dan turned off the engine and then reached for the bottle of red wine, opened the car door, and climbed out.

Stepping over the curb onto the freshly mowed green grass and then onto the sidewalk, he made his way to the narrow cement walk leading up to the front porch, looking forward eagerly to a home-cooked meal. Soft music made its way through the screen door and open window as he stepped up onto the porch. Glancing at the white, wooden swing for two suspended by chains from the porch ceiling as well as the two yellow metal chairs that faced it, he pushed the doorbell.

Jack Brolin, looking comfortable in a pair of gray slacks and black turtleneck shirt, was at the door wearing a big grin. He unlocked the screen door and pushed it open, noticing the sack Dan carried. "What's in the sack?"

Dan shoved it against Jack's stomach as he stepped inside. "A bottle of wine."

As he took the wine, Jack smiled appreciatively. "You didn't need to do that."

"It's a cheap bottle," said Dan as he glanced around the familiar living room. "Don't make more out of it than it is."

Jack grinned, knowing it was not cheap, and gestured to a comfortable looking pale yellow floral, stuffed chair. "Have a seat. I'll tell Lori you're here and put this on ice." Then he walked toward the dining room, talking over his shoulder. "Can I fix you a drink?"

Dan sat down in the stuffed chair, getting comfortable. "I could use a bourbon on ice." His eyes roamed the room of fine furniture, including a console with a seventeen-inch television screen next to the radio and record player where the soft music was coming from, thinking he should get a bigger television.

Lori Brolin walked in from the dining room dressed in a pink, print dress covered by a white apron and bearing the fruits of her labors in the kitchen. She was a pretty woman of five-two, a little on the heavy side but not fat. Her face was oval with nice features, full lips, brown eyes, and long, brown hair that swayed as she walked.

Dan stood while returning her smile. "Hello, Lori."

They casually embraced as she gave him a small kiss on his cheek and then wiped the lipstick off with her thumb. She turned to her husband, who was at the liquor cabinet, pouring two bourbons over ice. "Where are your manners, Jack? Take Dan's coat."

Looking embarrassed and a little irritated, Jack put the bottle down while Dan slipped out of his brown suit coat. After taking the coat, Jack pointed at Dan's tie. "The tie."

Lori smiled as she watched Dan take off his tie. "I'm so happy you could make it tonight."

"Thanks for the invitation." He handed his tie to Jack and glanced toward the dining room and kitchen beyond. "Something smells good."

She looked unsure. "I hope you enjoy it." Then with a concerned look asked, "How have you been?"

Dan nodded a few times, feeling glad that was out of the way. "I'm good, Lori. Thanks for asking."

She glanced at her husband. "I'll leave you two to talk." She turned to leave but stopped and looked at Dan with a smile. "Thanks for bringing the wine."

Jack grinned. "Dan said it was a cheap bottle."

She laughed softly. "I'm sure it's just fine." Then she disappeared into the kitchen.

While Jack hung Dan's coat and tie in the hall closet, Dan unbuttoned his shirt's top button and rolled up his sleeves, getting comfortable.

Jack returned to the liquor cabinet and poured the bourbon. "Did you get the package yet?"

Dan shook his head. "Must be lost."

"It'll show," said Jack with certainty. "What did you do today besides sitting around on your ass?"

The music stopped, and Dan glanced at the record player as the next record dropped, followed by the needle's scratchy sound finding its way along the grooves of the record. "Cleaned house."

Jack looked surprised. "I thought you had a housekeeper for that."

The sound of soft music from the record filled the room. Dan grinned. "I do, but the place still gets messy."

Jack chuckled as he picked up the two drinks. "Shit, there's only one of you. How messy can it get?"

Dan returned to the stuffed chair, ignoring the question, and looked out the window at the curtain-covered, lighted windows of the house across the street.

Jack handed him a drink and then sat down on the sofa under the big picture window that Dan had been staring out and held his glass up. "Here's to us." He took a drink while noticing Dan's hair. "You got your haircut?"

Dan chuckled. "I think Foley was getting a little pissed, so I thought I'd better before he had me walking a beat downtown."

Jack chuckled, knowing the captain would never do that to his senior detective. He took a sip of his drink, trying to think of something to talk about besides the dead girls and Dan's lonely life. "Think the Dodgers will win the pennant this year?"

Dan gave him a look, wondering why he would ask that, knowing that an argument always followed anything about the Dodgers. "Are you serious?"

Jack shrugged. "Why not?"

"They're bums, and you know it."

Saving the two from the eternal argument about the Dodgers and baseball, Lori appeared at the dining room door. "Dinner's on the table."

As they ate dinner, the two men talked about high school, Friday night football games, and some of the harmless trouble they got into in those days. As they ate dessert and drank more coffee, the subject of the war and their time as MP's with the Rangers in Europe became the topic of conversation. Neither mentioned the 90-foot climb up the cliffs at Pointe du Hoc in Normandy, which had taken the lives of several of their friends.

Though she had heard these stories more than a dozen times over the years, Lori laughed at them anyway, thankful their stories took her husband and Dan away from the reality of their jobs and Dan's loneliness. She smiled affectionately and watched as they recalled some of the men they had known and the good times that brought tears of laughter to their eyes.

The evening flew by, and in a moment of pause, the grandfather clock in the corner of the dining room tolled eleven. Dan looked at it, resenting its accuracy, knowing the time had come for him to leave. Wanting to hold onto the moment and the company a little longer, he asked for one last cup of coffee.

Detective Morgan got out of his car, stepped into the cool night air, tossed the cigarette he had been smoking onto the pavement, and quietly shut the car door. After locking it, he walked to the curb and stepped onto the sidewalk, colored in various colors from several neon signs in windows or above doorways. Soft music from the jukebox inside the '16th Street Bar' accompanied Dan as he walked toward the alley where the young Sally Crowder's body had been found last Monday night. Walking past two drunks sharing a bottle of cheap wine in the doorway of a closed store, he paused at the alley entrance under the red neon sign, 'Rooms,' noticing the second 'o' was still burned out. He turned from the sign and looked up the dark alley filled with islands of light from light fixtures hanging above locked rear doors. Glancing up and down the empty sidewalk of 16th Street and the bent legs of the two derelicts in the doorway, he unbuttoned his suit coat, pulled his Thirty-eight from its holster with his right hand, and stepped into the dark alley.

The music and noise of the street behind him grew faint and were replaced by his footsteps on the cold cement as he walked farther into the alley. A faint car horn and trolley bells filled the black night as he walked past the metal grates where the warm air of the sewer met the chilly night air, creating an eerie mist. Stepping in and out of the islands of light, he walked toward the spot where he had first looked down at Sally Crowder's body and her lifeless blue eyes. He thought of her mother, sobbing while standing over her in the morgue, and of Leonard Crowder's wish for vengeance.

Standing over the spot that had lured him into the alley, he stood a few feet from the circle of dim light that lit up the cement from a fixture above the rear door of the building. He stood there for several minutes, going over the scene, the photos, lab report, and coroner's report he had memorized. It all added up to zero. He thought about Diane Wagner, Gail Thomas, and Sally Crowder, all dying in the same manner, which also added up to zero. The only things common were the army blankets and the girls themselves, who were all about the same height and weight and with dark brown hair. Whoever was doing this was very careful at leaving nothing that could be used as evidence or lead the police to him. He felt sorry for the families, fearing there would be no closure for them, the same as there would be no closure over his daughter Nancy or his twin brother, and that bothered him.

His mind returned to the pictures of Diane Wagner's body in Rio Grande Park, of Gail Thomas's, in the alley behind the Pioneer Theater, and Sally Crowder's, whose body was discovered just a few feet away from where he was standing. 'There has to be a connection,' he thought. 'Are Jack and I missing something?'

"Lieutenant?" said a woman's voice breaking the silence.

Startled, he turned, pointing his gun at a dark figure standing in the alley just beyond the edge of an island of light.

The figure stepped from the shadows into the dim light.

"You scared the shit out of me, Ruth."

She laughed softly. "I thought it was you." She looked at the gun. "You aren't going to shoot me, are you, Dan?"

He put his pistol away. "I should, just for the hell of it."

She smiled as she looked past him into the blackness of the alley and frowned. "Ever find out who killed that poor girl?"

Dan walked the short distance between them, took her by the arm, and gently escorted her toward 16th Street. As they walked, he could smell the cheap perfume she was wearing, and it excited him. "I thought you'd know better than to follow a stranger into a dark, lonely alley."

She smiled at him as he hurried her along the alley toward the street. "I knew it was you, Lieutenant."

Reaching the street, he let go of her arm. "You could have been wrong."

She smiled. "But I wasn't."

Not wanting to enter into a losing argument, he changed the subject. "How old are you, Ruth?"

"You know I'm twenty, Lieutenant."

"You're nineteen."

She laughed softly. "Ain't you the smart one?"

"Just a cop." He looked at her face reflecting the red color of the neon sign 'Rooms,' thinking she was pretty and could have a nice life if she'd get off the street. "Where's home, Ruth?"

The question irritated her. "What does that matter?"

Dan shrugged. "I guess it doesn't. Why do you do this?" he asked, knowing he was breaking his own rule about never getting personal.

She looked up at him through a long moment of irritated silence, trying to understand his asking. "You mean, why do I work?"

He stared at her, thinking of the others, knowing that she could end up the same way.

Ruth shrugged as she glanced up 16th Street and then looked into Detective Morgan's blue eyes and shrugged. "It's what I do, Lieutenant."

'There had to be more to it than that,' he thought, and then he wondered, 'Maybe she just likes the sex.' He looked around. "You be careful tonight. I wouldn't want you ending up like Sally Crowder."

Ruth glanced back up the alley. "So, that was her name?"

He nodded. "Like you, she was young and pretty."

As if she did not get the connection, she smiled. "I'm glad you think I'm pretty, Lieutenant." Then she turned and walked away only to pause after a few steps, half turn, and looked back over her shoulder. "Go home to your wife and family, Lieutenant, and stop chasing ghosts."

Wishing he could do as she said, he stood at the edge of the alley and watched as she crossed the street toward the corner. A car starting its engine across the street caused him to look at the dark, late model Chevy or Pontiac that slowly drove away. Dan turned in time to see Ruth disappear around the corner, and then he stepped into the street to watch the taillights of the car grow faint as it traveled down the empty street of neon lights and dim lampposts. When he could no longer see them, he walked to his car and paused to glance back at the corner where Ruth had disappeared, hoping nothing would happen to her.

Eight

Turning into the driveway, Dan Morgan stopped his car next to the house where the walk met the front porch. He turned off the headlights bringing darkness to the driveway, and as he turned off the engine, the silence was quickly replaced by the soft song of a hundred crickets. Sitting back in the car seat, staring into the dark night, he thought about the whore Ruthie and the dangerous world she lived in. He wondered what had brought a beautiful girl like her to such a life.

Deciding there was nothing he could do about it, he took the keys out of the ignition, got out of the car, locked it, and walked toward the front porch. As his footsteps mingled with the noisy crickets, he looked up the street of houses that had become dark shadows with an occasional porch light or window offering an alluring, warm orange glow. Climbing up the three steps to the front porch, he pushed his key into the front door lock while glancing around the empty porch for a package. Not seeing one, he stepped inside, turned the light on in the foyer, and then closed and locked the door. Looking down at the mail scattered on the foyer floor beneath the mail slot, he bent down and gathered it up, finding a postcard with a picture of Chicago, Illinois. Excited about getting a card from his son, he turned it over, hoping to read more than 'Doing fine,' but that was the message scribbled in ink. Disappointed, he tossed his keys in the glass bowl on the table next to the three envelopes he had put there earlier that day, laid his topcoat over the back of the chair, and hung his hat on the hat rack with the others.

He walked into the living room, reached under the shade of the table lamp sitting on the desk, and pulled the chain, filling the desk with light and the room with shadows. Moving the chair away from the small desk, he sat down, opened the center drawer, and pulled out the small stack of nine postcards. He untied the small blue ribbon he used to bind them together, put the new card on top, retied the ribbon, put the stack back in the drawer, and closed it. Sitting back in the chair, he looked at the black telephone on the corner of the desk wanting to hear his son's voice, wishing that there was some way he could call his son and talk with him. But there wasn't.

Feeling tired as the day now caught up with him, he stood, replaced the chair, turned off the light, and went upstairs, where he changed into a pair of pajama bottoms and a clean undershirt. Finding his slippers under the chair he had once slept in while watching Norma die of cancer in their bed, he slipped them on and picked up her pillow and the folded blanket from the bottom of the bed. Tucking them under one arm, he looked at the empty bed and thought of the dark shadows under her eyes as death came to visit and her ghostly, thin, pale face that no longer looked like his Norma. Turning away from the bed, he turned out the light, stepped into the dark hall, closed the door, and walked down the stairs without looking at the closed doors of Nancy's and Robert's bedrooms.

He turned off the light in the foyer at the bottom of the stairs and walked into the living room toward the sofa where he had been sleeping since Norma's death. He tossed the pillow on the sofa, laid down, covered up with the blanket, and looked out the window at the streetlamp before closing his eyes. While Dan Morgan waited for sleep, his mind filled with Norma, Nancy, and finally, Robert.

Sunday morning found Dan, still dressed in his pajamas and undershirt, at the dining room table nursing a cup of black coffee while looking through the pictures of the three murdered girls. His belly grumbled as hunger found him, so he went into the kitchen, and while considering what to fix for breakfast, he decided that eggs, bacon, and pancakes at the White Spot on East Colfax was a better idea. Setting his near-empty cup down, he went upstairs, took a quick shower, and put on a pair of Levi's and a black t-shirt.

The White Spot Restaurant on East Colfax was crowded, and it took a few minutes for a stool to empty at the counter. Smiling, he said good morning to the waitress and ordered coffee and breakfast.

While he ate, he read the sports page from the paper he had brought with him, hoping no one would bother him with meaningless conversation. After eating, he enjoyed a second cup of coffee while he read about the Denver Bears baseball team losing their third game in a row. His cup empty, he put some change on the counter for the tip, picked up his check, paid the cashier at the end of the counter, and walked outside.

Standing in the warm sun next to his car, he watched the light traffic travel up and down Colfax Avenue while contemplating what to do with the rest of the day. After a few moments, he came to a decision, got into the car, and drove east on Colfax with soft music from the radio as his passenger.

Pulling into the parking lot of the cemetery where both Norma and Nancy lay buried, he shut off the engine. After climbing out of the car, he closed the car door and suddenly realized he had no flowers for their graves. While thinking of the flower garden at home, Dan noticed the beautiful, colored flowers in an older home's front yard across the street. After a moment of considering the flowers, he made his way through the light traffic, walked up the narrow walk, and knocked on the front door.

A kind looking but suspicious elderly woman opened the door. "May I help you?"

Dan smiled. "Pardon me, madam, but I was about to visit my wife and daughter across the street and realized I had no flowers."

She glanced at the cemetery across the street and then, giving him a skeptical look, glad the screen door was locked and wondered what his lack of flowers had to do with her.

Dan turned and gestured to the flower garden. "You have such pretty flowers, and I was wondering if I could pick just a few to brighten their graves."

She stared at him in silence, considering whether or not he was crazy.

"I'd be happy to pay you."

After a moment, the elderly woman decided he meant her no harm and smiled. "No need to pay me, young man. Help yourself to whatever you need. They'll all grow back."

He grinned. "Thank you."

An elderly man's voice from somewhere in the house called out, "Who's at the door, Elsie?"

She turned her head and yelled. "A young man wanting some flowers." She looked at Dan. "Did you say your wife and daughter are both buried across the street?"

"Yes, ma'am."

The voice from inside called out, "What's that?"

She turned her head, looked into the house, and yelled louder. "I'll tell you all about it later, Arthur."

She turned and smiled warmly. "I have a couple of small canning jars you're welcome to if that would help."

He looked appreciative, knowing she would not take any money. "I hate to take your jars, ma'am. The flowers will do."

"Nonsense," she said. "Cut flowers won't last a day in this heat. Now you wait right here, and I'll get a couple. I have plenty that I never use."

He watched her through the locked screen door as she disappeared into another room, returning a few minutes later with two large, clear, glass canning jars, each containing a little water. She unlocked the screen door, pushed it open, and handed them to him. "These should do just fine."

Appreciative, Dan thanked her as he took the two jars.

She smiled. "Pick all you want, young man."

He thanked her again, stepped off the porch, and began to fill the two jars with different colored flowers, and when he finished, he walked across the street to Norma's and Nancy's graves. He placed the jars of flowers next to their headstones and sat on the grass between them, talking to Nancy for a short time and then to Norma about Robert, wishing he would come home. Several minutes passed before he finished visiting and stood. After brushing off the back of his Levi's, he touched both headstones, said he would come back another day, then walked to his car. Not wanting to go home to an empty house, he drove around town for a while, filled his car with gasoline, and stopped at the store for a six-pack of beer to keep him company while listening to a Denver Bears baseball game on the radio.

Early Monday morning, Captain Foley leaned out of this office. "Morgan, Brolin, come in here a minute?"

Jack looked at Dan with a concerned look. "He doesn't look very happy."

Dan grinned, "Don't look at me. I got my haircut."

Jack followed Dan into the captain's office. "Want me to shut the door?"

"You won't be in here that long." He looked at Jack and then Dan. "How are you coming on the Sally Crowder case?"

"Nothing new," replied Dan, wishing he had some good news that would satisfy the captain.

Foley thought about that. "Have you talked to Littleton and Englewood law enforcement to see if they've come up with anything?"

Dan nodded. "We're talking to anyone we think might help." He looked troubled. "This guy cleans everything, Captain, and leaves no prints. It's like he's a ghost."

Foley looked irritated. "You know I don't believe in ghosts. Hargrove and Mueller are out of town on a special case. That leaves the two of you, Jeff Arnold and Harry Cross, and Arnold's home, sick with something." The captain looked at Dan. "There's been a holdup and shooting at a pawn shop not far from here." He handed a piece of paper with the address to Detective Morgan. "Have a look. You can get back onto your case this afternoon. There's already a black and white at the scene."

Dan looked at the paper and read aloud, "18th and Stout."

Jack headed for the door. "I'll drive."

Jack Brolin parked behind the black and white police car parked on Stout Street while Dan looked out the window at the green neon sign 'Pawnbroker' hanging from steel struts protruding from the dark, red bricks of the building. Getting out of the car, they walked past a large, plate-glass window filled with various items for sale. Dan pushed the door open, which caused the tiny bell above it to ring. They stepped inside to the scene of a man lying on the floor in a pool of blood and Officer's Sam Price and Charley Moore talking to an elderly man who was holding a bloody towel against the left side of his head. He looked nervous and afraid.

Detective Brolin knelt next to the body, checked for a pulse, looked up at Dan, and shook his head as he stood, indicating that the man was dead.

Dan glanced around and then looked at Officer Price, who was walking toward him. "What's going on, Sam?"

Officer Price shrugged while holding a pad in one hand and a pencil in the other. "Looks like a robbery gone bad."

Dan looked at the old man standing next to a glass counter near the cash register. "Who's the man with the bloody towel?"

Officer Price turned his head, looked at the man, and then at the notepad he held. "The owner, a Mister Benjamin Rothstein."

"The man on the floor?" asked Dan.

"A customer, according to Mr. Rothstein," replied Officer Price.

The front door opened, ringing the tiny bell, and two men from Forensics walked in carrying their black bags of equipment and cameras. They immediately knelt next to the body.

"He's dead," Jack said.

"Thanks," said one man with a smile. "I never would have guessed."

Jack grinned and then turned to follow Dan and Sam Price across the small store to where Mr. Rothstein and Officer Moore were talking.

"Hello, Mr. Rothstein," said Dan. "I'm Detective Dan Morgan, and this is my partner Detective Jack Brolin."

Mr. Benjamin Rothstein was dressed in dark blue dress pants and a white, long-sleeved dress shirt with rolled up bloody sleeves and no tie. He was a heavyset man in his late sixties with balding black hair, brown eyes, a large nose, and a weak chin. He looked at Detective Morgan and spoke in a heavy accent. "Them little punks killed that nice man Mr. Hathaway. What about his family?" he asked angrily. "Who will tell them?"

Dan looked at the body. "We'll take care of that." He turned back to Rothstein and gestured at his head. "Can you tell us what happened?"

"Got hit on the head by one of them punk kids. That's what happened."

Dan noticed the numbered tattoo on the old man's right forearm and knew it was from one of the many German death camps. He recalled walking through the gates of the Dachau concentration camp, finding men that looked more like skeletons than men.

Mr. Rothstein looked at the body and spoke in his heavy accent. "I had just given Mr. Hathaway fifteen dollars for an old gold watch he pawned. He was leaving when those two no goods came in and asked for his money." Benjamin Rothstein looked like he was proud of Mr. Hathaway. "He refused and hit one of them in the face. That's when the other punk shot him."

Dan turned to the man from Forensics. "Check to see if he has any money."

Rothstein gestured with one hand. "No need to look; those no-goods took it."

Jack wrote everything Rothstein was saying in his notepad. "Can I have your full name?"

Officer Price looked at Jack. "I already have that information."

Jack looked at Price and smiled. "Now, I'll have it as well." He looked at Mr. Rothstein and waited.

Mr. Rothstein looked from Officer Price to Jack. "But I already told all this to that officer."

Dan smiled. "You're going to have to tell us again, Mr. Rothstein."

Benjamin looked irritated. "Benjamin Rothstein." Then he spelled it.

"What did the robbers look like?" asked Jack.

"Like punks," Benjamin said. "They all look like punks."

Jack smiled at Dan and then looked at Mr. Rothstein. "Can you be a little more specific, sir?"

Looking more irritated, he began describing the two men. "They both had those red bandannas over their mouth and noses. But I think they were in their mid-teens, with black hair, one long and the other in one of those crew-cut things. Both were wearing jean pants and white T-shirts with cigarettes rolled up in the sleeves, looking like gangsters."

Jack thought for a moment. "How could you tell they were young with half their faces covered?"

Mr. Rothstein looked at Detective Brolin with narrowed eyes. "The eyes, Detective. The eyes tell the age." He paused a moment and then continued. "I refused to open the register, and that's when the one with the short hair hit me. The next thing I remember is getting up from the floor. The register was open, the money gone, and so were those no goods."

Dan glanced back at the body. "The young boys these days are crazy, Mr. Rothstein. You need to be more careful."

Rothstein looked at Dan while remembering the young boys helping the Nazis in the concentration camps. "I guess that's true enough. Next time I'll hand them the damn register."

"Or shoot them," offered Jack jokingly.

Benjamin Rothstein nodded in silence, thinking that was a damned good idea.

Dan looked at the glass cabinets. "They take anything besides the money?"

"They just wanted money; it's always the money."

The front door opened, and as the tiny bell above the door rang, two men from an ambulance walked in with a gurney and knelt next to the man on the floor.

"He's dead," offered the man from Forensics.

Dan turned from the two men with the gurney to Mr. Rothstein. "Can I take a look? Head wounds always bleed a lot."

"I suppose," replied Benjamin.

Dan gently removed Benjamin's hand that held the towel. "That's a nasty wound, Mr. Rothstein." He turned to the two men examining the body. "Could one of you take a look at Mr. Rothstein?"

The man with the bag of medical supplies and instruments walked over, set his bag on the glass counter, opened it, and started looking at Mr. Rothstein's head.

"Can we call anyone for you?" asked Jack.

"I called my wife already."

The medic from the ambulance cleaned the wound and put a large bandage on it, telling Benjamin that he required stitches and offered to take him to the hospital.

"My wife, Ester, will take me." Then he looked at Detective Morgan. "I already lost the day." His expression turned to disappointment. "Aaron, in the next block, will make the money today."

Dan tried not to smile as he gave him his card. "Sometimes, a person remembers something a few days later, Mr. Rothstein. Should anything come to you, please give my partner or me a call."

Hearing the bell above the door, they turned, seeing a heavy-set middle-aged woman wearing a worried face pause to look down at the body and then hurried across the floor and embraced Mr. Rothstein.

Figuring it was Mrs. Rothstein, Dan and Jack stepped back and watched in silence as she kissed him on the cheek and then gently touched the bandage on his head. She stepped back and shook a crooked finger at him. "I keep telling you to be careful, Benjamin. Are you alright?"

"Do I look alright?"

Dan smiled, turned away, and watched the men from Forensics packing up their equipment. "You boys finished here?"

"All done, Detective," replied one officer.

"Come, Benjamin," said Ester. "Lock up, and I'll take you to see nice Dr. Silverstein."

Jack turned to Mr. Rothstein. "Do you happen to have an address or telephone number for Mr. Hathaway?"

Mr. Rothstein turned from his wife, opened a drawer under the register, and handed Dan a receipt that he passed to Jack to copyinto his notepad. When done, Jack gave it back to Mr. Rothstein.

Mr. Rothstein took the receipt and then looked at Dan. "Wait a minute."

Dan watched as Mr. Rothstein opened a drawer and took out a gold watch. "Give this to Mr. Hathaway's family. I couldn't sell it now."

Dan took the watch, thinking that it was a nice gesture. "I'm sure they'll appreciate this, Mr. Rothstein."

"If you will excuse us," said Ester Rothstein. "I have to take my husband to see our doctor."

Jack reminded Mr. Rothstein that if he thought of anything else, to call him or his partner. Then he and Dan waited while Mr. Hathaway's body was covered and put into the ambulance.

The ambulance drove away, heading for the city morgue while Dan and Jack got into Jack's car. As they drove away from the curb, Dan told him to drive down toward Larimer Street.

Looking curious, Jack asked, "What's on Larimer?"

"I want to check on something."

Still curious, he let the subject drop, then turned at the next corner, drove west, and as they approached Larimer Street, he asked, "Which way?"

Dan thought a moment. "South."

Jack turned the corner heading south. "Mind telling me what we're looking for?"

Dan ignored the question as he looked from one side of the street to the other, searching for Ruth.

Irritated at no response, Jack drove for several blocks, wondering what his partner was up to, and then he pulled over next to the curb and stopped. "What the hell are we looking for?"

Dan glanced at both sides of the street. "I'm looking for Ruth?"

"The prostitute?"

"That's right."

"What the hell does she have to do with our holdup and murder?"

"Nothing, I just need to see if she's alright."

Jack looked suspicious, hoping his partner hadn't started something with a whore. "You aren't getting mixed up in something, are you?"

Dan gave him a look. "No. I want to see if she's alright, that's all. Now keep driving."

Jack wondered what Dan was up to as he put the car in gear, pulled away from the curb, and drove down Larimer, worried about his partner. "Why the interest?"

Dan was considering the question when he saw Ruth's pimp George Peterson, also known as Curley, walk out of a cheap hotel. "Pull over."

Looking at Curley, Jack pulled up next to the curb and stopped.

Dan stuck his head out the window. "Hey, Curley!"

Curley gave the two detectives an uncertain look and kept walking.

"Come over here," demanded Dan.

Curley stopped, glanced around, and then looked at Dan.

Afraid that Curley was about to run, Dan yelled, "I just want to know if you've seen Ruth."

Curley was tall and skinny, dressed in expensive brown slacks, a tan sports shirt, and brown and white saddle shoes. His hair was curly and black with a little gray, his face clean-shaven, and he had tired, bloodshot brown eyes. Looking unsure, Curley took a drag off his cigarette and cautiously approached the car, stopping at a safe distance. Glancing from Dan to Jack and then back at Dan, he knelt and looked at him through the open window. "What do you want with Ruthie?"

Dan motioned for him. "Come closer."

Curley looked at Dan, remembering another time he asked him to come closer, and decided to stay where he was.

"I'm not going to hurt you," said Dan, looking irritated. "I just want to know if you've seen Ruth today, and I don't want to have to yell. Now get the hell over here before I get out of the damn car."

Not wanting that, Curley cautiously walked to the car, stooped next to the door, and looked in at Jack and then Dan.

"Have you seen Ruth today?" asked Dan again.

Curley took a drag from his cigarette and blew the smoke away from the window. "Saw her a couple of hours ago."

"She's alright, then?"

Curley looked puzzled but not as puzzled as Jack Brolin. Curly shrugged. "She's fine. We had breakfast at Mindy's Café earlier."

"You know where she is now?"

Curley thought a minute. "Best be working."

Feeling relieved, Dan said, "Alright." Then he turned to Jack. "Let's go."

A confused Jack drove away, leaving an equally confused Curley standing on the sidewalk. They drove in silence for several blocks when Jack looked at Dan. "Why the hell are you checking on the whore?"

Dan knew Jack would not let up until he told him about visiting the crime scene on Saturday night after leaving his place and running into her. "After all that's happened lately, I just thought I would check up on her."

Jack thought for a few minutes. "She's picked her life, Dan. I know you've tried, but you can't save her from herself."

Dan knew that was true, but just the same, he did not want what happened to these three girls to happen to anyone else, not even a prostitute like Ruth. Feeling a little foolish, he looked out the window at the people walking along the sidewalk, knowing he could not change Ruth any more than he could change her pimp.

The rest of the week, the two detectives talked to possible witnesses in surplus stores, running down leads on the robbery and also talking to several high school students about Sally Crowder. None of them had heard of the other girls. No one saw Sally in a car with a stranger the day she disappeared, and none jumped out as suspects.

Nine

Late Friday afternoon, Captain Foley walked out of his office, stopping at Dan's desk, and as he slipped into his suit coat, he looked down at him. "Anything new on the robbery?"

Dan looked up and shook his head. "Not much to go on. Jack and I will visit Mr. Rothstein on Monday. Maybe by then, he'll remember something that will help."

Foley did not look happy with the answer. "And what about Sally Crowder?"

"Nothing new on the girl either, Captain," replied Dan. "We're still talking to people, but it's a damn void. We're going to check a few more army surplus stores about those army blankets. Maybe we'll get lucky."

Foley looked doubtful while adjusting his coat, and then he looked at Detective Brolin. "Anything on that hit and run last month?"

Jack grinned. "Dead-end street, Captain."

Not appreciating the humor, Foley gave him a look. "Cute. I want better results." He looked from one to the other and then at the clock above the stairs, thinking about his dinner waiting. "We'll talk on Monday. If anything comes up, you can reach me at home."

Captain Foley looked at Dan. "As Homicide's senior detective, Morgan, appearances mean a lot. Your hair looks good. Let's keep it that way." Then he turned and walked toward the stairs.

Dan touched the back of his hair, testing its length as he stared after the captain, wishing he would forget about the length of his hair.

Jack looked across the two desks at his partner. "You ever get that package?"

Dan turned to Jack. "Never did."

Jack thought about that for a moment. "I wonder what happened to it." Then he asked, "Any big plans this weekend?"

Dan shook his head. "No. I need to get some stuff done around the house."

"What sort of stuff?"

Dan gave him an irritated look. "You know, stuff."

Jack grinned. "If you get bored, you know where I live." Then Jack looked excited. "Hey, come over Sunday for hotdogs and beer. We can sit on the patio, drink beer, and listen to the ball game on the radio."

"Who's playing?"

"The Dodgers."

"Those bums." Then Dan smiled. "Maybe. I'll think about it."

Looking slightly discouraged, Jack took his gun from the drawer, shoved it into its holster, and slipped it into his coat. "See you when I see you, I guess." Then he turned and walked toward the stairs.

Dan watched him for a moment and then called out, "Hey, asshole."

Jack stopped and turned.

"What kind of beer should I bring?"

Jack grinned. "The kind you like. Cheap."

Dan smiled and watched his partner until he disappeared down the stairs, then opened the bottom left-hand drawer of his desk and took out the three envelopes. Setting them on his desk, he pushed his chair back, stood, and after shrugging into his coat, he got his gun from the desk drawer. Putting on his gray fedora, Dan grabbed the envelopes and his topcoat and headed for the stairs, looking forward to Sunday with Jack and Lori. Smiling, he hoped the Dodgers got their asses kicked.

It was dark when Dan drove into his driveway, stopped the car, shut off the engine, and turned off the headlights. Still anticipating a package, he stepped onto the porch, hoping to find it next to the front door. Not finding one, Dan opened the screen door in disappointment, unlocked the front door, and went inside. After locking the door, he picked up the mail from the floor, quickly went through it, and then set it on the table in the foyer with yesterday's mail. Picking up a folded note with his name on it leaning against the table lamp, Dan unfolded it, seeing it was from his housekeeper, Mrs. McDowell. In the note, she told him she had an emergency in her family and needed to return to Brooklyn. Mrs. McDowell said she would be away for at least two weeks. If she stayed longer, she would call.

Hoping her emergency was not too serious, he laid the note down, went upstairs, changed into a pair of Levi's and a white t-shirt, went back downstairs to the kitchen, and cooked the meatloaf Peggy Schaffer, next door, had given him two days ago. He ate in the living room while watching television, and after he finished his meal, he cleaned up the dishes and the kitchen, put the rest of the meatloaf in the refrigerator, and settled onto the sofa with a beer to watch television.

Dan was about halfway through a second beer and enjoying a 1938 Humphrey Bogart movie when the telephone rang. He turned from the television and looked at the black telephone sitting on the desk, hoping it was Robert. Setting the beer on the coffee table with the other empty, he got up, hurried to the desk, and picked up the receiver. "Hello."

"This is Foley."

Disappointed and knowing something was wrong, Dan said, "Yeah."

"There's been another murder."

Dan looked at the clock, seeing it was almost ten. "Shit," he said. "Where?"

"In the alley behind the Paramount Theater. I'll call your partner. Meet us there as soon as you can."

Dan hung up the telephone, turned off the television, grabbed his holster with his Thirty-eight, put it on his belt, and then went to the hall closet. Taking out a light black jacket, he slipped into it as he walked toward the front door, thinking that the three envelopes sitting on the dining room table would soon have company.

Uniformed police officers were trying to deal with curious onlookers and reporters when Dan approached the alley next to the Paramount Theater on 16th Street. Stopping his car at the entrance to the alley, he rolled down his window and waited as a uniformed officer approached his car. Dan showed the officer his badge, and the officer and two others began moving the crowd away from the entrance. Dan slowly drove past the curious onlookers asking questions as flashbulbs from reporters lit up the inside of his 49 Ford. Parking behind Captain Foley's 48 Chevy, he climbed out, walked between the captain's car and the coroner's van past their headlights that lit up the crime scene in the alley like a stage. Flashlights were bouncing off trashcans and racing along the alley, occasionally swallowed up by flashbulbs from Forensics and the men from the Coroner's Office.

Dan walked past Captain Foley, talking to Pete Lange, and knelt next to a young girl's body. She was wearing girl's blue jeans, white tennis shoes, bobby socks, and a man's white dress shirt posed just like the other bodies. He looked into her open eyes, examined the cauterized stub of the little finger of the left hand without touching it, and finally, the puncture in her neck.

Foley turned from Lang and knelt next to Dan. "How many cases are you and Jack working on?"

Dan thought a moment. "Eight or nine. Most are cold cases we're looking into."

The captain stared down at the face of the young girl whose dead eyes stared up at the night sky. "We've one sick son of a bitch after our young girls, Dan. I can see the headlines in tomorrow morning's paper. If we don't catch him soon, the mayor's going to be all over the chief's ass, and shit flows downhill if you get my meaning."

Understanding the meaning, Dad said, "We're doing all we can, Captain."

"Well, we've got to do more," said Foley.

Not disagreeing with that, Dan looked at the captain. "Who found the body?"

Foley stood and pointed at two frightened looking young girls standing next to a black and white patrol car, talking to a police officer.

Dan stood and hollered at the officer. "I want to talk to them, so don't let them go anywhere."

The officer waved, opened the rear door of the police car, and told the two girls to get inside.

Captain Foley looked past Dan up the alley. "Here's Brolin."

Dan turned, seeing his partner walking toward them, swallowed up by the bright headlights of the captain's car and Coroner's van.

Captain Foley turned to Detective Brolin. "I was asking Dan about your cases. Drop all the cold cases for now and concentrate on these girls and that robbery." The captain thought for a moment and then looked at Dan. "Dan, you're Senior Detective, so you stay on the murdered girl's full time." He looked at Jack. "You work the robbery with the murder and let the hit and run go for now. I'll assign the housewife knifing to another detective for a few days. I want you to stay with Dan on these girls." He paused in thought, looked at Jack, and then Dan. "The two of you can figure out how to split Jack's time between the robbery, the murder, and these girls. You're Senior Detective, so you're in the hot seat on this one, and you better come up with some results fast."

Dan nodded as he looked down at the body, thinking about the position the captain had just put him in. Not one clue has been found at any of the crime scenes that could lead them to the murderer or his reasons.

The captain looked worried. "You two stay in close contact with Chief Travis in Englewood and Sheriff Brumwell in Littleton." Foley paused. "Let's hope we don't have to get the other suburbs in on this thing."

Dan was staring down at the body. "Alright, Captain."

Foley looked from Dan to the body. "If the two of you need any more men to help run down leads, or anything else, just ask, and I'll see if we can borrow a couple of foot patrolmen."

Dan glanced at the patrol car, where the two girls waited, and then at Foley. "I think we'll be alright for now, Captain, with you taking the other cases off our load."

Jack was looking down at the body. "I agree."

Foley looked from one to the other. "I have two men on special detail and one out sick. The department is pretty thin right now. Keep me up to date. I want to have answers when the chief calls, and I'm sure he will do so several times a day." He looked at both ends of the alley, crowded with curious gawkers and reporters. "The press is going to have a field day with this one." Then he looked first at Jack and then at Dan. "I'm putting forensics and Pete's department on overtime for the weekend. We'll see what they come up with on Monday."

Dan wasn't very optimistic.

Captain Foley turned and walked away, talking over his shoulder. "Enjoy your weekend."

As Captain Foley walked toward his car, Dan gestured toward the police car. "Two girls that found the body are in the back of that patrol car."

Jack looked toward the patrol car, then knelt, and looked at the latest victim's body, thinking she was so young and pretty. "Such a shame."

Dan turned and borrowed a flashlight from one of Pete's men, knelt, and put the light on the girl's left hand. "Pinky finger's missing, and the hand has been cauterized around the knuckle."

Anger filled Jack as he looked into the girl's open eyes and thought about her family, remembering the Crowder's at the city morgue. He took the flashlight from Dan and put the light on the rope burns and bruises on her wrists and ankles. Then he moved the flashlight up the girl's body, stopping at her neck to examine the puncture wound.

"This is Friday night," said Dan. "The son of a bitch changed days."

"I wonder why?" asked Jack thoughtfully as he looked at the girl's face.

Dan shook his head. "I don't know. Throw us off, maybe?" Then he turned and looked up at Todd Anderson of Forensics. "Can I move the body to check her pockets for identification?"

"We already did that," replied Todd. "Wasn't anything in any of her pockets."

Dan looked back down at the body, thinking of Gail Thomas in Englewood and the student ID card in her back pocket, and figured the killer would not make that mistake again. He took the flashlight from Jack and gave it back to the officer. "Let's see what these girls can tell us."

The officer stood away from the car he was leaning against and walked to meet them while tearing a piece of paper from a small notepad. "I wrote down their names, telephone numbers, and their addresses." Then he handed the paper to Dan.

Dan looked at the paper and read their names aloud. "Betty Donahue and Sybil Franklin." He shoved the paper into his shirt pocket, bent down, leaned inside the open car door, and smiled at the two girls who looked afraid and worried. "Hello, ladies. We want to ask a few questions, and then the police officer will take you home."

With arms intertwined, they nodded in unison and then moved closer to one another.

"Which of you is Betty?"

"I am," said the taller of the two.

He smiled at the other girl. "Then you must be Sybil."

She nodded yes.

"Are we in trouble?" asked Betty.

"No," said Dan softly with a small smile. "We just need to ask you a few questions, and then you can go."

Betty looked scared. "We told the police officer everything."

"I know you did," said Dan. "But we have to ask you a few questions, even if you've already answered them. Okay?"

"Why?" asked Sybil.

Dan smiled at her. "Because you may remember something you didn't tell the officer. That happens a lot. Nothing to be ashamed of."

They looked at one another, and both said, "Okay."

"I'm Detective Dan Morgan, and the good-looking fellah behind me is Detective Jack Brolin, my partner."

Jack leaned toward the car door looking over Dan's shoulder and winked. "Hello, girls."

They smiled, looking a little embarrassed.

Dan looked from one girl to the other. "May I ask how old you are?"

"Fourteen," said Sybil.

"Fifteen," said Betty.

Dan's face held a reassuring smile. "What were you doing in the alley?"

Betty spoke first. "The movie just got out, and we were walking up the street to catch the streetcar to go home. We were talking about the movie, and as we passed the alley, I saw a van parked in the middle of it with its headlights out."

Becoming hopeful of their first break, Dan leaned further into the car. "Do you know what kind of van?"

Betty shook her head. "It was too dark, but I do for sure know it was light-colored, maybe white."

"That's good," said Dan, trying to raise their spirits. "What happened next?"

Sybil said, "I could see a man bent over next to the taillights doing something, so we stopped and watched for a minute."

"If it was dark," asked Dan. "How do you know it was a man."

Sybil looked at Dan. "He stood, looked at us, shut the rear door of the van, hurried to the driver's side, got in, and drove away. That's when Betty said that we should go see what he was doing, so we walked into the alley and ----"

"That's when we saw the girl," interrupted Betty.

"We got scared," said Sybil. "And ran back to the street."

Betty pointed to the police officer standing a few feet away. "That's when we saw the police car and started yelling."

"Could you see anything about the man?" asked Dan. "What kind of clothing he was wearing, a hat maybe, or how tall he was?"

"No," said Betty. "He was dark, like a shadow."

"Yeah," agreed Sybil while nodding her head, repeating, "Like a shadow."

Dan stepped away from the car in disappointment and turned to Jack. "You have anything you want to ask?"

Jack leaned inside the patrol car. "You said a light-colored van."

"Maybe it was white," said Betty.

Sybil nodded in agreement.

"How could you tell that in the dark alley?" asked Jack.

Betty pointed to a light hanging over the rear door of a building up the alley. "He drove under that light."

Jack looked at the light above a rear door further up the alley and then smiled at Betty. "Good."

Dan looked past Jack's shoulder into the car. "Do you think you can remember what the back of the van looked like?"

They thought about that for a few moments, and then Sybil shook her head no. "He drove away too fast."

Betty looked at Sybil and then at Dan with a frown. "I have three older brothers." Then she smiled. "Maybe I can."

"That's good," said Dan. "Would you mind coming to the station tomorrow and look at some pictures? It would help us in our investigation."

Betty nodded. "If it's okay with my mom and dad."

"Can I come?" asked Sybil.

"Of course," smiled Jack. "We want both of you."

Betty looked uncomfortable. "My mom and dad won't be back from Cheyenne until Sunday night."

Dan leaned inside the car. "Someone will call your parents and arrange a time, and then a patrol car will pick you up." Dan smiled. "Thanks, ladies, you've been a big help." He turned to the police officer. "You can take these two ladies home now, officer."

As the officer climbed into the patrol car, Jack leaned into the car. "Thanks, you're both brave girls." Then he closed the door and stood next to Dan as the patrol car drove up the alley toward 17th Street.

Dan watched the patrol car for a few moments. "Ain't much, but it's more than we got from the other crime scenes."

Jack nodded. "Let's hope that little girl can recognize tail lights and the rear of the van from a book."

Hoping the same thing, Dan said, "I'm going home. Forensics can finish up here, and hopefully, Todd and Pete will have everything by Monday morning."

Jack looked at his watch. "Me too. It's after midnight, and I'm tired as hell."

They walked to their cars, said goodnight, and as Jack opened his car door, he paused to look at Dan. "We still on for Sunday?"

Dan stopped and turned. "What time?"

"Anytime. The game starts at one."

Dan got into his car and drove slowly down the alley past the crime scene, thinking he would call the front desk at headquarters when he got home and give them his home phone in case someone came in to file a report on a missing teenage girl.

Ten

Dan Morgan lay on his side on the sofa staring out the window of the living room, waiting for the sun to come up, thinking about the young girls that would never grow up and have children of their own. He thought of Leonard and Sylvia Crowder the night he had shown them the picture of their daughter and then Mrs. Crowder falling to her knees in the morgue when she saw her daughter's body. His thoughts turned to the latest victim, and he was not looking forward to telling her parents that their daughter would never come home again.

Turning onto his back, he looked out the narrow window high on the east wall at the morning sky of oranges, pinks, and purples above the treetops beyond Al and Peggy Schaffer's house next door. As he watched the sky slowly turn lighter and the darkness of the living room slowly fade away, he thought about the pictures in the envelopes and of those taken last night that he would get from Pete and Todd on Monday or Tuesday. For some reason, his mind turned to that terrible day he had found the crime scene pictures of his twin brother hidden in his father's garage.

1936

It was two days before Nancy Ann Morgan's first birthday in the summer of 1936. Dan and his wife Norma and their two children lived only a few blocks away from his parents. Dan stopped by their house to borrow some of his father's tools he needed to work on his 1932 Ford. He parked next to the curb, walked up to the front door, and finding it locked, he knocked and then rang the doorbell. When no one answered, Dan walked around the house to the garage, found the side door unlocked, stepped inside, and flipped the light switch filling the garage with dim light. Knowing his father would not mind, he poked around until he found the tools he needed, and then he turned the light out and stepped outside. The door was hard to close, so he pulled at it hard several times until it closed. Hearing something fall inside, he pushed the door open, poked his head inside, and in the dim light, saw a small piece of the wall had fallen from the corner behind the door.

Stepping back inside the garage, he flipped the light switch on and saw a small wooden box lying on its side, next to its lid. Several black and white photographs of what appeared to be the body of a nude boy were lying on the floor. Curious as to why his dad would hide pictures of a nude boy in the garage, he placed the tools he was borrowing on the counter, knelt to one knee, and picked one up. To Dan's astonishment, it was a picture of his identical twin brother, Donnie lying nude in the snow.

Looking at the picture was like looking at himself, making the hair on the back of his neck stand. He picked up another, then another, and realizing the pictures were of his brother's crime scene, he knew that his father had lied to him about the cause of his brother's death.

Hearing car doors slam, he stood and looked out the windows of the big garage door and down the driveway in time to see his mother and father walk into the house. Filled with anger about being lied to for years about Donnie's death, he knelt, scooped everything up, shoved it back into the box, and put the lid back on. Leaving the piece of wall lying on the floor, he stood and walked out of the garage holding the box under his left arm, and without closing the garage door, he hurried across the lawn to the back door.

His mother was in the kitchen, and as she looked up from fixing lunch, she smiled. "There you are."

"Where's Dad?" asked Dan in an angry tone."

Paulette Morgan saw the anger on her son's face and then noticed the small box he was carrying. "He's in the living room. What's wrong, Daniel?"

Without answering, he walked past his mother into the living room.

Wondering what her son was angry over and what was in the box, Mrs. Morgan put down the bread and knife and then followed her son to the living room door. Stopping, she watched from the doorway as Daniel approached his father with the small box in his hand.

Charles Morgan was sitting in his chair reading the funny papers, stopped reading, and looked up. "I thought that was your car --"

Dan tossed the box onto his father's lap, interrupting his father. The lid came off, and everything spilled onto his lap, with a few landing on the floor. "You've lied to me all these years about how Donnie died."

Surprised and unprepared, Charles looked down at the pictures of his dead son, then reached down and began picking them up and putting them back into the box. When done, he looked up at Dan. "Yes, we've lied to you, son."

"Why?" asked Dan. "Why did you lie to me?"

Mrs. Morgan moved from the doorway and stood beside her husband's chair, placing one hand on her husband's shoulder. "We thought it best, son." She looked down at the pictures she knew existed but had never looked at and then at Dan. "Your father and I felt it best that you never knew the real truth about your brother."

Dan glared into his mother's soft eyes. "You've known he lied all these years?" Then he pointed to the box. "Have you seen what's in that box, Mother?"

His father looked up. *"I wouldn't let your mother see them."* Charles placed the lid on the box and set it on the table next to his chair. *"Your anger should be directed at me, not your mother."*

Dan looked from his mother to his father, turned, and stomped out of the house.

Mrs. Morgan started to call after her son but knew he needed some time, so she stared at the closed door listening to the sound of a car door slamming, followed by an engine starting and then tires squealing. She looked down at the top of her husband's balding head. *"I'll finish fixing lunch."*

"I'm not hungry," he said in a soft voice as he picked up the box, stood, and walked out of the room to put it back.

Several days later, Charles and Paulette Morgan pulled into the driveway of Dan and Norma's home. While Charles remained in the car, Mrs. Morgan got out and walked to the front door of her son's home and pushed the doorbell. Norma opened the front door, and when Dan heard his mother's voice, he got up from the chair he was sitting in, walked into the kitchen, took a beer out of the refrigerator, and walked out the back door. Norma invited Mrs. Morgan in and asked if Charles was coming in. Paulette said that Charles thought it would be best if he stayed in the car, thinking there would be less chance of an argument. Believing that to be true, Norma showed Mrs. Morgan to the sofa, excused herself, and went into the backyard to look for her husband, finding him sitting on the workbench in the garage nursing a bottle of beer. Her efforts to get him inside brought about a very intense argument between the two of them. Norma held her ground that day, and in the end, she convinced him to come into the house and talk to his mother.

Once inside, Norma sat down on the sofa next to Mrs. Morgan and held her hand while Dan got another beer from the refrigerator. He sat in a chair that faced the empty fireplace with his back to his mother and wife.

"Son, can I explain?" asked Mrs. Morgan.

"What's to explain, mother?" he replied angrily. *"You and dad have lied to me all these years."*

"Dan, please," pleaded Norma.

He turned, giving her a stern look. *"They've lied to me all these years about how Donnie died, and damn it, I still don't know the truth."* He looked at his mother. *"Isn't it about time for the truth, mother?"* Then Dan returned his gaze to the empty fireplace and took a drink of beer.

Mrs. Morgan let go of Norma's hand and stared down at her own hands for a moment. *"It isn't something that one wants to discuss, Daniel. What happened to Donnie is a terrible thing, son."*

"And I should have been told what it was." Dan recalled the day Donnie had died and the feeling he had experienced all day that something was terribly wrong. "What happened?"

Mrs. Morgan's eyes welled as she looked at Norma. "You may not want to hear this, dear."

"She can stay," barked Dan. "She's part of this family and deserves to know the truth. We've had enough lying."

Paulette opened her purse, took a white handkerchief, and wiped the tears from her eyes. "As you wish, son."

Feeling sorry for her, Norma watched as she dried her eyes.

Paulette paused a long moment trying to gather the words, then suddenly said, "Your brother had been raped." She lowered her head and began to sob. "Then he was murdered."

Dan turned in shock. "Raped?"

His mother looked at him with welling eyes. "Yes." Her voice quivered as tears ran down her face. "After they raped Donnie, "she said, "his naked body was placed in the snow like some piece of trash next to a small stream in Englewood." She paused and then softly said, "Sand Creek, I think it was."

"The creek that winds through Englewood Park?" asked Dan.

"I believe so. I will not go there. To this day, I wake up at night thinking about the horror he must have gone through at the hands of the maniac that took his life."

Dan turned his chair and looked at his mother. "How did he die?"

She wiped the tears from her eyes. "I don't know. Just knowing he was murdered was too much for me to bear back then, and it still is." She paused a moment as she stared out the living room window at her husband sitting in the car and wiped her eyes with the white hanky. "Your father took the file out of the cold case files when everyone had given up." She paused in thought, turning from the window to her son. "I think your father knew what pain the pictures would have brought to us, Daniel, so he kept them from us."

In a calm voice, Dan asked, "Did you know he had them?"

"Of course," she said softly. "Your father and I hold no secrets from one another. I never asked to see them, and furthermore, I never wanted to see them, nor do I want to know how Donnie died. I prefer remembering Donnie as he was the last time I saw him when he was full of life and always happy."

Dan hadn't cried in years, but now he wiped the tears from his eyes. "Someone should have told me, mom. He was my twin brother, and I had the right to know."

Mrs. Morgan looked down at the crumpled hanky she held. "Looking back, maybe we should have. It was a terrible thing for your father and me to endure, and we just wanted to save you from that."

"What about when I got older?"

"We should have told you, I guess, but we thought it was best left alone. You and Norma married and were happy together, and then the grandchildren came." She stared into her son's red welling eyes. "That cold, snowy January day in 1918 changed our lives forever. Your father was never the same, and I didn't want it to consume you as it had your father. He's blamed himself all these years for not catching the man that took Donnie from us." She paused to wipe her cheeks and eyes. "He spent most nights and weekends trying to find Donnie's killer, talking to drunks and prostitutes. Every time someone was arrested for the smallest infraction, he hurried down to the jail to interrogate him. He spent hours in the garage going over the evidence, which was very little. There were times when he would come in from the garage with red, puffy eyes, and I knew he'd been in the garage crying while going over the evidence."

Norma had been sitting on the sofa next to Dan's mother, quietly listening. Until this moment, she knew very little about Donnie's death because the family never talked about it, and while she had thought that was strange, now she understood.

Mrs. Morgan wiped her eyes. "Forgive your father, son. He loves you, and he was only trying to protect you from an awful truth."

Dan stared at the dead fireplace in silence.

Paulette stood and looked at the back of Dan's head. "I should go. Your father's waiting in the car." She turned to Norma. "Thank you, dear."

Norma's eyes were wet with tears, wishing she could do more to ease the tension between them, but she knew that in the end, it was up to her husband.

"Mom," he softly said while staring into the fireplace.

She paused at the door and turned. "Yes, son."

"Tell Dad I'll stop by tomorrow."

Dan opened his eyes, realizing he had fallen asleep, sat up, and looked at the grandfather clock standing in the corner of the living room. Seeing it was nine-thirty, he tossed the cover back, put his feet on the area rug, and looked out the window, hearing the quiet sound of a push mower and children playing. Sliding his feet into his leather slippers, he stood and made his way down the hall to the kitchen, where he opened the refrigerator, pulled out a bottle of beer, and opened it by using the opener attached to the side of the cabinet. He took a drink while walking down the hall, opened the front door, and stepped onto the porch, where he bent over and picked up the morning newspaper. With the bottle of beer in one hand and the paper in the other, he walked back inside, closed the door, went into the living room, and sank into a plush chair. He took a sip of beer, set the bottle on the coffee table, and unrolled the newspaper. Listening to Al Schafer's push mower next door, he decided he would mow his lawn when the telephone rang. He stood and picked up the receiver. "Hello."

"Detective Morgan, please."

"This is Detective Morgan."

"Detective, this is Desk Sergeant Petry, and I see we have a note to call you if anyone reports a missing teenage girl."

Excited, Dan looked out the window. "That's right."

"Well, we have a Mr. and Mrs. Edward Phillips here wanting to report their daughter missing."

Dan's memory found the girl lying in the alley last night. "Show them into an empty room, offer them coffee, and give them the paperwork to fill out. I'll be there as quick as I can get dressed."

"Sure thing, Lieutenant."

Detective Morgan walked into the lobby of the police department and glanced at the empty benches along the wall as he walked up to the desk sergeant.

On recognizing Dan, the officer smiled. "Good morning, Lieutenant."

"Where is Mr. and Mrs. Phillips?"

The desk sergeant stood and walked around from behind his desk. "I put them in room 104 with the paperwork to fill out." He paused. "Neither wanted coffee."

Dan thanked him and then walked down the hall to the same room where he had told the Crowder's about their daughter. He paused at the door, took a quick breath, opened it, and stepped inside, finding a worried couple sitting on the far side of the long oak table. He closed the door. "Good morning, Mr., and Mrs. Phillips. I'm Detective Dan Morgan."

Mr. Phillips was heavyset, balding, dressed in blue, wrinkled slacks and a dress shirt with sleeves rolled up to the elbow. Mrs. Phillips was built much the same, and her brown and gray hair was in a braid that wrapped around her head. She was wearing a faded, floral housedress with a full apron and looked worried as she wiped her red, tearing eyes with a white hanky.

Mr. Phillips stood and shook Dan's hand. "Edward Phillips." He gestured to his wife. "This is my wife, Grace."

Dan smiled. "Please be seated, Mr. Phillips."

Mr. Phillips looked fearful as he returned to his chair. "Any news about our daughter?"

Dan pulled a chair from the table and sat down. "What is your daughter's name?"

"Marie," said Mrs. Phillips. "Marie Susan Phillips."

"And how long has your daughter been missing."

Grace looked worried, and her voice quivered as she spoke. "Since last night." She wiped the tears from her eyes and cheeks with her hanky and then leaned forward, hugging her large black purse. "She was supposed to be home by midnight. But we haven't seen her." Fear filled here face. "We are worried with these murders in the newspapers. We've called all her friends, but no one knows where she is."

Mr. Phillips looked at Dan. "Can you help us find our daughter?"

Dan looked at the missing person's report sitting in front of them. "Can I see that?"

Mr. Phillips slid it across the table.

Dan picked it up and began reading to himself: *Marie Susan Phillips. Address: 955 Lipan Street.* Dan figured she went to West High School and continued reading. *Race: Caucasian. Age: Fifteen. Height: Five Feet. Weight: 88 lbs. Hair: Brown. Eyes: Blue.* Everything matched the description of the girl in the alley behind the Paramount Theatre. He set the paper down, contemplating his next few words, and then he looked at the worried couple. "There's no easy way to say this, but the body of a young girl matching your daughter's description was found downtown Friday night."

In the silence of the room, Mrs. Phillips let out a soft sob as she bent over and buried her face in the elbow of her arm resting on the table.

Mr. Phillips looked at Dan. "You think that girl is our Marie?"

Dan nodded. "Yes, sir, I do. The girl fits the description in the report you filled out." He paused, thinking how much he hated this part of his job. "The only way to be certain is for one or both of you to make an identification."

Mr. Phillips closed his tearing eyes and put his arm around his wife.

Dan stood. "I'll give you a few minutes. I'll be just outside the door." He turned and stepped into the hall, pulled the cigarette package from his shirt pocket, took one out, and lit it. Blowing a puff of smoke into the air, he tossed the dead match into the sand of the ashtray standing next to the door. Then he put the package back into his shirt pocket and listened to the muffled crying on the other side of the door. Minutes passed, and after he took a final drag, he blew the smoke into the hallway and shoved the butt into the sand-filled ashtray. After taking a deep breath, he opened the door and stepped into the room.

Mr. Phillips looked up with weeping eyes. "Where is my little girl?"

"If this is your daughter, she is over at Denver General." Dan paused. "I can call ahead and make the arrangements if you feel you're up to it. If not, we can do this another time."

Edward's eyes welled with tears. "She's all we had."

"I'd like to see my daughter," said Mrs. Phillips as she stood.

"I'll go and make the arrangements." He opened the door, stepped into the hallway, walked down the hall to the front desk, and looked at Sergeant Petry. "I'd like to use your telephone."

Dan pushed his old mower back and forth across his yard, thinking of Mr. and Mrs. Phillips holding onto one another while identifying their daughter's body. He occasionally stopped to empty the grass clippings into a thirty-gallon can sitting on the edge of the driveway, then continued the task of mowing the yard. The sun was warm, and by the time he finished mowing, his face and shirt were wet from perspiration. He edged the lawn along the sidewalk, driveway, and around the base of the elm tree and then carried the 30-gallon can of grass clippings to the compost pile near the alley. Thinking of Mr. and Mrs. Phillips, he dumped the clippings, put everything away, and headed for the back door.

He washed up at the kitchen sink, dried with a dishtowel, made a bologna sandwich, filled his plate with stale potato chips, and got a beer out of the refrigerator. With the plate of food in one hand and his beer in the other, he managed the front screen door and stepped out onto the covered porch, letting the door close with a bang. Setting his plate and beer onto the small, white, wooden table, he eased into one of the two white wooden chairs on either side.

The air was calm and warm and carried the muffled but happy sounds of children playing somewhere in the neighborhood, mixing with the sounds of push mowers and sprinklers watering lawns. He took a bite of the sandwich, washed it down with a drink of cold beer, and thought of past Saturday mornings playing catch with Robert in the front yard. Nancy would sit on the porch railing, tormenting her older brother when he missed the ball.

Al Schafer from next door walked around the corner of the house and stepped up onto the porch. "Hello, Dan."

"Albert," grinned Dan, pleased with seeing his neighbor. "Can I get you a sandwich and a beer?"

Al sat down in the other white wooden chair and looked at Dan's plate of food. "Already had my lunch," he said while eyeing the bottle of beer. "But a beer sounds inviting."

"Won't be but a minute." Dan stood and disappeared inside.

Al looked down at the plate of food, reached out, took a chip, and put it into his mouth.

Returning a few moments later with a cold bottle, Dan handed it to his neighbor.

Al thanked him, took a healthy drink, and rested the bottle on his right thigh while letting out a small belch. Al Schafer, at forty, was a big man of six feet with a friendly face and a nice smile. He had big hands and broad shoulders that were perfect for a carpenter.

Dan recalled how hard Al had worked putting in the shower upstairs for Norma after she got sick with cancer. He watched his neighbor take a drink of beer, wondering if he had ever worn his hair in anything other than a flat top. Deciding he probably never had, Dan took a bite of his sandwich. "How's Peggy?"

Al sipped his beer. "She's good. I can't keep up with her anymore."

Dan smiled while remembering how busy Peggy always seemed to be, doing this thing or that while going here and there. "How's work?"

"Always busy this time of year." Al looked concerned, adding, "Good thing too. Have to make up for the time I lost this past winter." He took a drink of beer. "Saw your picture in today's newspaper."

Surprised and a little angry, Dan thought about the flashbulbs and cameras from last night. "I haven't looked at the paper yet."

Al turned. "Good likeness. I've been reading about these vampire killings."

Dan was pissed about the picture and was in no mood to talk about the case.

Al looked at Dan. "I suppose you can't talk about all that."

Dan shook his head. "No, Al, I really can't."

Al chuckled softly. "I didn't think so." He paused. "Had to ask, though."

"I understand." Dan shoved the last of his sandwich into his mouth and washed it down with a drink of beer.

Al looked at Dan. "What are you hearing from Robert these days?"

Dan's mind found the postcards tucked away in the drawer of the desk inside. "I get a postcard from him now and again."

Schafer took a drink of beer. "How's the boy doing?"

Embarrassed at not knowing, Dan simply said, "Okay, I guess."

Al sipped his beer. "Still not talking to one another?"

"No, we hadn't talked much since before he left."

Thinking how lonely Dan must be in this big house, Al said, "That's too bad."

Dan agreed with a silent nod, then took a drink of beer.

Al took a drink of his beer and then turned to Dan. "Ever figure out what it was that got him so upset?"

Dan considered the question. "I think maybe he blames me for Nancy's death since it was me that bought the bicycle she was riding the day she was struck and killed by that car."

Schafer took a drink of beer and looked at the bottle in thought. "Did Norma place the blame for that on you?"

Dan considered that while he took a drink of beer. "She never said she did."

"Maybe Robert doesn't either but instead blames you for not finding the person that killed her since you're a cop and all. That makes more sense to me."

"Maybe," replied Dan remembering how hard he and Jack had worked to find the driver and the car. His next thought was of his mother telling him how his father worked endlessly to find the man who killed his twin brother Donnie.

Al finished his beer, set the bottle down on the white wooden table, and stood. "Well, guess I best be getting back before Peggy discovers I'm gone."

Dan chuckled. "Have a good day, Al, and give my best to Peggy."

"I'll do that," replied Al as he stepped off the porch, where he paused and looked back at Dan. "Sure hope you and Robert work things out. Each other is all the two of you have now."

Dan knew that was true as he watched Al disappear around the corner of the house. While the stillness returned to the porch, he took a drink of his beer, letting his mind reflect on how he and Jack Brolin had worked with other detectives and police officers running down every lead in Nancy's death. But as the days and weeks rolled by, the case got colder and colder.

His mind raced to the alley behind the Paramount Theater the night before and the body of Marie Susan Phillips lying on the metal table in the city morgue while her parents cried over their loss. Mrs. Phillips had wanted what belonged to her daughter and asked about her billfold full of pictures. He recalled how disappointed she was when he told her it was not with the body. He drank the last of his beer, knowing Marie's killer had taken the billfold as a trophy along with her panties and little finger.

A small summer breeze made its way across the porch from the street as his mind turned to the days when he and Norma would sit in these very chairs, drinking lemonade and talking about simple things. He missed those small, unimportant conversations that now seemed so very important and lost in time. Closing his mind from such things, he picked up the empty plate and two empty bottles from the table and walked inside, letting the screen slam behind him.

After the kitchen was clean, he walked into the living room, picked up the newspaper, and read the headline: '**Vampire killer strikes again.**' He looked at the picture below of him in his car, taken as he drove into the alley, and softly said, "That's just great." After tossing the paper onto the sofa, he walked into the foyer, picked up the three envelopes from the small table, and sat down at the dining room table. He opened the first envelope and dumped the pictures, crime scene, and coroner report of Diane Wagner on the table and then sorted through the pictures, studying each one, and finally put them back into their envelopes and set them aside.

Picking up the envelope that Pete had written the name Barbara No Name, Dan took a pencil, scratched that out, wrote Sally Ann Crowder, and dumped the contents on the table. After examining each picture carefully, he scratched out Barbara No Name on the typed reports and wrote in Sally Ann Crowder. When finished, he went through the envelopes of Gail Thomas, and when done, he sat back, feeling disappointed. He did not know what he expected to find, but whatever it was, it still eluded him. There was something in the pictures that bothered him, and no matter how hard he looked at each black and white photo, he could not discover what it was. It was like solving a jigsaw puzzle with missing pieces.

He put everything away and returned the envelopes to the table in the foyer for Monday morning's trip to the office. Then he returned to the stuffed chair in the living room and opened the paper to another page. '**Ridgeway promoted to General. Replaces MacArthur**'. Thinking it had been a mistake for President Truman to fire MacArthur, he began reading the article.

The time passed, and having read the Saturday newspaper, he tossed it on the coffee table and contemplated what he was going to do the rest of the afternoon and evening. He looked at the grandfather clock in the corner of the living room, seeing it was only four o'clock and too early for dinner. Thinking that he had not been to a movie in a while, he reached for the newspaper and glanced over the entertainment page. King Solomon's Mines starring Stewart Granger and Deborah Kerr, playing at the Gothic Theater in Englewood, looked interesting. Seeing the next showing was at six o'clock, he tossed the paper onto the sofa and headed upstairs to change and clean up.

Dan followed a small crowd of moviegoers out of the theater under the marquee's bright lights to the corner of the theater and gravel parking lot. The air was calm and warm under a moonless sky of stars, and as he walked toward his car, he was greeted by a pleasant aroma that made him hungry. Pausing, Dan looked across the parking lot at the long, narrow, white building with black letters on the side of it, spelling the word Rockybuilt. Thinking a hamburger sounded good, he walked toward the white building, stepped inside, sat down at the counter, and ordered two hamburgers.

Driving south on Broadway, he opened the white bag containing the hamburgers, took one out, unwrapped the paper, and took a bite. Driving past the Pioneer Theater, he thought of Gail Thomas lying in the alley behind it and continued through the intersection of South Broadway and East Hamden. Taking another bite of hamburger, he drove up the long hill past the army surplus store he had visited last week, past Flood High School, and continued south along Broadway while eating his dinner. By the time the second hamburger was in his stomach, he was driving across the railroad tracks by the county courthouse in Littleton, where he and Jack had visited sheriff Brumwell days earlier. As he passed it, he thought of the sheriff's pretty, married secretary, Cathy Holman.

The main street of Littleton's small, cozy town was not very busy. Several of the stores had closed, and only a few cars were parked along the deserted street. As he turned off Littleton Boulevard into the park, the headlights of Dan's Ford lit up the poplar trees lining the gravel road leading into Rio Grande Park. The sound of his tires on gravel broke the stillness as Dan drove into the empty parking lot and stopped in front of one of several old telephone poles laid end to end that marked the boundary of the lot. He turned off the headlights and the engine, listening to the crickets and other night sounds that flowed through the open window. A cool spring breeze caressed his face while his mind reviewed the pictures of Diane Wagner's body that had been found in this very place. The clanging bells at the railroad barrier drowned out the crickets, followed by the lonely whistle of a train approaching from the south. He turned toward the flashing red lights of the gates as they lowered across the boulevard and then watched as a locomotive engine speeding toward Denver passed through the headlights of waiting cars at the crossing. As tankers, boxcars, and flatbeds followed the speeding engine, another car turned into the park, turned off its headlights, and stopped several yards away with its radio challenging the roar of the train.

The caboose suddenly came out of the darkness chasing the rest of the train north, and in the sudden stillness, music from the other car replaced the roar of the train. As the now silent barriers rose to let the traffic cross Littleton Boulevard, Dan felt the fool sitting all alone in the parking lot near a dark car that was probably full of teenagers. After asking himself what he had hoped to accomplish by coming here, he whispered, "I'm losing my mind." He started the car, backed away from the telephone pole barrier, drove out of the parking lot into the lights of downtown Littleton, and turned the car toward home.

Eleven

Sunday was a warm, quiet day as Dan and Jack Brolin sat on Jack's back patio drinking beer while listening to the Dodgers ball game on the radio. Neither had spoken about the Phillips family Dan had told Jack about earlier. The ball game was in the top of the ninth, with the New York Dodgers trailing by one run with two outs and no one on base. Dan took a small sip of his third or fourth beer and listened to the baseball announcer on the radio, screaming with excitement as the batter hit a fly to third base ending the game. Feeling sorry for his partner, who loved his Dodgers, Dan could not bring himself to tease Jack about his favorite team losing, so he sipped his beer in silence.

A disappointed Jack reached over, turned off the radio, and looked at his partner. "You ready for another beer?"

Feeling the effects of the beers he had already consumed, he shook his head no. "I think I've had enough."

Lori pushed the screen door open with her hip and stepped out of the house onto the cement patio carrying a platter of hot dogs and buns in one hand and a large bowl of potato salad in the other. Hearing the screen door slam closed, Dan turned, thinking she looked lovely in her blue and white dress that was similar to one Norma used to wear. Feeling guilty for taking it to the Goodwill last year, he wondered who was wearing it these days. Lori set the platter and bowl on the picnic table and looked at her husband with a cute, pouty face. "Your Dodgers lose again, hon?"

Looking dejected, Jack moved from the lawn chair to one of the benches at the picnic table. "Idiots."

Dan grinned as he stood and crossed the porch from his white wooden lawn chair toward the table and sat down on the bench across from Jack. He smiled at Lori, thanked her for the food, and then asked if she would join them.

She looked at her husband. "Depends on Grouchy."

Jack looked up, smiled, and patted the bench seat next to him. "I promise I won't bite."

Unsure, she looked down at the table. "Oh, I forgot the condiments, and we need napkins."

After she disappeared inside, Jack looked at Dan. "I'm getting another beer. You sure you don't want one?"

"No, but I'll take a soda."

Jack got up from the bench. "Shitty picture of you on Saturday morning's front page." He grinned. "Had you been drinking?"

Dan grinned. "Up yours. You're just jealous because your picture wasn't on the front page." He filled a bun with a hot dog, placed it on his paper plate, and filled the plate with potato salad.

Lori walked out of the house carrying a tray of chopped onions, jars of relish, mustard, and napkins.

Jack followed her out of the house, carrying a beer and two sodas, handed one to Dan, gave Lori the other, and took a drink of beer as he sat down.

Lori looked at Dan with a sad expression. "I heard what Jack said about your picture," she smiled and laughed softly. "It was pretty bad."

Dan chuckled, knowing she spoke the truth. "Maybe no one will recognize me."

The table filled with laughter and then turned quiet while they went about the task of filling their plates.

With his hot dog full of condiments, Jack picked up the saltshaker, salted his potato salad, and looked at Dan. "You've been awfully quiet today. You feeling alright?"

Dan bit into his hot dog. "I've been thinking about the package."

Jack looked curious. "You never got it?"

"No."

"What package?" Lori asked.

Jack quickly explained it to her.

She looked at Dan. "A joke, perhaps?"

Dan took a drink of soda. "If it is, it's not very funny. I've been thinking about it for days."

Lori paused while eating. "Maybe it's from your son."

"I considered that," said Dan. "But I won't know until I get it."

"Speaking of Robert," said Lori. "Have you heard from him lately?"

Sounding disappointed, Dan said, "I got the usual postcard the other day."

She reached across the table and gently touched his arm. "I'm sure that one day he'll come home, Dan."

Appreciating her gesture, he smiled, hoping she was right and bit into his hotdog.

Wanting to get his partner's mind off of his son, Jack changed the subject to the war in Korea, and after that, they discussed the price of gasoline and other issues in the news while they ate. Jack's attempt at getting Dan's mind off his son worked, but only because Dan was thinking about the four murdered girls.

The afternoon passed quickly, the night was approaching, and it was time for Dan to leave. He thanked Lori for the food and hospitality of her home. She kissed his cheek, telling him to be careful going home, and assured him that Robert would come home one day, and they would sit down and talk this all out. Dan smiled, saying he hoped she was right, told her goodbye, and then walked with Jack to his car at the curb in front of the Brolin house.

While Dan climbed into his 49 Ford, Jack rested his forearms on the open window and leaned inside. "What's the plan for Monday?"

Dan thought about the thousand drug stores in Denver alone that sold chloroform, considering that finding out who bought it would be like asking the surplus stores about the army blankets, another lost cause. "I thought I'd stop at the morgue and see if Lange has anything for us on my way to the office tomorrow morning. I'll meet you there."

Jack thought for a moment. "Place gives me the willies. I'll see you in the office."

"Alright. I'll see you in the morning."

Jack stepped away from the door. "I'll bring some donuts." He watched Dan drive away and then went inside the house to help Lori clean the kitchen.

The street Dan lived on was deserted and quiet, as it usually was on Sunday evenings. Most families were in their houses listening to their favorite radio programs, or those who could afford a television were watching; 'The Show of Shows.' Turning into the driveway, the car's headlights raced across the front porch, chasing shadows up the driveway to the white doors of the garage. Stopping next to the small sidewalk leading up to the porch, he shut the car off, rolled up the windows, got out, locked the car, and walked to the front door.

Once inside, he locked the front door, tossed his keys into the glass bowl, ignoring his reflection in the mirror on the wall above the table, and walked into the living room. Feeling tired and a little woozy from the beers he had earlier at Jack's, he looked at the grandfather clock in the corner of the living room, seeing it was only six-thirty. Knowing that was incorrect, he looked at his wristwatch, seeing it was eight twenty. After setting the time on the big clock, he closed the glass door covering the face of the clock and briefly considered turning the chimes back on. He had turned them off before because they had bothered Norma during her final days. Thinking they would make the house feel emptier than it already was, he decided to leave them off.

Knowing tomorrow morning would come early, he went upstairs, changed into his pajama bottoms, and came back down with the blanket and Norma's pillow. After turning off the lights, he lay down on the sofa and covered himself with the blanket, his head buried in the pillow. Staring out the window at the Martin house's warm, lighted windows across the street, he suddenly became envious of Tom Martin. As his eyes grew heavy, he imagined them watching television together and laughing while being a family.

Dan walked into headquarters with the manila envelope containing the autopsy and photographs of Marie Susan Phillips he had picked up from Coroner Pete Lange and Todd Anderson of CSU, along with the other envelopes. He gently tossed Marie's onto Jack's desk. "Pictures of Friday night."

Jack opened the manila envelope from Todd Anderson first, took out the eight-by-ten black and white pictures, and started going through them.

Dan put the other envelopes in the top drawer of his desk, picked up his cup, and headed for the small kitchen at the back of the office. Minutes later, he returned with a full cup of hot, black coffee and sat down at his desk. He took a sip, thinking it tasted terrible, and glanced around for his donuts. "Where are the donuts?"

Without looking up from the pictures, Jack opened the top left drawer of his desk, pulled out a partially mashed sack from Grandma's Donuts, and tossed it across his desk onto Dan's.

Dan reached for the sack, opened it, and looked inside at two chocolate-covered cake donuts. He took one out and bit into it, tasting the sweet, dark chocolate while considering the day ahead. Studying the donut while chewing, he said. "I'm going to take a ride out to Littleton and have a visit with Sheriff Brumwell."

Jack looked up from the pictures and scoffed. "What for?"

"I want to visit the crime scene."

Jack grinned. "Who you shitting? You just want to see that good-looking Mrs. Holman?"

Dan had not considered Mrs. Holman until now and decided she was very good-looking, but it was too bad she was married. He took another bite of the donut and looked at Jack while talking with his mouth full. "She's married, asshole."

Jack chuckled. "You can still look." Then he said, "Seriously, what do you hope to gain by visiting Rio Grande Park?"

Dan considered that while he washed the donut down with the hot, bitter coffee. "Probably nothing."

"Then why waste your time?"

"Can't explain it, Jack. All I can tell you is that I want to put my feet on the same ground where they found the body and the killer walked."

Jack set the pictures down, picked up his coffee, and stared at his partner over the rim while taking a sip. "You aren't going psychic on me, are you, Dan?"

Dan chuckled, finding his partner funny. "Yeah, that's exactly what I'm doing, you big ass."

Jack smiled, but he was always worried about his partner and thought the ride might do him some good. "Well, if you don't mind, I'll stay here and get some work done, like trying to catch these two little assholes that robbed Mr. Rothstein and put a bullet in his customer's heart."

Glad that Jack was not coming, he said, "Suit yourself, and while you play around here, make sure those two girls come in." He stood. "Let's take those pictures into the captain, and then I'll be on my way."

Dan and Jack sat in silence as they watched Captain Foley look through Marie Phillips' pictures. Finished, he handed them to Dan Morgan. "You boys have got to catch this bastard, and soon."

Dan took the pictures. "Yes, sir, we know."

"Well," said Foley. "What are your plans?"

Feeling on the spot, Dan glanced down at the envelope and then looked at the captain. "There's not much to go on, Captain. We've got no fingerprints, all the bodies were washed clean, and no one has seen the killer except the two girls that found our latest victim, and they only saw him and the van he drove from a distance up a dark alley."

Jack leaned forward in his chair. "We're bringing the girls in later to have them look at some photos of vans. Maybe we can get the make and model."

Captain Foley thought about that. "Well, let's hope that leads to something."

Dan stood. "Anything else, Captain?"

"No, just keep me informed."

Jack followed Dan out of the captain's office, and when they got to their desks, he sat down and watched as Dan put the envelope in the top drawer of his desk and pulled out another envelope. "Who's that?"

"Diane Wagner. I want to compare the pictures to the park."

Not sure what his partner hoped to accomplish, Jack stared at the envelope and then looked at Dan. "You know what I've been thinking?"

Dan shut his drawer and looked at his partner, expecting some sort of wisecrack about Mrs. Holman. "No."

"I've been thinking about that fellah in England they called Jack the Ripper."

Dan considered that for a short moment. "You think we're dealing with our own Jack the Ripper?"

Jack shrugged, "Don't know, but it's a thought." Then he smiled. "Actually, that was Lori's idea."

"Not a bad one," said Dan. "Except for the postmortem knife wounds in Diane and the missing fingers, our other victims were not mutilated, and they're not prostitutes." Then he looked at the clock remembering the two girls. "Betty and Sybil will be here soon."

"I'll handle it," said Jack. "You go ahead."

Dan glanced toward Foley's office. "If the Foley asks where I am, tell him I'm checking on something." Then Dan held up the envelope bearing Diane Wagner's name and headed for the stairs. "Be back in a couple of hours."

Jack grinned. "Be sure and say hello to Mrs. Holman."

It was one-thirty when Dan's 49 Ford's front wheels touched the sidewalk's curb in front of the county courthouse in Littleton. Tossing his hat in the passenger seat, he climbed out of the car, hurried up the steps to the courthouse doors, and stepped inside the large lobby. The air was full of quiet voices that softly echoed off the white granite walls and ceiling, mixing with the soft sound of footsteps on the granite floor. He paused at the door of the sheriff's office, wishing Mrs. Holman was not a Mrs., then opened the door and stepped inside.

Cathy Holman looked up and smiled. "Detective Morgan, how good to see you."

Dan smiled, thinking she looked very nice in her short-sleeved, yellow dress with dark green piping. Her hair was up instead of long and flowing over her shoulders, as it had been the first time they had met. "Hello, Mrs. Holman. Is Sheriff Brumwell in?"

She looked regretful a s the smile left her face. "I'm sorry, but the sheriff and a friend from Wyoming went fishing in the mountains somewhere near Cripple Creek. They won't be back for a couple of days."

Disappointed, Dan stood in silence while considering what to do next.

Seeing his disappointment, she asked, "Is it important?" Then she gestured to another closed door. "Maybe one of his deputies could be of assistance."

Dan shook his head. "It's only important to me."

In the moment of silence that followed, she said, "If I knew what it was you wanted to see the sheriff about, Detective Morgan, perhaps I could help you."

He considered that. "I was just going to ask if he would mind showing me where they found Diane Wagner's body."

She thought about that for a minute, and then she picked up the receiver of the black rotary telephone and dialed a number. "Evelyn, this is Cathy Holman." She paused while smiling at Dan. "I have some errands to run, and I'll be back in about an hour. Would you mind taking my

101

calls? You're a dear. Thank you, Evelyn. I'll call you when I get back." She hung up the phone, opened the bottom drawer of her desk, and took out a dark brown handbag. She tucked it under her left arm as she stood smiling. "Feel like a walk, Detective?"

Somewhat confused, Dan asked. "To where?"

She smiled at him as she walked around the desk. "The park, of course. Isn't that what brought you to Littleton?"

"You know the spot where they found Diane Wagner?"

"Of course," she said, opening the door. "I'm not as fragile as I look, Detective. Shall we go? I have to be back in an hour."

"I guess," said Dan as he followed her out of the office and waited for her to lock the door.

They walked in silence across the lobby with its echoing footsteps, out the front door and down the steps toward the sidewalk.

At the bottom, Dan pointed to his car. "My car is right there."

She stopped, looked at his car, and smiled. "It's such a lovely afternoon. Let's walk. It's only a couple of blocks."

"Alright, but I need to get the pictures of the crime scene you gave me the other day. They're in my car."

"I'll wait here."

They walked along South Court Place to where the corner met Littleton Boulevard, turned west, and walked across the railroad tracks toward downtown Littleton.

Dan felt a little uncomfortable walking with a married woman down the main street of Littleton. "What does your husband do, Mrs. Holman?"

There was a long pause. "My husband died in the Philippines soon after the Japanese invasion. I had hoped he was a prisoner, but it wasn't until January 1946 that I learned he had died during the Bataan Death March."

Feeling the fool, he regretted asking, but at the same time, he was glad that he had. Dan looked along the boulevard lined by three-story buildings toward the Rocky Mountains in the distance. "I'm sorry, Mrs. Holman. I didn't mean to bring back any sad memories."

She looked at the side of his face as they walked. "Please call me Cathy, Detective."

He grinned. "If you call me Dan instead of Detective."

She smiled with a quiet laugh. "Alright, Dan, but there is nothing for you to be sorry over. You couldn't have known, and it was a long time ago." She paused, looking at the mountains in the distance above the rooftops of the buildings of downtown Littleton. "We were married

102

September 3rd, 1941, two weeks before the army sent him to Bataan." She paused in memory as she looked down at the sidewalk while they walked. "I found out I was pregnant a few weeks after he left, but I lost the baby in late January 1942. I sometimes wish I would have carried the baby full term so I would have something of Jim's to hold onto." She looked at him. "What about you, Dan?" she asked. "Are you married?"

Dan thought of how quickly his own family had fallen apart and reflected on his wife for a moment. "Norma, my wife of twenty-three years, died two years ago of cancer."

Cathy looked sad. "I'm sorry to hear that," and then she smiled. "But you had twenty-three wonderful years together." She looked away. "I'd sell my soul to have had just half that time with Jim."

Watching the traffic pass, he knew what she said was true, and he felt lucky for having had those years with Norma.

"Any children?" she asked.

"We had two children, a girl we named Nancy after Norma's great aunt." He paused. "Nancy was twelve when she was killed by a hit-and-run driver two blocks from our house. That was five years ago."

Cathy felt sorry for him and didn't know what to say.

"I have a son, Robert." He paused again. "We haven't spoken in over two years. He's in Chicago doing whatever it is he's doing. He'll be twenty soon." Dan suddenly realized he was talking to someone he barely knew about the most private things in his life.

She stopped and looked up and down the boulevard. "Let's cross here." They made it across the busy street, dodging honking cars and a truck driver who stuck his head out of the window, yelling, "Damn crazy fools!"

Safely on the sidewalk, Cathy laughed a nervous laugh. "I'm going to get run over one of these days."

Dan chuckled without humor. "Do this too often, and I'm sure you will."

She glanced at the truck as it sped away. "Do you hear from your son?"

"I get a postcard now and then."

At reaching the edge of Rio Grande Park, she pointed to a group of cottonwood trees in the southeast corner. "It's over there."

Dan looked to where she was pointing, seeing a weathered picnic table and benches looking lonely and neglected, sitting alone on a tiny knoll in the shade of several tall cottonwood trees. Beyond the table, the knoll was full of shrubbery and weeds separating the park from a tan brick building about a hundred yards beyond.

103

They walked through the park past a couple sitting on the green grass talking, a teenage boy and girl lying on a blanket laughing, and a young girl sitting against a tree with legs crossed reading a book while sipping on a straw stuck into a bottle of soda pop. Moments later, they were standing in the park's secluded corner with the table and benches he had seen before.

Dan stopped and looked up at the tops of the trees, knowing they would soon let loose their tiny pieces of cotton resembling a light, spring snow that the wind would soon blow across the park. He glanced around, noticing a worn path through the underbrush and weeds of the vacant lot that led toward the railroad tracks thirty or forty yards to the east. Dan suddenly recalled the train that had passed the other night while he sat foolishly in the parking lot. Figuring it was a path often used by teenagers, he wondered if the killer had used it as well to place the body. While Cathy made herself comfortable on one of the weathered benches, he imagined the killer carrying Diane and the army blanket from the parking lot on the other side of the park in the darkness to this spot while cars with shining headlights rolled up and down Littleton Boulevard.

Opening the envelope with the crime scene's pictures, he knelt and took them out, and placed them on the grass before him. Methodically he looked from the pictures of Diane's body to the real-life scene. After a few moments, he picked up another picture and stepped to the left a few steps and then a little closer to the trees.

Cathy put her purse on the weathered table next to her and watched with interest. After several minutes had passed, she finally asked, "Why do you want to do this?"

Dan paused from what he was doing, turned, looked at her puzzled face, and smiled. "I'm not really sure."

She smiled. "That's encouraging."

He grinned, feeling foolish, but continued with what he had come here to do while she watched. After several minutes, he picked up the pictures and put them back into the manila envelope. When he reached the table, he set the envelope down and sat next to her, getting a slight whiff of her perfume. He took a pack of cigarettes out of his suit coat pocket. "It's difficult to explain."

She watched while he tapped the top of the pack against his left hand until a couple of cigarettes emerged from the pack.

"Cigarette?"

"No, thanks," she said. "I'm a little curious, though. What did you hope to accomplish by comparing the pictures to the actual spot?"

Dan considered that while he lit his cigarette. Turning his head away from her, he blew smoke into the air and then looked at her. "I don't think the killer just happened to pick this place." He glanced around. "He's been here in the daylight. Maybe more than once."

"How do you know?"

Dan took a drag from his cigarette and blew the smoke away from Cathy. "This is the most secluded spot in the park. It wasn't by chance he chose it in the dark." He paused. "He knew he could take as much time with Diane Wagner as he wanted." He looked at the table. "He may have had lunch on this very table while planning what he was going to do." He paused to look at her. "He could have sat where we're sitting and watched the café across the street where Diane worked while he ate a sandwich he may even have ordered from her."

Cathy looked at the weathered table and then at the café across the street. "Feels creepy when you think about it."

"Yeah, it does." He looked at her, thinking she looked lovely. "I don't mean to make you feel uncomfortable."

She looked at him for a moment. "It just sounds so eerie when you talk about him."

He quickly considered what she had said. "There's no way for me to explain any of this to you. I just wanted to see what the killer saw and be in the same places he has been. It is hard to explain, but I feel the need to get closer to him in some way." Looking embarrassed, he smiled softly. "That sounds strange, I know, and I can't explain any of it." He took a drag from his cigarette. "Maybe I just want to catch the SOB too badly."

Cathy stared at him. "It doesn't sound all that strange. Psychiatrists do similar things with their patients to try and understand why they do the things they do."

He thought about what she said and wondered if a psychiatrist would help him understand the man he hunted. In the moment of silence that followed, the perfume she was wearing made the short journey between them, and he wanted to kiss her. Suddenly, guilt over Norma found him, so he stood from the bench and headed for the path. "Be right back."

"Where are you going?" she asked.

"Not far."

She watched with curiosity as he walked the worn path between the weeds for several yards to a dirt road.

Standing at the edge of the field, his eyes followed the narrow dirt road on this side of the railroad tracks that ran from the boulevard on the left and then south along the tracks for about a hundred yards before it turned west, disappearing into the trees.

Curious, Cathy softly hollered, "What do you see?"

Dan walked back to the table, turned, and looked toward the railroad tracks. "You can't see it from here, but there's a dirt road on this side of the tracks."

"It ends up at Santa Fe Drive," she said.

Dan gestured toward the dirt road. "He could have parked in the weeds and carried her here." He paused in thought. "But there were no photos of wheels flattening down the weeds."

She thought of the pictures she was familiar with. "I don't recall any pictures like that."

He glanced back at the field. "Doesn't matter now, I guess, but it would be nice to know if he had."

She looked past Dan to the empty field, wondering if anyone had even thought about that when they found the body.

Dan looked at the spot where the body was found and pictured the killer placing Diane on the blanket and then back to where the killer's car may have been waiting. He looked back at the parking lot. "The dirt road is closer than the parking lot." He thought for a moment longer, looked at his watch, and smiled at her. "Guess I better get you back to work. I'd hate to be the cause of you getting fired."

She laughed softly. "Sheriff Brumwell would never fire me."

He smiled. "You sound sure of that."

She smiled with confidence. "He's my uncle."

Dan chuckled at that, picked up the manila envelope, and offered his hand. When she took it to help herself up, her hand felt warm and soft in his, and he knew that he wanted to see her again. But in doing so, he would have to find a way to deal with the guilt about Norma. They walked back to the courthouse steps, where he shook her hand and thanked her for her time and company.

"My pleasure. I only hope it helps in your investigation."

Dan looked unsure. "So do I."

"Well," she said, "I best be getting back." She offered her hand again. "Good afternoon, Dan."

He gently shook her hand. "Thanks for showing me the crime scene."

She turned to walk up the steps but paused and turned with a shy smile. "I hope you won't think I'm too bold, but would you like to have coffee with me some evening after work?"

Wishing he had done the asking, he was thankful she was being a little bold and grinned. "I would."

She walked back down the steps while opening her purse, took out a pencil and a small red telephone book. "I hope you don't think I'm too forward, but I'm long past being coy, Detective."

"I don't mind," he said, watching as she tore a piece of paper out of the red book. "I thought we agreed to call one another by our first names."

She looked up from the paper, smiled, and continued writing.

"The truth is," he said. "I wanted to ask you, but I hesitated."

Pleased by that, she smiled and handed him the paper. "You have my number at work. This is my home telephone and my address in case you're ever in the neighborhood."

He took the paper, glanced at the name and number, and slid it into his shirt pocket. "I'll call you."

"I hope you do. I think it would be nice to have a cup of coffee and talk about things that don't include murder and dead bodies."

He chuckled. "That might be different."

She smiled as she turned and started up the steps.

He watched her for a moment and then turned toward his car, and after he opened the car door, he looked up in time to see her disappear into the courthouse.

Norma's memory was always in the midst of any thought Dan had about seeing another woman. And by the time he drove into the parking lot of Denver Police Headquarters, he'd had several arguments with himself about having an innocent cup of coffee with Cathy Holman.

As he turned the car engine off, he looked at the image of his eyes in the rearview mirror, knowing he would like more than a cup of coffee with her. Thinking he might talk to Jack about her, he picked up Diane Wagner's envelope, got out of the car, walked across the parking lot to the main entrance, opened the door, and stepped inside.

Looking at his partner while walking toward his desk, second thoughts about confiding in Jack rushed at him like the trains passing Littleton Boulevard. And by the time he reached his desk, Dan was convinced that he would be better off leaving Jack out of it.

Jack looked up from what he was doing and then at the clock above the stairs. "You've been gone a long time."

Dan pulled his chair from under the desk, sat down, and looked across the two desks at his partner. "Did the two girls make it in?"

Jack nodded. "With their parents. The photo of the van she picked out is a 1948 Ford."

"So, we're looking for a white 1948 Ford van." Then looking frustrated, he said in jest, "Can't be too many of them around." He looked at his partner. "But that's more than we had. Anything new on the robbery?"

"Mr. Rothstein called and said he remembered the kid with the crew cut had a scar on the front left side of his forehead about three inches long. So, I decided to look through these juvenile mug shots." He grinned. "Just might get lucky and find our boy has a record."

Dan looked doubtful. "Life isn't going to be that easy for us, my friend. How about the other dipshit?"

"Nothing. But if we catch one, we catch the other."

"I hope so," said Dan. "I'd like to get these two little bastards."

Jack stood from his swivel chair, walked around the desk, and sat on the edge of his partner's desk. "How did you make out with Brumwell?"

Dan wished he hadn't asked. "Sheriff Brumwell was gone, but Mrs. Holman took me to the park."

Jack considered that for a long moment. "Took you to the park, did she?" He nodded thoughtfully, wearing the smile of a Cheshire cat. "Interesting."

Dan looked up at his partner's brown eyes and grinned. "Sit down, damn it."

Jack chuckled as he returned to his desk, wishing his friend would find someone to fill the emptiness in his life, even if just for a little while. Jack worried about Dan being alone too much and was afraid he would get used to it. He picked up a mug shot book and tossed it across his desk onto Dan's. "It's only three. Start looking."

As Dan pulled the book towards him, the telephone rang, so he pushed the book aside and picked up the receiver. "Detective Morgan."

"Did you like the latest package I left?"

Not recognizing the voice, Dan asked, "Who is this?"

"A friend. Did you enjoy it, Detective?"

Dan slammed the receiver down. "Asshole."

"What was that?"

"Someone is asking me if I liked the package."

"It wasn't Robert?"

Dan shook his head. "No, I'd know Robert's voice. This idiot had some sort of accent."

"Sounds like someone's messing with you. You piss anybody off lately?"

Dan thought about that as he glanced around the department, wondering if someone in the office was trying to be funny, and thoughtfully said, "Not any more than usual." Then thinking of his picture in the paper, he returned to the mug book. "Let's see if we can find your robber."

Dan sat on the sofa in front of the television, eating the Chinese food he had picked up for dinner while watching 'You bet your Life,' starring Groucho Marx. When the show ended at eight-thirty, the coffee table was a mess of small paper containers partially filled with food, several dirty paper napkins, and two empty bottles of beer. Filling his mouth with the broken fortune cookie, he unrolled the tiny piece of paper and read the fortune that could pertain to anyone. He tossed it on the table, got up, turned off the television, picked up the containers and his empty beer bottles, and headed for the kitchen. He put the leftovers in the refrigerator so he could reheat them another night.

He gathered up the four envelopes of the victims from the table in the foyer, spread their pictures across the dining room table, and then walked up and down the table, staring at them. Pausing now and then to study each group of pictures, he still did not know what it was he was looking for. Something about the pictures troubled him, and he thought that if he looked at them long enough, he would eventually figure out what it was, not realizing it was slowly becoming an obsession.

After an hour of looking at the pictures, going over the forensics and coroner's reports, he looked at his watch, noticing that it was approaching ten o'clock. Tired and angry about not getting anywhere, he thought about his father looking at the pictures of Donnie all those years. Looking down at the mess on the table, he thought this must be how he had felt while going over and over the same pictures and evidence, day after day, month after month, and year after year, getting nowhere. Stepping back from the table, he whispered to himself, "No wonder dad drank." Then he put the pictures away and went upstairs to change into his pajamas.

After tossing the blanket and Norma's pillow on the sofa, he checked the doors, turned out the lights, lay down, covered up with the soft blanket, and snuggled his head into Norma's pillow. While staring out the window, his mind jumped back and forth between Norma and Cathy Holman. He looked at a picture frame sitting on the table across the darkroom, and while he was unable to see the photograph of Norma in the darkness, he could see it in his mind's eye. As sadness filled him, he stared out the window and thought of how pretty Cathy Holman looked sitting on the bench in Rio Grande Park until his eyelids began to feel heavy.

Twelve

It was almost ten o'clock on Tuesday morning when an excited Jack Brolin pushed his chair back from his desk with the back of his legs as he stood. "Got the little bastard."

Startled, Dan looked up.

Jack picked up the mug book he was looking through and hurried around his desk, slammed the book down on top of the mug book Dan was looking through and pointed to the picture of a young juvenile. "Jimmy Obrien. See the damn scar?" Leaving Dan to look at the picture, Jack hurried back to his desk for his coat hanging from the back of his chair. "We'll take the book with us and visit Mr. Rothstein and see if he can identify this Jimmy Obrien as one of the robbers."

Thinking that was a good idea, Dan stood and shrugged into his suit coat.

Jack walked back to Dan's desk, picked up the book, and waited while Dan took his gun out of the drawer of his desk.

Dan looked at Jack. "You have the address on the little shit?"

"We'll stop by records and get it on our way out. I'll drive."

"Let's hope it's current," said Dan as he followed his partner toward the stairs.

The tiny bell above the door chimed when Dan followed his anxious partner inside the pawnshop and closed the door, ringing the same tiny bell again. He followed Jack down a narrow aisle between long glass cases filled with other people's treasures that they had sold or used to borrow money.

Benjamin Rothstein was sitting behind the glass counter in the rear of the store, watching two men in overalls installing a metal mesh screen across the front of the counter. Hearing the bell above the door, he looked up, and seeing the two detectives, he stepped past the two workers into the narrow aisle. Rothstein stopped and smiled as he pointed toward the men building a cage with a door next to the cash register. "Got the idea from a cousin in New York City," he said proudly with his heavy accent. "They always have trouble with crooks back there. Very dangerous place, New York City." He looked at the two detectives. "Have you come to tell me you've arrested those two hoodlums?"

Dan looked at the men working and knew the cage wouldn't help if someone wanted something and decided not to say anything to Mr. Rothstein.

"Not yet, Mr. Rothstein," said Jack. "But we'd like to show you a photo."

"Sure," said Rothstein as he reached up with both hands to pull his glasses down from the top of his head. "What is this photo you have?"

Jack put the book onto one of the glass counters and opened it to a page containing several photographs of juvenile criminals. "I'd like you to look at a few pages and tell me if you see anyone that looks familiar."

Rothstein looked at him with a curious face. "You mean familiar, as in robbing me?"

Jack glanced at Dan, looked at Rothstein, and grinned. "That's the idea."

"Sure," said Rothstein as he bent over the book and started going through the pages very carefully. Coming to Jimmy Obrien's picture, he put his hand over the picture covering the mouth and nose. Getting excited, he pointed to it. "That's the one. That's the boy that hit me with his gun and took my money." He pointed to the picture again. "See the scar?"

"You're positive?" asked Jack.

Wanting Mr. Rothstein to be sure, Dan said, "You told us the two men that robbed you were wearing bandannas over their faces; are you sure?"

"Absolutely," replied Rothstein with authority. "I'd recognize him with a sack over his head." Then his eyes narrowed. "It's the eyes, detective. I looked into those eyes, and I saw death."

Jack looked at Dan. "Satisfied?"

With a wry smile, Dan nodded that he was.

Proudly, Jack thanked Mr. Rothstein.

Benjamin Rothstein looked puzzled. "You gonna arrest that hoodlum now, I hope?"

Jack slammed the book closed. "Soon as we find him." He picked it up. "We'll be in touch."

Rothstein looked puzzled. "What does that mean, you'll be in touch?"

Jack smiled. "When we make the arrest, we'll call you, and you can come down to Police Headquarters and make a positive ID."

As they walked toward the door, Rothstein yelled. "Don't take too long, Detective. I'm an old man, and I don't care about the money. I want the little criminal in jail." He paused, then yelled. "And throw away the key!"

Jack drove to the address on Grant Street he had gotten from Records and parked in front of the apartment house next door. He and Dan got out of the car, walked up the sidewalk to the solid glass door, and stepped into the foyer. Off to the left was a table used for mail too big to fit in the regular four rows of mailboxes above it. Each mailbox had a name with a black button that would ring the doorbell in that apartment.

Jack ran his index finger up and down the names until he found Juliet Obrien. He looked at Dan. "Number thirteen." He chuckled as he pushed the button. "Is that fate or what?"

Dan grinned just as a woman's voice said, "Who is it," through the small black speaker next to the mailboxes.

Jack put his mouth close to the speaker. "Is Bob home?"

"There's no one here by that name."

Jack stepped away from the tiny speaker and looked at Dan. "Just wanted to see if anyone was home."

Dan watched with interested curiosity while his partner pressed another button, got no answer, and then another that produced a young female voice, "Who is it?"

"Package," said Jack. The buzzer sounded. Jack opened the door and then looked at Dan. "You don't think Mrs. Obrien would have let us in, do you?"

Dan grinned. "No, but the manager would have."

Jack gave Dan a disappointed look. "Now, what fun would that have been?" Then he followed his partner down the dim corridor looking for apartment thirteen. Finding the apartment in the rear of the building next to the fire exit, they stood on either side of the door, pulled out their badges and guns, and gave each other a quick grin. Jack pushed the button next to the door, hearing the muffled buzz of the doorbell inside the apartment. Several moments passed before they heard the sound of the lock in the door turning and when the door opened. A surprised Jimmy Obrien saw their badges, quickly turned, and ran back into the apartment.

"Police," yelled Jack as he and Dan ran after him.

Jimmy headed for the side window that was open but tripped over an area rug and went flying across the floor, knocking over a small table, and breaking the lamp that sat on it. Dan and Jack grabbed Jimmy to handcuff him when a heavyset woman ran out of another room. Afraid for her son, she picked up a decorative pillow from the sofa and hit Dan on the head, knocking off his fedora. "Leave my son alone."

Dan raised one arm, swatting at the pillow while taking out his badge. "We're the police, Mrs. Obrien."

Seeing Dan's badge, she stopped swinging the pillow, and realizing her son was being arrested, Mrs. Obrien sat on the sofa and hugged the pillow to her chest. As her eyes welled with tears, she watched Jack put handcuffs on her son. "What is it this time, James?"

Jimmy never answered his mother, so Dan showed her the arrest warrant. "Your son's wanted for armed robbery and murder, Mrs. Obrien."

She stood with the pillow, stepped past Dan, and hit her son over the head with it. "You're just like your no-good father."

Jimmy flinched and gave his mother a mean look.

She looked at Dan. "His father died in prison." Then she looked at her son. "I warned you something no good would come from hanging around with that Alan Trotman."

Realizing they now had the name of the second suspect, Dan showed her the search warrant. "Which room belongs to your son?"

"That one," she said, pointing to a closed door. Then looking defeated, she stepped back and sat down at the dining room table, dropped the pillow on the floor beside her chair, and wiped her red, welling eyes with her apron. "I knew something like this would happen."

Dan kept an eye on their prisoner while Jack went into Jimmy's bedroom.

Jimmy Obrien looked at Dan. "How'd you find me anyway?"

Dan chuckled. "You dumb shit, the owner of the pawnshop identified you."

"I wore a mask."

"It's the eyes, Jimmy," said Dan with humor. "It's the eyes."

Having no idea what Dan was talking about, he gave him a baffled look.

Dan glanced back at the bedroom door, wondering if Jack was having any luck finding a weapon, and then he looked at Jimmy. "Where's Alan?"

Jimmy looked out the window. "I don't know anybody named Alan."

"Don't lie," said Mrs. Obrien.

Jimmy gave his mother a dirty look. "Shut up, Ma."

Dan swatted Jimmy on top of the head. "Don't disrespect your mother."

Jack returned from Jinny's room with a twenty-two-caliber pistol wrapped in his handkerchief and handed it to Dan. "Found this under his pillow."

Dan took the gun wrapped in Jack's handkerchief and shoved it into his suit coat pocket.

Jack reached down, helped Jimmy up from the sofa, and looked at Mrs. Obrien, feeling sorry for her. "I'm sorry, Mrs. Obrien."

Tears filled her eyes, then ran down her face. "I don't know where I went wrong with Jimmy. His older brother works hard, has a nice family, but Jimmy---" She never finished.

Jack guided Jimmy Obrien toward the apartment door while Dan looked at Mrs. Obrien, feeling sorry for her as well. "Sometimes they go down the wrong road, Mrs. Obrien. I'm sure you did all you could, but in the end, he's the one who makes the bad decisions." He tipped his hat. "Good afternoon, Mrs. Obrien." Then he turned and followed Jack and Jimmy out of the apartment.

It didn't take long for Jimmy to give up his friend's address, and within the hour, they had arrested Alan Trotman, who still had the murder weapon on him. When both perpetrators were in a cell in the basement of Headquarters, Jack and Dan Morgan went upstairs to their desks.

A happy, smiling Captain Harold Foley greeted them while shrugging into his suit coat. "Good work, you two."

Dan gestured to his partner. "Jack did most of the work on this one, Captain."

Foley looked at Jack. "Good work." Then he looked at a smiling Dan Morgan. "Don't get confident, Morgan. You two still have more than a couple of murders to solve." Then he looked at Jack Brolin. "You can get back on that hit and run now while you help Dan on the murders." Then he walked toward the stairs talking over his shoulder. "I have a doctor's appointment. See you both in the morning."

Dan sat down and started to say something to Jack when his phone rang. Picking up the receiver, he said, "This is Detective Dan Morgan."

"Good afternoon, Detective."

Dan recognized the voice as the caller from yesterday and decided to see what he had to say. "Good afternoon."

Jack looked on with curiosity.

The caller said, "That was not a very good picture of you in Saturday's newspaper."

"Yeah," replied Dan. "I didn't much like it either." He stood, glanced around the busy office of typewriters, and ringing telephones, wondering if someone was playing a practical joke. "How did you know the picture was of me? My name wasn't in the paper."

"I know everything about you, Detective."

Irritated, Dan asked, "Who is this?"

"The person who gave you the gifts."

"I haven't received any gifts, and I don't have time for this bullshit." Then he slammed the receiver down. "Asshole."

"What was that?" asked Jack.

"The same asshole who called the other day about the package."

Jack grinned. "These cases always bring out the idiots and crackpots."

114

Believing that was true, Dan stood, picked up the four envelopes, and pushed his chair under his desk. "I'm heading home."

Jack stood. "Me too."

Dan unlocked the front door to his house, stepped inside, turned on the light, and locked the door behind him. He picked up the mail that lay on the floor, tossed his keys into the glass bowl on the table, and set the four manila envelopes next to it. Hanging up his hat, he walked into the living room, turned the desk lamp on, and glanced through the mail, seeing nothing of importance. Disappointed that there was nothing from his son, he placed the mail in a neat stack next to the telephone, wishing his son would come home or at least call.

Feeling hungry, he turned off the lamp, walked down the dim hall to the kitchen, turned the light on, and then the radio that sat atop the refrigerator. He spent the next three-quarters of an hour listening to soft music while he set the table for one and went about the task of cooking dinner. When it was ready, he opened a bottle of wine, sat down at the kitchen table, poured himself a glass, and listened to the music while he ate. During the silent moments between selections, he quickly entered into a silent argument with himself about whether or not he should call Cathy Holman.

When the last of his meal was gone and the argument still unresolved, he cleaned the kitchen, turned off the radio, picked up the bottle of wine, his empty glass, and walked into the living room. Collapsing into his chair, he filled his glass with wine and sat back, wondering what Cathy Holman was doing. As he took a sip of wine, his eyes found the picture of Norma, smiling as she stood by a giant red boulder in The Garden of the Gods, taken three and a half years ago. He smiled at remembering how full of life Norma had been before cancer took her, leaving only sadness to fill his life. He had always loved her smile and the way her nose wrinkled when she laughed, but in her final weeks, she neither smiled nor laughed.

He sipped his wine and remembered sitting upstairs in the chair next to the bed, wrapped in a blanket while holding her hand, unable to sleep the night she took her last shallow breath. Shoving that from his mind, he poured a little more wine into his glass, got up, turned on the television, and returned to his chair. He sat back and sipped his wine while watching the Burns and Allen Show, but instead of listening to the show, he thought about the murders and lack of evidence and leads he and his partner had. The only real lead they did have was the white 1948 van, and he had never noticed how many there were in Denver until now.

His mind soon found the envelopes sitting on the table in the foyer, and as the credits at the end of the show rolled up the seventeen-inch

115

television screen, he realized that he could not remember anything about the show. He looked at his watch and, seeing it was eight-thirty, set the near-empty wine glass down and picked up the newspaper to see what other programs were on tonight. Nothing interested him, so he tossed the paper onto the coffee table, picked up his glass of wine and the half-bottle, and walked into the foyer for the manila envelopes. He emptied the envelopes on the dining room table, and while putting them in an order that made sense to him, he wished he had more room. Sitting down, he took a drink of wine as his eyes roamed the table, examining each photo while his mind soaked up every detail.

When the wine glass and the bottle were both empty, he stood and stared down at the pictures through tired, sleepy eyes, wondering what it was that he kept searching for. Looking at his watch and seeing that it was nearly ten, he carefully put everything away, stood, and pushed his chair under the table. Feeling a little woozy from the wine, he picked up the envelopes and walked into the foyer. After returning the envelopes to the small table, he returned to his chair and the television in the living room.

The test pattern displayed on the television screen of an Indian in full headgear in the center accompanied by soft, wavering static was what Dan Morgan saw when he opened his eyes hours later. Groggy and a little hungover, he stood, turned off the television, and picked up the alarm clock. Seeing that he had forgotten to pull the pin to set the alarm. It was six-thirty Wednesday morning, and Dan felt like shit. Holding his head, he slowly made his way down the dim hall to the kitchen, where he filled the percolator coffee pot with water and coffee grounds. He set the pot on the burner and lit the gas with a match, making sure it was on low before he went upstairs to get some aspirin for his headache and get cleaned up for work.

When he was shaved and dressed, he returned to the kitchen, turned the burner off, set the coffee pot on a cold burner, put two pieces of bread in the toaster, and poured himself a mug of coffee. When the bread was toasted, he generously spread grape jelly on both pieces and ate them while standing over the kitchen sink, looking out the window into the backyard, going over the pictures in his mind. While taking a bite of toast in the stillness of the kitchen, he watched the cat that lived in the house beyond the alley stalk a bird that proved too quick. The cat sat on the grass in disappointment as it glanced from this to that before it retreated through the fence into the alley.

Shoving the last of the jellied toast into his mouth, he considered getting a cat or a dog to greet him when he came home but quickly decided the idea of a pet was not a good one. Then deciding it was time to go, he gulped down the warm coffee and cleaned up the kitchen. He picked up his brown suit coat folded over the back of the red kitchen chair, walked into the foyer, grabbed the envelopes, and walked out the front door.

Thirteen

Dan hung up the phone with a frustrated expression and pushed the telephone's black base to the back of his desk.

Jack looked up from what he was doing. "Sheriff Brumwell, have anything?"

Dan shook his head. "Brumwell just got back from his fishing trip and hasn't had the chance to go over the case with his men to see if they have anything new." Dan sounded disappointed. "I'm not sure how hard they're working on their case."

Jack grinned. "He's probably hoping we'll solve the case and make him a hero."

The phone rang, and Dan being in a bad mood, hoping it was not the wise ass who had called the day before. "Morgan."

"Good morning, Dan."

Recognizing the voice, Dan said, "Good morning Joyce."

"I have a package for you."

"A package?" Then he thought about the message and the telephone call the other day.

Jack looked up in curiosity.

Joyce asked, "Want me to have someone bring it up?"

"No, I'll be right down." He hung up the phone, looking puzzled. "I have a package downstairs."

Jack looked curious. "Maybe it's from that guy you hung upon." He grinned, recalling how rude Dan was to the man. "Wouldn't that be a shitter?"

Hoping it was something from his son, Dan stood. "Be back in a minute." He hurried downstairs, and as he approached Joyce's desk, she smiled and held up a flimsy, brown paper package tied with the kind of white string one would use on a kite. "Here it is."

He took the small package lacking postmarks or addresses, seeing his name written in black ink on the outside. "Who gave this to you?"

"It's the craziest thing, Lieutenant," she said while gesturing at one of the benches. "That package had been sitting on that bench over there for quite a while. I thought someone left it when they went to the bathroom, so I got up to take a look, saw your name, and that's when I called you."

Looking a little confused, Dan glanced around the lobby and then looked at Joyce. "You never saw who left it?"

She shook her head. "No, I didn't. Sorry. But there was a bum wandering around the lobby, and I asked him to leave."

118

Dan turned in silent confusion and walked up the stairs, wondering who had sent it and what was inside.

"Who's it from?" asked Jack as Dan approached his desk.

Dan looked puzzled as he sat down. "I don't know."

"Open it."

Dan stared at the package for a few moments, untied the string, and pulled the brown paper apart, exposing a pair of girl's yellow panties. As if they were a fatal disease, he abruptly stood and stepped back from his desk. "What the hell?"

"What is it?" asked Jack, who hurried around his desk, and at seeing the panties, said, "What the hell is right."

Dan looked at Jack. "Didn't Brumwell say Diane Wagner's mother told them her daughter's yellow panties and bra were missing?"

Jack nodded. "Yeah, but Brumwell knew where the bra was." Then he asked, "Any note?"

Dan picked up a pencil from his desk, put it through one of the leg openings, and lifted them to look for a note. "Doesn't look like it." Then he laid them back on the brown wrapping paper and carefully picked up the paper package by the corners.

"Where you going?" asked Jack.

"Forensics."

Todd Anderson looked up, noticing the brown wrapping paper Dan was carefully carrying as the two walked in, and being curious, asked, "What's that?"

Dan set the package down on Todd's desk and carefully parted the brown wrapping paper, exposing the panties. "This was left on a bench in the lobby with my name on it. I think it has something to do with Diane Wagner, the girl murdered in Littleton."

Anderson leaned forward and looked at the panties. "Why would anyone send you her panties?"

Dan shook his head, wondering the same thing, and then thought about the telephone calls. "You got me there. I'm not even sure at this point if they belong to Diane Wagner."

Todd picked up a letter opener from his desk, pushed the paper apart, and carefully lifted the panties with it. "Looks like there's a little blood on them."

Dan remembered the picture showing over seventy stab wounds. "Can you do anything with the spot of blood?"

Anderson nodded as he set them down. "If I had a sample of the victim's, I could run a match for blood type." He looked at Detective

Morgan. "But if I recall correctly, she died of exsanguination, so there was no blood left in her body."

Dan nodded in agreement. "And the body was washed clean by the killer."

Todd examined the panties. "Tell you what, leave them here, and I'll check the paper for prints and let you know what I find."

"You'll find at least two," said Dan. "Joyce's at the front desk and mine."

"Well," said Todd. "Let me see what I can come up with, and I'll give you a call later."

Dan's phone was ringing when he and Jack returned to their desks from Forensics. Dan hurried to his desk and picked up the black receiver. "Morgan."

"Did you get the package?"

Dan recognized the slight accent from the other calls, looked at Jack, and pointed to the receiver, "Yes, I got the package a few minutes ago."

Jack sat up in his chair, looking interested.

"That's a relief, Dan," said the caller. "I was afraid someone would steal it off the bench."

"Isn't coming here a little dangerous?"

Jack hurried around his desk and sat close to Dan, who held the telephone away from his ear far enough so that Jack could hear what the caller was saying.

"Oh, I never delivered the package myself. I paid some poor soul to do that for me."

Dan thought about the bum Joyce had asked to leave, wondering if maybe she could identify him. "Took him long enough."

The caller considered that. "What do you mean?"

"You called about the package a week ago."

Laughter filled the telephone. "This isn't the same package, Dan."

Dan's mind filled with items missing from the victims as he looked at Jack. "There's another package?"

"Oh, Dan," said the caller with laughter. "You are a rare one, Detective, but not as bright as I thought you were."

That irritated Dan, but he let it pass.

Then the caller's voice changed. "Was it you that called me a vampire?"

"No," replied Dan, still curious about the other package. "I had nothing to do with that. We don't talk to the press."

The caller sighed. "I'm glad to hear that. Must be that terrible reporter, but I suppose sensationalism sells a lot of papers."

120

"I'm sure it does," replied Dan. Then deciding to test the caller, he asked, "Whose panties are these?"

"Playing dumb does not become you, Detective," said the caller in an angry tone. "That irritates me."

Fearing the caller was about to hang up, Dan said, "Alright, they belonged to Diane Wagner. But why send them to me?"

"The last time we talked, you thought I was some crackpot, and now with the panties, I hope you think differently."

"That's true. I did believe you were a crackpot, and I apologize." Dan decided to try for a name. "If you're going to keep calling me, it would be nice if I knew who I'm talking to."

"I guess that's true enough." The caller paused in thought. "You can call me Paul."

"Paul, it is. Look, Paul, I would still like to know about the other packages...." Hearing the dial tone, Dan looked at the black receiver, hung up the telephone, and stood as he looked at Jack. "Let's talk to the captain."

Captain Foley looked up from what he was doing and, seeing Dan and Jack at his closed door, motioned them in.

Dan opened the door, and as he and Jack stepped in, Dan asked, "Can we talk to you, Captain?"

Foley put his pen in the inkwell. "This about the killings, I hope."

"Sort of," replied Dan as he and Jack sat down. "Last week, while I was out, Irene took a call from someone asking if I liked the package. There was no package, and then on Monday, I got another call, and I thought it was some crackpot with an accent, so I hung up. Today, I got a package containing the yellow panties belonging to that murdered girl in Littleton, Diane Wagner. And I just got a call from the same guy asking if I got the package."

Foley had a worried face as he looked at Dan. "Why didn't you tell me the killer has been calling you?"

Dan shrugged. "I never realized it until I got the package today and this last phone call. I thought it was one of those crackpots we get now and then that saw my picture in the paper."

Jack looked at Foley. "Guy sounds like a nut to me."

Captain Foley looked from Jack to Dan. "What sort of accent did he have?"

Dan shrugged. "Sounded European to me. German, maybe, I'm not sure."

Foley leaned forward, looking interested. "Where are these panties now?"

"Todd in Forensics has them," said Dan. "He's checking the paper they were wrapped in for prints."

Captain Foley nodded. "I doubt he'll find any that will be useful." He sat back, shaking his head. "Takes some nerve to walk into Police Headquarters and leave a package of evidence of a murder."

Dan leaned forward in his chair. "He said he hired some poor soul to do that, and Joyce said there was a bum hanging around in the lobby until she ran him out."

The captain thought on that for a moment. "Maybe she'll recognize him."

"That's what we were thinking," said Jack.

"Right," said Dan. "Jack and I can drive her around to see if she recognizes anyone."

Foley looked at Dan. "Alright, but I'm curious, why would this Paul, and I doubt that's his real name, call you in the first place?"

Dan Morgan looked puzzled. "You got me there, Captain."

Foley picked up his telephone and dialed the operator. "Irene, could you check with the other girls and find out who took the message for Detective Morgan on Monday and see if he asked for him by name? I'll hold."

"That was me, Captain," said Irene. "And the caller asked for Detective Dan Morgan."

"Thanks, Irene." Foley hung up the telephone and looked at Dan. "This Paul character asked for Detective Dan Morgan."

Dan was surprised. "How would he know my name or that I was working the case?"

"Your picture was in the paper," offered Jack.

Foley looked at Jack. "But the article never mentioned Dan's name, and we don't release names of detectives working open cases to prevent this sort of thing." Foley turned to Dan. "No, this guy knows you. I'm sure of that." He gestured to Jack. "Your partner is working the case too, and in fact, he was first on the scene at the Crowder crime scene. Why didn't he get the call?"

Dan gave Jack a puzzled look. "I don't know, Captain."

"Neither to do I," replied Foley. "This Paul fellow chose you for some reason, Dan, and I'd like to know what that reason is."

"So would I," replied Dan thoughtfully.

Foley stared at Dan as he sat forward, placing his arms on his desk. "I'll call the DA's office when we're done here and see about getting a wiretap on your telephone." Foley paused a moment. "We need someone to help us understand what sort of character we have on our hands."

Dan remembered what Cathy Holman had said at the park about a psychiatrist. "You mean a psychiatrist."

Foley nodded yes as he stood. "I'll go up and talk to the Chief about bringing someone on board." He looked at Dan. "There's a recorder somewhere in the building. Find it and have it put on your telephone. I want these calls recorded." He looked at them with a stern face. "Keep quiet about this. I don't want it leaked to the press."

They followed Foley out of his office, and while he went upstairs to see the Chief of Police, Dan, and Jack returned to their desks.

Dan sat down, reached for the telephone, and pulled it closer. "Guess I should call Brumwell and tell him about the panties."

Jack picked up his telephone. "I'll see if I can find the recorder."

Dan picked up the receiver of his telephone and started dialing the sheriff's office.

"Sheriff Brumwell's."

"Cathy, this is Dan Morgan."

Jack looked up, thinking that was friendly.

"Well, hello, Dan. How are you?"

Dan smiled, "Fine, thanks, and you?" He glanced across the desks at Jack, who was staring back at him, turned away, and asked if the sheriff was in.

Disappointed that Dan was not calling her, Cathy put him on hold and told the Sheriff he was waiting.

Moments later, a gruff voice was on the line. "This is Brumwell."

Dan told the Sheriff about the package containing the yellow panties but not about the phone calls.

Brumwell sounded a little jealous as he asked, "I wonder why he sent them to you instead of me."

"I don't know, Sheriff, but I'd like to keep them a while if it's alright with you?"

The phone was silent for several seconds while Brumwell considered Dan's request. "I think it best if we have them here in Littleton since they pertain to our investigation. We'll need them as evidence if we ever catch the bastard."

Disappointed, Dan said, "I understand, Sheriff. It may be a day or so before I can bring them out. The crime lab is checking the wrapping paper for prints."

"If there are any, I'd like a set for our evidence file."

"Alright, Sheriff, if there are any, I'll see that you get a set when I bring the evidence out."

"That sounds just fine," said Brumwell. "We appreciate the help of the Denver Police."

123

Dan hung up, wishing he hadn't called Brumwell and thinking that he didn't want to give the evidence to Littleton, but in reality, any evidence regarding the Littleton murder should be with the Littleton Sheriff's Office.

Jack Brolin hung up his telephone. "The recorder will be brought up later today and put on your phone." Then he stood, walked around his desk, sat on the edge of Dan's desk, glanced around, and lowered his voice. "What's going on with you and Mrs. Holman?"

Dan looked surprised and a little guilty. "Nothing."

Jack grinned. "When did you start calling her by her first name instead of Mrs. Holman? That seems a bit friendly."

Knowing that Jack would not let this drop, Dan leaned forward in his chair and lowered his voice. "Remember when I went to Littleton on Monday, and she took me to Rio Grande Park because Sheriff Brumwell was fishing?"

"I remember."

"Well, I found out that she's a widow. Her husband died during the Bataan Death March."

Jack looked sad. "That's too bad. The war made a lot of young widows." He paused, and then he smiled. "You should ask her out to dinner."

Dan thought of the arguments he's had with himself over that very subject. "I don't know..." he let the sentence die.

"Why not ask her?" Jack wanted his friend to have some resemblance of a normal, happy life. He lowered his voice to a whisper. "Look, pal, Norma's been gone for over two years. At some point, you have to start living again instead of spending all of your damn time in that mausoleum you call home."

"It's not a mausoleum," argued Dan angrily.

"Alright," said Jack with regret. "And I'm sorry about that. But damn it, Dan, you need something in your life besides an occasional few hours with Lori and me or a movie by yourself."

"I've had a few dates," argued Dan.

"Yeah, right," scoffed Jack. "How many? Three? Four?"

Dan shrugged, feeling his face get warm.

Jack could see his partner was getting angry, so he backed off. "Look, buddy, all I'm trying to say is Mrs. Holman seems like a nice lady, and she sure showed an interest in you."

Dan thought for a moment. "I just don't know if I'm ready right now." Then he looked around. "Shouldn't we be having this conversation someplace else?"

Jack looked at Dan and considered that. "No one's listening. Maybe you're not ready for a relationship, so start small." He put his hand on Dan's shoulder. "Call her up and ask if she'd like to get a cup of coffee when she gets off work."

Dan recalled her asking him if he would like to have a coffee some evening. "I don't know."

Jack chuckled, picked up the telephone, and handed it to him. "Call her. I'm going downstairs to the coffee shop, so you won't have to worry about me listening in." Then he grinned. "Shit, she may even turn you down."

Listening to the dial tone, Dan looked up at his partner. "You're not very good at building my confidence."

Jack grinned as he got up from Dan's desk. "Call her. A couple of hours with a nice woman like Mrs. Holman will do you some good. You've been talking to yourself and those damn manila envelopes far too long. You could use some intelligent conversation other than mine."

"Who the hell said you were intelligent?" Dan watched his partner until he disappeared down the stairs before he dialed the Littleton Sheriff's Office.

It was a little after five when Dan turned from Littleton Boulevard onto a busy South Court Place next to the Arapahoe County Courthouse. Seeing Cathy Holman standing on the third step of the courthouse steps, he pulled up next to the curb, reached across the passenger seat, opened the car door, and pushed it open.

Cathy climbed in and smiled as she closed the door. "Your call was a nice surprise."

Dan smiled as he pulled away from the curb and drove north on Court Place, away from the courthouse. "Actually, I surprised myself."

She laughed softly. "Well, I'm glad you called. Where are we going?"

"Your city, your choice."

She thought for a moment. "There's a nice little place a few blocks from here. Take a right at the next corner and then left onto Littleton Boulevard."

The restaurant was crowded, but they managed to find a small table next to a window that looked onto the side street, and as they sat down, he glanced around the restaurant. "Busy place."

Cathy glanced around. "It usually is."

A thin waitress of forty with long, black hair and red lipstick approached with two glasses of water and menus.

Dan looked up. "Do you have a bar?"

125

The waitress smiled, looking regretful. "No, we don't."

Cathy ordered hot tea and Dan black coffee.

As the waitress left, Dan glanced at the menu, making his mind up quickly, but Cathy, on the other hand, patiently looked over the menu. He smiled at how she seemed to study every word.

Having made her mind up, Cathy set the menu down and looked at him. "Were you born in Denver?"

Before he could answer, the waitress returned with their drinks, asking if they were ready to order.

They ordered, and as the waitress walked away, he answered her question. "I was born in a little house in the 1500 block on South Pearl Street." He smiled. "It's still there and looks much the same as it did back then, but it appears a little smaller for some reason. Are you a Denver native?"

She dipped her tea bag into the cup of hot water, looking reminiscent. "In a little house not far from City Park, and like you and most kids back then, I was born at home." She looked up. "Do you have any family living in Denver?"

"No, I don't. Both of my parents passed away a few years ago. Within a few months of one another, actually." He paused, looking sad. "I don't think my mother liked being alone."

"I'm sorry to hear that. No uncles, aunts, or cousins?"

"Both of my parents were only children." Dan picked up his cup of coffee and took a drink. "You?"

"I have a brother in Los Angeles." She looked down into the cup of tea while she played with the tea bag. "I haven't seen him in five or six years. We write occasionally, but we're not close." She paused. "I guess we never were."

He watched as she placed the tea bag on a spoon, wrapped the string around it, and squeezed the bag, watching the tea drip into her cup. After she finished, she took a sip. "You have any siblings?"

The waitress suddenly appeared with their dinners, and as she set the plate down, the aroma of chicken fried steak and mashed potatoes reached him. Feeling hungry, he placed the napkin on his lap, picked up the knife and fork, and looked across the table at Cathy as she cut into a nice-looking pork chop.

She looked up, paused with his knife, and again asked, "Any siblings?"

Dan cut a piece of meat. "I had a twin brother who died when we were eight."

"A twin?" She smiled. "Fraternal?"

Dan shoved a piece of meat into his mouth. "Identical." He grinned. "I was the oldest by twenty-three seconds, and Dad used to say that Donnie was always the stubborn one."

She smiled. "Dan and Donnie, how sweet."

Dan nodded. "Poetic, huh?"

"Mind me asking how he died?"

He thought of a way to answer the question he knew would come up at some point if they continued to see one another. He stuck his fork into the mashed potatoes and moved it around in thought, letting the gravy mix with the potatoes. "Donnie was murdered when he was eight years old. That was in 1918."

Not expecting that, she stared at him while thinking about the loss of his wife and daughter. "I'm sorry if I brought up a bad memory."

He took a bite of the mashed potatoes and smiled warmly. "As someone told me recently, it happened a long time ago, and you couldn't have known."

She smiled with relief, and while she wanted to know more, she changed the subject. "I graduated from East High in 1933, and then I attended the university for two years." She took a bite of her dinner and asked where he had gone to school.

"I graduated from South High in 1928, the same year Norma and I were married."

She smiled. "So, you were high school sweethearts."

Dan smiled. "We were the last year of school. I had seen her around, but..." he paused in memory and smiled again. "I just never had the courage to ask her out."

Cathy laughed while thinking she had to make the first move by giving him her number. "We were all a little afraid and shy of relationships back then."

He nodded, "I know I was."

She took a bite of food and watched as he attacked the chicken fried steak on his plate with his knife and fork. "How did you manage to get up the nerve to ask her out?"

He grinned. "I didn't. My partner, Jack Brolin, and I ran around together back then. You met him the other day when we came to see your uncle, the Sheriff. His girlfriend Lori, who he married, lined Norma and me up on a blind date." He grinned again. "I think Lori enjoyed the drama. It was a little awkward at first."

"Why was it awkward?"

He paused with the knife in one hand, the fork in the other. "It seems that Norma didn't like me all that much."

Cathy laughed. "Why on earth not?"

Dan shrugged. "She thought I was egotistical."

Cathy covered her mouth with one hand as she sat back and laughed.

Dan chuckled. "That's true. I asked her about that years later, and she said I just had that look about me." He gestured at her with his fork. "How did you and your husband meet?"

"In high school. Ted was on the football team, and I fell hopelessly in love with him." She paused in memory for a moment and then cut a piece of food with her fork. "We broke up soon after graduation, but we met a few years later at a bank in downtown Denver where I was working. He came to my teller window, and after a couple of weeks, he asked me out." She paused. "Time went on, and one day he asked me to marry him." She shrugged, looking sentimental. "I accepted, and two years later, we were married." As sadness grabbed her, she looked out the window for a brief moment. "I haven't talked about Ted to anyone in a long time."

Dan sat back in his chair and picked up his coffee cup. "And I haven't talked about Norma and my family in a long time."

She smiled. "And what does that say about us?"

He took a drink of coffee. "We're private people, maybe?"

She thought about that. "I think it's good that we talk about the past once in a while. I think it keeps the memory of those we lost alive. I also think it helps the healing process."

He was not as sure about that as Cathy seemed to be, but he smiled and nodded in agreement before taking a bite of steak.

They ate dinner and talked about other things, such as school and what mischief they had gotten into while growing up. Cathy wanted to know where he spent his time during the war, and he told her some funny stories about Jack Brolin from when they were serving as MP's in England, but not about the battles or the cliffs of Normandy. She asked him why he became a police officer, and he told her that his father was a police officer, and it was something he had always wanted to do. He smiled while telling her how he would put on his father's policeman hat and walk around the house, carrying his nightstick, pretending to be a policeman. He laughed when he told her how he would lock Donnie in the closet they used as a jail.

Their dinner eaten, and another cup of coffee and hot tea consumed, Dan paid the bill and left a tip on the table. He helped her into the car, then climbed behind the wheel, drove out of the parking lot, and followed her directions to her house on South Pennsylvania in Englewood. He parked in the driveway, walked her to the front door, and while she unlocked it, he glanced around the neighborhood of small houses, picket fences, and warm, lighted windows.

She opened the door, turned the lights on in the living room, and invited him inside. While he closed the door, she set her purse on a small, blue cloth chair resembling a half barrel. "Would you like a glass of wine?"

"I better not, but thanks all the same."

The moment turned quiet and awkward, so she held out her hand, thanking him for dinner. "I had a nice time."

Dan took her hand and gently shook it. "Me too." Reaching behind him, he found the doorknob with his right hand. "Can I call you tomorrow?"

She smiled warmly. "I'd like that."

"Great." Then he opened the door, stepped outside into the evening shadows, and gestured at the door. "Make sure your door is locked."

"I will."

"Goodnight," he said while backing away from the door and then, turning, walked through the open gate in the picket fence to his car.

She watched him get into his car before she closed the door, locked it, leaned her back against it, and listened to the sound of his car engine starting. When she heard the sound of the car backing out of the gravel driveway, she turned the porch light off and walked into the living room, where she turned on the television. Kicking off her shoes, she sat on the sofa with her feet up and considered Dan Morgan while she watched 'What's My Line.'

Fourteen

Officer Joyce Moore was busy at the front desk when she looked up at a man of five-eight, medium build, and brown, graying hair combed straight back. He was wearing a rumpled brown suit, white shirt, and brown and white striped bowtie. "May I help you?"

The man pushed his wire-rimmed glasses back up from his nose with his index finger and smiled. "I'm Professor George Pappel," he said, and then he glanced at a piece of paper he was holding. "I'm here to see Captain Harold Foley."

Joyce looked into the professor's brown eyes, thinking he seemed a little odd, and smiled pleasantly. "Is Captain Foley expecting you, Mr. Peppel?"

"Pappel," corrected the Professor as he handed her his card. "It's Pappel, and I believe he is."

Joyce gestured to one of several empty oak benches along the wall. "Please have a seat Mr. Pappel, and I'll inform Captain Foley that you're here."

Professor Pappel turned and looked at the benches, then smiled at Officer Moore, said thank you, and sat down.

Officer Joyce dialed Captain Foley, telling him that a Professor Pappel was here to see him, and hanging up, she looked toward the Professor. "Captain Foley will be right down."

Pappel returned her smile. "Thank you."

Minutes later, Captain Foley walked down the stairs and across the lobby. "Doctor Pappel?"

"It's Professor," replied George as he stood.

The captain corrected his mistake and introduced himself. They shook hands, and then Foley invited him upstairs to his office, where he asked the Professor if he would like a coffee or soda.

"Water would do nicely if it wouldn't be a bother."

"No bother, Professor," said Captain Foley as he walked to his open doorway and asked one of the file clerks to bring a glass of water for their guest. Then he turned to the professor and gestured to three chairs. Please, have a seat."

The professor sat down on the end chair near the corner and glanced around the office of wood walls with large glass windows covered by open Venetian blinds that gave the captain a good view of what was going on in the squad room. A glass case filled with plaques and photographs covered most of the wall behind the captain's desk.

Foley picked up his telephone and dialed Detective Morgan, telling him to get his partner and the files on the recent homicides and then to come into his office. Hanging up, he smiled at the professor. "Thank you for coming, Professor."

"If I understood Chief Roberts correctly," said the professor, "you need some advice on one of your prisoners."

"Suspect," corrected Foley.

Pappel frowned. "Of course, suspect."

While they waited for the water and Detectives Morgan and Jack Brolin, Foley asked, "So you're a professor of psychiatry?"

The professor pushed his glasses back up his nose with the index finger of his left hand. "I'm a professor of psychology."

The captain smiled. "I'm not sure I understand the difference."

Pappel considered that for a moment. "To put it simply, a psychologist deals in the science and theory of the psyche or mind, whereas a psychiatrist deals with the individual and his mental state, or problems if you will." He shrugged. "There's more to it than that, of course, but that's the short version."

Foley smiled and nodded as if he understood and was relieved when Detective Dan Morgan tapped on the doorjamb of the open door. "You wanted to see us, Captain?"

"Come in," gestured Foley.

Entering the captain's office, Dan and Jack wondered who the man in the crumpled brown suit was.

The Professor stood as Foley introduced them, and while they shook hands, the clerk returned with the glass of water. As the others sat down, Pappel took the water, thanked her, then took a drink as he sat down.

The door closed, and Foley turned his attention to Dan and Jack. "Professor Pappel teaches psychology at the university, which I just found out is not the same as psychiatry." He looked at Dan. "I had asked the chief for some help in understanding your friend, and the chief called on his friend Professor Pappel." He turned to the professor. "How do you prefer being addressed? Mr. Pappel or Professor?"

"Whichever you are comfortable with, Captain. It makes no difference to me." He turned to Dan. "The man you're seeking advice on is your friend?"

Foley chuckled. "Just a little office humor, Professor. They're not really friends. The man is a suspect in a couple of killings the detectives are working on."

Pappel's eyes went from Foley to Dan, and then he let out a small chuckle. "Oh, I see. A joke."

"As I said, the person in question," began Foley. "Is a suspect in at least four murders, and I was hoping you could help us understand what kind of wacko we have on our hands."

"Wacko," chuckled the Professor as his index finger pushed his glasses up his nose. "That's a good one." Sitting up straight in his chair with knees together, holding the glass of water on his lap with both hands, he looked from one to the other. "I will do my best, gentlemen. However, you must understand this is 1951, and while a lot of knowledge has been gathered over the years, there is still a lot we do not understand or know about the human psyche or human behavior." He looked at Foley. "Is it possible for me to talk to the individual?"

"Well," replied Foley. "That's part of the problem. We don't have him in custody."

"I see," said Pappel with a puzzled look. "That may make it difficult, to say the least." He took a sip of water.

Foley gestured to Dan. "Perhaps it would be best if I let Detective Morgan tell you the story since he's the only one who has had a conversation with the suspect."

Pappel looked at Dan. "You've met the man?"

"No," replied Dan. "We've only talked on the telephone." Dan cleared his throat and then started with the first murder in Littleton, ending up with the latest victim in the alley behind the Paramount Theater. He gave the professor most of the details, including how they died, their missing fingers, that each victim had been washed, and where the semen was found on the bodies by the coroner. Then Dan told of the message about a package he never received, the first telephone call he thought was a prank, and then of actually getting a package containing the underpants of the first victim. He also told him about the second telephone call from a man who identified himself only as Paul, who had an accent he believed to be European.

Professor Pappel considered all that Detective Morgan had told him for a few moments, took a sip of water, and then looked at him. "May I see the pictures?"

Dan took Diane Wagner's pictures out of the manila envelope and handed them to the professor, who studied each one for several moments. Without saying anything, he gave those back and went through the other pictures examining each one thoroughly. When he finished with the last picture of Marie Phillips, he took a sip of water and looked at Captain Foley. "I'd say that you're dealing with a psychopathic killer."

The term "psychopathic killer" was a little unnerving to the captain, as well as to Dan and Jack.

"Psychopath?" repeated Dan.

132

Pappel looked at him. "I'm sure of it. These murders have all the traits of a psychopath, including the taking of souvenirs."

Foley leaned forward, resting his elbows on his desk. "What does he do with a finger?"

Professor Pappel thought about that. "Treasures it. Each time he looks at it, he will recall every moment spent with his victim while getting the same, how should I say, excited emotions out of it."

"I thought psychopaths," said Jack, "mutilated their victims like Jack the Ripper. Except for the missing fingers, these girls were bled out by a small cut to the neck."

Professor Pappel smiled at Detective Jack Brolin. "Not all psychopaths are like Jack the Ripper."

The room was quiet for several moments when Foley said, "We come up against a lot of crazy people high on cocaine or booze, but I don't recall ever dealing with a psychopath. I want to learn a little more."

Pappel nodded. "Of course. I teach that there are three types of psychopaths: organized, disorganized, and mixed." He paused to take a sip of water. "Disorganized psychopaths often have average or below-average intelligence. They are usually impulsive, use whatever weapon is available at the time, and usually do not try and hide the bodies of their victims." He paused again to sip his water and push his glasses up his nose. "They are often quite violent. In contrast, an organized psychopath is above average in intelligence and often plans his crimes methodically by abducting his victims. He then tortures or kills them in one place and disposes of them somewhere else by either hiding them, so they are found later, or burying them so they can never be found."

He sipped his water. "This type maintains a high degree of control over his victims while he has them, and that is very important to him. He also has the unique ability to get rid of any evidence. Another trait they have is they tend to follow the news media to bolster their ego." He paused to look at Dan. "You see, they have real pride in their work. They feel superior, and some contact the authorities and gloat over the police's inability to capture them." Pappel took another sip of water while the room remained silent, and then he smiled. "But, sometimes, an organized killer descends into a disorganized killer or becomes a mixed killer that has both traits." He paused. "Personally, I believe the latter is the most dangerous."

"What causes someone to become a psychopath?" asked Dan.

"People don't just become a psychopath and start killing. No, they are born that way. You have to understand, Detective, the psychopath is not like us in this room, and they live in a world where there is no conscience or remorse for what they do. Men such as this are often solitary individuals, don't hold steady jobs, and are driven to do the things they do to feel better about themselves or get sexual gratification. As a child, they often torture small animals for the pure enjoyment of it and later graduate to the human race."

Thinking of Paul, Dan asked, "How does an organized psychopath choose his victims?"

"Good question," smiled Dr. Pappel. "Some target young children, either boys or girls and others." He paused as he glanced at Jack. "As in the case of Jack the Ripper you mentioned, some prefer prostitutes while still others prefer men and, or women. Each is different in what drives or pleases them." He looked at Dan. "From talking to him, how old would you guess this Paul to be?"

Dan sat back in his chair. "Hard to tell over the telephone, but I don't believe he is a young man, but not an older man either." Dan paused. "The accent throws me, but I'd say he's close to my age, perhaps a little older, probably in his forties. Is that important?"

Professor Pappel nodded. "If he is an older man, then he has been doing this for quite some time." He looked at Dan. "It appears the mark on each girl's throat in the picture is small. Is that correct?"

"Less than half an inch," replied Foley. "They are clean cuts, no jagged edges. We suspect he used a scalpel."

Pappel looked thoughtful. "A wound that small would take a few minutes before the victim passed out. Exsanguination can be a slow death, which means he can torment them further during their last moments. He has complete control, and he thrives on the power that gives him."

"That must be frightening to his victims," said Jack.

George Pappel looked at him while pushing his glasses up. "I'm sure it is."

Dan Morgan leaned forward and rested his elbows on his knees, clasping his hands together, trying to process everything as he looked at Pappel. "Are there any signs that would give this guy away if we do suspect someone?"

Dr. Pappel shook his head. "No. You must understand that he appears as normal as you and I. In talking with him, you would never suspect him of being anything other than a normal human being. He could be a policeman, your postman, even a deacon at your church, or the guy next door whom you like." He paused, looking at Foley. "You could be such a person, Captain, and none of us would suspect."

Foley glanced at his two detectives. "Are you serious?"

Pappel smiled as he nodded. "I'm very serious, Captain. To put it in perspective, a man such as this could be your best friend, your brother, or even your father, and you would have no suspicions of him being anything other than what he appears to be. They are very good at hiding who they are and what they do."

"Now that's scary," replied Foley.

George Pappel sipped his water and nodded as he leaned forward in his chair to look at Dan. "Did I hear you correctly earlier that he washed all of the bodies?"

"That's right," responded Dan.

"Hmm," said Pappel softly.

"What?" asked Foley.

"That's interesting, is all. Various cultures wash the bodies of the dead before burial." He looked at Dan. "You said earlier that you believe his accent is European. There are several European countries with that culture."

Jack looked at Pappel. "What about the semen he leaves in the pubic hair?"

Pappel shrugged. "He may have trouble completing a normal act of sex, which is common among certain psychotics, and he could also feel inadequate when it comes to sex. That could explain his masturbating on them after they are dead."

Foley leaned forward, resting his forearms on his desk. "What would bring on this feeling of inadequacy?"

Pappel thought a moment. "Could be many reasons." He looked at Captain Foley. "But I would not get lost in the sexual part of these crimes, Captain."

"Why is that?" asked Foley.

"Sex is secondary," said the Professor. "Control and power are what is important to your man." He paused while looking at Foley. "That and causing mental or physical pain. Psychopaths thrive on causing pain. Performing this particular act of sexual gratification could simply be an act of final insult to his victim."

Pappel turned to Dan. "I have been thinking about your relationship with this Paul, and I believe he has contacted you because he knows you."

That worried Dan. "Knows me?"

"I'm quite positive. Has anything out of the ordinary happened in your life lately?"

Dan considered that for several moments. "No," he said with a nervous chuckle. "Just these damn telephone calls."

The Professor smiled. "I believe your Paul is an organized killer who may be descending to either a disorganized or a mixed psychopath." He paused to take a drink of water. "We don't know what he had done before because he probably hid the bodies of his victims. But now we know that he stabbed the first victim postmortem but not the others. This leads me to believe he had the urge to mutilate but not since." He paused in thought. "I'm certain he has been killing for several years and hiding the bodies, but for reasons known only to him, now he chooses to display them." Pappel stared into his glass of water for a moment and then looked at Dan. "I believe that he is entering a state of morphosis." He paused. "I think he wants you to see his work, Detective."

Jack looked from Dan to the professor. "Why would he want Dan to see his work?"

"Only he knows the answer to that." Pappel paused and turned from Jack to Dan. "Sending you the package containing one of his trophies would have been difficult for him. Those are vivid reminders of each victim, and he treasures them dearly."

Dan wasn't so sure. "He sent it to prove that he killed Diane Wagner because I doubted him?"

"Perhaps, but you must understand that it would have been difficult for him to part with any trophy." Pappel stared at Dan for a long moment. "He wants something from you."

Dan looked puzzled and a little concerned. "Like what."

"Again, only he knows, but it could be recognition, or he may even want you to stop him. I don't know at this point, nor do I believe he does." Professor Pappel thought for a moment. "Psychopaths are quite complicated, and their reasons for doing what they do are difficult to ascertain."

Dan considered that. "I can't believe this Paul creep and I know one another."

"You may never have spoken," explained Pappel. "Or if you had, it might have been a passing word or two, but that could have been enough to make the connection for him. Whatever the bond he feels toward you, I believe it to be quite strong. He has certainly pulled you into his little private game, and it's a game he wants only you to play."

"That's kind of spooky," said Jack Brolin while looking at Dan.

"It is a little spooky, Detective," agreed Pappel. "Most psychopaths are spooky."

Foley sat back in his chair, looked at Dan with concern, and then at Pappel. "Do you believe this Paul wants Dan to investigate these murders?"

Pappel looked at the captain and then at Dan. "I'm certain of it."

Dan looked at Foley. "I agree with Jack. This whole thing is spooky."

136

Professor Pappel looked concerned as his eyes found Dan's worried face. "I'd be careful, Detective." He paused. "There may be something very evil waiting for you in the days that follow."

Dan stared at the professor in silence while thinking about what he had just said.

Concerned about his senior detective, Captain Foley looked at Dan. "Maybe I should pull you off the case and assign it to someone unknown to this Paul character."

Pappel considered that only briefly. "I wouldn't suggest doing that, Captain. If you want to catch this man, I'd say Detective Morgan is your best chance. He is the key to unlocking the mystery. I don't believe your detective is in any danger at the moment, and Paul has already made contact with him for whatever reason. Taking him off the case may anger your suspect to the point that he may kill quickly and then disappear to another city or go back to hiding his victims. Right now, I believe he has entered into a cooling-off period, and he may contact Detective Morgan before he kills during his next cycle or soon after."

"Cycle?" repeated Jack.

Pappel turned to Jack. "It is like he has this." he paused in thought. "Beast inside him that must be fed. Once he kills, the beast is satisfied for a time, but it will always need feeding. This Paul has no choice in the matter and has probably fought the urge as a young man, as many of them do. He may even have caused pain unto himself in an effort to control the urges, but sadly, they all succumb to the beast. It appears his normal cycle is two weeks, but for some reason, he killed the girl he left in the alley behind the theater in Denver before his normal cycle."

Captain Foley considered how the whole situation seemed so unreal. "Any thoughts on that?"

"As I said previously, I believe he is entering into a state of morphosis and may be escalating." He looked at Dan. "Part of him may want to stop, and he may be reaching out to you to stop him."

Dan and the others considered that in silence.

Foley looked worried. "Any suggestions on how we handle this maniac the next time he calls?"

Pappel thought for a short moment. "Let him do most of the talking. If he asks you a question, don't lie." He paused. "He is very intelligent and will know by the tone of your voice if you lie. Stay calm, no matter what your personal feelings are or how angry you may become." He drank the last of his water. "Don't get anxious or personal with your questions. Remember, he wants to be in control, so let him have that control. Who is in control is not important at this stage. It's who's in control at the end that matters."

Dan sat in his chair, staring at the floor, wondering what terrible thing he had gotten himself and Jack into.

Pappel looked at Dan. "He already knows more about you than you would like, which enforces my belief that he knows you, and I'm certain he knows who and what you are. It might be a good idea to put a recorder on your telephone and tape all your conversations. I may be able to give you a good guess at what he's thinking."

Foley nodded. "That's already being taken care of, Professor."

Professor Pappel pulled out his pocket watch and opened it. "Oh my," he said. It's going on ten, and I have a class soon." He stood and set the empty glass of water on the edge of the captain's desk, reached into the side pocket of his coat, and handed Captain Foley a business card. "Call me when you have a recorded conversation." Then he gave a card to Jack, and before he handed one to Dan, he scribbled his home phone number on the back. "Since this, Paul has chosen you," he said, handing Dan the card. "If anything comes up, or you have questions, the number on the back is my number at home. Please, don't hesitate to call me, no matter what the hour."

Dan's head was reeling with thoughts about Paul as he took the card and looked at the name and the telephone numbers.

Professor Pappel shook Dan's hand and then Jack's and smiled as he shook the captain's hand. "I'm looking forward to helping the police with this. My life has been a little boring of late." He nodded as he smiled at them. "Gentlemen." Then he opened the door, stepped out of the office, and walked across the noisy room of typewriters and muffled voices toward the stairs that led down to the main entrance.

Foley stared after the professor. "Funny little guy."

Dan quietly thought of everything the professor had said while putting the pictures back into their manila envelopes.

Captain Foley noticed his silence. "Are you alright, Dan?"

Dan closed the flap of the last envelope and looked at the captain for a long moment. "I had no idea what kind of a monster we were dealing with."

Jack looked worried. "None of us did."

"Well, we know now," said Foley. He looked at the Professor's card lying on his desk. "And we have an authority on the matter at our disposal."

Just then, the telephone rang.

"Foley." The captain listened for a moment and then grabbed a pencil and paper. "Give that to me again."

Dan and Jack watched as Foley wrote something on a piece of paper.

"Who is this?" Foley asked. Hearing a click, he hung up his telephone and looked at Dan and Jack. "We have a body at this address."

Dan took the paper and looked at the address. "Who was that?"

Foley shrugged. "I don't know. The caller didn't give his name but said there was a body in the garage at that address."

"Male or female," asked Jack.

"The caller didn't say," said Foley. "But in case it is another girl, I want you two on it."

Dan and Jack walked out of the captain's office to their desks, where Dan put the envelopes in the middle drawer of his desk. He had started to get his pistol when he saw a note from Irene at the switchboard asking him to call her.

Seeing the note, Jack asked, "What's that?"

Dan picked up the telephone and dialed zero. "Irene, at the switchboard, wants me to call her."

Jack took his Thirty-eight out of his desk and slipped it into his holster as he watched Dan.

"Irene, this is Dan Morgan." He looked at Jack as he listened to Irene, thanked her, and hung up the telephone. "Paul called. I had told Irene to hold my calls while we were in with the captain."

"He leave a message?"

Dan nodded. "Said he had a couple of presents for me."

Jack looked at him. "More panties?"

"I don't know, maybe," said Dan as he took his thirty-eight out of his desk, slipped it into his holster, and then taking his coat off the back of his chair, he said, "Let's go check out that body."

"Maybe it's with a finger this time," said Jack, half joking.

Dan frowned, not finding the humor as they walked toward the stairs, passing Detectives Hargrove and Mueller, who was shrugging into their suit coats, looking like they were in a hurry.

Mueller looked at Dan. "Bum with his throat cut was found floating in Cherry Creek River near 6th and Speer Boulevard."

Something told Dan that Paul had gotten rid of his poor soul delivery boy.

Fifteen

Jack Brolin parked his car in front of the house belonging to the address pm the paper Dan had been handed from Captain Foley. "This is it," he said as he turned the key, shutting off the engine.

Dan opened the car door, noticing a 1948 dark blue Mercury sitting in the driveway. "I have a funny feeling about this." As he climbed out of the car, he glanced around the nice upper-class neighborhood, wondering what they were going to find inside the garage. While Jack closed his car door, Dan walked up the narrow sidewalk separating the overgrown green lawn toward the front door.

Jack looked up and down the affluent, quiet street while following Dan up the four steps of the big, covered porch to the front door.

Dan pushed the doorbell, setting off a set of chimes inside, and after several moments passed and no one opened the door, he pushed it again. After a few moments, Dan leaned close to the door window and cupped his hands around his face trying to see inside, but the thick lace curtains made it difficult. "Looks like no one's home."

"Didn't the note mention the garage?" asked Jack.

Dan nodded. "I just wanted to see if anyone was home before we go poking around in someone's garage. This whole thing could be a prank."

Jack quickly considered that.

They stepped off the porch and walked along a narrow walkway beside the house to the driveway and the dark blue 1948 Mercury. While Jack checked the driver's door, finding it locked, Dan continued to the garage at the end of the driveway. He stopped at the window of one of the garage doors and put his face with cupped hands against the window while Jack did the same on the other door. Dan stepped away from the door. "The windows are covered with something." Thinking that was strange, he walked to the corner of the garage to a side door finding the inside of that window covered as well. With Jack standing behind him, Dan drew his pistol, turned the doorknob, pushed the door open, and cautiously stepped inside the dark garage.

Jack pulled his gun as he stepped into the dark garage standing next to Dan.

Dan looked for the light switch finding one on the wall next to the door and turned on the light. As the dim light from the single bulb filled the garage with dark shadows, he stepped back. "What the hell?"

Seeing the bloody body of a naked man hanging from the rafters by his arms over a pool of blood, Jack made the sign of the cross on his body and said, "Mary, Mother of God."

"Jesus," said Dan in a soft voice as she quickly glanced around the dim garage making sure they were alone. Seeing two fluorescent lights above the workbench, and a second light switch, he turned the lights on, filling the garage with light. Stepping closer to the body, Dan was careful not to step into the pool of blood. He looked up at the victim's bloody, beaten face, seeing that somebody had cut his throat so severely it had almost decapitated him. Blood that had flowed from the arteries of the neck covered the front of the naked body, pooling on the cement floor. Seeing blood splatter marks extending for several feet, he slowly walked around the body, finding what looked like burn marks on the back and buttocks. "Looks like someone used his body as an ashtray." He stopped when he reached the front of the body and leaned a little closer. "Jesus, Jack, someone did a job on his penis and scrotum." Then he stepped back and looked down at the pool of dark blood and the blood splatter that had reached the workbench several feet away. "Amazing how much blood the human body holds."

Pushing away the need to vomit, Jack looked at the splatter marks, the pool of blood, and then at the body. "From his size, I'd say close to one and a half gallons."

Dan looked at him with surprise.

Jack shrugged. "I read things."

Dan smiled. "Anyone ever tell you that you're a little strange?" Then he looked down at the pool of blood. "Splatter marks are everywhere. Be careful not to step on any. Todd wouldn't like that."

Jack glanced around the garage and then back at the open doorway, thinking they needed to find a telephone and get some help. "Let's get the hell out of here, Dan, and call this in."

"In a minute." Dan glanced around the garage, which looked similar to any other garage. There was a tool chest in the corner, a radio on the workbench, a lawnmower in the back corner, and a couple of tires leaning against the back wall. Seeing a blow torch sitting on the far end of the workbench along with a piece of rebar, he asked, "Want to bet those were used to make the burns on the body?"

Jack looked at them, imagining the horror. Let's get out of here, Dan, and call this in."

"Alright," replied Dan. "I'll go next door and see if they have a telephone."

"Don't be too long," said Jack as he turned back to the victim.

141

Reaching the doorway, Dan stopped and turned. "Don't touch anything."

Jack turned to an empty doorway and then turned back to the nude, bloody body and softly asked himself, "What the hell would I touch?" Thinking the place was creepy, he decided to wait outside.

Dan walked up the steps to the house next door, rang the doorbell, and waited. A few minutes later, an elderly woman wearing a colorfully flowered housedress and clean apron opened the door and gave Dan a curious look. "Yes?"

"Good morning, ma'am," greeted Dan while displaying his badge. "I'm Detective Dan Morgan with the Denver Police, and I was wondering if you had a telephone I could use."

She looked past him to the street. "Where is your police car?"

Wondering what difference that made, Dan said, "I'm a detective, ma'am. I don't drive a police car."

She smiled. "Then how do you get around?"

Getting a little irritated with her, Dan pointed to Jack's car. "In that."

She raised her head a little higher, looked past him, and then said, "We don't have a telephone, but Mr. Trenton, next door, might."

"Mr. Trenton?" asked a surprised Dan, wondering if that was him in the garage.

She smiled proudly. "Why Howard Trenton, of the Denver Daily News, of course."

"Of course," said Dan while thinking about breaking in the back door to use the telephone, but that would only corrupt the crime scene. "Well, I can't use his phone because he's not in the house at the moment."

She pointed across the street. "The Warren's across the street have one, I believe."

Dan glanced across the street, tipped his hat, and smiled. "Thanks for your trouble. Have a nice day."

Dan walked down the porch steps, across the street, and up the sidewalk to the front door. Not seeing a doorbell, he knocked, and after a few moments, the door opened, and a woman in her thirties dressed as though she were going out for dinner smiled at him. "May I help you?"

"Mrs. Warren?" asked Dan while holding up his badge.

"Yes," she said with a curious look.

"I'm Detective Dan Morgan of the Denver Police. Do you have a telephone I could use?"

Looking worried, she glanced past him and asked, "Is everything alright?"

"I can't say, ma'am, but I need to use your telephone."

Not quite sure about him, she asked, "How did you know my name?"

Dan could not believe all the questions as he gestured to the house across the street. "The kindly, elderly lady across the street told me and said that you might have a telephone."

She stepped away from the doorway, looking worried. "It's there," she said, pointing down the narrow hall to a black telephone on a small table. He thanked her, hurried down the hallway with its dark hardwood floor and walled pictures, picked up the receiver, and started turning the rotary dial to call his captain.

"This is Foley,"

Dan glanced over his shoulder as he lowered his voice. "Captain, this is Dan Morgan. That body you sent us to check out?"

"What about it?"

Dan glanced around to see where Mrs. Warren was and spoke in a whisper. "It could be Howard Trenton."

The phone was silent for a moment, and then the captain asked, "The columnist, Howard Trenton?"

"I've never met or seen the man, so I don't know for sure, but the body is in his garage, and no one is answering the front door."

"Shit," said Foley. "Todd Anderson and Pete Lange will be there as soon as they can. You and Jack sit tight."

Dan hung up the receiver and turned, almost bumping into Mrs. Warren. Wondering if she had been eavesdropping, he excused himself, thanked her for the use of the telephone, and stepped outside.

Jack Brolin was standing at the corner of the garage, smoking a cigarette, and seeing Dan walking up the driveway, he took a drag, dropped it on the driveway, and stepped on it. "Find a telephone?"

"The house next door didn't have one, so I had to go across the street. Foley is sending Todd and Pete over." Thinking Jack looked a little pale, Dan asked, "You alright?"

Jack thought of the body inside the garage and nodded that he was.

Dan glanced around and then looked at Jack. "I think I know who the victim is."

That brought life to Jack's somber face. "Who?"

"The lady next door said that her neighbor, Howard Trenton," Dan pointed to the house belonging to the garage. "Had a telephone."

Surprise filled Jack's face. "That's Howard Trenton hanging in the garage?"

Dan nodded. "I think so."

Jack looked puzzled. "Why would anyone do that to Howard Trenton?"

"Beats the hell out of me," said Dan, then he took out his cigarettes and offered one to Jack. "A man like that makes a lot of enemies."

After what seemed an eternity for the two detectives, Todd Anderson of Crime Scene and Pete Lange of the Coroner's Office finally arrived with their teams. Curious neighbors began to pour out of their houses to see what all the fuss was about as Dan led Todd and Pete toward the side door of the garage.

Todd stepped inside the garage, stopped, and turned from the body to Dan. "I hope you two were careful where you were stepping."

"We stayed out of the blood," said Dan. "And the prints on the floor are neither of ours." Then he and Jack stood next to the workbench with Pete while Todd and his men walked around the body, taking pictures. When they finished, Todd told Pete that he and his men needed to wait to have a look at the body while he and his men processed the garage. Dan and Jack leaned against the workbench watching with interest as the group took pictures of blood spatter, measured its distances, dusted for prints, and collected anything that resembled evidence.

Dan pointed to the piece of rebar and the small blowtorch at the end of the workbench. "You may want to bag that up. Our killer may have used them to make the burns on the body."

Captain Foley stepped into the busy garage, stood next to Dan, Jack, and Pete, and gestured at the body. "Are you certain that's Howard Trenton?"

Dan shrugged. "Neither of us has ever seen Howard Trenton, but if he lives in the house out front and this is his garage, it's him."

Foley saw Todd Anderson standing a few feet away. "Is it okay if I have a closer look at the body, Todd?"

He turned to the captain. "Watch where you step. We have one set of bloody footprints that probably belong to the killer." As Foley walked toward the body, Todd walked over to Dan and Jack. "Did either of you find blood on the doorknobs?"

Dan looked at his hands. "No, the killer must have wiped them clean before he left."

Captain Foley stepped closer to the body, and then he slowly walked around it, making sure he did not step in any of the blood. After he made a complete circle, he stopped next to Lange, who was standing by Dan and Jack at the workbench. "What can you tell me, Doc?"

"Not much more than you can see right now. Todd asked me to wait until he processes the crime scene." Lange looked at Foley. "Took me a moment, but it looks like Howard Trenton, the reporter."

"Which means this is suddenly a high-profile case," offered Foley. "And everyone from the mayor on down is going to be on my ass."

144

Lange considered that. "I'll know more when I get a chance to look at the body, but right now, all I can tell you is what we see." Pete stepped away from the bench and pointed to the bloody tape. "The victim's mouth is taped shut with what appears to be surgical tape. His throat is cut so deep it came close to decapitating him." He paused. "Whoever did the cutting was full of rage." Pete paused again, trying to stay out of the way of Todd's men. "From the angle of the cut, I'd say you're looking for a man that is right-handed, and from the position of the body, I'd say the killer was at least five foot ten." Pete gestured at the victim. "The body is full of burns that may be from that blowtorch and piece of rebar on the workbench Dan pointed out. Oh yeah, his penis and scrotum are full of tiny cuts."

"Why would anyone torture Howard Trenton?" asked the captain more of himself than anyone else.

"That's your department, Captain," said Pete. "I'll give you a more detailed report after Todd and his men have finished, and I get the body on one of my tables."

"Alright, Doc," said Foley. "Thanks. Give me something as soon as you can." Then Foley saw Todd Anderson a few feet away talking to one of his men, walked over, and lowered his voice. "That body is Howard Trenton, and I need something just as fast as you can get it to me."

Todd Anderson glanced at the body behind Foley. "No shit?"

"I need something fast, Todd," repeated Foley.

Todd nodded quickly. "As soon as I can, Captain."

Foley gestured to Pete Lange, "How soon can Doc have the body?"

Todd looked past the captain to Pete. "Shouldn't be much longer."

Foley smiled and patted Todd on the shoulder. "Thanks, Todd."

Officer Sam Price appeared in the open doorway and started to step inside.

Dan stopped him. "There's blood everywhere, Sammy."

Officer Price looked at Dan, then the bloody floor, and seeing Foley, called out. "Captain Foley." He waited until the captain approached and lowered his voice. "The press and television people are here asking for you. Do you want to do an interview?"

"Hell no," replied Foley looking and sounding angry. "How the hell did they find out so fast?"

Officer Sammy Price shrugged, "I don't know, Captain."

Dan considered Mrs. Warren across the street.

Foley looked at the young officer. "Go on, get back to your post, and keep the riffraff out of here."

"Yes, sir," replied Price, looking embarrassed as he turned and walked out of the garage.

Foley looked at his watch. "It's after two. I'm heading back to tell the chief. You two don't have to stick around while Todd and Lange do their work." Then he turned and walked out of the garage and down the driveway toward his parked car, ignoring the questions from the reporters.

Jack looked from the body to Dan. "You ready?"

It was almost three-thirty when Captain Foley stepped out of his office, looking irritated. "Morgan, you and Jack, come into my office."

Dan looked up, then glanced around the office, seeing that everyone had stopped what they were doing, and looked at him. Looking at Jack, he stood. "Now what?"

Dan opened the door, then he and Jack stepped inside, closed the door, then he and Jack waited for the captain to speak.

Foley stood behind his desk with his hands on the back of his chair. "Have a seat." He waited until they sat down. "The chief wants this Trenton thing wrapped up quickly." He pulled his chair away from his desk and sat down with a worried, thoughtful expression as he looked from one face to the other. "Trenton was severely tortured before he died, and both the chief and I would like to know why."

"Maybe he was blackmailing someone," offered Dan.

"That'd be my guess," agreed Jack.

Foley thought about that for a moment. "Well, he sure pissed someone off." He paused. "The two of you are going to find out what got Mr. Trenton killed. You two don't talk to anyone but me about this case. Understand?"

"What about the murdered girls?"

Foley thought for a moment. "We're shorthanded, so the two of you will have to handle both cases, but luckily, two other police departments are looking for Paul. Let them carry the weight for a few days."

Dan considered that having little faith in the other police departments. "We'll manage both, Captain."

Foley looked at his watch. "Todd and Lange are probably still there, but I want the two of you back at the crime scene right now. Check the house and that damn garage again." He looked at Dan. "I want you two there for the rest of the day and all night if necessary. Go over the place with a fine-toothed comb. We'll talk in the morning."

Deciding to take two cars, Jack followed Dan to Howard Trenton's house, arriving there a little before four in the afternoon. The street was empty now as they parked in front of the house, got out of their cars, and walked up the driveway just as Todd Anderson was getting ready to leave the scene.

"You the last one?" asked Dan.

Todd waited next to his car. "Lange left with the body about thirty minutes ago."

Dan looked at the house. "Your men do any looking around inside?"

Todd nodded. "Dusted for prints and nosed around a bit. We spent most of our time in the garage."

"Is the house still open?" asked Jack.

Todd reached into a bag he was carrying and pulled out a set of keys. "Found these in the pants we recovered from inside the garage."

Dan reached out and took them.

Todd gestured to them. "House, garage, and car keys. There's a couple of keys I don't know what they're for. Possibly his office."

"Okay, Todd," said Dan. "Thanks."

Todd started to get into his car but stopped. "We found traces of chloroform in that Mercury. I don't want to tell you how to do you're investigating, but that seems like a good place to start."

Dan glanced at the Mercury, looked at the keys Todd had given him, selected the car key, and looked at Jack. "Let's start where it probably began." Then as Todd drove away, Dan softly asked, "You thinking what I'm thinking?"

Jack nodded. "It can't be Paul. He only goes after women."

Dan considered that. "You may be right. Anyone can buy chloroform." Then he thought about the phone call. "Paul was upset about Trenton's remarks about a vampire." He unlocked the driver's door of Trenton's Mercury, reached around, unlocked the rear door for Jack, and then climbed into the front seat.

Jack opened the rear door. "I can't see Paul killing Trenton over a headline." Then he climbed into the back, sat down on the rear seat, and looked under the front seat. "Smells like a hospital back here."

Thinking Jack may be right about Paul, Dan opened the glove compartment and started going through things. "Someone must have been waiting in the back seat for Trenton. I wonder where he was off to."

"Good question."

Not finding anything, Dan got out of the car and waited for Jack to climb out of the back seat. "Once Howard Trenton was immobilized, he was carried into the garage through the side door." Dan looked toward the garage. "Let's take another look at the garage before we go inside."

"Okay," said a reluctant Jack Brolin.

Stepping inside the garage, Dan turned on both lights and saw a flashlight on the workbench. He picked it up and walked to a ladder resting against the side of the garage. He picked up the ladder and opened it up next to the pool of sticky blood. After climbing up a few steps, he shined the flashlight on the rafters, finding the spot from which Howard Trenton's naked body had recently hung. "There were wear marks from the rope on the rafter where he had been hoisted up." He climbed down, left the ladder in place, walked back to the garage door, and stepped outside. He looked back down the driveway to Trenton's Mercury, thinking about the lack of black heel marks from Trenton being dragged along the cement driveway. He turned to Jack. "Trenton was not a big man, and it's possible for a bigger, stronger man to carry him up the driveway and into the garage." Then he and Jack stepped back inside the garage. Dan imagined the killer undressing an unconscious Trenton, tying his hands, tossing the rope over the rafters, and then pulling the rope, lifting the body above the cement floor.

Jack looked up at the rafters. "Hell of a job for one man."

Dan considered that. "Yeah, but it's doable." Then he looked around, seeing an old, wooden, two-wheel dolly leaning against the wall. "He could have used that."

Jack looked at the dolly. "I've been thinking," he paused. "If someone was waiting for Trenton in his car, how would he or they know what time he would be leaving?"

"Good question," said Dan thoughtfully. "One explanation is the killer would know if he had set up a meeting with Howard. Let's go inside the house and see if Trenton has a calendar or datebook."

They walked out of the garage, turned off the lights, closed the door, and walked to the back door. After trying a couple of keys in the door, Dan opened it, and then they stepped into a small, dark room off the kitchen.

Jack's hand found his Thirty-eight out of habit, while Dan's hand found the light switch that gave light to the small room.

Jack closed the door and followed Dan through the kitchen into the living room.

Dan glanced around. "No desk in here."

Jack saw a closed door to his left, walked over, opened it, and stuck his head inside. "In here."

Dan followed Jack into Howard Trenton's office, pulled the chair away from the desk, and sat down. Glancing over the top of the desk for a datebook he didn't see, he opened the center drawer, found one, and opened it to Wednesday. "Nothing."

Jack sat on the edge of the oak desk. "Well, there goes that theory."

Dan stared at the empty calendar. "Not necessarily. It could have been a meeting set a few hours before."

Jack thought about that. "Maybe it was a meeting he didn't want anyone to know about, so he never wrote it down."

Dan looked up at Jack. "You could be right." Then he put the datebook back. "Maybe there's something about a meeting in his office at the newspaper. We'll check that out tomorrow." Then he turned the desk lamp on and started going through the desk drawers." He paused and looked at Jack, watching him. "See if our friend Mr. Trenton was a drinking man."

Jack grinned and headed for what looked like a liquor cabinet in the corner of the room, pulled the two small doors of the cabinet open, and turned with a grin. "Can I pour you a drink, Sir?"

Dan smiled as he opened another drawer and began rummaging through it. "Ice if you can find any."

Jack turned, looked through another doorway, and, seeing the kitchen beyond the dining room, walked away in search of ice.

Dan went about the task of pulling drawers out of the desk, looking under each one for an envelope taped to the bottom, and looked for secret compartments on the sides. Finding none, he put everything back without leaving a mess.

Jack set a glass of ice and bourbon on Trenton's desk. Then he sat down in a comfortable chair in front of the desk, draped one leg over the armrest, and took a small drink. His eyes roamed the walls of reproduced paintings, old, dated pictures of Denver, and people he assumed were either friends or family of Howard Trenton.

Dan found several envelopes from a bank containing bank statements. "If Trenton was blackmailing someone, he either never got paid, or he has a secret account someplace." He took a sip of bourbon. "According to his savings and checking, he's not that wealthy."

Jack thought about that. "Maybe we should check his bank and see if he has a deposit box."

Dan thought that was a good idea as he put the bank statements back where he had found them. Then he sat back and sipped his drink while looking around the room at pictures of Howard with several different men and wondered why there wasn't one with a woman. Dan put his glass down, walked to a wall of pictures, and checked behind each one for a small wall safe or something taped behind a picture. After he had checked the entire room, he returned to the desk and drank the last of his bourbon. Setting his glass on the desk, Dan looked at a photo showing Howard

Trenton and another man taken in front of Buffalo Bill's grave on Lookout Mountain, west of Denver. He leaned forward, picked it up, and looked at Trenton. "Talk to us, Howard. What the hell were you into?"

Jack stood and picked up Dan's glass to fill it again, but Dan looked at his watch and then at his partner. "Let's start looking around. I don't want to stay here all night."

Three hours passed, and they still had not found anything that looked like or even resembled dirt on anyone or anything else that would give someone cause to torture and kill Howard Trenton.

Jack pulled another drawer out of the chest in the master bedroom, took the shirts out, and turned the drawer over, looking again for an envelope taped to the underside. Not finding anything, he put the shirts back in the drawer and continued with the other drawers. When he finished searching the dresser, he turned and looked at Dan, who had just looked behind the final picture in the house. "I'm tired, Dan."

"Yeah, I am, too," admitted Dan. "So far, we haven't found one thing that Trenton could be using for blackmail."

Jack picked up the glass of bourbon whose ice had melted, drank what remained, and as they moved to the final room, he said, "I have a theory."

Dan paused at the door, curious if it was another of his far-out theories.

"Maybe Howard was having an affair with a married woman, and her husband found out."

Dan considered that. "A jealous husband and a crime of passion?" He opened the door to the final bedroom. This one smelled musty and unused.

Jack followed Dan into the dimly lit room, stopped, and glanced around.

Dan walked to the window and raised the shade, thinking about the men's pictures in the study. "No, I don't think so, Jack." He opened a drawer filled with women's undergarments. "What the hell do we have here?"

Jack walked over and looked into the drawer. "Women's underwear?"

Dan stepped away from the drawer and walked around the room, looking at the pictures on the nightstands, dresser, and walls. "I think this room belonged to Trenton's mother."

Jack closed the drawer, picked up a picture, and looked at the woman wearing clothes from another era. "I think you're right."

Finding nothing in the room, they walked downstairs, where Jack fixed them another small drink while discussing where they may not have

150

looked. Jack took a sip of bourbon. "We've been all over this place, Dan. There's nothing here."

"There has to be something hidden someplace, Jack. Trenton wasn't treated the way he was over nothing." He took a small drink and then added, "Somebody was pissed at him, or he had something someone wanted, and that's why he was tortured. And I don't buy your theory about a jealous husband."

"Why not?"

Dan gestured with one hand. "Look around. All the pictures of Trenton are with different men."

Jack glanced around. "Oh, yeah." He took a drink while considering that fact. "Maybe they got what they were after, and we'll never know." He paused while thinking of the way the body looked in the garage. "I'd have started spewing the moment they headed for my testicles."

Dan smiled at the look on his partner's face and went back over the house room by room in his mind, from the kitchen and rooms on the main floor to the bedrooms and bathrooms upstairs. Dan looked at Jack. "The basement."

"Aw, shit," complained Jack. "I want to go home and eat."

Dan put his glass on the table and stood, thinking he had no one waiting for him. "Go home. I'll check out the basement."

Jack stood and downed the rest of his drink. "Not on your life." Then he jokingly said, "You might find fifty or sixty thousand dollars and then leave town."

Dan grinned and headed for the doorway to look for the basement.

Jack followed Dan to the basement door in the small room off the kitchen. Opening the door, greeted by musty basement smells, they walked down the stairs to a dark, musty basement.

Paul was sat on the sofa with his knees pulled against his chest, rocking back and forth with red, welling eyes. Tears ran down his face as he hummed a senseless tune that kept time with the movements of his body. As the clock on the wall chimed, Paul stopped and watched as the little door opened, and a tiny wooden bird popped out, sang its quick song, and disappeared back inside, the door closing behind it. He stared at the tiny door of the clock, let go of his knees, and stood. After wiping the tears and sweat from his face with his hands, he wiped his hands on his pants and walked to the basement door, opened it, turned on the light, and walked down the stairs.

At the bottom, he paused a moment to look at the closed door to the room where he kept his guests, then walked across the basement floor to another closed door. Taking the key from above the door, he unlocked it, opened the door, replaced the key, and stepped inside, closing the door behind him. He stood in the pitch-black darkness of the room for a long moment, imagining what awaited him across the floor. He reached out in the dark, finding the light switch on the wall, and turned on the light. Hesitating for a moment, he looked across the room to a wall of several twelve-inch square bins. As excitement filled him, he stepped across the cold cement floor to the wall, stopped at the first bin, put his hand inside, and touched its contents. Closing his eyes in memory, he moved on to the next and the next and the next until he stood before the last bin, next to other rows of empty bins waiting for his trophies.

From the last bin, he took out a fruit jar filled with blood, held it up to the overhead light, and shook it lightly until the finger inside rested against the side of the jar. He stared at it for several moments while touching the jar with affection as he turned it around, watching the finger slide along the glass. He placed it back in the bin, took out a billfold, opened it, and looked at the name Marie S. Phillips on a student ID card. He smiled as he looked at each photograph in the wallet as if he knew everyone in the pictures. He closed the billfold, put it back, took out a pair of white panties, placed them against his face, and smelled them. Feeling the soft, silky material against his skin, he remembered a naked Marie Phillips hanging upside down over the bathtub in the other room.

Several minutes passed, and then Paul looked at the white panties as tears streamed down his face. He carefully put the panties back in the bin just as they were before he took them out and wiped the tears from his eyes. Turning from the bins, Paul walked to the corner of the room, turned his back against the wall, slid down to the floor, wrapped his arms around his knees, and whimpered like a child.

Dan pulled into his driveway, shut off the car, and grabbed the bag containing a sandwich he had picked up at Oscar's Deli. He locked the car, went inside the house, and after locking the front door, he bent down, picked up the mail, and quickly glanced through it. Finding nothing from Robert, Dan set the mail on the small table in the foyer, tossed his keys in the glass bowl, hung up his hat, and headed for the kitchen. As he poured a glass of milk, he looked at the clock above the refrigerator, seeing it was almost eight, and wondered what was on television. Picking up the glass of milk and the bag with his sandwich, he headed for the living room, turned the television on, and then changed the channel to one of his favorite shows, 'What's My Line,' and settled down on the sofa to eat.

It was nine twenty Thursday night when Dan opened his eyes. Seeing a different program on the television, he sat up, feeling groggy and in a bad mood. Dan looked down at his stocking feet as they touched the floor, not remembering when he had taken off his shoes. Getting up, he left the television on, went upstairs, brushed his teeth, put on his pajama bottoms, and returned to the living room, where he checked the television guide in the newspaper. Deciding on Martin Kane, Private Eye, his thoughts suddenly turned to Cathy Holman. Wondering if he should call her, he looked at the big clock in the corner and, after quickly debating the question with himself, sat at the desk and dialed her number.

"Hello," answered Cathy.

"Did I wake you?"

She laughed softly. "No. I'm just lying here on the sofa watching TV in my pajamas."

Dan wondered what she looked like in pajamas.

Her voice changed. "I saw on the news that Howard Trenton was found dead in his home. How terrible. It makes you wonder what kind of a world we live in."

"I know."

"Do you know what happened?"

Remembering what the captain said about talking to anyone, he said, "No. These things usually take a few days."

Cathy yawned. "Excuse me."

Dan thought of how nice she looked the last time he saw her. "It's almost ten; we both better get to bed."

"I'm glad you called," she said.

"If it's alright, I'll call you sometime tomorrow night."

"Why wouldn't it be alright," she said, and then she smiled. "But could you please make it a little earlier?"

Dan laughed. "I'll try. Goodnight."

Sixteen

Dan was standing on the sidewalk watching his young daughter, Nancy, riding the new bicycle he gave to her on her birthday. She was smiling at him as she rode the bicycle in circles in the driveway, ringing the bell on the handlebars repeatedly, and with each passing, the bell became louder and louder.

Opening his sleepy eyes, he lifted his head and looked across the dark room at the telephone bathed in the dim light of the streetlamp. Pushing the cover away, he got up, stumbled across the floor to the desk, and picked up the telephone. "Hello."

It was Captain Foley. "We have another body."

Thinking they were piling up quickly, Dan turned the desk lamp on and looked at his wristwatch. It was 3:47 Friday morning. Trying to clear his head from the little sleep he'd had, he asked, "Where?"

"You know where Edwards Lumberyard is on South Santa Fe?"

Dan thought for a moment as he scratched his head. "Yeah," he said thoughtfully. "I think so, across from the golf course."

"That's right," said Foley. "There's a gravel road that runs from Santa Fe along the chain-link fence of the lumber yard to the northeast gate. Call your partner, and I'll meet the two of you there."

Dan started to ask if it was a man or woman when he heard the click, followed by a dial tone. He pulled the chair away from the desk, sat down, and dialed his partner's number.

The telephone rang several times before Lori Brolin answered with a sleepy voice. "Hello."

"Lori, this is Dan. I need Jack?"

"Just a minute."

Dan could hear Lori trying to wake her husband, remembering that Jack had always slept very soundly, even in the army.

"Yeah," said Jack sounding drunk.

"Foley just called. They discovered another body outside the fence of Edwards Lumber Company on South Santa Fe."

"Paul again?"

"Foley didn't say, but I'm guessing it is."

"Damn it, couldn't your friend take a few days off? What happened to that cooling off period Professor Pappel mentioned?

Dan wondered the same thing.

"What time is it?" asked Jack.

"Almost four a.m."

Jack sat up on the edge of his bed and rubbed the sleep from his eyes. "Where did you say it was?"

"Edwards Lumber Company on South Santa Fe Drive. About the 1500 block, I think."

Still sounding half-asleep, Jack said, "I'll get dressed and meet you there."

"There's a gravel road on the north side."

"I know where it is," interrupted Jack.

Dan set the receiver on the telephone base, feeling tired, and then looked at the sofa wishing this Paul guy would take a few days off. Getting up from the desk, he shoved the chair under it and headed upstairs to change from his pajamas into a pair of Levi's and a shirt.

Dan turned off South Santa Fe Drive, following the headlights of his car along the gravel road that ran along the chain-link fence of the lumber yard. Taillights and headlights of police patrol cars lined the road, making it difficult for him to maneuver between them. Surprised at seeing Jack's car, he parked next to the fence behind it, turned off his lights and engine, and got his flashlight from the glove box. After climbing out of his car, he started walking toward the dark images of several men standing in the dim light from a single bulb atop a telephone pole at the far end of the fence and gate to the lumber yard.

Seeing Jack walk toward him, he grinned. "You take an airplane to get here?"

"It's Ruth," said Jack ignoring Dan's question.

The grin left Dan's face as he stopped in disbelief and then hurried past Jack toward several men gathered around the ditch beneath a cottonwood tree across from the gate. Stopping at the edge of the ditch that separated the road from the far bank and cottonwood tree, he turned his flashlight on Ruth's nude body lying in the ditch. The automobile lights behind him cast moving shadows over Ruth as men moved around the crime scene looking for evidence. He stepped into the shallow, dry ditch, knelt next to the body, and looked at her face covered in a mass of cuts, bruises, and dried blood. He looked into her swollen blue eyes, recalling the last time he had looked into them when she told him to go home to his wife and stop chasing ghosts. Dan stood. "That son of a bitch, Curley." Then he yelled, "Cover her up, damn it, and get her out of there."

Todd Anderson of the crime lab was behind him, standing on the gravel road. "Sorry, Dan, but my men aren't through here yet."

Dan turned with an angry look. "I said to get her out of the damn ditch."

"I can't do that, Dan," argued Todd. "My men have a job to do."

155

Jack was at Dan's side. "Todd has to process the scene, Dan. You know that."

Dan's demeanor softened as he looked down at Ruth, and then he turned to Todd. "I apologize, Todd. Just be careful with her." Then he stepped out of the ditch and headed for his car.

Jack stepped in his way. "I know what you're thinking, Dan, but don't go after Curley while you're pissed."

Dan placed one hand on Jack's chest, gently pushed him aside, and walked past him. "Damn right, I'm pissed."

Captain Foley was standing nearby and yelled, "Detective Morgan!"

Dan stopped, turned, and looked at Foley walking toward him.

"Where the hell are you going?" asked the captain.

Dan pointed at Ruth's body. "To bring in the bastard that did that for questioning."

Foley quickly considered that it might be a bad idea in his current frame of mind. "Jack's going to follow you back downtown."

"I don't need Jack to do this, Captain."

Foley stepped closer to Dan, looked him in the eyes, and lowered his voice. "Either Jack goes with you, or you don't go." He paused. "Don't challenge me on this, Detective. You'll lose. Now take a deep breath, settle down, and act like the detective you are."

Dan nodded and took a deep breath. "Yes, sir."

Foley relaxed and stepped back. "That's better. Now, your partner will follow in his car, and you don't go near Curley unless Jack is with you." He paused with narrowed eyes. "Are we clear on that?"

"Yes, sir."

Foley stared at Dan. "You don't lay a hand on this, Curley." He turned to Jack. "Get in your car and follow Dan."

Curley sat up in bed, startled and afraid, as the door to his dark hotel room burst open, and two men rushed in. He reached for his .22 pistol in the drawer of the nightstand, but Jack was too quick and kicked the drawer shut on Curley's hand. Yelling in pain, Curley let go of the pistol and moved back to the headboard with fear on his face. It was not until Dan turned the light on that he recognized who had broken into his room. "What've I done?" he asked, looking from one to the other.

Dan and Jack grabbed his arms and pulled him off the bed while he kept repeating, "What've I done?"

Afraid Dan was going to hit Curley, Jack stepped between them and looked at Curley. "Get dressed."

Curley gave each a worried look, got dressed, and then the three hurried down the stairs to the lobby, with Jack holding one of Curley's arms and Dan the other.

Reaching the front door, Jack pulled Curley safely away and headed for his car.

Dan stopped and started after them. "What the hell you doing with Curley?"

Reaching his car, Jack opened the rear door, pushed Curley into the back seat of his Ford, slammed the door, and turned to Dan. "I'm just protecting you from yourself."

Dan gave Jack a dirty look, then looked at Curley sitting in Jack's car, turned, and walked back to his, and then followed them to headquarters.

Jack put Curley into one of the interrogation rooms on an uncomfortable chair at a small wooden table. He looked at Dan and motioned him out, and as he closed the door, Curley was still asking why they were arresting him. In the hall, Jack looked at Dan. "You ready to ask Curley about Ruth now?"

Dan gave Jack a dirty look. "What the hell do you think?"

Jack opened the door, letting Dan walk in, and while Dan headed for another chair across the table from Curley, Jack closed the door keeping a close eye on Dan. Neither spoke.

Curley stiffened in his chair, looking nervous and afraid as his eyes went from Jack to Dan, remembering times in the past when Dan had roughed him up. His eyes followed Jack as he walked past the table and stood against the wall behind him with arms folded. Then he turned and looked at Dan, sitting across the table, staring back at him. "What the hell's going on? I ain't done nothing."

Dan leaned forward with his arms on the table and stared into Curley's brown, bloodshot eyes, imagining him hitting Ruth until she passed out. Knowing Curley was right-handed, Dan reached across the table, grabbed Curley's right wrist, and pulled the hand toward him. Curley protested and started to stand, but Jack moved away from the wall and put Curley in a chokehold while Dan examined the knuckles on his right hand.

"What are you looking for?" asked Curley in a choked voice.

Finding no marks, Dan ignored the question and examined the left hand. Disappointed, he looked at Jack and let go of Curley's hand.

Jack let go of the headlock and moved back to the wall.

Curly rubbed his neck as he looked up at Jack and then at Dan Morgan. "What is it you think I've done?"

Dan leaned across the table. "Ruth was beaten to death, Curley, and you're our prime suspect."

Curley looked surprised and started to get up. "What?"

Jack put both of his hands on Curley's shoulders and pushed him back into the chair. "No one told you to stand, asshole."

Curley looked upset. "Ruth's dead?" he asked, looking from one to the other. "I haven't touched Ruthie in a while. Sure, I've knocked her around a bit when she got mouthy, but that's all."

Dan stood and slapped the top of the oak table with his open hand. "I think you and Ruth got into one of your little spats, and it went too far."

Curley looked scared as little beads of perspiration formed on his forehead. "No, that ain't true, Detective. I swear it." Then he held up his hands, showing his knuckles. "You saw for yourself. I ain't hit nobody, least of all Ruthie."

"Maybe you wore gloves," suggested Jack.

Curley turned and looked at Jack. "No, I swear."

Dan stood and walked around the table and leaned close to Curley. "By the time you realized you had gone too far, Ruth was dead. So, you put her in your car and dumped her body in a ditch like a piece of garbage."

Curley's eyes went from one to the other, ending at Dan's angry eyes. "I couldn't have taken her body anyplace. I don't own a car." He wiped the sweat away with his hand. "I didn't kill Ruthie." He looked from Jack to Dan. "You gotta believe me."

Dan glanced at Jack, and both wondered how he could have dumped Ruth's body on the south side of Denver without a car.

Jack sat down on the edge of the table next to Curley and offered him a cigarette. "When did you last see Ruth?"

Curley's hands were shaking as he took the cigarette. "At dinner before she and the others went out." He paused with a sad look. "I can't believe she's gone." He looked from one to the other. "Who'd do such a thing?"

Dan watched while Jack lit the cigarette hanging from Curley's mouth.

"Who were the others?" asked Jack.

"Penny and Evelyn."

The faces of the two prostitutes crossed Dan and Jack's memory as Dan leaned on the table. "Was Ruth going to meet anyone special?"

Curley sat back, trying to distance himself from Dan. "She and the others were going to walk Larimer Street to try and turn a trick or two."

"What time was that?" asked Jack.

Curley took a deep drag from his cigarette and blew the smoke toward the overhead light. "We finished eating about nine. They left shortly after that."

Dan looked at Jack, nodded toward the door, then followed him out of the room. As Dan closed the door, he asked, "What do you think?"

Jack sighed. "I don't think he's good for it."

Dan looked at the closed door, imagining Curley sitting alone in the room smoking the cigarette Jack had given him. "Yeah, me neither." Feeling tired, Dan looked at his wristwatch, seeing it was close to 6:00 a.m. He looked at Jack. "Sorry for the way I acted."

"No need to apologize. I know you liked Ruthie and have tried to help her."

Dan put his arm around Jack and guided him down the hall. "Let's let Mr. Curley Peterson spend the rest of the day in a cell while you and I get some sleep. We'll look for Penny and Evelyn later tonight."

Dan bent down, opened the lid of the milk box next to the front door, took out the two bottles of milk left by the milkman, and then while holding the milk, managed to unlock the front door and step inside. He closed the door, locked it, and headed for the refrigerator in the kitchen. He set one bottle on the counter, peeled the paper lid from the other, and took a long drink of cool milk. Wiping his mouth, he put the lid back onto the bottle, opened the refrigerator and made room for the two bottles, then closed the door. He looked up at the round, red clock above the refrigerator, seeing it was ten minutes to seven in the morning.

Feeling even more tired than before, he headed for the blanket and pillow waiting for him on the sofa, turned off the lights, kicked off his shoes, and lay down in his clothes. He covered up with the blanket and closed his tired eyes, but instead of sleep, his mind filled with visions of Ruth's naked body lying in the ditch. Turning over, he pushed the images away, only to be replaced by the murders of Howard Trenton and each of the four girls. Turning over for the third time, he tried to think of Cathy, but the other visions kept pushing her away. Finally, the battle won, the ghosts of the dead faded into a black void as sleep overtook him.

It was 9:45 a.m. when the bright sunlight coming through the small east window woke him. He tossed the cover back, slowly sat up, put his stocking feet on the area rug in front of the sofa, and looked out the front window. Thinking it looked to be a nice day, he stood, walked upstairs carrying the pillow and dragging the blanket, showered, shaved, and got dressed. After a breakfast of coffee and toast, he gathered up the envelopes, his gun, and his hat and then headed out the front door. As he backed his car out of the driveway, he thought of Ruth lying in the cold, dark ditch with her face beaten and got mad at himself because he couldn't even remember her last name.

Detective Morgan set the four envelopes of the murdered girls on top of his desk and looked around for his partner. Seeing Jack's desk was clean, he looked at the clock on the far wall, seeing it was 11:30 a.m. Sitting down, he pulled the telephone toward him, noticing the recorder hooked up to his phone. Making sure it was turned off, he dialed the Littleton Sheriff's Office.

"Sherriff's Office."

Dan smiled at hearing Cathy's voice. "Good morning."

Surprised by the phone call, she smiled. "Good morning. I didn't mean you had to call me this early."

Dan laughed. "When I say I'll do something, I do it."

She laughed. "That's good to know."

"It's Friday, and I was wondering if we could have dinner this evening."

She paused a moment, not wanting to appear anxious even if she were. "What time?"

Dan looked at his wristwatch. "How about I pick you up from work, and we'll decide where to eat then?"

"Alright. See you at five."

Dan said goodbye, hung the phone up, and stared at it for a moment, thinking of how she looked the last time he saw her.

Jack walked past his desk. "Who was that?"

Not wanting to discuss Cathy with Jack, he lied, saying he was making a dental appointment.

Doubting that, Jack pulled his chair away from his desk, wondering if his partner was okay. But instead of sitting down, he walked around his desk and sat on the edge of Dan's desk, noticing the tape recorder. "I'm sorry about Ruth, Dan."

Dan sat back in his chair, staring at the top of his desk. "Ruth was someone I knew, Jack." He looked up at him. "She wasn't a friend or anything like that, but all the same, I worried about her. You probably don't understand, but I wanted her to leave the streets before something like this happened."

Jack considered what he said. "I know you did, and I don't mean to sound cruel or uncaring, Dan, but as I said before, she chose her life."

"I know she did, but damn it, Jack, she was a young, beautiful girl who could have had anything she wanted."

Jack sighed, hoping Dan had not replaced his dead daughter with Ruth, a prostitute. "It's obvious she wanted what she had, Dan." He paused. "And that was the street." Then Jack patted him on the shoulder.

160

"Let's go downstairs, and I'll buy you a cup of coffee and a sweet roll before we cut Curley loose and head over to Howard Trenton's office."

As Dan stood, his telephone rang. Wondering if it was Paul, he reached over, turned on the recorder, and then picked up the telephone. "Morgan."

"This is Foley. Would you come in for a moment?"

Sensing something was wrong, Dan shut the recorder off, thinking it was going to be inconvenient. "Foley wants to see me."

Jack looked toward the captain's office. "What about?"

Dan frowned. "I don't know, but he didn't sound too happy. Why don't you cut Curley loose, and after I see the captain, we'll get that coffee and head to the newspaper office."

Jack nodded, remembering how mad Foley was last night, thinking it probably had something to do with that.

Dan tapped on the glass of the door of the captain's office.

Foley looked up and motioned him in.

Dan opened the door and stepped inside. "You wanted to see me, Captain?"

"Yes, I did, Dan." He gestured to the chairs in front of his desk. "Have a seat." He waited until Dan shut the door and sat down. "Are you alright? I was a little concerned about you last night."

Dan looked regretful. "Sorry, Captain. I guess I lost it when I saw her body discarded like a piece of trash in the ditch with her face cut and bloody." He paused. "She was someone I knew, not a stranger like the others. It just got to me."

Foley understood, but all the same, he was worried about his best detective. "You've been through a lot the past few years, Dan. I want to make sure you can keep focused on your job. If you can't, say the word, and I'll reassign you." He paused briefly. "There will be no ramifications or hard feelings if you don't think you can, and I'll appreciate the honesty."

"Don't do that, Captain. I'm alright now." Dan looked at him. "As I said, I never saw a girl I knew lying in a ditch looking like that before." He paused. "I just lost it."

"We all have at one time or another," said Foley with a small, understanding smile. Then the smile left his face. "Was there something between you and this girl?"

Dan sat back in his chair, looking surprised. "No sir, Captain, there wasn't. I knew Ruth from the streets. I had arrested her a few times and knocked her pimp Curley around more than once for roughing up his girls, her included."

Foley looked unsure. "Seems to me that there is something more to this."

161

Dan shrugged. "I don't know what to say, Captain. There was nothing between Ruth and me. I wanted her to get off the streets and go back home, wherever that was." He looked at Foley. "I didn't think she belonged there. Most of them do, but---" He let the sentence die.

Foley smiled. "I knew a crazy young boy of thirteen once when I walked a beat that I tried for a long time to help."

Dan looked interested. "What happened?"

Sadness held the captain's face. "Got shot by a patrolman during a robbery." Foley looked at him. "Some people just can't be saved, Detective." Figuring they had talked enough about the girl, Foley changed the subject. "You find anything at Trenton's last night."

Dan shook his head. "No, sir. We tore the place apart and couldn't find anything."

"No hidden safes?"

"No, sir, we checked for safes behind pictures and in the basement. We checked for taped envelopes under every drawer in the house. I even went through his bank statements to see if he had a lot of money. He didn't."

Foley thought for a moment. "He could have it hidden any place." Then he said, "See if he has a safe deposit box. If he does, I'll get a warrant, and we'll open it."

"Jack and I discussed that last night. We'll stop at his bank today."

Foley nodded his approval. "Okay, what's your next step?"

Thinking that he and Jack needed to talk to Evelyn and Penny tonight without telling the captain, he filled Foley in on what might have happened at Trenton's home. "Jack and I are going to interview his boss and some of the people he worked with, and then we'll check out his desk and filing cabinets in his office."

"Sounds good. Keep me posted, and don't talk to anyone about this Trenton thing."

"No, sir. Is that all, Captain?"

"Yeah, go on, get out of here."

Dan walked out of the captain's office, closed the door, and headed for his desk.

Jack was waiting. "Well?"

"We'll talk on the way."

They stopped at the coffee shop on the first floor, where Jack bought Dan a coffee. While Jack drove and drank his coffee, Dan ate his sweet roll and filled him in on the captain's concerns about him and Ruthie. Then he looked at Jack. "Do you recall what her last name was?"

Jack shook his head. "No, I don't."

Howard Trenton's editor of the Daily News and several of his fellow employees were of little help in the investigation. Getting permission from the editor, Dan searched the drawers of Howard's desk. At the same time, Jack rummaged through the five-drawer filing cabinet, a task that included looking for any envelopes taped to the undersides of drawers but found nothing. When Dan finished, he went through Howard's datebook, finding that several days before his death and after were blank. Dan sat back in the plush leather chair and looked at a notepad he had missed. He pulled it closer and saw that the paper held an imprint of something Trenton had written on the missing piece of paper. Getting hopeful, he took a pencil from the pencil holder on the desk and began rubbing the side of the lead across the notepad while Jack watched with interest. The words "Jefferson Park 9 PM" appeared. Dan set the pencil down, tore off the piece of paper, and looked up at Jack. "Do you know where Jefferson Park is?"

"No."

"I do. It's a little park on the west side that sits between Eliot and Clay on 23rd Street." He smiled. "Just a few blocks from Trenton's house."

Jack looked interested. "He was meeting someone at the park?"

Dan grinned as he stood. "That's right, but he never made it."

After Jack parked his car on Eliot Street next to Jefferson Park, Dan got out of the car, and as he closed the door, he watched a man with a big dog walk into the park and throw a ball for the dog to chase.

Jack climbed out, closed his door, and walked around the car to the sidewalk. He stood next to Dan and leaned against his car, wondering what this place had to do with Trenton.

Dan was watching the dog return the ball to the man who threw it again. "Too bad Trenton never wrote down a name."

Jack watched the same dog. "We're never that lucky."

Dan stepped away from the car and crossed the sidewalk onto the green grass, leaving Jack to glance up and down the sidewalk before he followed Dan into the quiet park. The morning was filled with the lazy sounds of pulsating sprinkler heads watering the far side of the park. They walked through a part of the park not yet wet with water to a bench near a half-filled trash can, six empty swings, and two teeter-totters and sat down. He watched Jack take a pack of cigarettes out of his pocket, and as Jack offered him one, he said no with a slight wave of the hand. While Jack lit his cigarette, Dan watched a young mother as she and her daughter approached the swings. The woman lifted the little girl into one of the swings and gently pushed her. Hearing the giggles from the child reminded Dan of his daughter and the tire swing he had put up on the elm tree in the front yard.

Jack blew a puff of smoke in the air and looked at the lit end of the cigarette. "I wonder who Trenton was meeting here."

Dan put one arm on the back of the bench behind Jack and watched the little girl in her swing glide back and forth. "This whole thing is crazy."

Jack took another drag of his cigarette and stared across the park at the sprinklers pouring water onto the grass.

"We have four murdered girls, and we know who's guilty, but we can't find him." He paused. "We have two more victims with no suspects, and the one least likely to be solved is the one the captain wants us to spend most of our time on." He looked at Jack. "We still need to talk to Penny and Evelyn."

"You want to try and find them now?"

"No, they're probably sleeping. We'll look later tonight." Dan looked at his watch. "This ain't doing us any good. Let's go to Micky's. I need a drink."

Micky's was not very busy when Dan and Jack walked in, letting their eyes adjust to the dim light as they made their way to a small table away from the jukebox, where it was a little quieter. A short, thin girl they knew as Rita took their order and then delivered their drinks.

Jack took a quick drink as he looked at his partner, thinking he looked troubled, set his glass down, and looked at Dan. You, okay?"

"Just thinking of how Foley chewed my ass out over Ruth."

"Well, you were pissed last night, partner. I was worried you'd kill Curley."

He looked at Jack. "Thanks for last night." He smiled. "I wouldn't have killed him, but I might have beaten the shit out of him."

"I'm not so sure," Jack said, "You were pretty upset."

"I guess I deserved an ass chewing."

Jack chuckled, sat back in his chair, and played with the ice condensation on the side of the glass. "I think your father image got the better of you."

Dan laughed softly but knew Jack wasn't far from being wrong.

Jack grinned. "Foley is a pretty good Joe."

Dan agreed in silence, took a drink, and stared into his glass of bourbon and melting ice. "I don't know what the hell I'm doing or thinking anymore."

Jack looked into Dan's worried face. "You have to let go of the past, Dan." Then he leaned with his forearms on the table and lowered his voice. "Norma's dead, and she isn't coming back." He took a drink. "Get involved with someone, Dan. Go to bed with Cathy Holman. Shit, Dan, the world won't end if you do." His worry over his friend and partner showed clearly on his face.

Dan stared at the ice in his glass, thinking of all Jack had said, took a drink, and shrugged. "Maybe."

Deciding they needed to talk about something else, Jack grinned. "Let's drink up and go cut Curley loose."

Dan looked surprised. "You didn't let him out this morning?"

Jack smiled. "I was worried about you and the captain and figured Curley could stew a while longer. What else does the son of a bitch have to do?"

Dan laughed, looked at his watch, finished his drink, and stood. "Let's let Curley spend another night in jail."

"Where we going?"

"We aren't going anywhere, asshole. You're taking me to my car. I have a date with Cathy at five."

Jack looked up at Dan. "What about Penny and Evelyn?"

"This is Friday night. It shouldn't be too difficult finding them later tonight." He grinned. "I'll call you after dinner."

Dan stood on the sidewalk, leaning against the fender of his car, waiting for Cathy to exit the courthouse. He took a drag from his cigarette and looked up the steps just as she walked out of the big glass doors. Taking another quick drag, he tossed the cigarette into the gutter and stepped away from the car.

Seeing him, she smiled, waved, and started down the steps. "Hello, been waiting long?"

"A few minutes." Then he took her arm, escorted her around the car, opened the door, helped her in, and then hurried around to the other side. "I hope you're hungry," he said, starting the car. "Because I am."

"I am hungry. Where are we going?"

As he drove north on Court Place, recalling the last time he and Cathy went to dinner, he said, "The same place as last time?"

She thought of another place that was a little more romantic. "When you get to Littleton Boulevard, turn right. I know a quaint, little place just off the Boulevard."

"Sounds interesting."

She smiled. "I don't know if it's interesting, but the food is delicious."

The table covered with a red and white checkered tablecloth sat near the window, looking out on the busy street. An empty Chianti wine bottle in a basket with a lit candle sat in the center of the table.

"I hope you like Italian food."

He smiled. "I love it."

The waiter, dressed in black dress pants, a white shirt with a black bowtie, and a long white apron, appeared at the table asking if they were ready to order. They ordered dinner, and Dan also ordered a bottle of red wine, but Cathy asked if they could have a lighter rose`.

Dan smiled and looked at the waiter. "Make that a bottle of rose`."

The waiter smiled and nodded. "Yes, sir."

As the waiter walked away, Dan glanced around the dim room of candles and checkered tablecloths, listening to the soft music coming from a handheld concertina played by a short, heavyset man as he walked from table to table. "You are right. It is quaint."

She smiled. "Then, you like it?"

"I do. It's very nice."

The waiter returned with a bottle of wine, showed them both the bottle, popped the cork, and offered it to Dan, who waved it away, saying it was fine. The waiter poured a small amount into a wine glass and waited while Dan sipped the wine, pronouncing it perfectly.

Pleased by that, the waiter poured a half portion into each of their wine glasses, set the bottle on the table, and left, leaving them to sip their wine and listen to the music of the concertina while waiting for their dinner.

After the food was on the table, they ate and talked about their lives, the things they liked and disliked, as people do when getting to know one another. Finished with dinner, Dan sat back, looking at the food left on his plate, and noticed Cathy's plate,wondering where she had put it. The waiter approached and asked if they were finished eating. Dan said he was, then Cathy nodded yes, and they waited in silence as the waiter took their plates.

Cathy glanced around at the other people enjoying their dinners. "I love it here." Then she softly laughed. "It's a good thing. I don't come here very often, or I would weigh two hundred pounds."

"We'll have to come here again," said Dan, and then he looked at his wristwatch.

Sensing he was in a hurry, she asked, "Do you have to leave?"

He set his cloth napkin on the table and looked at her. "Unfortunately, I do."

Just then, the waiter approached and looked at Cathy. "Would the lady like dessert?"

Cathy smiled. "No, thank you. I couldn't eat another bite if my life depended on it."

He looked at Dan. "And you, sir?"

"No, thank you."

"Very well," said the waiter. "I'll be back shortly with your check."

Dan picked up his glass of wine. "I have to meet Jack downtown. We're working on a case and have to find a couple of ladies."

She smiled. "That doesn't sound too good."

Dan smiled. "That came out wrong." He leaned forward, glanced around, and lowered his voice. "We need to question a couple of ladies about a case Jack, and I are working on."

She became interested. "Are they suspects?"

He shook his head. "No, we just need to ask them some questions." He smiled. "Because of their profession, it's best to catch them at night while they're working."

Cathy thought about that, imagining what the girls looked like.

The waiter returned and placed a small tray with the check on the table. "When you're ready, sir." Then he turned and walked away.

Dan looked at his watch. "But I have time. I don't want that to interfere with this just yet. I'm enjoying myself too much."

She smiled, feeling glad. "So am I." Then she looked interested. "Mind me asking what sort of case you're working on?"

Dan shifted nervously in his chair. "A woman was murdered last night."

Cathy looked worried. "Another teenager?"

"No," said Dan, reaching into the inside pocket of his gray suit for his wallet. He looked at the check lying on the tray and took out several bills to cover the cost of dinner and the gratuity. "This girl was a teenager, but the circumstances are different."

Interested, she asked, "In what way?"

Dan smiled and put his wallet away and looked at his watch. "I guess I better take you home so I can meet Jack." He stood and pulled her chair away as she got up from the table and then followed her out of the restaurant.

Dan opened the car door, helped Cathy into his car, got in, and drove out of the parking lot onto Littleton Boulevard. He had driven a short distance when he said, "The girl that was murdered the other night was a prostitute I knew as Ruthie."

Cathy looked away from the street ahead at Dan. "You knew her?"

Dan considered the question, becoming fearful of what she may think. "Not well. I had arrested her a few times for solicitation." He left it at that but was not sure he should have.

167

Cathy looked at the side of his face lit up by the dashboard's lights while he stared out the windshield at the road lit up by the headlights of his car. "How did she die?"

Dan hesitated. "Someone beat her to death."

Cathy looked away. "Oh my God, how horrible."

While he drove, Dan explained that he and Jack were going to talk to two of her coworkers later and see if they could give them any leads, though he doubted they could.

Pulling into her driveway, he shut the car off and turned to her. "In truth, I knew this young girl. Yes, she was a prostitute selling sex, but there was something about her that made me see a different girl." He paused and chuckled. "Jack seems to think I was replacing Nancy with someone else to worry about." He shrugged. "Maybe he's right; I don't know what it was, but I talked to her several times about getting off the street and going home. I even offered to pay for her bus ticket." He smiled softly. "But she would just look at me and smile, saying this is what she did, and walk away." He looked out the windshield into the night of shadows. "Now, her parents, wherever they are, will never know what happened to their daughter."

"I'm sorry, Dan. But you did try, and that's all you can do."

He looked at her face in the dim light of the neighbor's porch light, thinking she looked beautiful, and then he leaned toward her, put his arm around her waist, and kissed her.

The tender kiss quickly became passionate, and Cathy pulled away and sat up, fussing with her hair as she smiled. "You have someone to meet."

Wishing he didn't have to meet Jack, he smiled. "Guess I better go."

She smiled. "I think so."

He got out of the car, opened her door, helped her out, and walked her to the gate of the picket fence.

She smiled as she stood on her toes and kissed him. "Be careful."

"I'll call you tomorrow." Then he watched her step through the opened gate. "Be sure your doors are locked." He waited until she was safely inside, and the lights were on before he got into his car, backed out of the driveway, and drove toward his rendezvous with Jack Brolin.

Cathy locked the door, walked into the bedroom, lay across the bed with her arms around her pillow and contemplated Dan Morgan.

Seventeen

It was almost eight-thirty Friday evening when Dan drove into the Police Headquarters parking lot and parked next to his partner's car. Jack got out, locked his car, and after he climbed into Dan's car, they drove up and down Larimer, Blake, and Lawrence Streets, looking for the prostitutes, Penny, and Evelyn.

Jack rolled down his window and looked at the people walking up and down the sidewalk. "I've never seen so many girls out and about. Must be a busy night."

Dan smiled. "I'd say it's a slow night, or they'd all be off the street."

Finding that humorous. Jack grinned in silence while Dan drove up Blake Street looking along the sidewalks on his side of the car, searching for Ruthie's two friends.

"There's Penny," said Dan, and then he slowed and made a U-turn, ignoring the verbal abuse of the driver he had just cut off. He pulled up next to the sidewalk and drove slowly along the curb.

Jack stuck his head out of the car door window. "Penny."

She kept walking as she looked over her shoulder to see who had called her name.

"Penny," yelled Jack again. "Stop. We want to talk to you."

She stopped but kept a safe distance from the curb as she bent down to see who was in the car. Recognizing the two detectives and afraid she would be arrested, she asked, "About what?"

As Dan stopped the car, Jack motioned for her to approach the car. "Come closer. We want to ask you a few questions about Ruth."

Penny was a short, thin, black woman dressed in a short, black skirt, high heels, and a white long-sleeved blouse that hid the needle tracks on her arms. Though she looked older than her twenty-five years, she was still very attractive. She put one hand on the top of the car, the other on her hip, and bent over, looking at Jack and then at Dan, leaning toward Jack. "What about Ruthie?"

Jack turned, reached into the back, and opened the rear car door, telling her to get in.

"Am I under arrest?"

"No," said Dan.

She glanced around to see who was watching, then reluctantly did as she'd been asked, and once seated, she looked from one to the other. "What about Ruthie?"

Dan had his right arm on the back of the front seat as he turned to look at her sitting in the middle of the back seat. "When was the last time you saw Ruth?"

She looked from one to the other with a curious look while chewing her gum. "She in trouble?"

The car filled with silence, and then Dan said, "Ruth is dead, Penny."

Penny stared at Dan with a surprised look. "Dead," she repeated, and then she began to cry. "How did she die?"

"Someone beat her to death," replied Dan in a soft voice.

Penny rocked from side to side as she cried. "Oh, my Lord, that poor child," Then her sadness quickly turned to anger. "Is that why you arrested Curley? Did that son of a bitch kill that child?"

Jack turned. "No, Curley didn't kill Ruth. He was our prime suspect, but we don't believe he hurt Ruth."

"I tried to get her to go back to Wichita," said Penny.

"Is that where she was from?" asked Dan.

She nodded yes.

Dan hoped he could contact her parents. "Do you know what her last name was, Penny? I seem to have forgotten."

Penny's face held anger as she looked at Dan. "Check out her rap sheet. You arrested her enough."

Dan suddenly felt regretful about those arrests. "To get to her rap sheet, I'd need to know her full name, and I can't recall what it was."

Feeling sorry for getting angry, she wiped the tears from her face. "Spencer, it was Spencer. She has a mother living in Wichita. She gets a letter from her once in a while."

"I'd like her mother's address," said Dan. "So, I can write to her and tell her about her daughter."

Penny looked at him for a moment. "Alright. Take me to my place, and I'll get that for you. Go to the next corner and turn left."

While they drove Penny to her place, Dan said, "Curley told us that you and Ruth had dinner with him before you hit the streets."

She wiped her eyes. "That's right. After dinner, me, her, and Evelyn walked Larimer for a time, and then we split up."

"Which way did Ruth go," asked Dan.

Penny thought for a moment. "I think she went over to Lawrence."

"You never saw her leave with anyone?" asked Jack.

"Hell no," she said as she cried. "If I had, I'd be telling you. Once she turned that corner on 17th, I never saw her again."

170

Dan felt sorry for Penny, knowing that whores don't have anyone but one another.

"Here it is," said Penny.

Dan stopped the car in front of an old boarding house.

Penny climbed out of the back seat, saying she'd be right back, and then disappeared inside. Moments later, she stepped out of the door to the boarding house where she and Ruth had shared a room, walked toward the car with a stack of letters tied with a string, and handed them to Jack.

"You want a ride back to where we found you?" asked Dan.

She wiped the tears from her face and looked up the street. "I can walk. It ain't that far."

"You be careful out there," said Jack.

"Anyone messes with me, I pull out that straight razor I carry and make him a girl." Penny leaned in the window and handed Jack a small pile of money. "This is three hundred dollars that Ruthie was saving." She paused, fighting her sorrow. "Maybe her mother can use it so's she can take Ruthie back home where she belongs."

Jack handed the money to Dan.

Penney stepped back from the car and looked up the street of colored neon signs, streetlights, and people aimlessly walking along the sidewalk. She wiped the tears from her eyes and softly said, "I'm gonna miss that girl."

"You be careful," said Dan, then he drove away from the curb.

A short time later, they interrupted Evelyn scaring off her young male customer. Mad at losing the customer, Evelyn told much the same story that Penny had told them.

Dan drove away, leaving Evelyn, who was a few years older than Ruth, standing on the sidewalk in tears at the news about Ruth.

Jack looked at his watch. "How about a drink."

"I thought you were tired."

Jack shrugged. "I am, but I would like a drink unless you're too tired."

Dan smiled. "Micky's?"

Dan stepped onto the porch and lifted the lid of the milk box with his foot. In the dim light of the old bulb above his head, he saw it was empty and remembered that the milkman hadn't come yet. Having a hard time putting the key in the lock, Dan dropped his keys on the porch. While staring down at them, he put one hand on the door for balance, bent down, and, while picking them up, dropped the four envelopes.

171

Laughing as he bent down to pick up the envelopes, he stood on wobbly legs and played with the keys and the lock. Finally, getting the key into the lock, he unlocked the front door and stepped into the darkness of the foyer. He locked the door and flipped the light switch that turned on the overhead light. Raising his hand with the envelopes to shade his eyes from the light, he stepped away from the door and tossed his keys into a glass tray on the small table. Watching as they bounced, coming to rest inside the bowl, he chuckled at this difficult feat and then tried to hang his hat up, but it fell to the floor. Staring at the hat a moment, he gestured at it, and while holding the four envelopes under his left arm, he slowly bent down to one knee to pick up the mail lying on the floor, managing then to fall against the door. Laughing, he slowly got up with the help of the doorknob, grabbed the chair next to the table that now held his keys, and waited for the spinning to stop.

Walking into the living room, he stopped at the desk and placed the mail on top of it along with the four manila envelopes. Placing his hands on the desk, he closed his eyes, thinking of sleep when the clock in the corner struck the quarter-hour. Standing, he looked at it, sitting smugly in the shadows of the corner, seeing it was two-fifteen in the morning. He turned and looked at the black telephone sitting on the desk next to the mail and the crime scene envelopes and considered calling Cathy. Realizing that it would be unwise in his current condition, he stumbled to the sofa, plopped down, and with his shoes and clothes on, closed his eyes and went to sleep.

Dan Morgan lifted his head from the sofa and glared at the black telephone sitting on the desk, wishing it would stop ringing. He pushed himself up, put his feet on the floor, and stood with the help of the sofa arm and coffee table. Still groggy, he walked the short distance to the desk and picked up the ringing telephone. "Hello," he said as he pulled the chair from the desk and sat down.

"You sound like shit," said Jack.

"I feel like shit," said Dan, with a dry mouth. "What time is it?"

"Almost noon."

"Shit," said Dan softly. "What day is it?"

Jack chuckled. "It's Saturday, ass hole."

"How much did I have to drink last night?"

"Well, let's just say I haven't seen you that drunk since Norma's wake."

Dan remembered that day as he looked out the living room window, remembering he was so drunk that he had passed out under the elm tree in his front yard that night.

"I followed you home to make sure you were okay."

172

"I don't remember. Thanks."

Jack chuckled. "I thought you never would get into the house."

Dan was sitting at the desk with his head supported by his left hand and his eyes closed. "If you don't have anything important to say, I'm going back to bed."

Jack chuckled. "Goodnight."

Dan hung up the telephone, got undressed, went to the bathroom, and then lay down on the sofa and covered up with the afghan.

When Dan next opened his eyes, it was after three in the afternoon. He tossed the afghan over the back of the sofa, sat up, and stared out the window with a pounding headache. Standing, he went into the kitchen, made a pot of coffee, and then went upstairs to clean up.

Dressed in a pair of Levi's and a cotton plaid shirt and feeling a little out of sorts, Dan put his half-eaten breakfast on the counter by the sink. He filled his cup with coffee, went out onto the front porch, and sat down in one of the white wooden chairs. The afternoon sun was low in the sky, and the neighborhood was quiet except for the birds arguing as they sprang from one branch to the other, avoiding a young gray squirrel. A woman he didn't recognize, and her small, tan dog walked along the sidewalk past the elm tree and the squirrel.

She smiled, waved, and said, "Hello."

Dan returned the smile, said hello, and thought that he would like a dog to help with the loneliness, but dismissed the idea as quickly as he had thought about it. His life was no life for a dog. He sipped the coffee as the silence returned to the porch, and he thought about Cathy and the kiss they shared in the car. He smiled and decided he would call her later. Then he thought about Penny and Evelyn crying over Ruth's death, of the money he would send with a letter to her mother, and then of Ruth lying on the cold metal slab in the city morgue. He turned his stare to the screen door, feeling drawn to the big manila envelopes sitting on the desk in the house. He got up and went inside, and as the screen door slammed behind him, he closed and locked the door. Glancing out through the lace curtains covering the window of the door to the empty street and sidewalk, he turned, picked up the envelopes, and grabbed a box of tacks from the desk. After dropping his cup off at the kitchen counter, he headed for the back door.

The musty smell of the garage greeted him as he opened the side door of the garage. Stepping inside, he flipped the light switch filling the garage with bright fluorescent lights mounted in the ceiling and then closed the door. He stood by the door looking around the empty garage until his eyes settled on the far wall of unpainted drywall and the few tools hanging from it. Thinking it would do since it had no window, he set the four envelopes and box of tacks on the workbench and started removing the tools. When finished, he pulled the nails from the wall with his hammer. When finished, he brushed the wall with an old rag, picked up the box of tacks and the four envelopes, and set them onto a stool with wheels. He pushed the stool toward the wall, knelt on the cement floor, and sorted through the envelopes, putting each one in the order of the girl's deaths.

Picking up Diane Wagner's envelope he had been given by Sheriff Brumwell in Littleton, he took the pictures out and placed them on the floor in front of him, and quickly glanced over them. Then he tacked them to the wall in an order that made sense to him. Finished, he repeated the process with Gail Thomas from Englewood, Sally Crowder from the alley near Larimer Street, and Marie Phillips from the alley behind the Paramount Theater. When he finished, he stepped back and looked at the collection of photos of the crime scenes, as well as those taken at the city morgue. Filled with the mystery of what haunted him about these pictures, Dan sat down on the wheeled stool and slowly rolled from one end of the wall to the other, pausing now and then to look at a picture. He didn't know how long he slid from one side of the wall to the other until he noticed it was dark outside the windows of the big garage doors. Looking at his watch, he got up from the stool, his mind still filled with the worry that something was not right and the need to find what that was. Pausing at the door, he looked back at the wall of pictures for a long moment, turned out the lights, locked the garage door, and headed for the house.

Inside, he opened the refrigerator door, took out a bottle of beer, popped the cap on the opener, and took a drink. Tossing the cap into the trash, he thought about fixing something for dinner and suddenly realized that he had not called Cathy.

After several rings, a sleepy voice said, "Hello."

"Did I wake you?"

"That's okay." She thought about how upset he had been over this prostitute's murder. "I was worried. Are you alright?"

"I'm fine."

"I didn't hear from you last night, and I was getting concerned. I started to call you, but ..." she let the sentence trail off.

"Probably better that you didn't. After Jack and I found a couple of Ruth's friends and questioned them, we stopped for a drink that turned into several."

"You don't have to explain."

"I want to," he said. "I had too much to drink, and that's why I didn't call you. Plus, it was late, or should I say too early."

She chuckled softly. "You're telling me you were drunk?"

174

He thought for a moment. "Don't know what else to call it. We didn't start out to, but the night and drinks crept up on us." He paused. "When I got home, I thought about calling you, but I wasn't sure you would want to talk to a drunken police detective."

She laughed softly. "That might have been interesting. Did you make any progress on Ruth's murder?"

"No."

"That's too bad."

"Look," said Dan. "It's late, and I better let you get back to sleep."

"What are you going to do?"

He considered that. "Watch the ten o'clock news and then go to bed."

The phone went silent for a moment, then Cathy asked if he would like to come over for dinner Sunday afternoon.

"I would."

She smiled, feeling glad. "Come over around three."

"See you then."

"Goodnight, Dan."

Dan hung up the telephone, picked up his bottle of beer, turned on the television, and returned to the sofa.

It was a little before three-thirty Sunday afternoon when Dan pulled into Cathy's driveway, shut the car off, grabbed the flowers he had stopped to pick at a small park, and got out of his car. As he walked along the picket fence toward the gate, someone said hello. When he turned, he was looking at a little girl of six or seven standing by the fence of the house next door on the other side of the driveway. He smiled, "Hello."

"Are you a friend of Cathy's?" asked the little girl.

"Why, yes, I am.'

"Are those for Cathy?" she asked, eyeing the flowers.

Dan opened the gate to Cathy's yard wanting to put some distance between him and the nosey little girl. "Yes, they are."

The door to the house next door opened, and a plump, dark-haired woman around thirty stuck her head out. "Come in the house, Carla."

Dan smiled at her and tipped his hat, but she ignored him and called out to the little girl again. "Carla, come into the house."

Feeling the chill she projected from the door, he closed the gate, walked to Cathy's front door, and rang the doorbell.

A smiling Cathy opened the door, then unlocked the screen door, and stepped back. "Come in."

Dan stepped inside, greeted by soft music, and as he smiled, he noticed her hair was in a ponytail. He handed her the flowers. "I met your neighbors."

"Carla?"

Dan nodded. "That's the one."

"They're a nice family," she said. "Carla wanders over here once in a while, and I have to take her home."

She took the flowers. "They're beautiful, thank you." She closed the door while looking at them. "Where did you get flowers on a Sunday?"

"I raided a nearby park."

She chuckled as she turned and walked toward the kitchen, talking over her shoulder. "You're a detective. You're not supposed to steal."

"I suppose you're right, but I couldn't help myself."

She laughed, "Would you like a drink?"

"Sure."

"The liquor cabinet is next to the television," she said, disappearing into the kitchen. "Help yourself."

Dan walked toward the cabinet, asking if he could fix her one. She declined, saying she was nursing a glass of white wine. He heard the water running in the kitchen and imagined her putting water in a vase for the flowers while he poured a small amount of bourbon into a short, wide glass. Taking a sip, he headed for the kitchen while his eyes roamed the room of nice but inexpensive furniture. Seeing a picture of Cathy and a good-looking man in uniform, he assumed he was her late husband. He stopped at the kitchen door, leaned against the jamb, and watched her busy over the gas stove. Thinking she looked very nice in her blue skirt and white, short-sleeved blouse, he asked, "What are we having?"

She turned and smiled. "Chicken fried steak, corn on the cob, and a small salad when I get around to it."

Dan sipped his drink and walked into the kitchen. "I make a mean salad."

She smiled. "Everything is in the refrigerator."

Dan put his fork on the edge of his empty plate, sat back, and picked up his cup of coffee.

"Get enough to eat?" Cathy asked while eyeing his empty plate.

Dan took a drink of coffee, said he was full, and then set the cup of fine china onto its saucer. "In fact, I may have overdone it."

She smiled. "Dessert?"

Dan shook his head no. "I'm full thank you."

She stood. "You go on into the living room and watch television while I clean up the dishes."

Dan stood. "I'll help, and then we'll both watch television."

Pleased at that, she smiled.

176

Dan's mind was on the pictures hanging on his garage wall, hearing very little of what was said on the television. He took his arm from around her, sat forward, and looked at his watch. "It's getting late."

She looked at the small, round clock inside a dark wooden sailing ship with silver sails sitting on the television. "I forgot about the time. Tomorrow is Monday, and we both have to get up early."

He took her hand, stood, and then helped her up. Smelling her perfume, he thought about their kiss Friday night, and as he looked into her soft eyes, he gently kissed her.

She let go of his hand and put her arms around him, feeling his arms around her waist, gently pulling her body against his. After a few moments, she pulled away and smiled. "It's late."

Dan smiled and asked where his coat and hat were.

She got them from the hall closet, handed him his coat first, and watched as he put it on, then his light gray fedora.

He smiled, taking the hat. "I enjoyed dinner."

"So did I." she smiled. "You're right. You make a mean salad."

Grinning, he took her hand and led her to the front door, opened it, turned with his back against the screen door, and looked into her soft, brown eyes. "Goodnight."

She reached out with one hand taking the lapel of his suit, stood on her toes, and kissed him. "Goodnight."

A moment of silence filled the doorway while each considered him staying the night, but neither wanted to bring it up, so Dan backed out of the door. "Make sure you're all locked up?"

Cathy leaned against the edge of the door with her cheek and softly said, "I will."

He walked to the fence, opened the gate, and stepped onto the driveway and his waiting car. Dan turned, looked back at the closed door, and thought about going back, but instead got into his car and drove away.

Eighteen

Dan opened his eyes to the sound of the alarm clock sitting on the coffee table, raised a lazy arm from under the blanket, and pushed the button on top of the clock. The morning pallet of pinks and oranges painted the quiet room as he rested his head on the soft pillow. Opening his sleepy eyes, he found the family picture taken before Nancy's death. The clock's continual ticking seemed unusually loud in the morning stillness as he looked from the picture to the window and the early morning.

He thought about last night with Cathy, and while his mind played it over like a ten-cent movie, he regretted coming home. Tossing the blanket back, he put his feet on the floor, buried his face in his hands, and thought of Ruth's naked body lying in the ditch. He thought of Penny and Evelyn crying, then of Penny giving them the money Ruth had been saving. He looked out the picture window at the empty street and thought that prostitutes were no different than anyone else. They just had different occupations. He stood, folded the blanket as he had done every morning for the past two years, picked it and the pillow up, and slid his feet into his leather slippers. He dropped the blanket and pillow on a chair in the foyer to take upstairs later and then walked down the hall to the kitchen to make his coffee.

Dressed in a dark blue three-piece suit with a white shirt and black tie, he picked up the suit from the foot of the bed to drop it off at the cleaners and walked out of the bedroom. Pausing at the top of the stairs, he looked at the closed doors of his children's bedrooms, and while the memory of their laughter filled his head, he walked to Nancy's room. He stood at the door with his hand on the knob for a moment, almost afraid to open the door and look inside. But when he did, the room was the same. The bed was made, her favorite book was still on the nightstand, and her dolls were sitting in a row on the top shelf of the bookcase his dad had built for her. He closed the door and then opened the door to Robert's old room, finding it in much the same condition, filled with things that Robert liked. He felt the same emptiness every time he looked into their rooms, and Dan wondered why he bothered to torture himself.

Closing Roberts's door, he descended the stairs, dropped his clothes on the chair in the foyer, and headed for the kitchen. He drank a cup of coffee and ate a piece of buttered toast while glancing through the morning paper to see if there was any mention of Ruth. Seeing a lengthy article about Howard Trenton but no mention of Ruth, he closed the paper, thinking a prostitute beaten to death and her nude body dumped in a ditch must not be a worthwhile story. He drank the last of his coffee, cleaned up the kitchen, and headed down the hall for his gun he had left on the desk in the living room. Putting it on, he picked up the suit and stepped out onto the porch.

Jack was nowhere in sight when Dan got to his desk, and as he took his coat off and hung it on the back of his chair, he noticed a folded note under his telephone. Wondering if it was from Irene at the switchboard again, he pulled his chair away from his desk and sat down. He unfolded the note, seeing it was from Jack informing him that he had let Curley out of jail, and was taking him back to his place. After that, he was going to nose around a little more to see if anyone had seen Ruth the night she died. Thinking he, too, should be following up on Ruth's death, Dan crumpled the note and tossed it into the trashcan. Seeing two ten by twelve manila folders in his inbox, he picked them up, noting that one was from Todd Anderson and the other from Pete Lange. Deciding to open Lange's first to read the autopsy report on Ruth, opened the envelope from Lange and pulled out a folder. Reading the name 'Ruth Unknown' on the tab, he picked up an ink pen, crossed out Unknown, and wrote Spencer. Then he dumped the eight-by-ten black and white photographs onto his desk and began looking through them.

    The first photo was of a nude Ruth lying on the metal table in Pete Lange's morgue. He stared at the picture for several moments, looking at her bruised and swollen face and her wet hair combed straight back against her head, tucked behind her ears. As he stared at Ruth, the thought occurred to him that they all looked alike in death after Pete finished with them. Their hair wet and combed straight back, their faces void of lipstick and rouge, all looking like they were sleeping except for Ruth, whose face carried the bruises of her attacker. He quickly glanced through all the pictures showing the crude stitches on her chest from Pete Lange's autopsy and bruises on her arms, hands, and back, where her assailant had beaten her unmercifully. Knowing she was a small girl, Dan wondered how strong a fight she had put up and quickly decided it probably wasn't much of one. Setting the photos on his desk, he picked up the typed coroner's report that Pete had painstakingly typed on his big, black, Royal typewriter.

    First Name: Ruth. Last Name: Unknown. Dan crossed that out and wrote in Spencer. *Race: Caucasian. Height: 5'3'. Weight: 110 pounds. Hair: Dark Brown. Eyes: Brown. Cause of death: Multiple fractures to the head.*

    "You son of a bitch," whispered Dan. Then he noticed Pete had circled an entry farther down the page. '*Victim's wrists and ankles bore the marks of being bound. There was no trauma to the vaginal or rectal area suggesting rape. However, small traces of semen were in the pubic*

179

hair, and it appears someone tried to wipe it off, which is not consistent with the other victims. Further note: the body was not washed clean before being dropped at the scene, as were the other victims.' Dan stared at the entry as anger filled him, thinking this was Paul's work. His heart pounded against his chest as he stood and walked in a tight circle next to his desk, reading it again and again, curious as to why Paul would wipe off his semen.

He looked toward the Captain's Office, but seeing it was empty, he sat back down and reread the report. He opened the second manila envelope from Todd Anderson, dumped the black and white pictures of the crime scene onto his desk, and started going through them. He had been so upset at seeing the body that night that he had never noticed its position or similarities to how Paul had left the bodies of the other girls. He quickly glanced through the photos, searching for the army blanket but found none. He looked at the report stating that her clothes were missing, and Todd made no mention of an army blanket. Reaching for the telephone, he picked up the receiver and dialed Todd Anderson's extension.

"This is Todd."

"Todd, this is Dan Morgan. First, I want to apologize for the way I acted the other night."

Todd said he understood.

"Did you find an army blanket under Ruth's body?"

"No," replied Todd. "We didn't. Do you think this prostitute was killed by the same person that killed those teenage girls?"

Dan paused in thought, thinking the other girls were not nude and Ruth was not missing a finger. Not wanting to explain himself, he said, "I'm not sure. Maybe I'm just grasping at straws. Thanks." He hung up the telephone and looked at the report where Lange had circled the part about the semen and knew that Paul had killed Ruth. He got a piece of paper out of his desk and scribbled a quick note telling Jack that he was going to run down a lead and that he would check in later. He shoved everything back into the envelope, shrugged into his coat, and headed for the stairs with the envelope under his left arm.

Dan paced back and forth in front of the university's entrance waiting for Professor Pappel, and while he paced, he wondered when he would get the two packages from Paul that contained Ruth's panties or bra. He turned, hearing his name called, seeing the Professor dressed in his usual brown wrinkled suit walking down the steps. Dan walked to meet him. "Sorry to bother you, professor."

"That's quite alright, Detective." Then he looked worried. "Is everything alright?"

180

Dan glanced around at the many students passing and lowered his voice. "Is there somewhere we can talk?"

Puzzled, Pappel glanced to his left and then to his right. "There's a lonely spot," he said, pointing to a small bench in front of several lilac bushes in full bloom. Reaching the bench, Pappel looked at Dan as they sat down. "How may I help you, Detective." He paused. "You sounded upset on the telephone."

Morgan glanced around and then turned so that he faced the Professor. "When you came to headquarters, you mentioned that these psychopaths change from organized to unorganized and even become both at times."

"Yes, that happens sometimes."

"I agree with what you said earlier that Paul might be. . .how did you put it?"

Pappel looked at him. "Entering into a stage of morphosis?"

"Yes," said Dan. He glanced around and lowered his voice. "I believe he beat a prostitute to death last Thursday night."

The professor looked stunned. "Are you sure?"

Dan spoke in a low voice. "According to the autopsy, this girl was not sexually assaulted, she wasn't washed like the others, and he did not take her little finger." He paused and glanced around, making sure there were no students nearby. "However, the coroner found semen in her pubic hair, and it appeared that he tried to wipe it away."

Pappel looked toward the brick building of the university in thought. "That is interesting. Tell me, was anything of hers missing?"

"All of her clothes. If Paul did do this and he has changed, will he become a different killer?"

"Oh yes," said Pappel. "When he cut those girls, causing them to bleed out slowly, it was the power of the moment he fed on. Sexual gratification came later. The longer it took them to die, the better it made him feel. It's as if he makes the journey with them but does not die, and that is what excites him sexually."

Dan considered that. "You once said that Paul had a beast in him that needed to be fed."

"It's a matter of speech, Detective. The beast is in his psyche."

Understanding that, Dan asked, "Is it possible that his beast is changing?"

Pappel looked into Dan's eyes. "Oh yes, I believe it is Detective, and it is becoming dangerous, very dangerous, indeed. If this Paul of yours is changing to a mixed psychopath, I'm afraid the beast we talked about has developed a larger appetite. Remember, he has been feeding it for years."

While Dan sat in silence digesting what the Professor had told him, Pappel took his pocket watch from his suit coat, looked at it, and then stood. "I'm sorry, Detective, but I have a class in a few minutes."

Dan looked apologetic as they stood. "Of course, I'm sorry, Professor."

Pappel shook his head with a frown. "Oh no, Detective, don't be sorry. I want you to call me at any time of the day or night. I happen to have a class starting in a few minutes." He put one hand on Dan's shoulder. "You have my home number, so don't hesitate to call."

Dan smiled, "I will, and thank you for seeing me on such short notice."

"I must go. Call me any time." The Professor took a few steps, stopped, and turned, looking concerned. "Be careful of this man, Detective. I don't want to alarm you any more than you already are, but now that he's changing, you could be on the beast's menu."

Dan thought about that. "Will this change his personality?"

"If you mean, will he appear different to those around him? The answer is no. Only the beast within has changed, and the only difference is that if he has a wife and family, he will have to make up more excuses to be out of the house."

Dan thought about that while he watched the Professor hurry up the steps to the university's doors, and as the professor disappeared inside, Dan turned and hurried to his car.

Jack looked up while talking on the telephone, gave Dan a nod, then turned away, lowered his voice, and continued his conversation.

Wondering if Jack was talking to Lori, Dan tossed the two manila envelopes of Ruth onto his desk and pulled his Thirty-eight out of its holster. After putting the gun in his desk, he sat down, waiting for Jack to get off the telephone.

Jack hung the telephone up and looked at Dan. "What lead were you following up on?"

Dan picked up the envelope from Pete Lange,took out the coroner's report, and reached across the desk, handing it to Jack.

Jack glanced at it and then looked at Dan with questioning eyes.

Dan pointed to it. "Read the part that Pete circled with his pencil."

Jack's eyes wandered over the paper until he found the circle and began reading. When he finished, he looked up at Dan. "You're shitting me."

Dan was filled with anger and hate. "It was Paul that beat Ruth to death, Jack."

Jack looked confused as he sat back in his chair. "But why? I thought it was young teenage schoolgirls that got him off."

Dan stood from his chair, sat on the edge of Jack's desk, and lowered his voice. "The lead I referred to in my note was talking to Professor Pappel."

Jack glanced around to see if anyone was listening and then leaned closer as he looked up at his partner.

Dan lowered his voice. "I stopped by the University, and Professor Pappel confirmed what I believed when I read that report. That Paul might be changing into that mixed psychopath the professor talked about when he was here. Remember?"

Jack gazed across the room for a minute, and then he looked at Dan. "I remember. There were three types."

"That's right," said Dan. "Organized, disorganized, and mixed, which is a combination of the first two." He looked at Jack's thoughtful expression. "Pappel says the beast's appetite has to be fed in other ways."

"You mean he won't kill the same way that he has in the past?"

"That's right, and it may be more often." Dan paused. "He also said that Paul is a very dangerous person right now." Not wanting to worry his partner, he left out the fact that he could be on the beast's menu, as the professor had put it.

Jack unconsciously reached for his coffee cup and lifted it to his lips, finding it empty. Setting the cup down, he looked at Dan. "You gonna tell Foley?"

Dan nodded. "As soon as he comes back."

Jack looked at the clock above the stairs leading down to the first floor. "It's almost three-thirty."

Dan considered that, stood, grabbed his coat, and the two manila envelopes of Ruth. "Let's get a drink."

Micky's was not very crowded, so Jack picked a table in the back, and after their drinks were delivered, he asked, "I wonder why Paul hasn't delivered the presents."

Dan thought about the bum floating in Cherry Creek. "Maybe he's having a hard time finding someone to deliver them."

Jack grinned, knowing what Dan meant. "What did you do on Sunday? I tried calling, but there was no answer."

Debating whether he should say anything, he took a drink of bourbon. "I had dinner with Cathy Holman Sunday."

Jack looked surprised, and then he smiled, looking happy for his friend. "That's great. Where did you take her?"

Dan took a sip of bourbon. "She fixed dinner at her place."

Jack quietly sang, "Oh, Danny Boy," and then he smiled. "Best be careful of this one."

Dan grinned, then he took a drink, thinking Jack was the same Jack he knew back in high school and that he would never change.

Knowing he had embarrassed his friend, Jack said, "Mrs. Holman seems like a nice lady."

Dan nodded as he stared at his drink and thought about their kiss as he left Sunday evening. "Yeah, she is."

Hoping for some success in their relationship, Jack smiled. "I don't know what you're expecting or want out of this relationship, but whatever it is, I hope it works out."

Dan smiled, thinking he didn't know what he wanted just yet but knew Jack meant well.

Nineteen

Dan walked into the office in a bad mood on Tuesday morning, said hello to Jack, picked up his cup, and headed for the kitchen to fill it with coffee.

"Pretty bad stuff," warned Jack.

When Dan returned, he set the coffee on his desk, took off his suit coat, draped it over the back of his chair, sat down, and took a drink of the strong, bitter coffee. Making a face, he said, "Holy shit!"

Jack grinned, and then he opened his desk drawer, pulled out a white sack from Grandma's Donuts, and tossed it onto Dan's desk. "Those should help."

Dan opened the sack finding two glazed donuts, took one out, tore it in half, and dunked it into his coffee as he looked at Jack. "Did you say anything to Foley about Ruth?"

Jack shook his head. "No, I thought you should tell him."

Dan finished his donut, opened the envelope from Lange, took out the autopsy report, and stood. "Let's go see Foley."

They walked to the captain's office, where Dan tapped on the window of the closed door and waited.

Foley looked up from what he was reading and motioned for the two to come in. He glanced from Jack to Dan. "What's on your mind?"

"I'd like you to read this, Captain." Dan handed him the autopsy report. "Read what Pete circled."

Foley started reading, and when he finished, he looked at Dan. "Don't tell me you think this is Paul's handy work?"

Dan nodded. "That's exactly what I was thinking, Captain."

"So do I," said Jack in support of his partner.

Captain Foley looked from one face to the other, gestured to the three chairs, and told them to have a seat.

Dan told Foley about his meeting with Professor Pappel and the professor's warning that Paul may be changing into a mixed psychopath with a bigger appetite.

Worry filled the captain's face as he sat back, staring at the autopsy report. "This changes things." He looked at Dan. "Then the guy you wanted to beat up had nothing to do with her death?"

Looking sheepish, Dan shook his head. "No, Captain, he didn't."

Foley gave Dan a knowing stare. "Alright, move Ruth's case into the Paul column with the other girls. I know it's early, but have you run across anything while looking into her death that may help us with the others?"

Dan shook his head. "We've questioned her two closest friends and a few other girls that work the street, but Jack and I both came up empty, same as before." Dan leaned forward in his chair. "He's like a ghost, Captain. No one sees him. Those two girls that found the body behind the Paramount are the closest anyone has come, and that was by accident."

Foley didn't look happy. "Sooner or later, he'll slip up. Until then, keep digging."

Dan shifted nervously in his chair. "One of Ruth's friends gave me three hundred dollars Ruth had been saving and some letters from Ruth's mother. If it's alright, I'd like to write to her mother and send her the money."

Captain Foley quickly considered that. "Go ahead, but remember, you're writing to a mother that lost her daughter. I'm sure she didn't know Ruth's profession, so be careful."

"Yes, Captain."

A woman knocked on the captain's door, and after he motioned her in, she walked to his desk and handed him a large manila envelope. "Dr. Lang sent this over."

"Thank you," said Foley as he took the envelope and set it on his desk. After she left and closed the door, he opened the envelope, pulled out what was inside, and looked at Dan. "The coroner's report on Howard Trenton from Lange." He picked up the report, put on his reading glasses, and started reading. "Cause of death was from exsanguination from the cut on his throat." He looked at Dan and Jack. "That's no surprise. Lange thinks the weapon may be a large hunting knife, and the killer was probably right-handed, standing about five feet ten."

Dan leaned forward in his chair. "What is Lange's estimate on time of death?"

Then Captain Foley looked at the paper. "Time of death was between one and three a.m. Thursday morning. Why?"

"Just curious," answered Dan while thinking of how Trenton was tortured before he died.

Foley continued. "Lange counted twenty-seven burns on his back and stomach." He looked at Dan and then Jack. "There were fifteen small cuts on the penis and scrotum." He paused to take off his glasses and tossed them on his desk as he set the report down. "Semen was also found in Howard Trenton's rectum."

Dan looked at Jack and then Foley. "He was raped?"

Foley gestured to the report up. "That's what it says. According to Lange, whoever raped Trenton also shoved a piece of pipe up his ass."

"Damn," said Jack. "How does Lange know it was a pipe?"

Foley looked at Jack. "There was severe trauma to the area, and Todd's men in forensics found a bloody pipe at the scene. Lange matched the blood type to Trenton."

"Any prints on the pipe?" asked Dan hopefully.

Foley shook his head. "No." Then he picked up Todd Anderson's report. "They found Howard Trenton's clothing piled in the corner of the garage, along with his wallet, keys, and some cash." He looked at them. "We can rule out a robbery." Foley looked down again at the report. "They dusted the garage, the car, and the house, and they only found one set of prints. My guess is they will be Trenton's." Foley shoved everything in his desk, locked it, and then got up from his desk and shrugged into his suit coat.

Dan and Jack stood while Foley walked around his desk toward the door. "I know you two are doing all you can, but you need to do more somehow. Go back to the crime scene and ask all the neighbors again if they saw anything. Maybe you'll get lucky. Now, if you'll excuse me, there's someplace I have to be."

Dan looked at Foley. "Would you mind if Jack and I had a look at the files, Captain?"

Foley returned to his desk, unlocked the drawer, gathered up all the files, and handed them to Dan. "You're getting quite a collection of these." He paused as he looked at Dan. "Have you seen this morning's paper?"

Dan shook his head. "No, Captain, I haven't."

Captain Foley looked unhappy. "Get a copy and read about what a poor job we're doing."

Dan went downstairs and got a copy of the Tuesday morning newspaper and took it up to his desk so he and Jack could read it. The paper was having a field day over the murder of Howard Trenton, questioning the Denver Police Department's ability to solve the case after five days. It appeared to Dan that the murder of Howard Trenton overshadowed the murders of the teenage girls, the same as it had Ruth's murder. Dan tossed the newspaper into the trash can, and then he and Jack left to canvas Howard Trenton's entire neighborhood. But after interviewing people on the block where Howard Trenton had lived and those across the alley as well as the houses around Jefferson Park, it all proved completely unproductive.

Dan spent the last hour at work Tuesday afternoon on the telephone locating Mrs. Gloria Spencer, Ruth's mother, to tell her the sad news about her daughter without telling her the truth about how she died or what Ruth Spencer did for a living. Once the initial shock and tears were over, Dan told her about the money, saying it would help pay to have the

187

body returned to Wichita for burial. Mrs. Spencer thought about that for a moment and then told him that she knew what her daughter did for a living and that it might be best if the money was used to pay for her burial in Denver, explaining that she was a widow with limited funds. Understanding how she felt, Dan said that he would take care of the arrangements and let her know where her daughter had been buried. She thanked him, and after she hung up the telephone, he called the mortuary that had handled Norma's funeral. Then he called Pete Lange, telling him not to release Ruth's body to the county cemetery for the indigent.

The next few days were without incident, and no bodies of teenage girls turned up. Dan wondered whether Paul had disappeared as Pappel said he could or, perhaps, Paul was in a cooling down period after Ruth Spencer.

Friday afternoon found Dan and Jack at their desks, going over both the Trenton crime scene photographs and those taken in the city morgue by Lange.

Jack looked up from the picture he was holding. "Isn't that Professor Pappel?"

Dan looked up just as the professor and Captain Foley were shaking hands outside the captain's office. "Yeah, it is."

Moments later, Dan's phone rang.

"Morgan."

"This is Foley. Grab your partner and come in."

Dan hung up the telephone and picked up the two folders on Howard Trenton. "Foley wants to see us."

As they walked into the captain's office, Foley gestured to the professor. "You two remember Professor Pappel."

The three men shook hands, said hello, and then sat down while Foley called the operator, telling her to hold all calls. Then he leaned forward, resting his forearms on the top of his desk, and looked at the Professor. "I don't know how much you know about the death of Howard Trenton, but I would like your opinion on a few things."

"Of course." George Pappel frowned, looking regretful. "Too bad about Mr. Trenton. I liked his column. A little controversial at times but interesting reading just the same."

Foley stood with a surprised expression as he looked through the glass walls of his office. "What the hell are the mayor and chief doing here?"

Dan, Jack, and Professor Pappel stood as the Chief of Police opened the office door, stepped in, and looked at Foley. "We need to have a little talk, Harold."

Captain Foley watched as the mayor and several men in suits walked in behind the chief, crowding the office.

188

Chief James Roberts was a good-looking man in his early sixties, a little on the heavy side, standing six feet, and his head of once thick black hair was now pure white. Seeing his friend Professor Pappel, he smiled. "Hello, George," and then he introduced him to the mayor. After they shook hands, Chief Roberts asked Pappel, "What brings you down to headquarters?"

Pappel glanced at Foley. "I only just arrived. We hadn't got into what Captain Foley had asked me here for."

"Well, I hate to interrupt your meeting," said the Chief. "But we'd like to talk to Captain Foley privately if you don't mind."

Professor Pappel smiled. "Of course." He turned to Foley, said good afternoon, nodded at Dan and Jack, and then looked at Chief Roberts. "Hope to see you soon, James."

Chief Roberts smiled. "Tell the misses I said hello."

"I will," replied Pappel. "And the same to your wife." Then he walked out of the captain's office toward the stairs.

Chief Roberts looked at Dan and Jack. "If you'll excuse us, gentleman."

Dan and Jack walked out of the office, and before Jack could comment, Dan hurried toward the stairs, catching up with the professor on the steps outside the building. "Professor."

George turned and, seeing it was Dan, waited.

"I need to ask you a couple of questions if you have the time, Professor."

Pappel nodded. "Of course."

Dan glanced around as he gestured to a cement bench next to the building. "Let's sit down for a moment."

After they sat down, Dan again glanced around before looking at Pappel. "I'd like you to look at some pictures I have of Howard Trenton's body, and maybe you can tell me something about the killer."

"Glad to help, Detective, if I can."

"I hope I can count on your discretion by not letting this go any further."

Pappel nodded, looking puzzled. "Of course."

Dan glanced around again and lowered his voice. "The captain thinks Trenton may have been tortured over certain information he may have had about someone." Dan opened the folder from Pete Lange and gave the graphic photographs to Pappel. "As you can see, Professor, this Howard Trenton was severely tortured."

The Professor took his time examining every photograph of Trenton, and when he finished, he looked worried as he handed them back to Dan. "This is terrible. Whoever did this was filled with rage." Then he asked to see the coroner's report.

Dan pulled it out of the folder and handed it to him.

The Professor read the report carefully. "I'm not a policeman, and undoubtedly I am looking at this crime purely from a psychological point of view, but I don't believe Mr. Trenton was tortured for the reasons your captain believes." He handed the report back to Dan.

Dan took it and placed it back inside the envelope. "Why not?"

"What I am about to say is purely an opinion, you understand, Detective? Without talking to the man who did this, an opinion is all I can give."

"I understand," said Dan.

"The burns on the body were pure enjoyment and, more than likely, the first of what was to follow. The cuts on the penis and scrotum, I am sure, were sexual and followed by fulfillment in self-gratification. The semen in the rectum is also sexual gratification."

"And the use of the pipe?"

"Simply a means of degrading the victim." He paused. "There is so much rage in the photos. I believe the man that did this was very angry and filled with rage and hate toward Mr. Trenton. And like some rapists who blame their victims for their desires, he blamed Mr. Trenton." He paused in thought. "As I said, this is purely an opinion."

Dan considered that as he looked across the parking lot and then at the Professor. "Are we dealing with another Paul?"

Professor Pappel frowned as he considered the question. "It's unusual to have two psychopaths operating in the same city at the same time, both leaving their victims where they can be found and examined."

Dan stared into Pappel's brown eyes. "Could Paul have done this?"

The Professor shrugged. "It's a strong possibility. We only have to ask ourselves why he would do it."

Dan looked at the parking lot and then at Pappel. "That's the question, alright, Professor. Now all I need to do is find the answer."

Pappel stood and looked at Dan for a long moment. "If this is Paul's work, Mr. Trenton may have angered Paul over his columns in the newspaper."

Dan stood while recalling Paul, asking if it had been he who called him a vampire. He shook Pappel's hand. "Thank you, Professor."

Detective Morgan walked upstairs, noticing the unusually quiet office, and could hear the muffled voices that were loud at times coming from behind the captain's door. Reaching his desk, he put Howard Trenton's folder down and looked toward the closed blinds of the captain's office. "They still at it?"

Jack looked toward the office, nodded, and then looked at Dan. "Where have you been?"

Dan started to tell Jack about his conversation with the professor when the captain's door opened, and the mayor, the chief, and the others walked out. They watched as the solemn parade walked across the room, disappearing up the stairs to the chief's office.

Foley stepped out of his office, looking angry while motioning for Dan and Jack, and when they walked into his office said, "Have a seat."

Dan closed the door, and then he and Jack sat down and waited.

Foley angrily shoved the papers off his desk. "Assholes."

Surprised by the sudden outburst, Dan and Jack slid off their chairs and began picking up the papers.

"Leave it," said Foley irritably.

Leaving the papers strewn over the floor, they returned to their chairs and waited while the captain walked to the side of his desk and sat on its edge. Looking regretful, he apologized for his actions. "The mayor is going to put a special task force together to investigate the Howard Trenton murder and those young girls."

Dan glanced at Jack and then looked at Foley. "Who will head up the task force?"

"One of the mayor's private investigators."

"Why?" asked Dan.

"Because he's the damn Mayor," said Foley angrily.

"Shit, Captain," said Dan. "We've been working hard on these cases." He looked at Jack and then back to the captain. "Paul doesn't leave any evidence lying around, and the mayor's men won't find any unless they manufacture it."

"I can't disagree with that," said Captain Foley. "But next year is an election year, and he doesn't want this Trenton murder biting him in the ass at the polls next November."

"That's bullshit," said Jack angrily.

Dan agreed. "If this is about Howard Trenton, he was just killed last Thursday."

The captain looked regretful. "There's nothing I can do about it. They'll be taking over Monday morning."

Dan Morgan shook his head, looking disappointed. "It always comes down to politics."

Captain Foley raised his brow and shrugged. "It usually does. You can keep working on that prostitute friend of yours."

Dan looked at him. "The whore's not worth their time?"

Foley looked at him and raised his voice. "I never said that."

"I know you didn't, Captain," said Dan. "While you were talking to the mayor and the chief, I was outside talking to Professor Pappel about the Trenton Case." While Jack and Captain Foley listened, Dan told them about the conversation he had just finished with the professor.

Foley returned to his chair and sat back, looking concerned. "Two psychopaths?"

Dan wasn't so sure. "I think it was Paul, and while the professor didn't say as much, I believe he thinks it a strong possibility."

Foley looked at Dan. "But why would Paul kill Howard Trenton?"

"Well," began Dan. "It could be the vampire shit Trenton put in the paper." He paused. "I think referring to the killer as a vampire pissed Paul off."

Captain Foley sat forward in his chair. "I need to pass that on to the chief. Write something up on that and give it to me."

Jack looked angry. "Why tell them? Let the bastards do their own work."

Foley looked at Jack. "I'll not put myself in that position, Detective. I'll not cross the mayor or the chief and lose my pension."

"So that's it?" asked Jack. "We just hand everything over to this task force created by the mayor?"

Foley gave Jack an angry look. "That's it, Detective. Learn to live with it the same as I have to."

Dan looked at the captain. "What about the warning Professor Pappel gave about changing detectives?"

Foley stood and began picking up the papers he had earlier pushed off the desk. "I tried that argument, but it got me nowhere." He paused. "Guess we'll see if the professor was right about that."

Dan and Jack knelt from their chairs and began helping. Dan handed what he picked up from the floor to the captain. "The suits who were with the mayor, were they the private investigators?"

Foley took the papers. "They'll come for the files on Monday."

"They're in my garage."

Foley took the papers from Jack and gave Dan a curious look.

Dan shrugged. "I have them pinned to the wall of my garage, so I can study all of the pictures at the same time." He paused. "There's something about them that bothers me."

The captain thought about that. "Well, bring them in Monday morning. But remember, both of you are off of everything but this Ruth Spencer case. I'll tell the chief about the Trenton thing on Monday. I don't think he was very happy about this either." Foley put the papers in a

192

pile on his desk, grabbed his suit coat, and shrugged into it. "It's late, and I'm going home to pour myself a stiff drink before dinner."

Dan felt betrayed and angry. "What do I tell Paul the next time he calls?"

Foley considered a moment. "Just play along. We don't want your friend to do anything rash."

Dan was sure Paul wasn't going to be happy about this and feared he might take another young girl. As he and Jack followed Foley out of his office, the captain headed for the stairs while he and Jack walked in silence to their desks.

Dan was sitting at his desk, gazing at the pencil he held in his right hand while tapping the top of his desk with the eraser.

Jack started straightening up his desk, getting ready to go home, when he looked at his partner. "You can still work on Ruth's case. That's still going after Paul. Maybe we'll beat the bastards to him."

Dan nodded in silence, watching the eraser of the pencil bounce as he continued to tap it on the top of his desk.

Jack stared at his partner for several moments, then asked, "What are your plans for the weekend?"

Dan shrugged and dropped the pencil. "I have some things to do around the house."

"Like what?"

"My housekeeper's in Brooklyn for another week." Dan leaned back in his chair. "The place is a mess, and I don't want her coming back with it looking the way it does."

"Unless you've been throwing a lot of parties I haven't been invited to, how messy can that house get?"

Dan smiled. "I'm a pretty messy person. Besides, the lawn needs mowing."

Jack got his gun from his desk drawer, put it on, and slipped into his suit coat. "If you get bored, call. Better yet just come over." Adjusting his coat as he looked at Dan, he knew he was taking this hard. "Get your mind off this crap, Dan, and call Cathy. Take her out to dinner or a movie tonight and forget about this place and that asshole, Paul. We'll both get on Ruth's case on Monday."

Dan looked at him. "You know what pisses me off? They didn't want Ruthie's case because she's a prostitute."

"So, what," said Jack. "That's in our favor. If Paul did kill Ruth as we suspect, maybe we can make the arrest before they do."

Dan considered that for a moment as a small smile crossed his face. Maybe." But he wanted to solve all the murders, not just Ruth's. He watched Jack disappear down the stairs, envious that he had someone waiting at home for him. As he turned back to his desk, the telephone rang. "Detective Morgan."

"Good afternoon, Dan."

Dan considered not turning on the recorder but reached across his desk and turned it on anyway. "It's late, Paul, and I want to go home. What can I do for you?"

"You can tell me how your investigation is going?"

"You know I can't talk about that." Thinking about having to give it up on Monday, Dan said, "But I will say it's going."

"Well, that doesn't sound too promising."

Dan sat back in his chair. "I've been thinking about the packages, and I'd like to talk about the first package you called about."

"Okay," replied Paul curiously.

"The package was Sally Crowder, wasn't it?"

Paul smiled. "Good for you. I was beginning to think you weren't going to figure that one out."

"The next package was Diane Wagner's panties. You threw me a bit with that one."

Paul laughed softly. "I thought it might."

"The next package was Marie Phillips, the girl you left behind the Paramount Theater." He sat up in his chair. "The next two were Howard Trenton and the prostitute, Ruthie."

The phone was silent for several moments.

Dan sat forward in his chair with his elbows on the desk. "I know you killed them both. Trenton, I get, but I don't understand why the prostitute."

"I'm very proud of you, Dan. There's hope for you becoming a real good detective one day."

Still wanting to understand about Ruthie, he asked again, "Why the prostitute?"

"The trace on your telephone will find me within a few minutes, Dan. I don't want to talk about my killing the prostitute or that queer, Howard Trenton."

Dan realized Paul had just confessed. "Was it because he called you a vampire?"

Paul laughed. "Dan, you are such a prize. You're wasting precious time with such questions."

Knowing he only had but a few moments, Dan said, "Okay, let's talk about you and me."

"What about you and me?"

Dan wanted to get to the heart of their relationship. "You're calling me for a reason, and I believe it's because we've met."

The phone was silent, then Paul said, "Think about the pictures, Detective. Think about the pictures."

Dan heard the click, followed by the dial tone. "Damn it." He hung up the telephone and turned off the recorder, knowing the wiretap didn't have enough time to complete its task. He sat back, staring at the telephone, thinking about the pictures, and wondered if Paul was leaving clues at the crime scenes that may be in the photographs. Looking at his watch and seeing it was just five, he wondered if Cathy was still at work, picked up the telephone, and dialed her work number. The telephone rang several times before she answered.

"Sheriff Brumwell's Office."

"Cathy, this is Dan Morgan. I was afraid I had missed you."

"I was out the door and had to unlock it to get back in. That's what took me so long to answer the telephone."

He smiled. "This is short notice, but I was wondering if you would like to go out to dinner tonight."

"I'm sorry," she said. "But I'm having dinner at my aunt and uncle tonight. But I'm free tomorrow night."

He smiled. "Tomorrow would work. Why don't I give you a call sometime after lunch?"

"Let me call you. I have a hair appointment at ten thirty, and I'm not sure when I'll get home."

Dan said goodbye and hung up the telephone. Staring at the black telephone, he didn't want to be alone tonight and wished she wasn't busy. Wondering what he was going to do the rest of the evening, he stood from his desk, got out his pistol from his desk drawer, and thought about stopping to get something to eat as he shoved it into its holster on his belt. Staring down at the manila envelope of Howard Trenton, he picked it up, grabbed his coat, and headed across the empty office for the stairs, feeling extremely lonely.

Twenty

Dan Morgan sat on the stool in his garage, eating the last of the sandwich he had brought home from the deli. He was looking at the pictures while thinking of Paul's last words and wondering what he had meant by '***Think about the pictures.***' He had thought about them and looked at them every day and night, trying to figure out what it was that bothered him. Now he was sure that Paul was leaving clues just for him at each of the crime scenes, thinking that he was the only person who could see them. Frustration and anger filled him as he walked along the wall, searching for what it was Paul wanted him to see. Taking a drink of beer, he walked the entire length of the garage wall as he studied each photo.

Another hour passed, and feeling tired, he looked at his watch, seeing it was after eight, and decided to get Paul and these pictures out of his mind by watching a little television. He picked up the three empty beer bottles, fixed the door so it would lock when he closed it and turned out the fluorescent lights. Closing the door, he pushed against it to make sure it was locked, and then he walked across the dark yard through the sound of crickets toward the lights in the kitchen window. Once inside, he put the empty bottles with the others and then went into the living room. Sitting down, he rummaged through the newspaper for the television guide and, finding it, saw that he had a choice of a local television talk show, Truth or Consequences, or Your Hit Parade. Thinking music would help get his mind off Paul and the pictures, he chose the latter. Turning the television on, he kicked off his shoes, sat down with his feet resting on the coffee table, and waited for the commercials to end so that the host could announce the number seven song of the week.

He looked from the television to the black telephone sitting on the desk, knowing that Cathy was just at the other end of it, got up, turned down the volume, and walked to the desk. Pulling the chair away, he sat down, picked up the telephone, and dialed her number.

"Hello,"

"This is Dan."

Sensing something in his voice, she asked, "Are you okay?"

"I'm just tired, is all. It's been a long day. I'm not interrupting anything, am I?"

"No, I was just watching a little television."

"Me too."

"What were you watching?" she asked.

"The Hit Parade."

"Me too," she said. "That's one of my favorites."

"How was dinner?" He could hear the song playing on the show over her telephone and noticed the words over the telephone and the picture on his television were out of sync.

"It was good. My aunt, Connie Brumwell, is the kind of cook I wish I were. She never cooks anything bad." She paused. "I love this song."

Dan turned from the television to the darkness outside the window. "I bet you're a good cook."

"Not really. It's difficult cooking for one." She paused. "But I guess you'd know all about that."

He chuckled. "Yeah, I think I do. I eat a lot over the sink staring out the kitchen window watching Mr. Squirrel or Mr. Cat from across the alley."

She laughed softly. "Sounds exciting."

"You have no idea."

They talked a while longer, and then he said, "Well, it's late, so I'll let you get back to your program."

Not wanting to hang up yet, she asked, "What are your plans for us tomorrow night?"

"I thought dinner and a movie sounded good."

"That sounds nice," she said. "If you don't have any place in mind for dinner, I know a nice little restaurant called Joey's, with white tablecloths and dim lighting downtown."

"That sounds interesting. Where is it?"

"On 18th Street. I'll call you when I get home from my hair appointment."

"Any preference in a movie?"

She paused. "Since I chose the restaurant, you pick the movie. Anything is fine with me."

"Alright, I'll see what's on."

"Goodnight, Dan."

"Goodnight." Dan waited for the click, followed by the dial tone, before hanging up, then turned up the television volume and returned to the sofa, trying not to think about the mayor and Paul. Then as his mind returned to the pictures on the wall in the garage of the girls and crime scenes, he glanced at his watch, seeing it was just after nine. Suddenly he stood, turned the television off, retrieved his pistol from the top of the desk, grabbed his wallet and badge, and walked to the hall closet. Finding a lightweight, dark-colored jacket, he picked up his keys from the glass bowl on the foyer table and walked out the front door.

Dan drove south on Colorado Boulevard to Hamden Avenue, where he turned right and headed west toward Englewood. The two-lane paved road was empty as he followed the headlights of his car. Filled with the mysteries contained in the photos, he drove past the golf course hidden in the darkness, then past the tall, steel radio towers with their blinking red lights. He continued west for several minutes down the long sloping hill of streetlamps until he approached the alley between Lincoln Street and South Broadway in downtown Englewood. Slowing, he turned right into the alley and followed his car's headlights up the dark alley until he reached the rear of the Pioneer Theater. Stopping, he looked at the trash cans where Gail Thomas's body had been found and then drove to one side of the alley and parked.

Turning off the engine and then the headlights, he sat back in his seat in the dark, listening to the muffled voices and music coming from inside the theater. Knowing the dark alley would not give up her secrets he studied the fifty-gallon barrels used as trashcans, bathed in the dim light from the fixtures placed above the two exit doors of the Pioneer Theater. Reaching over to the passenger seat, he picked up his holstered pistol, slipped it on, and climbed out of the car. He closed the door as he glanced up and down the alley and the islands of light created by the light fixtures. Then his tired eyes settled on the seven fifty-gallon barrels once again, and he thought of Gail Thomas's body lying between them in the photos tacked to the wall of his garage. Turning, he looked at the dark, red brick at the rear of the theater. The two rear exit doors and the words Pioneer Theater, painted in big, black letters, were barely visible in the dim light.

Looking back down the alley toward Hamden, he stepped away from the car and started walking until he reached the end of the alley. Turning, he stood on the sidewalk, looking back up the dark alley with its islands of light, and softly said aloud, "No one could have seen you placing Gail in the alley." The stillness was broken by the hum of a streetcar as it rounded the corner from Broadway onto Hamden, then rattled along the tracks behind him until it turned into the Loop across Hamden. As it disappeared into the Loop with its bell loudly announcing its arrival, Dan lit a cigarette, tossed the match onto the sidewalk, and started walking back up the alley. He had walked but a short distance when a car pulled up behind him, flooding the alley in bright light. Dan half turned, exposing the left side of his body, raising his left hand in front of his face to shield his eyes from the spotlight that suddenly lit up the darkness. Tossing his cigarette down, his right hand found the butt of his Thirty-eight Special hidden from the lights by his body and dark jacket.

"You have business in the alley, Mister?" asked a voice.

Figuring the voice belonged to a police officer, Dan quickly identified himself as a Denver police detective.

The spotlight went out, and then the headlights, returning darkness to the alley but for the car's parking lights. "The chief said you guys might be nosing around. Have anything like a badge on you?"

Dan pulled his badge out of the back pocket of his Levi's and held it up.

The officer approached, looked at the badge, and then grinned while extending his hand. "I'm Officer Russ Cook."

Dan shook his hand. "You startled me the way you drove up."

"I believe that's the point." Officer Cook glanced up the alley, wondering what he was doing in the alley. "I was first on the scene that night."

Dan thought that was a break. "Would you mind walking with me back up the alley and telling me what you saw that night?"

The officer thought about that for a moment and then gestured toward the patrol car. "Hope in. We'll drive up."

Officer Cook was in his mid-twenties and had been a police officer for two years. He was nice looking, standing five feet ninewith brown hair,brown eyes, and a clean-shaven face. He drove up the alley, stopping behind Dan's Ford, turned off the headlights, leaving the parking lights on, covering everything in a soft amber color. He opened his door and stepped out while Dan climbed out of the passenger side.

Standing in front of the patrol car, Russ Cook gestured at the barrels. "That's the spot." Then he said, "I heard the chief gave you pictures of the crime scene, and I'm a little curious about what you think you might find here in the dark."

Dan smiled. "I'm not sure of that myself. I just wanted to see the place in the dark as the killer did."

"Trying to get into his head?" asked Cook.

Dan smiled again. "Something like that." Then he looked at Officer Cook. "Would you mind going over that night from when you first heard the call?"

Dan listened while Officer Cook related his approaching the scene from the other end of the alley. "Mr. Tindle was standing at the back door of the theater. He looked scared as hell and just stood there while I got out of my car with my flashlight, knelt next to the body, and checked for a pulse."

"What time was that?"

"It was ten after eleven. I happened to look at my watch as I got out of the car."

Dan filed that in his memory. "How far away were you when you got the call?"

"A few blocks. It took me about a minute to arrive on the scene."

Dan considered that, thinking the janitor had probably called it in just after eleven. "Have to ask this, and I don't mean any disrespect, but did you touch anything?"

Officer Cook shook his head. "No offense taken, Detective, and no, I never touched anything but the girl's neck for a pulse." Russ recounted his questioning of Ira Tindle and how he hadn't found out anything other than it was Ira that found the body. "Soon after I got here, the place was crawling. Every cop in Englewood showed up, including Chief Travis." He gestured around. "We checked everything we could find." He pointed to the lot behind the fence. "Including that parking lot."

Dan looked around, imagining the scene. "How many men were here that night?"

Cook thought a moment and then chuckled. "Just about every cop, on and off duty. A couple of dozen, I suspect."

Dan thought that was a hell of a lot of people in such a small space, and if there had been any evidence, they might have trampled it. "I'd like to poke around a little more if that'd be alright with the Englewood Police Department."

"I see no harm in that. Poke all you want, Detective." Officer Cook walked toward his car, talking over his shoulder. "Have a good evening, Detective." He climbed into his patrol car, started the engine, and waved as he drove past Dan, then disappeared around the corner at the far end of the alley.

Walking to the gateless opening in the fence, Dan stepped into the dark parking lot and made his way to Lincoln Street's sidewalk. The only car in the parking lot was a dark 1946 Ford Sedan parked next to the sidewalk. He stood next to the car while looking back toward the alley and the back of the theater, thinking it was too dark to see anyone from this viewpoint. The dim bulbs above the two exit doors of the theater gave little light.

Turning, he glanced across the street at a spattering of lighted windows of small houses, knowing it would be difficult, if not impossible, to see anyone in the lot or alley. He knew Paul could have carried the body through the empty lot without being seen. Driving a car down the alley would have been too dangerous, as it proved to be behind the Paramount Theater. He walked back to the opening, and as he stepped into the alley and looked at the fifty-five-gallon trash barrels, his memory remembered

200

the pictures of the body lying between them. He walked to his car, got in, and drove out of the alley and around the block to Broadway. He parked with the front wheels against the curb just a few yards from the entrance to the theater. Ne shut the engine off, turned off the headlights, and reached into the inside pocket of his jacket. Taking out his pad and stubby pencil, he wrote down everything Officer Russ Cook had told him, then closed the notepad, and put it and the pencil back into his pocket.

Getting out of the car, he closed the door glancing up and down a well-lit Broadway in downtown Englewood. The small downtown consisted of two city blocks of stores now closed, but with all their picture windows lit up showing off various items. The theater, two bars, and two drugstores, one in the middle of the block across the street and the other at the north end of the street on the corner, were the only businesses open. The street was empty except for five cars parked with their front tires against the curb, two on this side of the street and three on the other. A man and woman out for an evening stroll were the only people walking along the lighted sidewalk, stopping to look in the window of a dress shop across the street. A group of young boys walked out of the drug store across the street and stood under the marquis, laughing, talking loudly, and having a good time.

He turned, stepped onto the sidewalk, and walked toward the theater, thinking it looked out of place in a modern world with its walls of logs, looking more like an old frontier building than a movie house in 1951. Above the marquis of big red letters spelling out what was playing was a large painting of a covered wagon pulled by oxen. A small white sign in the empty cashier's window read, "Tickets Available at Concession." The red doors he walked toward were propped open, taking advantage of the cool evening air.

The familiar hum of a streetcar sounded as it passed on its way to the loop while he stepped through the open doorway into the small lobby. A young, dark-haired girl with big, brown eyes leaned on the small refreshment counter with an open copy of 'Hollywood' magazine. Setting the magazine aside, she stood from the stool she had been sitting on and smiled. "Good evening. Would you like a ticket for the movie?"

Dan glanced around the lobby as muffled sounds of the movie escaped through the closed, black curtains covering the entrance into the theater, one on either side of the small refreshment stand. He walked to the counter. "No, thank you. Is the manager in?"

The girl looked concerned. "No, sir, Mr. Watkins went home early tonight."

"I see," said Dan looking disappointed. "Is there an assistant I can speak with?"

201

She shrugged thoughtfully. "Mr. Watkins doesn't have an assistant."

Dan smiled. "Well, I guess you'll do." He showed her his badge. "What's your name?"

She looked worried but managed a small smile. "Mary Ann Jefferies."

"Mary, is Ira Tindle around?"

She hesitated, unsure if she should tell him, but then said that he was probably upstairs cleaning the manager's office.

Dan glanced around and then pointed to an open doorway and narrow staircase to his right. "Up there?"

"Is Mr. Tindle in trouble?"

Dan smiled, trying not to worry her. "No, I just want to ask him a few questions about the night he found the girl in the alley."

Two teenage boys pushed their way through the black curtains of the auditorium, laughing at something one of them had said. Then, while one went into the bathroom, the other approached the concession counter. Mary glanced at him, and then she looked at Dan with a worried look.

Dan motioned to the young man. "Go ahead and take care of your customer Mary."

The teenage boy gave Dan a curious look, then asked for a bag of buttered popcorn and a coke. Dan watched Mary as she went about the task of scooping up the hot popcorn from under the popcorn caldron and filling a white and red striped paper bag. She handed the bag of popcorn to the young man, who occasionally glanced at Dan, and then she filled a paper cup with coke then took the boy's money. As Mary gave the boy his change, his friend walked out of the bathroom and waited by the covered entrance. The boy with the coke and popcorn who had given Dan the once-over asked Mary if she was alright.

She smiled and said she was as the two boys gave Dan a final look before they disappeared through the curtain into the auditorium.

Dan smiled. "You know those two?"

She smiled, "They're in a couple of my classes at school."

"It's nice that they sort of watch over you."

Her smile turned into a small frown. "Dale's always asking me out, but I won't go."

"Why not?" asked Dan.

She shrugged, "I like someone else."

"I see," said Dan, thinking things in the teenage world hadn't changed all that much.

Sadness suddenly filled her pretty face. "My mom won't let me walk home when I get off work anymore. She makes my older brother come and get me when I work late."

"Sounds like you have careful, caring parents. Did you know Gail Thomas?"

Mary nodded. "We had a couple of classes together, and sometimes we would walk home from school together."

"What kind of a girl was she?"

"Oh, she was really nice and friendly." Then quickly added, "And really smart too."

Dan wondered if she might have been too friendly to strangers. "Do you remember the last time you saw her?"

Mary thought a moment. "I think it was Friday night at the Gothic. That's a movie theater up Broadway. Most kids go there because they have the latest movies, and afterward to the Buy 4 Less Drug Store across the street or Meyers Drug in the next block for a coke. I think I saw her at Meyers after."

"Who was she with?"

Shed shrugged, "A group of eleventh-grade girls."

"Did you see who she left with?"

Mary shook her head. "No."

Dan thanked her, told her to be careful and listen to her mother, turned away, and walked up the narrow staircase to the second floor, where he paused to look up and down a dim, narrow, carpeted hall. Seeing a closed door with a sign 'Projectionist,' he looked in the other direction at an open door, hearing soft music spilling into the narrow, dark hall. Poking his head in, he found a man wiping down a large oak desk. "Excuse me, are you Ira Tindle?"

The man looked up with a defiant face. "Who's asking?" Ira Tindle was a tall, thin man with balding brown and gray hair and an unshaven face who looked as if he had just decided to grow a beard. Bushy eyebrows sat above tired blue eyes and a long nose. He was wearing a faded red shirt under an old pair of gray coveralls.

Dan stepped inside, taking out his badge. "I'm Detective Dan Morgan from Denver Homicide, Mr. Tindle, and I'd like a word with you if you have a moment."

Ira glanced around. "I'm pretty busy at the moment." Then he looked puzzled. "What about?"

"I'd like you to tell me about the night you found Gail Thomas."

Still looking puzzled, Ira reached over and turned off the radio. "I done told all I knew to the Englewood police. What's the Denver Police doing investigating a crime that happened in Englewood?"

203

"I'm sure you did, Mr. Tindle, but I'd like to hear it myself. Mind if I close the door?"

Ira shrugged. "I prefer that you leave it open."

Leaving the door open, Dan approached the desk. "The reason I'm here to talk about Miss Thomas, Mr. Tindle, is we have an open homicide in Denver that is similar."

Looking despondent, Ira said, "How many times am I going to have to tell that damn story?" He looked at Dan. "Hate going over a thing like that."

Dan figured Ira was going to have to explain it all over again to the mayor's investigators at some point. "Sorry to bother you about this again, Mr. Tindle, but I promise this won't take long."

Tindle looked irritated as he glanced at his watch. "Guess I could spare a few minutes."

Dan pulled the notepad and stubby pencil out of his pocket.

Ira watched with interest as Dan turned to a blank page and wrote something. "What are you writing?"

Dan looked up and smiled, "Just your name Mr. Tindle. I find it's easier to write what a person says as they speak than to try and remember what they said later."

"I see." Then Ira gestured to the pencil. "You could use a new pencil."

Ignoring that, Dan said, "I appreciate your time, Mr. Tindle. Could you tell me what happened that night?"

Ira sat down on the table's edge behind the manager's desk and thought for a minute. "As I said before, it was a slow night. The place was empty, so around 9:30, the manager, Mr. Watkins, closed the place and took Mary Jefferies, the little gal that works the concession and sells tickets, home. Then after Gus, the projectionist, left, I locked the back door."

"They all left by the back door?" interrupted Dan.

Tindle nodded. "Always do. Mr. Watkins parks in the lot across the alley, same as me."

"What about this, Gus? What kind of car does he drive?"

"He doesn't own a car. He lives a few blocks east on Grant Street, so he walks."

"I see," said Dan. "What kind of car do you have, Ira?"

"Don't know what difference that makes, but I drive a dark blue 1946 Ford." Then he gestured in the direction of the lot. "It's parked out back, same as always if you want to look at it."

Dan thought of the car he had seen earlier. "What did you do after they left?"

Ira shrugged. "I went about doing my job." Then he looked puzzled. "What else was I going to do? The place has to be cleaned. People spill their drinks and popcorn and leave trash all over the place. I can't believe how messy people are."

Dan thought Ira was a little sassy but then remembered what Chief Travis had said about him and the war.

"Anyway," continued Ira. "I cleaned the place as I always do, making three trips taking out the trash instead of the four or five like I do on a busy night." He looked at Dan. "That poor girl's body wasn't in the alley then. I made certain the front doors were locked, and the lights were out in the concession, and then I went out the rear door like I always do. I locked it, and then I started across the alley to my car. That's when I noticed the trashcans pulled away from the fence. I figured some kids had been messing around, so I started putting them against the fence where they belonged, and that's when I found that poor girl. I could tell she was dead right off."

Dan looked up from the notepad. "How could you tell Mr. Tindle?"

"Saw plenty of death in the war, Detective. Some things you just know."

Dan knew what Ira was referring to. There is something in the way a dead person lies that tells you they're dead. "You never noticed a strange car in the alley or in the lot where you and the manager park when you took out the trash?"

"To tell the truth, Detective, I wasn't looking. Besides, it isn't any of my business who parks in that lot anyway. I was trying to get done so I could get home a little early and be with my wife and daughter."

"Do you remember what time it was when you found the body?"

Ira nodded. "I had just looked up at the clock above the left exit door to the alley as I was going home. It was three minutes after eleven."

Dan wrote that down. "How much time do you think had lapsed between your last visit to the alley and when you found the girl's body?"

Ira considered the question carefully. "Not sure." He looked at Dan. "I'm not a clock watcher, but maybe twenty or thirty minutes, I suppose, by the time I did everything, got my stuff, and headed toward the rear door." Ira looked at Dan. That's about all I can tell you, Detective."

"What happened after you found the girl?"

"I unlocked the back door, ran up here as fast as these old legs would carry me, and called the police (he nodded at the phone next to Dan) on that very telephone. When they got here, all hell broke loose out back, and I had to answer a lot of damn questions. I was fearful they believed I done killed that girl."

"Well, we all know you had nothing to do with what happened to Gail Thomas, Mr. Tindle." Dan thanked him for his time, put his notepad and pencil away, said goodnight, and headed for the door.

"Sure hope you catch that fella, Detective."

Dan was about halfway down the stairs when he stopped, turned, and looked back up the staircase, remembering Captain Foley telling him and Jack that they were off the case. Knowing that when the mayor's men talked to Ira, they'd find out he was still investigating the murders. "Shit he mumbled, then raced up the stairs.

Ira looked up as Dan walked in the door.

"One last thing," said Dan. "There may be a few private investigators from the Denver Mayor's Office stopping by in a few days asking the same questions." He smiled. "I'd appreciate it if you kept my little visit to yourself."

Tindle looked at Dan with a curious expression and then grinned. "You were never here."

Dan nodded his thanks, walked downstairs into the lobby, said goodnight to Mary Jefferies, and stepped outside into the night air and bright lights of quiet downtown Englewood. He paused at the door of his car, noticing the drug store had closed and the five boys were gone, as were the window shoppers and the other cars leaving the street. Dan looked across the street at the red, neon sign 'BAR' in the small window that disappeared behind a noisy streetcar as it hummed its way along the tracks toward the loop. After the streetcar passed and the sign reappeared, he thought about a drink but instead got into his car and followed the streetcar tracks north toward Denver and home.

Twenty-One

Dan opened his eyes early Saturday morning, and the first thing he thought about was the mayor's private investigators taking over his and Jack's case and the professor's warning. Tossing the blanket back, he sat up, put his feet on the area rug, and stared out the window at the morning sunlight in the Elm tree. His thoughts turned to the parents of the murdered girls when he had to break the sad news to them about their daughters. Pushing them from his mind, he thought of Ruthie and hoped the mayor's private investigators would hurry up and catch Paul.

Slipping his feet into his slippers, he stood, went to the front door, and peered out through the lace curtains just as the paperboy tossed the morning paper, missing his mark of the porch by several feet. Opening the door, he stuck his head out the screen door and yelled, "Is the front porch too small a target?" Watching the boy and his bike disappear up the sidewalk, he glanced up and down the street, wondering why he tipped the kid. Not seeing anyone, he stepped outside, hurried down the steps of the porch, picked up the paper, and hurried back inside. Walking into the kitchen, he tossed the folded newspaper onto the red Formica table, lit a gas burner, filled the coffee pot with water and coffee grounds, and went upstairs.

The sound and smell of percolating coffee greeted him as he walked back into the kitchen dressed in Levi's and a dark green cotton shirt not yet tucked into his pants. He got a coffee mug from the cupboard, placed it on the table, and thought about breakfast as he poured himself a cup of coffee. Undecided about what to fix, he sat down at the table, unfolded the newspaper, and read the headlines. '**Mayor Appoints Special Task Force to take over murder case of Howard Trenton, teenage girls.**' Worried about what would happen when Paul read the newspaper, he took a sip of hot coffee and started reading about the mayor's disappointment in the progress of the Denver Detective Squad. Angered by the article, Dan crumpled the paper up and then tossed it across the kitchen, watching it bounce off the cupboard beneath the sink. "Idiot!," he shouted. Then he slid off the chair and picked up the newspaper from the floor, picked up his mug from the table, and headed for the living room. He tossed the crumpled up newspaper onto the coffee table, pulled the chair away from the desk, sat down, and called his partner.

"Hello," answered Jack.

"Have you seen this morning's paper?"

"I figured this might be you calling. I just read it and was thinking about calling you."

"What the hell is the mayor thinking?" asked Dan.

Jack considered that. "He's thinking of re-election."

Dan sighed. "He's going to screw this thing up, Jack. Paul will either kill and disappear or disappear and continue killing. Only now he'll bury his victims."

"Well, there's not much we can do about that now," said Jack sounding frustrated. "I wonder if the captain and the chief have read it."

"I don't know," said Dan. "Paul called me just after you left yesterday."

That interested Jack. "What did he have to say?"

"Not a lot. The packages he was talking about earlier were Ruth and Howard. He admitted to killing them."

The telephone was silent while Jack processed that. "He admitted to killing them?"

"Pretty much," said Dan. "I tried to get him to tell me if we knew one another, but he never said one way or the other."

"Did you record the conversation?"

"Yeah."

"Good," said Jack. "What else did he have to say?"

"Just before he hung up, he said, 'Think about the pictures.'"

Jack chuckled. "Shit, that's all you've been doing."

"I know, and it makes no sense. I better get some breakfast and mow the lawn. I'll talk to you later."

Paul stared at the headlines of the morning paper, wondering why Dan had never said anything about this yesterday when they talked on the telephone. Figuring his boss must have told him to keep quiet about it, he leaned forward in his chair, dropped the newspaper on the coffee table, picked up his coffee mug, and walked into the kitchen. Standing in front of the old black, iron wood-burning stove, Paul picked up the coffee pot and filled the mug with hot coffee. Taking a thoughtful sip, he put the pot back on the stove and walked out of the kitchen, through the living room, and out the front door.

As the screen door slammed in the still, country morning air, the weathered boards of the porch creaked beneath his feet as he walked to an old chair that had once belonged to a fine dining room table. The chair moaned from his weight as he sat down and leaned it onto its back legs against the weathered wall of the house. As he took another sip of hot coffee, his eyes made the journey from the house north along the long, graveled driveway to the mailbox in the distance, standing like a sentry at the dirt road. The Rocky Mountains to the west looked majestic, with the third range still covered with the last spring snow. Sipping his coffee while he gazed at the weathered gray boards of the barn, he thought of happier days on this farm when his aunt and uncle were alive. A rusty, old tractor sat alone under the limbs of a big oak tree near the barn, abandoned and all but forgotten. Drinking his coffee, he remembered how as a boy, he would drive it across the fields, leaving deep furrows in the dark, rich Colorado soil.

In the warm, quiet morning on the front porch, he kept sipping his coffee and thought about both the newspaper article and the telephone conversation he had had with Dan late yesterday afternoon. Dan's aggressiveness and anger towards him brought a smile to his face, knowing now that Dan was not mad at him but at the mayor for taking the case away. He lowered the front legs of the old chair to the floorboard and took another drink of coffee. He had traveled too far in this journey and made too many plans that included Detective Dan Morgan. No, he would not let some stuffy mayor and his investigators ruin everything.

His mind reflected on Howard Trenton, and the enjoyable time they spent together. Now he wondered if perhaps killing him had not been such a good idea after all. "But Howard called you a vampire," he said aloud. Taking another drink of coffee, he felt very sure now that the mayor was about to ruin the plans he had that included Detective Dan Morgan, and he just could not allow that. He sat back in the chair, pushing its back against the wall again and raising the chair's front legs. With the back of the chair against the weathered wall, he contemplated his next move.

His mind recalled the bins in the special room in the basement and then the wide, shallow gully some three hundred yards south of the barn and those he had buried there. The minutes passed, and when the cup was empty, he let the chair down easily, stood, and walked to the edge of the porch. He leaned against a peeling porch post and stared across the land bathed in warm sunlight, thinking of Detective Dan Morgan.

A cat jumped onto the porch carrying a small mouse. Paul looked down, watching as it wriggled to get free. Smiling, he knelt. "Hello, Kitty. I see you've got a little friend."

Kitty dropped the mouse but quickly put a paw on it, preventing its escape. Paul watched Kitty play with the mouse for several minutes, fascinated by the cat's quickness, and chuckled when the mouse almost made it to the edge of the porch and freedom. The cat soon tired of the game and killed the mouse, pawed at it a couple of times, and then walked up to Paul and rubbed against his leg while speaking to him.

He looked down at Kitty, remembering other cats and small animals he had tortured, mutilated, and killed as a young boy. However, these days, small animals no longer interested him, as he had moved on to bigger prey long ago. Besides, Kitty, like him, loved the game before giving death. "Is Kitty hungry?" The cat looked up and spoke. Paul turned and opened the creaking screen door, stepped inside with the cat at his heels, and both headed for the kitchen with Kitty crying for something to eat.

After feeding Kitty, Paul walked down the stairs to the basement and visited his special room of bins. He stood in the center of the room, surrounded in memory, before he walked to the first bin that held the clothing of his first victim. He put his hand into the bin, felt the articles with his hand before taking everything out, looked at them, and tenderly touched each item. Paul visited each bin and touched each item while remembering the face and name that went with each one. Suddenly he felt tired, walked to the window high on the basement wall, and opened it just a crack. He turned the light off and lay down on the old, musty sofa under the window, and closed his eyes, thinking he would get the other room ready after his nap.

Having finished breakfast, Dan gathered his dirty clothes, put them in the washing machine, and cleaned the house, thinking he would be glad when Mrs. McDowell returned from Brooklyn. After the house was clean and the clothes put away, he ran a few errands that included dropping his dress shirts off at the laundry and picking up his clothes from the cleaners.

Returning home, he fixed a light lunch and ate in the garage while studying the pictures he would soon have to give up while recalling Paul's words, 'Think about the pictures.' Shoving the last of the sandwich into his mouth, Dan picked up his beer and stood from the stool. Walking up and down the wall while taking a drink of beer, he tried again to figure out what it was that Paul wanted him to see.

It was a little after one when Dan walked out of the garage and into the kitchen, cleaned his dishes, and poured a cup of coffee. With cup in hand, he walked into the living room, plopped down in his chair, and looked at the black telephone quietly sitting on the desk. Taking a sip, Dan wondered how long it took Cathy to get her hair done. Then remembering that he was supposed to pick out the movie, he set his coffee down and reached for the newspaper. He rustled through the pages until he found the movie section and scanned all of the theater listings, picking out two that looked interesting. The grandfather clock in the corner chimed one-thirty, and like a young boy about to go on his first date, he was feeling anxious and wondered what was keeping Cathy.

To his relief, the telephone rang, and he tossed the newspaper on the sofa, hurried to the desk, and picked up the receiver. "Hello?"

"It's Cathy."

"Hi, how's your hair look?"

"Alright, I guess. I'll let you be the judge of that."

He chuckled.

"What's so funny?"

"You know I'm not going to say anything other than it looks great. I don't believe in suicide missions."

She laughed. "What time are you picking me up?"

"Well, I've narrowed the movies down to two. The African Queen, starring Humphrey Bogart and Katharine Hepburn at the Denham. It begins at 8:00. Or, A Streetcar Named Desire starring Marlon Brando and Vivien Leigh at the Orpheum. It starts at 8:15."

"The Denham's on 18th Street, isn't it?"

Dan thought a moment. "I think it's 18th and California."

"Joey's restaurant is on 18th Street. We wouldn't have very far to walk after dinner."

"That's true, and we would not feel rushed. How about I pick you up at six? That should give us enough time to eat without having to hurry and make the eight o'clock movie."

"I'll be ready. Goodbye." Then she quickly said, "Dan?"

"Yeah."

"I'm looking forward to tonight."

He smiled. "Me too." He said goodbye, and as he hung up, his eyes found the picture of Norma and her soft eyes staring at him. Standing up from the chair at the desk, he picked the picture up and looked at it, remembering how frail she had become before cancer finally took her last breath in the bedroom upstairs. He would never stop loving her, but he knew that it was time for him to move on, and he was sure that she would want him to. He smiled at the picture, set it down, and then went upstairs to take a shower, shave, and put on his blue, three-piece suit.

Dan parked his car on 18th Street near Joey's restaurant and could see the big yellow sign with red letters 'DENHAM' in the next block above the marquee of white lights. After helping Cathy out of the car onto the sidewalk, he locked the car.

She was wearing a lavender floral dress that buttoned down the front with short, puffy sleeves, and he thought she looked beautiful.

"Have you eaten here before?" she asked.

Dan glanced at the quaint, pink neon sign 'Joey's' encircled by blinking lights above the door, giving the appearance that they were moving around the name. "I don't believe I have."

"I'm sure you'll like it."

He opened the door, and they stepped into the dimly lit restaurant, greeted by an attractive blonde hostess dressed in a black cocktail dress. She smiled. "Good evening. Lounge or dinner?"

"Dinner for two, please," replied Dan.

The girl picked up two menus and then led them through a maze of tables with white tablecloths and small, red glass jars with lit candles toward a table for two. While Dan pulled out a chair for Cathy, the hostess placed the two menus on the table, saying their waiter would be with them in a moment. Dan sat down across from Cathy and glanced around the dim room of couples enjoying their meal or quietly talking over a drink. He looked at Cathy. "Come here often?"

"Once in a while with a girlfriend."

"No dates?"

She smiled. "Not until tonight."

Dan smiled. "It's difficult dating after being married for several years. The world has moved on, and it isn't easy trying to catch up."

The waiter was at their table. "A cocktail before dinner?"

Cathy ordered a vodka collins tall and Dan a glass of bourbon straight up.

As the waiter walked away, Cathy leaned on the table with folded arms and smiled. "And what about you? Have you dated very much since your wife passed away?"

Dan frowned. "Not really. I've had coffee or a drink a few times, but that's about it. I've had a hard time with the guilt." Then he smiled. "Still do, I guess."

"Oh, I know what you mean. The sad part is we really shouldn't feel that way."

Dan noticed the absence of her wedding ring. "You're not wearing your wedding ring."

She smiled softly, looking embarrassed. "I didn't think it appropriate."

Curious about her husband, he asked, "Do you know how your husband died?"

"No," she said sadly. "I only know Ted was captured and died during the Bataan Death March." She paused. "I guess it was pretty awful."

Dan knew that quite a few American soldiers and Filipinos had been bayonetted or beheaded during the ordeal if they failed to keep up.

"I was terribly angry for a long time," she softly said as she frowned. "I was furious at the Japanese."

"I was angry about Norma, but there was no one to blame or get mad at but God." He paused. "And I did my share of that, regrettably."

"That's natural." Then she smiled and glanced around the room. "We sure know how to have a happy conversation on a date."

Dan smiled and nodded while trying to think of something else to talk about when the waiter with their drinks saved him.

The waiter smiled. "Ready to order?"

Dan grinned with embarrassment. "Sorry, we haven't looked at the menu."

The waiter smiled. "If I may, the prime rib is excellent."

Dan looked at Cathy. "Never argue with a waiter."

"I'll have the smaller cut," said Cathy. "And a little on the well-done side, if that's possible."

The waiter smiled. "It certainly is."

He looked at Dan. "A regular cut for you, sir?"

Dan picked up the two menus and handed them to the waiter. "That would be fine." And as the waiter left, Dan picked up his bourbon. "To a pleasant evening."

Cathy smiled and picked up her vodka collins. "To a pleasant evening."

Mary Ann Jefferies said goodnight to her friend Beverly Aikens, walked down the narrow walk from the porch to the sidewalk, turned, and waved. After Beverly waved back and closed the door, Mary walked along the lonely, dark sidewalk without streetlights toward her house on the next block. As she walked, she looked up at the black night sky filled with countless stars and sliver of a white moon. Her tennis shoes made soft sounds on the cement sidewalk while crickets filled the warm, quiet night air. In a hurry to get home, she hugged herself and walked a little faster. Moments later, she approached a white van parked against the curb and felt suddenly uneasy about it.

Mary opened her eyes, feeling groggy and disoriented in total darkness, and as her mind cleared, she realized a burlap bag was over her head, and her feet and hands were bound with rough, scratchy rope. Realizing she was inside that same white van and moving, she became frantic and tried to scream, but her mouth had a gag in it. Country music blared from the front of the van while Mary lay curled up on something soft that had an odor she didn't recognize. Managing to sit up against the van's wall, her mouth and nose were irritated from something, and she was very thirsty. As her head cleared a little more, she tried working free of the rough ropes tying her wrists together, but that only made the ropes hurt all the more. Then, thinking of Gail Thomas and unable to scream for help, she stopped her struggle and began to cry while calling out to her mother in a muffled voice that no one could hear.

Dan and Cathy stood just inside the balcony's closed door, letting their eyes adjust to the dark theater. Cigarette smoke floated upwards into the beam of the projector light, showing the previews of coming attractions on the silver screen. Seeing two empty seats a few rows down, they walked down the aisle of stairs and excused themselves as they made their way along the row of people to the empty seats. Knowing that Cathy did not smoke, Dan asked if she cared if he did.

"Not at all," she whispered.

Dan lit up a cigarette, and as the smoke floated into the beam of light above them, the movie began. He looked at the big clock's red illuminating hands above the green exit sign, noticing that it was eight o'clock. Getting comfortable, he took Cathy's hand in his.

Without looking away from the screen, she smiled, gently squeezed his hand, and moved closer.

Mary Jefferies lay on top of a pile of musty army blankets while the sound of country music drowned out her sobbing. The minutes passed, and as her sobbing turned to soft crying, she sat up and wondered what would happen to her. Then the music stopped, and after the announcer gave the time, she panicked and began screaming into the gag and kicking at the van's wall.

"Stop that damn kicking," hollered Paul from the front seat.

Mary kept kicking the side of the van and screaming into the gag.

Paul pulled to the side of the road, and with the motor running, he put on a hood and turned off the radio. Then, climbing between the opening of the two front seats into the back of the van, he grabbed her by the shoulders with his powerful hands. Pulling her away from the van wall, he shoved her to the van floor. "I said, stop yelling and kicking." Then he slapped the hood covering her face.

Fearful he was going to kill her, Mary lay curled up next to the pile of blankets and quietly sobbed, softly mumbling the words, 'please don't hurt me' into the gag covering her mouth.

As quiet returned to the van, Paul listened to Mary's soft whimpering and then spoke in a low, stern voice. "Listen to me closely, little girl. I'm not going to hurt you, but if you don't be quiet, you will be very, very sorry. Do you hear me?"

Struck with panic, Mary began her muffled screaming again and began kicking her bound feet into thin air.

Avoiding her kicks, he grabbed her shoulders and shook them, hitting her head on the side of the van. She stopped struggling and began to sob while he gripped her shoulders even tighter, pulled her close to his face, and spoke in a soft, calm voice. "Stop struggling, damn it. I don't want to hurt you, but if you don't stop kicking the side of the van, you won't like what I'll do to you."

She tried to ask him to let her go, but the gag muffled her words.

Not interested in what she had to say, he shoved her onto the pile of army blankets and watched as she curled up into a ball, whimpering like a child. "That's better. Now be a good girl, and I won't hurt you. I only need you for a couple of days."

She asked why, but the gag muffled her words.

"I can't understand what you're saying with the gag and hood over your head, so stop talking." Paul climbed into the front seat, took off his hood, and drove away with the radio blaring. The minutes passed, and she didn't know how long she had been in the van, but she could feel it begin to slow. As fear and terror of the unknown filled her, Mary sat up against the wall of the van. Looking into the darkness of the hood, she thought of Gail Thomas. When the van came to a stop, Mary heard a door open and close, and a moment later heard the rear door of the van open. Scooting against the side of the van, she turned her head toward the sound, and when she felt a hand on her foot, she pulled away and began kicking with her bound feet.

Almost getting a foot in the face, Paul stepped back, adjusted the hood he was wearing just in case hers were to come off, and watched as she kicked and rolled from side to side on the floor of the van. Getting angry, he reached into the van, grabbed her feet, pulled her to the edge of the van, and then grabbed her throat with both hands and squeezed. Realizing her state of mind and remembering what he needed her for, he let go, grabbed her feet, and tossed her back into the van. Slamming the door closed, he locked the van door, leaned his back against it, and said, "You can scream all you want, little girl, because there is no one to hear you." He paused. "I don't want to hurt you, Mary, so I'll come back when I feel you are ready to cooperate."

She lay curled up on the floor of the van crying like a child while Paul went inside his house, drank a beer, and returned twenty minutes later. He put the side of his face against the cold, metal rear door and closed his eyes, thinking it felt good against his skin. Then, with a calm, caring voice, he asked, "Are you alright, Mary?"

Mary slowly sat up and turned her head toward the voice and spoke into the gag.

"As I told you before," said Paul. "I don't want to hurt you, and I only need you for a couple of days to prove a point." He paused. "Make a sound when you are ready to be nice, so I can take you inside where you will be warm. Once I have done what I need to do, I will let you go unharmed. The hood over your face is, so you won't see what I look like, and that will keep you safe."

She yelled and tried to say that she would be nice through the gag.

Hearing her, Paul smiled. "I'll take that as a yes." Then he shoved the key into the lock. "I'm going to open the door now and take you inside the house." He unlocked the door and put the key into his pocket. "I hope you don't put up a fuss. I don't want to send you home injured."

The door opened, and Mary scooted away from the sound until she was against the back of the front seat. She huddled against it, filled with fear, and listened in the quiet to see where he was. Feeling the van move, Mary knew he was inside. Frightened, she curled up into a tighter ball.

"I don't want to hurt you, Mary," he said in a soft voice. "That may make your friend, the detective, angry, and I wouldn't want that. Now I am going to touch your ankles and help you out of the van. I'm not going to hurt you."

She didn't understand who he was referring to and flinched when he gently touched her ankles and slowly pulled her feet away from her body.

"How many times do I have to say this, Mary? I'm not going to hurt you. You are simply a pawn in a game of chess that I need to win. Now, I am simply going to pull you to the edge of the van, untie your ankles, and help you down. Then we'll go inside." Hearing her muffled words, he pulled her to the rear of the van. "I can't understand you through the gag Mary." He helped her put her feet on the ground. "Once we are inside, I will remove the hood, take off the gag, and untie your hands. I must tell you that I will have a hood on so you will not see my face. If you do, it will not go well for you. Nod if you understand."

Mary nodded.

"That's good. My hood is for your protection, so don't fear it."

Afraid of what might happen to her once inside, her legs gave way.

Paul held onto her and helped her walk while repeating that he wasn't going to hurt her. "Watch yourself," he said. "We have three steps to go up, then a short walk across a porch, and we're inside the house."

The night air was calm and warm when Dan and Cathy exited the theater amid the crowd. Dan half-listened to the other people talking about the movie while waiting for the light to turn green so he and Cathy could cross. The light turned green, and as they started across the street, Cathy took Dan's arm and held it tight, pulling herself into him. When they reached the other side of 18th Street, they walked toward Dan's car parked near Joey's restaurant.

She looked at the side of Dan's face. "Did you enjoy the movie?"

"I did," chuckled Dan. "Especially when Bogart's stomach started growling while Katherine Hepburn poured his tea."

Cathy laughed. "That was funny. Her brother's expression was priceless. I loved the way everyone tried to ignore the sound of poor Bogie's stomach."

"I liked the ending," said Dan as he paused in front of Joey's, not wanting the evening to end just yet. "Would you care for a nightcap?"

She looked at her watch. "I haven't been out this late in months." She smiled and held up her index finger. "One."

Dan grinned. "I promise, and then I'll take you home." He opened the door, and they stepped inside, met by the same blonde hostess that had seated them earlier. She smiled. "Back for a nightcap?"

"We are," answered Dan.

She led them to another door, and when she opened it, soft piano music rushed from inside a smoke-filled room with soft blue lights. She showed them to a table away from the piano. "Someone will be with you in a moment."

Cathy glanced around the crowded lounge and smiled. "I've never been in here before. This is a cozy little place."

Glad it was her first time, Dan smiled. "Yes, it is."

"Good evening," said the waitress. "What can I get you?"

Cathy ordered herself a vodka collins and Dan bourbon on the rocks. As the waitress walked away, they sat back and listened to the piano player as the music mingled with the soft buzzing of quiet conversations.

The waitress set their drinks on the small table. "Would you like to run a tab?"

Dan smiled, "I don't think so. We just stopped for a nightcap."

After the waitress told him how much for the two drinks, he handed her enough to cover a tip.

She took the money, thanked him, and walked away.

Cathy picked up her collins and smiled. "Thank you for a wonderful evening."

Dan smiled as he picked up his bourbon. "It was a nice evening, wasn't it?"

They each took a drink, and then Cathy looked serious as she leaned on the small table to talk over the soft piano music. "I read what the mayor said in this morning's newspaper."

Dan tried to smile but was unsuccessful. "So did I."

She looked concerned. "Why would the mayor say those terrible things about the police?"

Dan shrugged. "Jack and the captain both think it's because he is coming up for reelection next year and is trying to score some points."

"Well," she said. "I think it's terrible and a little unfair to you and the rest of the department."

He took a drink, set the glass down, and looked at her. "You'll probably be meeting the mayor's investigators in the next few days."

She looked puzzled. "Why?"

"I'm sure they'll be out to talk to your uncle, the same as Jack and I did."

Looking annoyed, she said, "I can hardly wait." Then she took a drink and decided to change the subject. "Where do you live?"

He told her, and they talked about his house and other things that would not lead back to the mayor or the cases. The minutes flew by too quickly for Dan, and the one drink he had promised her was gone.

Having no choice but to do what Paul told her and filled with hope that what he said was the truth and he would not hurt her, Mary Ann Jefferies did as she was told. She let her captor help her up the stairs to a porch of creaking boards. Stopping, she heard the sound of the screen door and then a door opening.

Kitty ran out, brushing against her leg, bringing a muffled scream from Mary as she backed up.

Paul laughed. "Just a cat wanting out of the house." He guided her inside to unfamiliar noises and odors that rushed at her. Hearing the sound of the screen door slam, followed by the door closing and the sound of the lock turning, she knew she was trapped. Terrified of knowing it would do no good to cry out, she felt his hand on her arm as he guided her across the floor that moaned eerily beneath their feet.

"Be careful of the stairs," he warned as he gripped her arm a little tighter.

They slowly walked down a flight of loose, moaning stairs and crossed a hard cement floor until they stopped, and he let go of her arm

Hearing another door open, she felt his hand on her arm once again.

"Be careful of the door," he said as he guided her through the open doorway and stopped.

"I'm going to untie you now, and after I close the door, I'll tell you when you can take off your hood and gag." He paused. "If you try anything before I close the door, you will never leave this room alive."

Fearful of his words, she felt the rope loosen from around her wrists, and then she heard the door shut and the lock turn and waited for him to tell her what to do.

"You can take the hood and gag off now, Mary Jefferies."

She pulled the hood off and then untied the gag from her mouth and looked around at a very nicely furnished bedroom and adjoining bathroom. Seeing the closed drapes on one wall, she hurried across the room and pulled them back, finding a windowless lime green wall. She panicked and ran to the door, where she tried the doorknob, and then she tried looking through a peephole, only to find it was for looking in, not out. She began to cry as she banged on the door with both fists yelling, "Let me out."

Paul was at the peephole. "None of that will do you any good. I'm the only one here, and we are a long way from the nearest house." He paused, listening to the quiet. "There is some salve in the bathroom for your mouth and nose. It will help the burning from the chloroform. You might also try some on your wrists and ankles. I'm sure they are sore."

As tears rolled down her cheeks, Mary leaned against the door and softly said, "What do you want with me?"

"I've already explained that to you, Mary. Don't you listen? Now put the salve on and go to sleep. I'm sure you're tired. Tomorrow we'll talk about you going home."

Filled with hope, Mary wiped the tears from her face and stared at the door. "Why can't I go home tonight?"

"Mary, Oh Mary," said Paul softly. "You keep asking foolish questions. Remember what I have told you. I have to make some calls tomorrow to prove a point, and if all goes well, I'll make the arrangements for someone to meet us later in the day and take you home to your mother and father."

"Who will meet us?"

He never answered.

She looked at the door. "Where am I?"

"Where you are, makes no difference, and that is a pointless question for me to answer. Now be quiet and get some rest since we've both had a hard day." He paused. "I'm going upstairs to get some sleep, and I suggest you do the same. I don't want you to worry, Mary. If I were going to hurt you, I would have done so long ago. Goodnight."

She leaned against the door. "Please take me home!" When no response came, she thought about her burning face and walked into the bathroom. Finding the salve, she put some on her lips and around her nose. When she finished, she applied a little to the rope burns on her wrists and ankles as her captor had suggested. As the burning eased, she went back into the bedroom, lay down on the bed, pulled the top spread over her, curled up, and cried, wishing desperately that her mother and father would come for her.

Paul walked across the floor of the basement to the door of the trophy room, unlocked it, stepped inside, turned on the light, and stood in the open doorway gazing at the wall of bins while fighting the desire he felt for Mary Jefferies. Unsure if he could resist her all weekend, he stepped into the room and walked along the wall of bins, each one containing clothing and miscellaneous personal items, including a glass fruit jar of blood and a little finger. He wanted Mary Jefferies to join the others in this room, but he had to convince the mayor to give the cases back to Detective Morgan. There would be another time for Mary Jefferies.

Paul slowly walked along the wall, eyeing each jar and piece of clothing of his victims. Reaching the last victim, the one he called The Detective's Prostitute, he stopped. She was different than the other girls because she wasn't a virgin and didn't deserve the love and respect Paul showed the other young girls. Taking an article of her clothing out of the bin, he held it against his face and then put it up to his nose, smelling the cheap perfume. Putting it back into the bin, he moved to the next bin belonging to the last virgin, Marie Phillips. Closing his eyes, he touched each article, remembering the moment the last drop of blood had fallen into the white, porcelain bathtub. As his fingers found the fruit jar, tiny beads of sweat formed on his forehead. It became difficult for him to breathe, so he pulled his hand out of the bin, and as desire filled him, he thought about young, innocent Mary Jefferies in the next room. Fighting the urge to take her, he turned from the bins, opened the door, turned out the light, and closed the door. After locking it and placing the key on the door frame above, he rushed past the bedroom where Mary was lying on the bed, covered with the bedspread, and crying.

Twenty-Two

Cathy Holman opened her eyes Sunday morning, looking out her bedroom window at the neighbor's tree bathed in sunlight against a blue, cloudless sky. Wrapping her arms around the spare pillow, she hugged it and thought about Joey's, the movie, the drink after the movie, and the goodnight kiss. She looked from the window to the door leading to the hall, picturing the black telephone sitting quietly on its small table. Hoping Dan would call her sometime today, she reached over and pushed the button on the alarm so it would not go off. Tossing the covers back, she put her warm feet on the carpet, thinking of Dan. Knowing her aunt and uncle would pick her up in a couple of hours to take her to church and then breakfast, she got up and walked into the bathroom to take a bath.

Dan set the sports page of the Sunday newspaper on the coffee table, picked up his empty mug, walked into the kitchen for more coffee, and then headed for the front door. Still wearing his pajama bottoms, tee shirt, and slippers, he opened the front door, pushed the screen door open, and stepped out onto the porch. Careful not to spill his precious coffee, he moved one of the white wooden chairs into the morning sunlight and sat down.

Enjoying the warm sun on this quiet Sunday morning, he watched the birds as they flew from branch to branch of the elm tree. Church bells in the distance reminded him that he had not seen the inside of a church since Norma's death. Taking a sip of coffee, he thought about Friday afternoon when Captain Foley told him about the mayor putting together the Special Task Force. That brought to mind the pictures covering the wall of his garage. As his next thought turned to Paul, he took a drink of coffee and considered the professor's warning regarding Paul that he might kill quickly and disappear because of the mayor's actions. He wanted to catch Paul as badly as anyone, maybe even more so because of Ruthie. But now, that was up to the Special Task Force of private investigators working for the mayor.

He turned from frustration to better thoughts of last night and sipped his coffee, thinking of Cathy hanging onto his arm as they walked down the sidewalk toward Joey's restaurant and how good that had made him feel. It had been a long while since anyone had held his arm like that. Her perfume still lingered in his memory as he took another drink of coffee and thought of her soft lips when they kissed goodnight. Swallowing the last of his coffee, he stood, pushed the chair back to where it belonged, and stepped inside, hearing the sound of a car door. Turning to look through the screen door, he watched the Martins across the street. They were all dressed up, getting into their car that would take them to church and then breakfast. Remembering Sundays with Norma and the children, he watched as Tom Martin backed the car out of the driveway and then drove down the street.

Paul looked through the peephole seeing his guest was sleeping, quietly unlocked the door, and placed the cardboard tray of food on the small table next to the door. He stared at Mary Jefferies for a long moment thinking how pretty she would be hanging over the bathtub in the next room. Forcing that picture from his mind, he stepped out of the room, closed the door not so gently, locked it, and then looked through the peephole.

Mary Jefferies opened her eyes and raised her head from the pillow, glanced around the room, remembering everything that had happened the night before. Sitting up, she saw the cardboard tray of food sitting on the small table near the door. Jumping off the bed, Mary ran to the door, grabbed the doorknob, and tried to open the door. Disappointed at finding it locked, she looked at the cardboard tray of food containing a paper cup of orange juice, a paper plate of toast, one scrambled egg, one piece of bacon, and a half glass of water. She looked at the door and yelled, "What do I eat with?"

Paul smiled while watching through the peephole. "You have two good hands with ten fingers. I suggest you use them."

While Mary was still afraid, she remembered what the man had told her about not wanting to harm her and the fact that up until now, no harm had come to her. Still, she was afraid, and anger was mixing with her fear as she looked up at the ceiling and screamed in frustration, "Please, somebody, get me out of here!."

Paul laughed as he watched her. "All in good time, my dear, but for now, you need to eat so you won't get sick. I want you healthy when your detective rescues you."

Frustrated at not knowing what he was talking about, she leaned against the door and tried to look through the peephole. "Who is this detective you keep talking about?"

"Eat your breakfast, Mary Jefferies."

She looked at the tray of food. "I won't eat this. It's probably poisoned."

Paul chuckled while he watched her. "You're such a foolish young girl, Mary. If I had wanted you, dead young lady, you would be dead. Now be a good little girl and eat."

Mary knew what he said was true, but the reasons he may want her alive were terrifying.

"Now eat," said Paul, like a kindly father. "I don't want to send you home looking skinny and abused."

She looked at the closed door, filled with hope. "When? When can I go home?"

Thinking she looked attractive with her long hair in disarray, he wished he did not need her to help his detective. He watched her for a moment, thinking of her nude body empty of blood while he washed and cleaned her. "When the time is right. Now please, eat your breakfast."

Worried about her parents, she asked, "Would you call my mom and dad and tell them I'm okay? I'm sure they're worried."

Paul looked at her distressed expression through the peephole and smiled. "You're not a very realistic person, are you, Mary?"

She wiped the tears from her cheeks with both hands while she considered his words. "What do you mean?"

Imagining her lying on the bed, drained of blood and all washed and cleaned before he made love to her, he spoke through the door. "I have to leave for a while. You'll find a tube of toothpaste you can put on your finger to clean your teeth after you have eaten. There is also soap and clean towels in the bathroom." He paused. "Did you use the salve as I told you to?"

"Yes,' she replied, and then out of desperation, she tried to look through the useless peephole. Unable to see anything, she put her ear to the door and listened to fading footsteps, one door closing and then another. Minutes later, she heard the sound of an automobile engine that quickly faded, and knowing she was alone, she tried opening the door. Giving up, she turned from the door and looked at the tray of food.

Dan dumped the last of the cut grass onto the mulch pile by the alley, put the thirty-gallon can, mower, and edger inside the garage, and then walked into the house. He opened the refrigerator door to find something to eat, but unable to find anything that appealed to his appetite, he glanced at the clock on the wall. Seeing it was almost four, he closed the refrigerator door and decided to go out. As he walked down the hall toward the front door and retrieved the car keys from the small bowl on the table, he thought about calling Cathy and asking her to join him. But knowing he would not be very good company, he decided against it.

+"Step away from the door," said Paul in a soft but firm voice while looking through the peephole. "I want you to get on the bed with your back against the headboard with your legs and feet straight out in front of you."

Mary did as told and closed her eyes. Hearing the lock turn and the door open, her heart pounded with the fear of what he might do to her, and fought the urge to open her eyes.

"You don't need to close your eyes, Mary."

Opening them, she saw a man standing in the doorway with a dark hood over his head. She could see his eyes looking at her through the two round holes and thought he looked creepy. A bolt of fear shot through her, and she wanted to run, but there was nowhere to run.

He picked up the tray from the table, backed out of the room, and when the door closed, Mary was immediately off the bed, standing with her ear against the door. "You promised I could go home." In the silence after the question, she heard footsteps going up the stairs, followed by a door closing. She stood glued to the door listening to the silence as tears filled her eyes. Moments later, she turned, fell onto the bed, and cried.

Cathy turned the television on to the evening news in her attempt to fill the empty house with voices as she went about the task of fixing a salad for one. She paused and looked toward the hall where the telephone sat and considered calling Dan to invite him over. But she quickly decided against it since he had not called her all day, and now she wondered if he was upset or maybe had grown tired of her. The salad ready and a glass of white wine, she sat down at the dining room table and ate while listening to the news coming from the television in the living room. Occasionally, she glanced at the telephone in the hallway while half-listening to the newscaster's voice. She ate her salad and drank the wine and wondered if she had done something to push him away. Maybe she should have asked him to spend the night, but that thought upset her, thinking that if that was all he wanted, too bad for him.

When both the plate and the glass were empty, she cleaned up the dishes, feeling a little angry at Dan Morgan. She opened the refrigerator, took out a half bottle of white wine, got a clean wine glass from the cupboard, and walked into the living room. She melted into the sofa, kicked off her shoes, put her feet up, and poured herself half a glass. After setting the bottle on the coffee table, she looked at the television, seeing that the news was over, and 'The Jack Benny Show' was just beginning. Startled by the telephone's ringing and hoping it was Dan, she got up, careful not to spill the wine, hurried into the hall, paused over the telephone, and then picked up the black receiver. "Hello."

"This is Dan."

She smiled with relief. "Where are you?"

"In a phone booth outside of a restaurant on Colorado Boulevard."

Cathy sat down on the chair that matched the small telephone table. "Have you eaten?"

"Just finished, but I think I would have been better off cooking something at home."

She smiled. "I wish you had called earlier. I would have fixed us both something to eat."

"I wish I had. Have you eaten?"

"I fixed a salad earlier."

"What are you doing now?"

She looked at her glass of wine. "Enjoying a glass of wine on the sofa while watching Jack Benny."

He looked out the glass window of the phone booth at the passing cars. "I thought about calling you earlier to see if you'd be interested in getting something to eat."

"Oh," she said, sounding disappointed. "I wish you had."

"To be honest, I didn't think I would be very good company."

"Because of the mayor?"

Dan felt awkward, letting silence fill the telephone. "What did you do today?"

"The same thing I do every Sunday. Church with my aunt and uncle and then out to breakfast."

"The sheriff, uncle?"

She smiled. "The sheriff uncle. After breakfast, they dropped me off, and I cleaned the house. What about you?"

He thought that maybe he should have cleaned the house instead of going for that ride in the country. "Nothing very exciting. I got up a little after seven, fixed breakfast, read the paper, and sat in the sun on the front porch with my morning coffee. Then I mowed the lawn."

"Sounds about as exciting as me doing some laundry and ironing my white blouse for work tomorrow."

There was a long pause, and then Dan asked, "Are you free Wednesday night?"

"I think so," she said, sounding unsure, so he wouldn't think her anxious.

"I was hoping I could pick you up at work, and then we could get something to eat."

"Alright," she said. "But call me at work Wednesday, just in case something comes up."

"I will."

She smiled into the telephone. "Goodnight, Dan."

He paused a moment. "I enjoyed last night."

She smiled, relaxing now. "So did I."

She heard the click followed by silence, then hung up the phone, and returned to the sofa with her glass of wine, relieved and happy that Dan Morgan had called.

Dan turned into his driveway, stopped the car next to the narrow walk leading to the front porch, and turned off the headlights and then the engine. He had stopped thinking about Cathy a few blocks back and had turned his thoughts to Sally Crowder and her parents when they had identified her body in the morgue. Dan thought of Sally, lying on the blanket in the alley with her dead eyes staring up into the black night. Now, sitting in the darkness filled with the sound of crickets, he imagined Paul placing her on the blanket, fussing with her, and then driving away in his white van. Then he thought of Diane Wagner never going home again, lying in the damp grass on her blanket, and Gail Thomas in the alley behind the Pioneer Theater surrounded by fifty-gallon trash barrels. Then of, Marie Phillips behind the Paramount Theater and all of the other grieving parents.

He thought of the body of Howard Trenton hanging from the rafters of his garage, having been tortured by Paul, and finally, he thought of Ruth's naked body lying in the ditch. Letting out a soft, angry sigh, he hit the steering wheel with both hands, then opened the car door and stepped out into the darkness. He locked the car and walked toward the garage to take everything down from the walls.

Mary heard a sound and got up from the bed she had occupied since Saturday night, hurried across the room, and stood with her ear against the door. Then, looking at the tray of partially eaten food, she wished that the man who held her prisoner would have given her a fork. She returned to the bed, where she lay on her stomach with knees bent, feet in the air, head resting on her arms, wishing she could go home.

Paul peered at her through the peephole, imagining her lying there while he undressed her and touched her soft, white skin as he hung her nude body upside down over the bathtub.

Hearing a noise at the door, Mary sat up. "Who's there?"

"Stay on the bed," said Paul as he put his hood on. "I'm coming in."

As the scary, hooded man entered, Mary slid back against the headboard.

Paul picked up the tray of partially eaten food and wondered if she was feeling ill. "Were you not hungry?"

"You promised I could go home." Trying to be brave, she fought back the tears. "When can I go home?"

226

He thought for a moment. "Tomorrow is Monday. You will be leaving tomorrow night."

She rose, looking hopeful. "I'm truly going home?"

"Your mouth and nose look much better. You might try the salve again." Then he backed out of the room. "I wouldn't want your detective thinking I had mistreated you."

Mary fought her tears and, with frustration, said, "I don't have a detective. Why do you keep saying that?"

He paused at the open door and looked at her through the two round holes in the hood. "I'm doing this to help your detective. You are merely a means to an end Mary Jefferies, nothing more. If it all works out, you will be home tomorrow night."

She looked at his piercing eyes staring at her through the round holes of the hood. "What if it doesn't?"

Paul thought of the trophy room. "Then things will turn out much different for you." He left the room, closed the door, and locked it.

Understanding what he meant, Mary wrapped herself in her arms, curled up on the bed, stared at the closed door, and thought of her friend Gail Thomas.

Twenty-Three

The grandfather clock standing in the dark corner of the Morgan living room chimed the quarter-hour. Dan had been awake for some time, staring out the living room window waiting for the morning and the alarm clock. He was thinking about Ruth's battered face as she lay naked in the dry ditch across the gravel road from Edward's Lumber Company. He was angry that the mayor had robbed him of giving her, the other girls, and their families justice and closure. He looked at the illuminating hands and numbers of the alarm clock sitting on the coffee table, telling him it was 5:15 a.m. He put his head back on the pillow and tried to go back to sleep, but instead of sleep, he thought of the envelopes he was going to give to Captain Foley in the morning.

He tossed and turned, trying again to sleep. The minutes passed, and the clock chimed the half-hour as the silent early morning filled with the familiar sound of bottles rattling on the porch. Opening his eyes, he waited for silence to return to the porch, and then tossing the blanket back, he got up and slid into his slippers, stretching the stiffness from his back. He walked to the front door, opened it, and retrieved the two milk bottles from the white box. While his eyes searched for the morning paper, he realized it was too early for the paperboy. Closing the door, he walked into the kitchen, put the milk in the refrigerator, and went about his usual routine of making coffee before retrieving the blanket and pillow from the sofa on his way upstairs.

After a quick shower, he shaved and dressed in tan slacks, a vest, and a white shirt with a brown tie. He carried his suit coat downstairs, placed it on the chair in the foyer, and rushed into the kitchen to turn the stove off. Then he walked to the front door, opened it, pushed the screen door open, and poked his head out looking for the newspaper and, not seeing it, stepped outside to have a look. Standing at the edge of the porch, he saw it stuck in the lilac bush at the far end. "This kid will never pitch for the Yankees." After retrieving the paper from the bush, he went inside, tossed it on the kitchen table, and put two slices of bread into the toaster.

With his toast buttered and heavy with grape jelly, he poured another cup of coffee, sat down at the kitchen table, and opened the paper to see if the headlines mentioned any of the murders or more of the poor performance of the Denver Police Department. Instead, the headlines were of the war in Korea, so he turned to the sports page and started reading.

Dan walked into the Detective Squad room, met by the sound of soft voices, typewriters, and ringing telephones as he walked toward his desk.

Jack was on the telephone, and seeing that the captain's office was empty, he dropped the manila envelopes onto his desk, picked up his coffee cup, and headed for the kitchen, wondering who his partner was talking to.

When he returned with his coffee, Jack grinned as he hung up the telephone, opened his desk drawer, pulled out a small sack from Grandma's Donuts, and tossed it at Dan. "Thought you could use some cheering up,"

Dan eyed the sack, picked it up, and looked inside, finding four glazed donuts. Taking two, he tossed the sack back to Jack, took a bite, and washed it down with the hot, strong coffee as he looked toward Foley's office. "Wonder where the captain is?"

Jack glanced toward the captain's office. "I don't know."

Taking another bite of his donut, Dan looked at Jack. "I told you about Paul calling just after you left Friday."

Jack looked concerned. "Yeah, you did."

Dan took a sip of coffee. "This shit is terrible." He set the cup down. "I asked Paul if we knew one another, and he just told me to think about the pictures, and then he hung up."

Jack looked puzzled. "I know you told me. He told you that before."

"I spent all weekend thinking about the damn pictures while I was looking at them, and I can't figure out what the hell he's talking about."

Jack shoved his cup away as he stood with a confused look. "It's something only he knows. I think he's playing with you. I'm going downstairs to the coffee shop for a good cup of coffee. Coming?"

The sweet aroma of fresh coffee wafted from the paper cup as Jack Brolin carefully lifted the lid from his cup, tossing it into the trashcan next to his desk. Taking a bite of the donut and then a sip of the hot coffee, he looked across the two desks. "That's better," referring to the coffee. Seeing the stack of manila envelopes that had become a part of his partner, he stood with his paper cup of coffee in one hand, his donut in the other, and walked around his desk to Dan's. "I tried calling you a couple of times." He sat down on the edge of Dan's desk. "I wanted to see how you were doing."

Dan took a bite of the donut as he looked up at Jack. "I took Cathy Holman out to dinner and a movie Saturday night."

Looking surprised, Jack smiled. "What movie?"

Dan picked up his second donut. "The African Queen with Bogart."

Jack looked interested. "I've wanted to see that myself. Is it any good?"

Dan took another bite of donut and nodded. "Yeah, it was. I liked it anyway, and so did Cathy."

"At the risk of being nosey," said Jack. "Where did you eat?"

Dan told him about Joey's Restaurant and the nightcap they had after the movie, leaving out the goodnight kiss.

Jack drank the last of his coffee, looked into his empty cup, and then at Dan. "I'm glad you took my advice and asked her out."

Dan grinned, knowing he had planned to anyway without his partner's advice.

Jack smiled. "You know, Lori has wanted to get you a puppy for a while now to keep you company."

Dan chuckled. "It ain't that bad, Jack."

"Well, maybe not," said Jack as he stood up from the edge of Dan's desk. "But it's not good to be alone all the time." Then he grinned. "Must have felt good having an intelligent conversation with a beautiful woman?"

Thinking that it had been, Dan's phone rang, saving him from answering his partner, asking whether he had kissed her goodnight. He picked up the receiver. "Morgan."

"This is Irene at the switchboard. I have a Chief Travis from Englewood on the other line for Captain Foley, and when I told him he wouldn't be in for a while, he asked for you."

Curious as to why Travis would be calling Foley, he told Irene to transfer the call to him and hung up from her call.

Puzzled, Jack sat back down on the edge of Dan's. "What was that?"

Before Dan could tell him, his telephone rang. "This is Detective Morgan."

"Detective, this is Chief Travis in Englewood. I'm giving you a courtesy call to let you know that we have a missing girl."

Dan looked at Jack. "When did she go missing?"

"According to her mother," said the chief, "she's been missing since Saturday night."

Dan thought about Saturday when he and Cathy were enjoying the movie. "What's the girl's name?"

"Mary Jefferies."

Remembering her from the theater, he leaned forward, looking worried. "I just talked to her Friday night."

Travis said, "Officer Cook said he saw you in the alley behind the theater." He paused. "But he never said anything about you talking to the Jefferies girl."

"Officer Cook," said Dan, "had already left when I decided to go inside the theater and talk to Ira Tindle. Mary was working behind the snack counter." He paused, listening to the silence. "I hope I didn't overstep, Chief, but I just wanted to get a look at your crime scene at night, and then I thought I'd talk to this Ira guy."

Travis thought for a moment. "No harm done, Detective; your captain called a few days ago, and we agreed that you could poke around. But I'd appreciate a telephone call the next time so I can alert my men."

"Of course," said Dan. "When I talked to Mary, she said her mother sends her older brother to drive her home. Is he missing also?"

"Mary wasn't working Saturday night. The way I heard it from her mother, she left a girlfriend's house a couple of blocks away and never made it home."

Dan quickly thought about Paul and his white van. "Can I be of any assistance Chief?"

Chief Travis thought about the article in the Saturday morning newspaper. "No, thanks, Detective, but we do appreciate the offer. If I find out anything, I'll call your Captain."

Dan started to say the same thing but remembered he was no longer on the case and figured the Chief must have read the newspaper article and that he had decided to call Foley. "Thanks for calling Chief. I hope you find Mary safe and sound." Dan hung up the telephone and looked up at his partner, sitting on the edge of his desk. "A nice young girl by the name of Mary Jefferies, who works at the Pioneer Theater in Englewood, is missing." He paused, looking worried. "Shit, I just talked to her Friday night."

"What the hell were you doing in Englewood Friday night?"

Dan was thinking of Mary Jefferies. "Nosing around."

Still sitting on the edge of Dan's desk, Jack glanced around the noisy office, leaned toward Dan, and lowered his voice. "Have you forgotten the captain reminded us Friday afternoon that we were both off the case? Your nosing around may piss a few people off."

Dan thought about that, but he was more concerned about Mary Jefferies at the moment. "Too late now, Partner. I guess if they get pissed, they get pissed. I really don't give a shit."

Jack looked at Dan. "You ready to throw your career away?"

Dan thought about that, knowing he wasn't.

Jack looked at Dan. "Did you find out anything that would help the case?"

Dan told him about the alley and meeting Officer Cook, what Mary had said about Gail, then everything that Ira Tindle had told him. When he finished, he gave Jack his theory about the parking lot across the alley from the rear of the theater where Paul may have parked the night he dumped Gail's body.

Jack considered everything. "Are you going to tell Foley that you were nosing around in Englewood?"

"I think I'd better before he hears it from Chief Travis."

Jack chuckled. "Foley is going to chew you a new asshole, buddy."

Dan didn't care about that at the moment. He was thinking about Mary Jefferies getting abducted and terrified while he and Cathy enjoyed a night out.

Captain Foley walked past their desks, looking upset. "In my office."

Dan and Jack glanced at one another, and while Jack followed Foley, Dan picked up his manila envelopes, wondering if the captain already knew about his little trip to Englewood.

Foley was taking off his coat when they walked into his office. "Close the damn door and sit down." Foley hung up his coat, walked around his desk, and sat down on its edge, wearing a troubled look. "I just got back from Chief Roberts's office," he said, looking at Dan.

Dan figured he would be lucky if he were about to start walking a beat on Larimer Street.

"Apparently, your Paul reads the newspaper," said Foley. "He called the mayor this morning."

Surprised, Dan looked at Jack and then at the captain. "He what?"

"I won't bore you with all of it," said Foley, sounding angry. "But Paul told the chief that he had taken another girl."

Dan nodded. "I know. Chief Travis called you and asked for me when Irene told him you were out. He said that a girl named Mary Jefferies, who works at the Pioneer Theater in Englewood, is missing."

Foley stared at Dan for a moment. "You sound like you know the girl, but I don't recall her name in any of your reports."

Jack felt uncomfortable for Dan, knowing he was going to get his ass chewed.

Dan stared up at Foley. "Hear me out, Captain, before you put me on a beat downtown."

Captain Foley gave Dan a puzzled look. "Start talking."

"I was bored Friday night, so I took a ride out to Englewood and did some nosing around behind the Pioneer Theatre."

Foley looked angry. "I remember telling you two that you were off the case." He looked at Jack. "Were you with him?"

"No, he wasn't," said Dan. "And he didn't know anything about it. While I was there, I went into the theater to talk to that janitor, Ira

Tindle, who found Gail Thomas's body in the alley. Mary Jefferies was working behind the concession stand."

Captain Foley chuckled while shaking his head. "You're a lucky bastard, Morgan."

Confusion filled Dan's face as he looked at Jack and then at Foley.

The captain stood, walked around his desk, and eased into his chair, wearing a big grin as he looked at Dan. "Your friend Paul told the mayor that unless he returns you to the case and keeps his Special Task Force out of the investigation, this Mary will die a slow, agonizing death. And so will the next girl and the next."

Dan wished that the captain would stop referring to Paul as his friend. Then he pictured Mary Jefferies standing behind the counter in the theater last Friday night while they talked. Then of her lying on an army blanket in some alley or park and felt a little sick to his stomach.

Foley continued. "Then the son of a bitch said that he would call the newspapers and tell them why she died. And that the mayor took two of the city's top detectives off the case and hired his own personal, private investigators to create a Special Task Force paid by the taxpayers."

"Holy Crap," said Jack wearing a big grin. "What's the mayor going to do now?"

Captain Foley chuckled without humor as he looked at Jack and then Dan. "He wants to be re-elected, so what the hell could he do? He agreed." Foley nodded at the envelopes Dan was holding. "You can keep your precious envelopes. You two are back on the case."

Though Dan felt relieved, he was still concerned about the Jefferies girl. "Did Paul say he was letting the Jefferies girl go?"

Foley shook his head. "He just hung up the telephone after the mayor agreed."

While Dan worried about Mary Jefferies, Jack asked, "Are the mayor's men totally out of the picture?"

Foley nodded. "Unless he kills the girl, or we ask for their help." He leaned forward with his forearms resting on his desk, looking from one face to the other. "We could use the manpower, but I don't want any of the mayor's men reporting back to him on our every move."

Dan looked relieved. "I'm glad to hear you say that, Captain."

Jack nodded in agreement. "Me too."

Foley looked from Jack to Dan. "You two better catch this bastard." He sat back in his chair, looking at Dan. "I think Paul's interest in you may be our best hope in nailing him."

Dan decided to tell Foley about the conversation he had entered into with Paul the previous Friday. "Paul called me on Friday just as I was getting ready to leave."

Foley looked interested. "What did he have to say?"

"He pretty much admitted to killing Trenton and Ruth."

Foley looked surprised. "Did you record it?"

Dan nodded. "Yes, sir."

"Good," said Foley. "I want to hear it later."

A detective knocked on the door, opened it, and looked at Dan. "There's someone on your telephone saying it's an emergency."

Thinking of his son, Dan rushed out of the captain's office and picked up the receiver the other detective had laid on his desk. "This is Dan Morgan."

"Sorry if I alarmed you, Detective," said Paul. "But the person that answered your telephone said you were in a meeting, and we need to talk."

Dan looked at Jack, standing at his desk, and mouthed for him to turn on the recording.

"I don't want this call traced before we have a chance to talk," said Paul. "There are two telephone booths on the back wall of Micky's Bar. I'm sure you know where that is."

Dan wondered how he knew about Micky's.

"If you want to see Mary Jefferies alive again, be there in five minutes."

The phone went dead; Dan hung up the telephone and reached for his coat on the back of his chair while telling Jack, "He wants me to be at the payphones in Micky's bar in five minutes." Putting on his suit coat as he hurried away, he added over his shoulder, "Tell the captain I'll be back as soon as I can."

Dan rushed out of Police Headquarters, running down Champa Street's sidewalk, racing a streetcar heading toward the corner and Micky's Bar. Losing the race and out of breath, he caught up to the trolley when it stopped to pick up passengers in front of Micky's Bar. Opening the dark brown wooden door, Dan stepped inside the dim bar, and without pausing to let his eyes adjust to the dim light, he hurried toward the back of the room. Rushing past tables and chairs partially filled with a late lunch crowd, he made his way toward the telephone booths. Hearing one of the telephones ringing and seeing a customer stand from a nearby table to answer it, Dan yelled, "Don't answer that."

Startled, the man sat down and watched Dan hurry past his table to the ringing telephone.

Stepping into the phone booth, Dan took the earpiece off the hook and put his lips close to the black mouthpiece protruding from the telephone. "I'm here," he said, sounding out of breath while he closed the wood-framed glass door turning on the overhead light.

Paul chuckled. "You sound a little short of breath, Detective."

"I don't run a lot," replied Dan, remembering that when Paul called him Detective, he was probably upset.

There was a pause, and then Paul said, "I hope you and the mayor have had time to talk."

"I haven't talked with the mayor, but my captain told me about your telephone call and the agreement to put my partner and me back on the case."

"I don't care about that partner of yours, but I am happy to hear that you're back on the case."

"Is Mary Jefferies alright?"

"She is for now." Paul paused, imagining how worried Dan was over the girl. "She's a very pretty girl, don't you think, Detective?"

"You told the mayor that if I were put back on the case, you would let her go."

"That's not what I said, Detective." Paul decided to have a little tormenting fun with his detective. "I told the mayor that unless he agreed to put you back on the case and forget about that task force, she would die a slow, agonizing death, as would the next." He paused and smiled. "I never said anything about letting her go."

Trying not to let his anger be heard, Dan gripped the black telephone cord, leaned into the mouthpiece, and lowered his voice. "Let her go, Paul."

Paul was enjoying Dan's agony. "She does appear to be a nice, sweet young girl." He chuckled softly. "But they all were nice and sweet, even that prostitute friend of yours."

Visions of Ruth lying in the ditch flashed in his memory, and he knew he didn't want Mary to end up like her or the other girls. "You got what you wanted from the mayor. Let the Jefferies girl go." Dan listened to the silence, trying to think of something that would have some effect on Paul's good side if he had one at all. "Are you there, Paul?"

"Does Mary remind you of your little Nancy, Dan? Is that why you are so interested in her?"

The question caught Dan by surprise, and Paul mentioning her name fueled his anger. "Don't talk about Nancy, you bastard."

"Temper, temper. I meant no disrespect, Dan."

The back of Dan's neck crawled, realizing just how much Paul must know about him as images of other men he knew flashed through his mind.

"It's just that I'm sure you miss your daughter as much as you do your late wife. I was curious, is all."

"How do you know about Nancy and my wife?"

"You would be surprised at what I know about you, Dan."

Dan remembered Professor Pappel saying Paul probably knew more about him than he would like. "We've met, haven't we?"

Silence filled the telephone.

"Not really. But I know about you and your family and the sorrow you felt when your little Nancy died all those years ago."

Dan was getting angrier. "This isn't about Nancy or my wife. It's about Mary Jefferies."

Paul considered that. "That may be true, but I'd still like an answer. Does she remind you of your Nancy?"

Hoping it might help Mary, he said, "Yes, she does. She reminds me of my daughter Nancy." There was a long pause, and while Dan waited for a response, he thought about the process Paul would follow and how Mary Jefferies would be dead in a few hours. "Paul?"

"What is it, Detective?"

Dan gripped the black mouthpiece with his right hand and put his lips close to it. "What about Mary Jefferies?"

Paul considered for several moments letting Dan hang on in agony while he became aroused. He envisioned her soft, white skin as her body hung upside down over his bathtub with her blood flowing from the small puncture in her neck. "I'm afraid Mary will be staying with me a while longer."

Knowing what Paul meant and fearing he was about to hang up, Dan struggled to say something that would change his mind. "If you kill Mary Jefferies, I will be taken off the case." The line went quiet, but Dan could hear Paul's breathing on the other end of the line and hoped he was thinking about what he had just said. "You started this game with me, Paul, and I want to finish it, one way or the other. If I'm taken off the case, our game is over. You can't win, I can't win, and we both want to win, don't we, Paul."

Paul thought about the plans he had set in motion weeks ago that included Detective Daniel Morgan. He chuckled softly. "Do you think you can win this game, Dan?"

As the dial tone filled the telephone line, Dan closed his eyes, rested his head against the black mouthpiece, and imagined Mary Jefferies lying on an old army blanket with her eyes open and her skin pale white. He slowly put the receiver onto the black hook, put his fingers through the brass handle of the door, and pulled it open, feeling the rush of fresh air as the tiny dim light above him went out. He sat in the dark on the wooden seat in the telephone booth for several moments while voices and laughter filled Micky's bar. Feeling years older from exhaustion, fearful for the Jefferies girl, and disappointed in himself for failing her, he imagined

236

telling her parents that he was unable to save their daughter. Self-anger rushed at him, as he hit the wall of the telephone booth with his fist. Stepping out of the booth, he walked toward the front door, oblivious to those around him. Fearing that Mary Jefferies had but a few hours left of her young life, he stepped outside into the warm morning sun. Feeling sick, he walked to the curb, put one hand on the steel pole of the 'No Parking' sign, leaned over, and vomited into the gutter.

Jack looked up from what he was doing as Dan made his way between desks toward the captain's office, looking like the world was about to end. Sensing it may surely be ending for the Jefferies girl, he got up and followed him into Foley's office. Closing the door, he watched while a troubled Dan Morgan flopped into one of the three chairs.

Foley looked worried. "Are you alright?"

Dan nodded. "Yeah, but I'm not so sure about Mary Jefferies."

Captain Foley considered that quickly as he slipped into his suit coat. "Chief Roberts wants to hear what happened firsthand. No sense in you telling it twice."

Denver Police Chief James Roberts was sitting behind his big, walnut desk dressed in his dark blue uniform, white shirt, and black tie. He looked up as his secretary opened the door, telling him that Captain Foley and two Detectives were here to see him. Thinking he knew what this concerned, he told her to show them in.

As Captain Foley, Jack, and Dan walked in, the Chief tossed what he was reading to one side and motioned to six leather chairs lined up in front of his desk. "Have a seat, gentlemen." He waited until everyone had sat down before he looked at Detective Morgan. "I was told that you had another call from this Paul character and went running off to Micky's."

Dan nodded. "He wanted to talk someplace where the call couldn't be traced."

Chief Roberts glanced at Foley. "Smart bastard." He looked at Dan. "What did he have to say?"

The chief and the others listened while Dan told them about the phone conversation, leaving out the part about his daughter Nancy. He told of his fears that Paul had never promised he would not kill her, but only that it would not be slow. Then he said that he was afraid the girl might be dead within a few hours.

Chief Roberts sat back in his big, black leather chair, looking sad and disappointed. "The mayor agreed to that bastard's demands, thinking he'd let the girl go." He looked at Dan. "You've talked to him before. What do you think he'll do?"

Dan shrugged. "I honestly don't know. But in talking to Professor Pappel, the way I understand things, Paul is in a continual battle with himself. I tried appealing to his good side if he had one, but I don't know if that did any good."

Chief Roberts thought for a moment. "Do you really think this animal has a good side, Detective?"

Dan considered the question. "He showed a sign of weakness, or humanity, whatever you want to call it, so yeah, I think there is a human being in there somewhere." He paused. "I'm just not sure I found it."

"Damn it," said Chief Roberts angrily. "If that girl dies, this case will be turned over again to the Mayor's Special Task Force." He paused, looking at Captain Foley. "I don't want to see that happen."

"Neither do I," said Foley. "For whatever reason, this Paul wants Dan to stay on the case, and maybe we are getting ahead of ourselves." He looked at Dan. "I don't think he's done with you yet."

Dan looked at the chief and then Captain Foley. "You're probably right, Captain. But I still don't know what the connection is between him and me, and it seems he definitely wants me to know."

Chief Roberts sat forward with his forearms on the desk, hands together, fingers entwined. "You have no idea what that could be?"

Dan shook his head. "No, sir, but I am sure he wants to continue this game he's been playing, whatever that is. I told him that if the girl dies, I'll be removed from the case, the game ends, and neither of us will win."

Foley sat forward in his chair and looked at his detective. "That was smart thinking, Dan. I don't think he'll kill her; you're too important to him for some reason. I only wish we could find out what that reason is."

Dan looked at him. "I hope you're right, Captain, but it depends on which Paul wins the battle over Mary Jefferies."

"So, we just sit back and wait?" asked a disappointed Chief Roberts.

Foley looked at the chief as he gestured at Dan. "Paul's connection with Detective Morgan is our best chance of catching the son of a bitch. I believe he'll contact Dan before he does anything to the girl."

"You may be right," said Chief Roberts. As he looked at Dan, he picked up a folder from his desk and opened it. "I see you've been a police officer since 1936."

Dan knew he was looking at his personnel file. "Yes, sir, except when I was in the military."

Roberts set the file down. "Your father was a police officer."

"Yes, sir," answered Dan. "He was."

"I never knew him," said Chief Roberts. "But his file tells of a dedicated police officer, and I'm sure he was a dedicated family man as well."

"Yes, sir, he was," replied Dan in pleasant recollection.

Chief Roberts sat back in his chair. "Is your father the reason you joined the force?"

Dan had pleasing memories of his father wearing a policeman's uniform. "I'm sure that played a big part in my decision."

Chief Roberts looked down at the file folder. "I also see that you served with the Rangers during the war."

Dan gestured at Jack. "We both did."

Roberts looked at Jack Brolin. "I've been looking in your file as well. What prompted you to become a policeman?"

Jack glanced at his partner. "Dan and I have known one another since we were kids. We went to the same school, played ball together, and even double-dated. It just followed that when he joined, I did too. Just as we both joined when the war came."

Chief Roberts pointed from one to the other. "You two look out for one another?"

"We do," said both Dan and Jack while looking at one another.

"Friendship is a strong thing," said Chief Roberts thoughtfully as he glanced from one to the other. Then he looked at Captain Foley. "These two work well together?"

"They do."

Chief Roberts thought about that for a moment, and then he looked at Dan. "Might serve you well to stay in contact with George Pappel. He's a little strange, but he is very intelligent and knows what he is talking about."

"How long have you known the professor?" asked Dan out of curiosity.

Chief Roberts thought again. "He and I go way back. Hadn't seen him for several years until a few months back when we ran into one another at a restaurant downtown." He looked at Dan. "Why are you asking?"

Dan shrugged. "Just curious, is all." He smiled. "He's very likable."

"Yes, he is." The chief leaned back in his chair, looking at Foley. "You have six detectives in homicide, Harold?"

"Yes, sir, I'm the seventh, I guess."

Chief Roberts thought about that. "We don't have a big homicide department like some other cities, Harold, and we can't afford a bigger one." He paused in thought. "Perhaps one day we will, but until that day comes, we'll do the best we can with what we have. I don't want these two working on any other cases. If you need a patrolman or two to help you out, call me."

"Yes, sir," replied Foley. "Thank you."

Dan leaned forward with his forearms resting on his knees. "Does that include the Howard Trenton case?"

Chief Roberts looked at Dan in silence for several moments.

Captain Foley silently wished that Dan hadn't brought that up.

Chief Roberts turned to Captain Foley. "Harold, what are your other two detectives, Hargrove and Mueller, working on?"

"Cases I took from Detectives Morgan and Brolin, plus the ones they were already working on."

"And what about Detectives Arnold and Cross?" asked the chief. "What are they working on?"

Foley shifted in his chair. "The files I took from Hargrove and Mueller."

Chief Roberts thought about that as he sat back again and looked at Dan. "Foley told me he listened to the conversation you had with this Paul fellow regarding Howard Trenton's murder. Work it with the others. Just catch this bastard." He glanced at his watch as he stood. "If you will excuse me, gentlemen, I have other issues to tend to." He looked at Captain Foley. "Keep me informed, Harold."

Twenty-Four

Mary Ann Jefferies opened her eyes, quickly sat up, and glanced around the room that had become her prison, not knowing what time it was or whether it was day or night. She wiped the sleep from her red, puffy eyes remembering the promise about her going home. Mary slid off the bed, walked into the bathroom, and closed the door. When she came out, the familiar tray and breakfast were sitting on the small table, and even though she was worried, she was also hungry.

"Glad to see you are eating, Mary," said the familiar voice on the other side of the door.

While licking the taste of eggs from her fingers, she stepped closer to the door. "You promised I could go home soon." Mary picked up the one piece of bacon, took a bite, and stared at the door, waiting for the man on the other side to say something.

"Do you know a Dan Morgan?"

Mary thought for a moment and then remembered the man that had talked with Ira. "I think he's a police officer in Denver."

"Detective," corrected Paul. "He's a detective."

She took another bite of bacon. "Yes, I know him." Then she asked, "Is he the one you keep calling My Detective?"

Paul ignored the question figuring she knew the answer. "I'm going to take you to him tonight."

Puzzled, she stepped closer to the door. "Why not just take me home?"

"Don't you like Detective Morgan?"

She considered the question and how she should answer. "I guess so. I don't know him that well."

Paul chuckled. "Well, it seems that he has an interest in your well-being."

Mary was glad but confused. "What sort of interest?"

"You're such a child at times, Mary. You'll have to ask him when you see him."

Mary did not like being called a child. "When will you take me to him?"

"Soon, but first you finish eating, drink your orange juice, and then get cleaned up. I have to leave for a while."

"Wait."

"What is it?"

"What time is it?"

He stared at her through the peephole, fighting his urge to touch her like he had the others. "It's early. Now, do as I say."

Detectives Morgan and Brolin were at their desks working on their inboxes when Dan's telephone rang. He put the pencil down and picked up the receiver. "Dan Morgan."

"Good afternoon, Dan."

Dan's heart raced as he looked at Jack. "Hello, Paul."

Jack reached across his desk, turning on the recorder sitting on Dan's desk.

"I'll have a package for you sometime tonight."

Dan thought about the packages of Ruthie and Howard Trenton, fearing for Mary's well-being. "Is Mary alive?"

Paul evaded the question getting enjoyment out of Dan's concerns about his precious Mary. "I'm going to put her someplace later tonight."

That put fear into Dan as he looked at Jack. "What do you mean, put her someplace? Is Mary alright?"

"Of course. Neither you nor I want anything to come between us and our little game now, do we?"

"No, Paul," said a relieved Dan Morgan. "We don't."

Humorously, Paul said, "I can almost hear the click, click of the tracers trying to find me, so this will be quick. I'll call you around seven-thirty on the same telephone we talked on earlier today to tell you where you can find her. You must answer by the fifth ring to find out where she is, or the deal is off, and then she will be mine." He paused. "You will never know what happened to her."

Dan knew what that meant. "I'll be there."

"Bring your partner, Detective Brolin. You may need him."

Dan thought about that. "Why will I need my partner?" Hearing a click followed by a dial tone, Dan hoped nothing would go wrong as he looked at Jack. "Paul says I'll need you along with me tonight."

Jack looked puzzled. "Why?"

Dan reached over, turned off the recorder, and looked at his partner. "I don't know."

Jack looked worried. "Do you think this Mary is alright?"

Dan looked at Jack and shook his head. "I don't know for sure." He looked at his watch and then at the big, white-faced clock above the stairs leading down to the first floor. "It's only four-forty."

"When is he releasing her?"

Dan turned from the clock. "He said he would call me at Micky's at seven-thirty tonight." He paused and looked at Jack. "I just realized something. He knows your name."

That concerned Jack. "How the hell does he know my name?"

Dan shook his head. "I don't know, but he seems to know everything." He leaned forward, glanced around, and lowered his voice. "When we were talking on the telephone at Micky's, he mentioned Nancy."

"Your daughter?"

Dan nodded his head.

Looking concerned, Jack stood from his desk, walked around it to Dan's, sat on the edge, and lowered his voice. "What did he say?"

"He asked if Mary reminded me of Nancy."

"Jesus," said Jack. "We gonna tell Foley about tonight?"

Dan thought about that for a long moment as he looked toward the captain's office. "No. Foley will tell the chief, and if Paul sees any police, we may never see Mary Jefferies again. We can't take the chance."

"Foley would never screw up our picking up Mary Jefferies," said Jack. "He isn't like that."

"I know," replied Dan. "But I can't chance the chief or mayor knowing, and Foley will feel obligated to tell them." He looked toward Foley's office. "Foley would probably go along with not telling the chief, and I don't want to put him in that position."

The day was quickly fading when Dan turned his car into the parking lot of Micky's bar, letting the front tires nestle against the sidewalk's cement barrier separating the parking lot from the stucco building. He turned off the headlights, shut the engine off, and in the stillness, neither he nor Jack spoke as they got out of the car. They walked toward the front of the building beneath the neon sign of blues, yellows, and reds spelling Micky's. Dan pulled the dark, wooden door open, and as they stepped into the quiet lounge, they saw that only a few of the thirty stools along the narrow bar were occupied. The familiar balding, heavyset male bartender nodded as they walked toward a table close to the two telephone booths in the back of the lounge.

Sitting down at a small, square table, Dan felt anxious and looked at his watch. "Six-fifty," he said softly, and then he glanced around the dim room at the few people sitting at tables or the bar talking and seemingly having a good time. Hearing a woman's loud laugh, he glanced across the room at a man and a woman in the far corner, enjoying a game of shuffleboard. The woman let out a shrill yelp followed by another loud laugh and then hugged the man spilling his drink. Dan wished they would leave.

A plump woman in her early thirties wearing a white blouse and short white apron over a dark blue skirt walked toward them. She smiled. "Hi, boys, the usual?"

Jack looked up, nodded, and smiled. "The usual." Then watched as she walked away to get their drinks.

Dan took off his fedora, set it on an empty chair, looked at his watch, and then at the telephone booths wishing it was 7:30.

Jack placed his hat on the other empty chair, glanced at his watch, and then turned to look at the noisy couple playing shuffleboard, wishing they would be a little quieter.

Still feeling anxious, Dan checked his watch again, hoping nothing had gone wrong. He wanted to get the Jefferies girl safely home to her parents. Then his thoughts turned to his earlier conversation with Paul, and he wondered who Paul really was and why he was so interested in him, his life, and his family. The minutes passed in silence, and by seven-twenty, they were working on their second drink. Dan began to fear that the beast in Paul wanted Mary Jefferies more than it wanted to continue his game. Dan looked at his watch. "It's 7:25," he said, looking at Jack. "I hope the bastard hasn't changed his mind."

The waitress had just stopped at their table to ask if they wanted another drink when one of the two telephones began ringing. Fearing the fifth ring, Dan jumped up, overturning his chair, rushed into the telephone booth, grabbed the earpiece, and put his lips next to the black mouthpiece. "Hello."

"Hello, Dan."

His stomach clenching, Dan asked, "Is Mary Jefferies alright?"

Back at the table, Jack looked up at Doris, who was watching Dan and smiled. "Big date."

She gave Jack a look and then turned and walked away.

Jack stood, picked up Dan's chair, rushed over to the booth, and stuck his head inside to listen.

Paul let Dan wait in agony for a moment. "You are so predictable, Detective. I almost know what you are going to say before you say it. Little Mary is waiting for you by the trash cans behind Micky's."

Fearing he may have killed her, Dan handed the phone to Jack, squeezed past him, and rushed toward the front door, imagining her lying on one of Paul's army blankets.

Jack put the receiver to his ear, and as he said hello, he heard a click, and the phone went silent. Putting the receiver back onto the black hook of the telephone box, he stepped out of the phone booth and rushed to the table. After tossing some money onto the table for the drinks and a tip, he picked up his and Dan's hats and hurried toward the front door.

Dan ran past his parked car and stopped in the alley, glancing left and then right. Seeing Mary sitting on the cold cement next to the trashcans with a hood over her head and her hands and feet bound, he ran to her.

By the time Jack got to Dan's car, he was already helping a weak, crying, and frightened Mary walk from the alley along the narrow sidewalk toward his car.

Seeing Jack in the parking lot's dim light, Mary Jefferies pulled away from Dan and stepped back in fear.

Dan held her close. "That's my partner Jack Brolin. He's here to help." Dan handed the hood he had taken off Mary along with the rope to Jack.

Mary looked tired as the tears ran down her cheeks. "Can I go home?"

"Right now," said Dan as he glanced around, knowing that Paul was watching from the shadows. He helped her into the back seat and gave the keys to Jack. "Head south toward Englewood. When we get close to her house, Mary can give you the directions."

Jack tossed the two hats, cloth hood, and ropes onto the passenger seat, climbed into the driver's seat, and waited for Dan to get Mary settled in the back.

As Dan sat next to Mary, he asked, "Are you sure you're okay?"

She managed a small smile as she wiped her cheeks. "I think so." Then she began to cry. "I was scared he would kill me like he did, Gail."

"Try not to think about that right now, Mary," said Dan. "You will be home soon, and no one will hurt you."

Jack backed the car up, drove out of the parking lot, and turned south on Champa Street toward Englewood.

Though she felt secure in Dan's arms, tears ran down Mary's cheeks. "All I could think about was Gail."

"I know, Mary, but try not to think about it. You'll be home in a few minutes." Then Dan handed her his clean handkerchief. "I'm sure your family is worried."

She took the hanky, wiped her eyes and cheeks, and smiled. "He kept calling you my detective."

Dan smiled. "And right now, I am."

Paul started the engine of his van, drove out of the shadows from the side street where he had been watching, and followed Dan's car at a safe distance along Champa Street. After a few blocks, he turned west toward the highway that would take him home. His mind soon imagined Mary Jefferies lying on the bed nude and then hanging upside down over the porcelain bathtub while her red blood pooled beneath her. He imagined washing her and then making love to her as he had the others. Paul hadn't driven but a few blocks when he became anxious, feeling warm and filled with lust. Beads of sweat formed on his forehead, so he rolled the driver's window down to let the cool, fresh night air inside the van. Unable to dislodge the image of Mary Jefferies' nude body, her soft white skin, and pubic hair, his desire for her became uncontrollable. His eyes filled with tears that blurred the road and traffic ahead of him. As they ran down his cheeks, he gripped the steering wheel so tightly his knuckles turned white, and then he pounded the steering wheel with his right hand and cried. "I had to let her go!"

Sobbing like a child, he turned the van onto a dark side street, stopped, and turned off the headlights and motor. Sitting in the quiet darkness, he closed his eyes and leaned forward, resting his forehead on his hands. Moments passed before he sat back and wiped the tears from his eyes and cheeks with the sleeve of his dark blue shirt. Trying to push the images of her out of his mind, he cried out, "Go away!" Then he softly whispered, "Please go away and leave me alone." Tears tasting of salt made their way down his face to the corners of his mouth. Closing his eyes, he slid down in the seat until his knees touched the dashboard under the steering wheel and sobbed.

Minutes passed before he opened his eyes and slowly sat back up in the seat, wiping his wet cheeks and welling eyes with his hands. "I'll find another girl tonight to take the place of Mary Jefferies, I promise." He sat taller in the van seat, turned the key, and pushed the starter button with his left foot. As the engine fired up, he turned on the headlights and shifted into low gear. Making a U-turn, he drove to the corner and turned right, thinking of the drug store on Federal Boulevard and the young girl who worked there. He followed the headlights of his van along the street, where streetlights cast round islands of light onto the dark pavement. He remembered that she had always been nice to him and often gave him a second Cherry Coke at no charge. Looking at his wristwatch, he knew he had to hurry.

The soft sound of the engine and tires whining on the asphalt filled the quiet car as Jack drove south on Broadway, occasionally glancing into the rearview mirror at Dan and Mary. Sounds of light traffic, an occasional horn, and the clanging bells of a streetcar going in the other direction filtered through the closed windows. Dan held Mary Jefferies and thought of his daughter as lights from passing streetlamps made their quick trips in and out of the car, illuminating Mary's face.

Entering the city of Englewood, Dan could tell by Mary's soft breathing that she had fallen asleep and wondered how much sleep she'd had in the past three days. Hating to wake her for directions to her house, he gently shook her shoulder. "Mary."

She opened her sleepy eyes, sat up, and looked out the window at the familiar lights of Englewood.

Dan smiled at her. "You need to tell us where you live."

Feeling tired and sleepy but anxious to get home, she looked past the front seat out the windshield and gave Jack the directions to her house. Several minutes later, the car slowed, and then she pointed at her house, telling him to stop. Jack pulled to the curb and stopped the car in front of a single-story, white, wood-framed house. He shut off the lights and engine, got out, and opened the rear door. Dan got out, helped Mary out of the car, and quietly closed the door. They stood on the sidewalk looking at the lights of the house that she had thought she would never see again. The excitement of being home was almost overwhelming for her.

Dan smiled as he gestured toward the house. "Your parents are waiting."

She looked disappointed. "You're not coming in?"

He shook his head. "No, Mary, this time is for you and your family. We need to ask you some questions, but we'll talk another time. Maybe tomorrow if you're up to it."

She put her arms around Dan, hugged him, and whispered thank you, turned to give Jack a quick hug as well, and then hurried up the narrow walk toward the front door. Finding it locked, she rang the doorbell.

The door opened, and at seeing her daughter, Mrs. Jefferies let out a scream of joy, took her daughter into her arms, and cried.

When the door closed, sounds of laughter and joy poured out of the open windows to the sidewalk where Dan and Jack stood. They looked at one another in happy silence, and while Jack opened the passenger door, picked up the hood and rope, tossing them in the back, got in, and closed the door, Dan took another moment to look at the figures inside. Moments passed before he opened the car door, climbed in, and started the engine.

Both men were silent as Dan drove north along South Broadway toward Denver. Jack stared at the headlights mixing with the neon signs and streetlamps on the street ahead of them. Turning from the scene out the windshield, he looked at the side of Dan's face immersed in the dim lights of the dashboard and noticed how worried he looked. "What are you thinking?"

"Just wondering who we traded Mary for."

Dan dropped Jack Brolin off by his car in the Police Headquarters parking lot and then drove home thinking about Mary Jefferies, the other unfortunate girls, Ruth, and Howard Trenton. Driving into his driveway, he stopped next to the dark living room window, shut the engine off, and then the headlights. As darkness consumed the car and the driveway, Dan stared out the windshield at the dark image of the garage doors bathed in the faint moonlight. He thought about the joy of the Jefferies family and the sorrow of the other families. Dan hated Paul and wanted to stop him, but Paul was outwitting him and Jack at every turn. It seemed as if Paul could do whatever he wanted, and no one could stop him.

Reaching over to the passenger seat to gather up the stack of ten by twelve manila envelopes, he thought of the rope and hood he had taken off of Mary. Looking at them sitting in the back seat, he would put them in the evidence locker as evidence if they ever arrested Paul. Then he picked up the envelopes, got out of the car, and once inside the house, he set the envelopes on the table in the foyer, his car keys in the bowl, and hung up his hat. After picking up the mail from the floor, he glanced through it as he walked into the living room. Tossing the mail on the desk, he picked up the telephone, dialed Captain Folcy, and told him about getting Mary back and why he had not told anyone else. Foley understood Dan's reasoning and agreed that too many people knowing about Mary could be dangerous. He then told Dan not to make of habit of keeping him out of the loop.

Telling the captain goodnight, he hung up the telephone and walked toward the kitchen, where he draped his suit coat over the back of a kitchen chair. He opened the refrigerator, took out a bottle of beer, opened it, and took a long drink, letting out a soft belch. Feeling hungry, he set the bottle on the red Formica table and opened the refrigerator door. His eyes roamed the inside for something to make a sandwich with, but before he could find it, the telephone on the living room desk rang. Hoping it was Cathy calling, he closed the refrigerator door, picked up his beer, and hurried down the hall to the living room.

"Hello," answered Dan.

"Hello yourself," said Cathy.

Glad that she called, he smiled. "What are you doing?"

"Sitting on the sofa watching television. What are you doing?"

"Not much," said Dan. "I just got home and was getting ready to fix a sandwich."

Cathy looked at her watch. "Kind of late, isn't it?"

Dan looked at his watch as he pulled the chair away from the desk. "I guess it is."

"Did you have a good day?"

He sat down and took a drink of beer. "Actually, it turned out to be a very good day." He told her about getting Mary first but not about Paul's telephone call to the mayor. He told her that Paul had called him and that he somehow had managed to talk him into letting her go.

Cathy smiled, feeling happy about the girl. "I would say you had quite a good day."

He took a drink of beer and looked out the window into the darkness. "Yes, I did."

"I bet you're tired."

"A little. It's been a long day."

"It's too bad you're so far away. I'd like to fix you something to eat."

"I'd like that, but in truth, I don't feel like the drive."

"I understand," she said, disappointed. "You sound tired. Perhaps you should get some rest."

"I think I will." He took a drink of beer. "I'll call you tomorrow night."

"Dan, I am so happy about that young girl."

He felt good about Mary himself and remembered how she had run up the sidewalk to the front door and then into her mother's arms. "Me too."

"You get some rest," said Cathy. "Goodnight."

He hung up the phone and went back to the kitchen to fix that sandwich, but instead opened another beer and returned to his chair in the living room.

Startled by the telephone ringing, Dan opened his sleepy eyes, looked at his wristwatch, and seeing it was a few minutes past eleven-thirty at night, he got up from the chair he had fallen asleep in and answered the telephone. "Hello."

"This is Foley."

"Yeah," said Dan fearing the news.

"Looks like Paul grabbed another girl after he let the Jefferies girl go."

Dan was wide awake. "Damn it. Where?"

"Smith Lake in Washington Park, near the hotel. I'll call Jack, and we'll meet you there."

Dan hung up, headed for his suit coat on the back of the kitchen chair, picked up his keys from the jar on the table in the foyer, and headed out the front door.

Thirty minutes later, Dan turned off of South Downing Street into Washington Park and drove along the paved street that snaked its way through the park. While rounding a curve, he could see headlights of cars across the lake looking like flickering dots that quickly disappeared and reappeared through the bushes that lined the winding road. Driving into a clearing, he could see the bright-colored neon sign, "Lane Hotel," on the roof of the eight-story hotel reflecting off the black lake. Beyond the lake shore were the headlights, exploding flashbulbs, and dancing flashlights of the police.

Turning into a gravel parking lot next to the lake, he parked behind Jack's car, grabbed his flashlight from the glove compartment, climbed out, and hurried past several patrol cars whose headlights lit up the scene. He hurried through the headlights into the chaotic world of bright, exploding flashbulbs, police flashlights, and voices. Seeing Jack standing next to Pete Lange, kneeling next to a body he knew would be another young teenage girl, he walked a little faster. Blinded temporarily by the flashbulbs, he looked down at the body, asking his partner how long he had been here.

"Not long. Five minutes maybe."

Dan glanced around. "Where's the captain?"

"Behind you," replied Captain Folcy, then quickly added, "I got lost."

Dan turned from Foley and looked down at the victim lying on the damp grass, dressed in a blue blouse, boys Levi's, tennis shoes, and white socks. He noticed her arm was lying in the lake up to the elbow, and the army blanket that had become one of Paul's trademarks was missing.

Pete Lange looked up at Foley. "There are no cut marks on the neck." Then he gently turned her over enough to lift her blouse and point to the dark skin. "Her blood has gathered at the lowest part of the body."

Foley knelt next to Lang, looked at the girl for a moment, and then at Dan, who was kneeling next to him. "Maybe this one has nothing to do with your friend."

Pete Lang looked at the captain and then at Dan. "Exsanguination is not the cause of death on this young lady."

Foley stood. "Let me know what the cause of death is as soon as you can."

The others watched as Dan pulled her blouse out from her pants and unbuttoned the front of her Levi's.

"What are you doing?" asked the captain.

He pulled her Levi's down a little and looked up at Foley. "Where are her panties?"

Knowing what Dan was thinking, Captain Foley knelt next to him. "That still doesn't prove Paul killed her."

Dan stood. "He killed her, alright, Captain. I'd bet my house on it." He looked at Lang. "Pete, can you tell if there is any semen on her pubic area?"

Pete looked at Dan for a moment and then at Foley.

"Well?" asked the captain.

Lang knelt, pulled her Levi's down a little farther, smelled the area, and then looked at Foley and Dan. "Can't say for certain until I get her on one of my tables, but it smells like semen."

Dan looked at Captain Foley. "It was Paul. He's changing just like Professor Pappel feared he would."

"Let's let Pete and Todd do their jobs," said Foley.

Dan watched Pete examining the victim. "When did the call come in?"

Captain Foley thought for a moment. "Someone called it in at eleven-seventeen. I got the call around eleven-thirty and called you."

"Did they give a name?" asked Jack.

Foley shook his head. "The officer at the desk told me that the caller just said we would find a body on the north side of the lake near the hotel and then hung up."

Dan shined the flashlight on his wristwatch, seeing it was almost one in the morning, and then he knelt next to Pete Lange. "Can you give an estimate of the time of death?"

Lange picked up the arm that was not in the water, bent it at the elbow, and touched various parts of the body, checking for rigor. "I'd guess three, four hours." Holding his watch under his flashlight, he said, "I'm guessing she died somewhere around ten." He looked at Dan. "It's just a guess at this point. I'll know more when I get her on one of my tables."

Dan thought of his daughter lying on one of Pete's tables as he looked across the dark expanse of the park to the lighted windows of the hotel rising out of the darkness. "I'm betting the lobby of the hotel has pay phones."

Foley turned around, looked at the hotel, and when he turned back toward Dan, he and Jack were already heading toward the hotel.

Dan and Jack hurried through the main door and walked across the empty lobby to the counter of the front desk, where they saw a solitary male clerk of thirty dressed in a dark suit looking bored.

Holding up their badges, Dan quickly asked, "Where are the pay phones?"

Curious about the two, the clerk pointed to his left. "There are two around the corner next to the bathrooms."

While Jack disappeared around the corner toward the telephones, Dan asked the clerk how long he had been on duty.

"Since nine o'clock last night."

"Did you see anyone who looked out of place in the lobby around eleven?"

The desk clerk thought for a moment. "There was a man who came from where the bathrooms and telephones are around that time and walked out the door. I was a little suspicious, so I stepped outside and watched him get into a white van and drive away. I figured he used the bathroom."

Jack walked up. "There are two pay telephones, one on the wall next to the men's bathroom and one on the wall next to the women's bathroom."

Dan turned back to the clerk. "Can you describe this man?"

The clerk thought for a moment. "About your height, I'd guess, maybe bigger."

"How about his hair," asked Jack.

"He had a red baseball cap on, but his hair was dark, either black or dark brown. He wouldn't look at me, so I never saw his face."

Disappointed, Dan asked, "How was he dressed?"

"Blue pants and shirt. The kind deliverymen wear. He had those black boots on," he paused in thought. "I think they're called Engineer boots. You know, the ones with the strap and buckle."

Dan knew exactly what he meant, hoping that this could be their first break. He looked at Jack. "Make sure no one else uses the telephones while I go back for Todd so he can dust them for prints."

While Todd worked the men's bathroom and pay telephones for prints, Dan and Jack returned to the lake, where Dan told Captain Foley everything the clerk had told him about the man in the lobby and his driving away in a white van.

"Your friend is getting sloppy," said Foley. "And that's good for us."

Wishing the captain would stop calling Paul his friend he watched Pete and one of his men as they lifted the young girl's body onto a gurney. He wondered if Paul was getting sloppy on purpose. "If it's alright, Captain," said Dan. "I'd like to drive out to Englewood before I come in tomorrow and see if Mary Jefferies feels like talking."

The captain nodded. "Good idea." Then he glanced at his watch, realizing it was late. "Nothing I can do here. I'll see you two in the morning." Then he turned to leave.

Dan called out, "One thing, Captain."

Foley stopped and turned.

"Chief Roberts said we could use a couple of patrol officers if we needed them."

"What's on your mind?"

"I thought that it might be a good idea for a couple of them to check the service stations between here and highway 85 & 87. Maybe Paul stopped for gas, and someone got a good look at him."

"Good idea," said Foley. "I'll use one of the police cruiser's radio to call dispatch right now and get someone right on it."

As Captain Foley disappeared into the bright headlights, Dan looked at the covered body and thought of the girl's parents. "This girl died in place of Mary Jefferies."

Having an idea of what Dan was thinking, Jack said, "You can't blame yourself for this, Dan. This sits on Paul's head." Jack put his hand on Dan's shoulder. "Don't take this on. It's not your fault. None of us had any idea Paul would grab another girl so soon."

Anger filled Dan as he looked at the covered body. "I did."

"Go home," said Jack. "You're tired, and so am I."

Dan looked at his partner. "Pissed is what I am, Jack."

"We all are." Jack put his arm around his partner's shoulders again and softly said, "Go see Cathy."

"She's sleeping."

"Wake her up. She'll be glad to see you."

Dan wasn't so sure as he glanced around at the hectic scene. "I'll see you tomorrow after I talk to Mary Jefferies." He turned and walked toward his car, thinking of the girl's parents.

"Go see, Cathy."

Cathy sat up in bed heavy-eyed and sleepy, having been startled by the sound of the doorbell, and looked at the green glowing numbers on the face of the alarm clock sitting on the nightstand. Seeing it was almost two-thirty in the morning, Cathy tossed the covers back and turned on the light. Putting her robe on, she reached into the drawer of her nightstand and retrieved her .32 caliber pistol. Then stepping into the small hallway that led to the bathroom and second bedroom, she held her robe together with one hand, and with her gun in the other, she entered the living room.
Stopping short of the front door, she called out, "Who is it?"

"Dan Morgan."

Wondering if he had been drinking, she said, "Just a minute." She unlocked the door and cracked it open without turning on the porch light. "Are you alright?"

Dan felt foolish, thinking that Jack's idea of coming here was not a very good one. "I'm sorry, Cathy, I should go." Then he turned to walk away.

Not wanting him to leave, she quickly said, "No, don't go." She unlocked the screen door and, while glancing around the neighborhood, softly said. "Come inside."

Feeling foolish and wishing he had gone home, he stepped inside the dim living room, bathed in the faint light from the bedroom down the hall.

Tense and a little nervous, Cathy closed the door and locked it. "What's wrong? Are you alright?"

He looked at her face in the dim light while smelling her perfume. He wanted to take her in his arms and hold her. "Paul killed another girl tonight after he released Mary Jefferies."

"Oh, God, no." She gestured to the sofa. "Sit down. I'll make us some coffee."

"Don't bother," he said as he stepped toward the door. "I should go home and get some sleep and let you do the same. I shouldn't have come. I just..." he let the sentence drop off.

Knowing why he came, she gestured to the sofa. "Sit down for a few minutes." Then she bent down to turn on a lamp.

"Don't," he said as he sat down on the sofa and, in the dim light, noticed the gun in her hand. "You know how to use that thing?"

She glanced at it as she sat down next to him. "My uncle taught me how to shoot years ago." She placed the gun on the coffee table and touched his arm. "Stay here tonight. You can sleep on the sofa, and in the morning, I'll fix a nice breakfast."

He started to get up. "I should go."

"Stay," she said, putting her hand on his arm.

He looked at the sofa, realizing just how tired he was. "What about my car?"

She considered the car. "I'll set my alarm a little earlier."

He considered that. "Are you sure you don't mind?"

"Of course not. I'll get you a pillow and blanket."

While Cathy disappeared into the short hall to the linen closet, Dan took off his suit coat, placed it on a nearby chair, and started on his tie just as she returned with a pillow and two blankets. She set them on the sofa and smiled. "These should keep you warm." She paused and asked, "Would you like a drink?"

He considered that as he laid his tie over his coat. "I don't think so." As he turned to her, the fragrance of her perfume filled his head, and he wanted to feel something warm, alive, and soft in his arms. He looked into her soft, dark eyes in the pale light coming from the hallway, took her in his arms, and kissed her.

Dan opened his eyes from a sound sleep and looked at the alarm clock sitting on the nightstand, seeing it was almost four-thirty in the morning. The clock's ticking seemed unusually loud in the quiet, unfamiliar bedroom as he turned and looked at Cathy's sleeping face in the dim light of the moon and relived their lovemaking over in his mind.

Startled by the alarm clock going off, he turned to reach for it, but Cathy leaned over him, grabbed the alarm, and turned it off. Holding the alarm in one hand, she laid her head back down on the pillow, closed her eyes, and combed back her hair with the other hand. "Don't look at me."

Dan chuckled. "Why?"

She turned away. "Because I look terrible."

"No, you don't." He reached over and took the alarm clock from her, set it on the nightstand, and then propping his head up with his hand, looked at her. "This is a little early for you, isn't it?"

She managed a small chuckle without humor. "Yeah." Then she snuggled back down under the covers. "I need to get up and fix us breakfast."

Dan felt his beard with one hand. "I don't suppose you have a spare razor."

She covered her yawn with one hand and rolled over, looking sleepy. "I use a razor on my legs, and there are new blades in the medicine cabinet."

Silence filled the bed as they looked into one another's eyes. Then Dan put his arms around her and pulled her warm naked body into his.

Dan lay on his back, staring out the bedroom window, watching the dark sky turning a light blue with the coming of dawn. He was thinking about the girl in Washington Park while Cathy lay curled up against him with her head on his chest.

She looked up at him. "Looks like we've missed breakfast." She sat up. "You go shave while I put the coffee on."

He tossed the covers back, sat up, put his feet on the small rug next to the bed, and looked at her over his shoulder. "I'll shave while you make coffee, and then while you get ready, I'll make us some breakfast."

She got up onto her knees and put her arms around him with her naked breast against his back, her face next to his. "Breakfast will be cold by the time I'm ready." Then she kissed his cheek, pushed him away playfully, and reached for her robe lying across the foot of the bed. He watched as she stood and slipped it around her slender body. She pulled her hair from under the collar of the robe as she walked toward the bedroom door. Pausing at the door, she smiled. "You'll find clean towels for a shower in the cabinet next to the toilet. Don't use up all the hot water."

Showered and dressed, Cathy paused at the kitchen door to watch Dan busy over the gas stove cooking breakfast.

He dumped the scrambled eggs onto a platter and set the platter on the kitchen table's yellow Formica top. Turning, he saw Cathy wearing a red polka dot dress standing in the doorway smiling. "You look nice." Then he pulled one of the yellow seated chrome chairs and backed away from the table. "Have a seat. It's a good thing we're in your kitchen and not mine."

As she sat down, she asked, "Why is that?"

Dan set the toast and sausage on the table. "We'd be eating bologna for breakfast or toast and coffee." He pulled a chair out, grinning as he sat down. "Your refrigerator is a cook's dream."

She watched him pour the orange juice she had made yesterday. "I'm one of those women who love to cook." She picked up the glass of orange juice. "The problem is there's no one to cook for but me."

He took a drink of orange juice and set his glass down. "I never liked cooking, but after Norma passed away, I had to learn."

Cathy took a bite of sausage. "Do you like to cook now?"

Dan bit into a piece of toast and grinned. "Not really."

"Well," she said with a big smile remembering last Sunday. "You make a mean salad."

Dan grinned as he took a bite of food. "That's true."

She glanced at the clock on the gas stove. "It's almost six-thirty."

"Neighbors?"

She looked worried as she nodded yes.

"I should go," he said, scooting his chair from the table.

Cathy reached out and touched his hand. "Stay and finish your breakfast." She smiled. "What are they going to do, stone me? Or even worse, talk to me less than they do now?"

"Just the same," he said. "I better go."

They got up and walked into the living room where he had left his suit coat the night before, slipped into it, shook his arms adjusting the shirtsleeves, and picked up his hat lying on the blue barrel chair. She took his arm, and they walked to the front door, where he kissed her and then unlocked and opened the front door. Hesitating before he opened the screen door, he glanced around the neighborhood, feeling a bit like a spy, then stepped into the warm morning sunshine.

She whispered. "Call me if you get the chance."

He smiled as he quietly closed the screen door and whispered, "I will." Then he turned, walked through the gate of the picket fence, and got into his car.

After his car disappeared up the street, Cathy closed the door, leaned against it, and thought about last night and this morning, having forgotten how very nice it was to have a man around.

Twenty-Five

Dan drove north on South Logan Street while his mind jumped from the young girl by the lake, to Cathy, to Norma, to Paul, and back to Cathy. The scent of Cathy's perfume still lingered in his memory, as did the softness of her warm body as they made love. He glanced at his watch, thinking that seven in the morning was a little early to stop at the Jefferies's house. Remembering a small café on South Broadway, he turned onto East Quincy and drove west.

After parking in front of the feed store that had just opened its doors, he walked across the gravel street and stepped into the Cherrelyn Café, taking a seat on the first dark, red stool at the counter. A heavyset woman of fifty dressed in a black dress buttoned down the front and a gray apron with white lace trimming filled a water glass. Smiling at him, she placed the glass of water on the counter along with a menu. "Good morning."

"Good morning," replied Dan adding, "Just coffee, please."

She turned to three glass coffee pots located on the counter behind her and poured a white mug with coffee, set the cup and a metal creamer in front of him on the counter. "How about a donut? They're fresh."

Dan quickly considered the offer, remembering he hadn't had the chance to finish breakfast at Cathy's. "Chocolate," he said, and then he watched as the waitress put his donut on a small plate she set in front of him. Taking a bite of the donut and a drink of coffee, Dan turned and looked out the window as a big flatbed truck loaded with bales of hay backed into the open doors of the feed store and wondered what time the Jefferies's got up.

Feeling anxious, he looked at the big, round, white-faced clock on the wall above the kitchen counter where the waitress picked up orders and noticed it was only a quarter after seven. He ordered another chocolate donut and a second cup of coffee, and by the time he finished both, it was twenty-to-eight. Refusing another free refill, he took some change out of his pocket and set enough on the counter for the donuts and coffee plus the tip. Standing, he told the waitress to have a nice day, then walked out of the café toward his car across the street.

Dan parked in front of a modest house painted white with black trim. Getting out of the car, he stepped over the curb to the sidewalk and made the journey up the narrow walk that separated the recently mowed green

257

grass. A white, wicker swing hung suspended from the rafters of the front porch roof, and a bed of multi-colored flowers spread from the porch along both sides of the house. Stepping onto the porch and front door, he pressed the doorbell, hearing the sound of chimes inside. Moments later, the door was opened by a plump, rather short woman in her late forties wearing a curious smile under her green eyes. "May I help you?" She had gray-streaked black hair and was dressed in a faded, rose-colored housedress and dirty white apron.

Dan started to take off his hat when he realized it was still in the backseat of his car. "Mrs. Jefferies, I'm Detective Dan Morgan and--"

"Oh yes," she said, cutting off his sentence with a slight Irish accent. "You're Mary's detective." A big smile filled her face as she unlocked the screen door and held it open while the hand with the dishtowel gestured for him to come in. "Come in, come in. Mary told us all about you."

He stepped inside. "It's a little early, and I apologize for that, but I was wondering if I could talk to Mary before she went to school."

She locked the screen door and the front door behind him and smiled as she gestured toward the dining room while speaking in her Irish accent. "Now, don't go worry'n none about the time of day, Mr. Morgan. We're all early risers around here. Brad, that's my husband, and Mary's pa leaves for work at six. Her older brother, Ronald, is out delivering newspapers, so don't concern yourself." She gestured to a chair at the oak table. "Have a seat Mr. Morgan, and I'll pour you a hot cup of coffee."

Having had enough coffee, he smiled. "No, thank you, Mrs. Jefferies."

"Nonsense," she said quickly. "You have a seat, and I'll go get Mary and then that cup of coffee." She turned to leave but stopped, turned, and smiled with welling eyes. "God bless you, Mr. Morgan."

Feeling awkward, Dan could only smile while thinking of the girl who had died in Mary's place, and while Mrs. Jefferies went to get her daughter, he glanced around the room with its modest furnishings. Photos of the family on the walls and an oak table filled with dirty breakfast dishes surrounded by six oak, stiff-back chairs told him that this was a happy house.

Mary walked into the dining room wearing a light green robe and looking like she had just gotten up. She smiled. "Good morning, Detective."

He smiled, noticing the redness around her mouth and nose left from the chloroform. "Good morning, Mary. Sorry if I woke you."

"I wasn't sleeping."

Worried about her, he asked, "How are you doing?"

She nodded with an unsure look. "Okay, I guess."

"Do you feel up to answering a few questions?"

Mrs. Jefferies told her to take Detective Morgan into the living room where they would be more comfortable, and then she smiled at Dan. "I'll bring that coffee now. How do you like it?"

Knowing she was not about to give up and not sure how strong the coffee would be, he asked for some cream.

Mrs. Jefferies disappeared into the kitchen while Mary showed Dan into the living room, where she gestured to a green chair with white lace doilies covering the back and both arms. As he sat down, Mary curled up on the dark green sofa playing nervously with the hem of her robe.

Dan reached into the inside pocket of his suit, pulled out his pad and stub of a pencil, and thumbed through the pad until he found a blank page. He jotted down her name and the date and then looked at her face. "Are you comfortable talking about what happened?"

She hesitated. "I guess so. It's not like he hurt me or anything."

Thankful for that, Dan said, "We can wait, Mary, but it's important that we talk while things are still fresh in your mind and they don't get distorted from other thoughts."

Hearing the faint clink of china, he looked up as Mrs. Jefferies approached with a cup and saucer of black coffee and a small white china creamer.

Setting them down on the coffee table, she smiled and, in her Irish brogue, said, "Have to warn ya, Mr. Morgan, I make a strong pot of coffee."

He lied, "I like my coffee strong, Mrs. Jefferies." Then he thanked her, picked the cup up, and took a drink, finding it exactly as she had said. He put the cup down on the saucer and poured a little cream into it, and instead of jumping right in with questions for Mary, he asked what Mr. Jefferies did for a living.

"Brad drives one of them big trucks." Mrs. Jefferies smiled. "He calls it a rig, but it's a truck to me. Sometimes he's gone two or three days at a time, but he was here last night when you brought our Mary home." Her eyes quickly welled with tears. "I'm forever thankful to you, Mr. Morgan." Looking embarrassed, she wiped her tears with her apron. "I'll let you and Mary talk."

Dan watched Mrs. Jefferies walk away, and then he looked at Mary. "Tell me what you first remember."

While Dan made notes, Mary told him about seeing the van parked next to the curb, and as she walked past, someone grabbed her, put a cloth over her mouth, and pulled her into the van.

"He put you to sleep with chloroform," offered Dan.

259

"It burnt my nose and mouth." She looked at Dan and thought about the chloroform. "Do you think he is a doctor?"

"We don't know at this point, but anyone can get chloroform at a drugstore. Can you tell me anything about the van?"

She thought a moment. "It was white."

"Do you know what kind of van?"

Mary shook her head and shrugged. "Just a white van."

Knowing the two girls at the Paramount Theater identified a Ford Van from photos Jack showed them to her as he asked, "You don't know if it was a Chevy or a Ford?"

"No," she said, shaking her head. "I'm sorry."

"That's okay," Dan told her. "Did you notice any dents or writing on the van when you walked past?"

She shook her head. "No, it was too dark. I just wanted to get home."

"Did he say anything?"

"He got mad when I banged my feet against the side of the van. He stopped once, came into the back, and pulled my hair, saying that he didn't want to hurt me, but if I didn't stop, he would." She paused. "I thought it strange that he knew my name."

Dan did not want to tell her that Paul had been watching her, knowing that she would have a tough time as it was. "You're doing fine, Mary. Anything peculiar about his voice?"

She frowned. "He had some kind of accent."

Dan wrote that down. "What about the ride?"

Mary thought for a moment. "It was uncomfortable. I was lying on a bunch of rags, and I was groggy, so I don't remember much."

Dan figured they might have been army blankets.

"The radio was loud and playing cowboy music from KFXX."

He continued writing. "What happened next?"

She told Dan about the man helping her out of the van and up the porch steps. She was very frightened and remembered something running past her leg, which turned out to be a cat, and then they walked downstairs to a bedroom.

He figured she must have been terrified. "Can you describe the room for me?"

"The bed was a canopy bed without the canopy but still had the posts. There was a blue bedspread and two pillows. White drapes covered a lime green wall that had no windows, and there was a small table next to the door where he would put a tray of food."

He wrote that down and then paused to take a sip of coffee.

"The door had a tiny peephole," she said. "But I couldn't see out."

"That's probably what he used to watch you. Tell me more about the bed."

She thought a moment. "It was a strange bed. The four bedposts were not as high as a real canopy bed." She paused a moment in thought, watching Dan as he wrote that down. "Each bedpost had a metal ring on the top."

Dan imagined Paul had used them to tie his victim's arms and legs. He looked up. "Tell me about the bathroom."

Mary shrugged. "One wall was full of mirrors."

Dan found that interesting and then realized that the girls could watch themselves as they bled out, thinking how terrifying that must have been for them. "Think for a moment, was there anything other than the mirrors that was peculiar about the bathroom?"

She thought for several seconds. "There was a big hook above the bathtub and those round things hanging down."

Dan looked puzzled. "What kind of round things?"

"You know, those things you put ropes through."

"Do you mean pulleys?"

"Yes, there were three of them." She paused. "What do you think he used them for?"

He lied, "I'm not sure. Tell me more about the bathroom."

She thought for a moment. "There were clean towels next to the sink and by the bathtub. A toilet, a medicine cabinet that had a tube of toothpaste but no toothbrush, and some salve. Everything was nice and clean. Oh yeah, there was a small radio on a table in the corner by the mirrored wall."

His mind went back to the salve. "You mentioned salve?"

She nodded. "He told me to put it on my nose and around my mouth to stop the burning."

Dan thought that was strange and looked up from the notepad. "Did the salve help?"

She bobbed her head. "Yes, it did."

Mrs. Jefferies walked into the room and sat down next to her daughter with a worried look. "Are you alright, dear?"

Mary looked at her mother. "I'm fine, Ma."

Mrs. Jefferies frowned. "Are you certain?" She looked at Dan. "She needs to rest, Mr. Morgan."

Dan felt guilty about all the questions, but he had to ask them.

Mary smiled at her mother. "I'm fine, Ma, really I am."

Worried about her daughter, Mrs. Jefferies held her daughter's hand while listening to Dan ask if she had ever seen his hands.

Thinking that was a strange question Mary said, "Lots of times. They were old looking."

Dan smiled. "That's good to know. How tall would you say he was?"

She shrugged. "Tall."

Dan stood. "I'm almost five feet nine. Was he taller or shorter?"

Mary looked unsure. "About the same."

Dan sat back down. "Can you tell me what he was wearing?"

"He wore blue pants and a blue shirt like some men wear when they're working."

Dan wrote that down.

"You need a new pencil," said Mary.

Dan smiled and looked at his stubby pencil. "You're right, I do." Then he asked, "You never saw his face?"

"No, he always wore this creepy mask with holes in it for eyes." She looked down at her hands. "He said it would be best for me if I didn't see his face."

Dan glanced at Mrs. Jefferies, suspecting she was about to ask him to leave. "We're almost done here, Mrs. Jefferies. Just a few more minutes." He looked at Mary. "What about the ride away from this place? What do you remember about that?"

"What do you mean?"

"Tell me about getting into the van."

"I had a hood over my head and a gag around my mouth. He helped me inside, then shut the door, and I could feel the van move when he got into the front. He started the engine and turned the radio on to KFXX again." She frowned. "I'll never listen to cowboy music again."

Dan smiled at that. "Was the road smooth or bumpy, straight, or curved?"

"At first, it was bumpy, and then we ran over something that vibrated the van, and then we turned."

Dan figured that could have been a cattle guard coming out of a long driveway on a farm in the country. "How long were you on the bumpy road?"

"Not long."

Dan wrote in his notepad and then asked, "Which way did you turn?"

Mrs. Jefferies looked at Dan. "How would Mary know that if she had a hood over her head?"

Dan looked from Mrs. Jefferies to Mary, "Do you remember which side of the van you were sitting on?"

"The same side as the driver."

262

"That's good. Now, were you facing the front or rear of the van?"

"I was sitting with my back against the side." She thought a moment. "He turned to the right because it pushed me back against the wall."

Dan smiled. "Good. Now was that road smooth?"

"No, but not as bumpy as the other, and it was noisy."

Dirt or gravel road, thought Dan. "That's good, Mary. Now try to think about how long he was on this road."

She thought for several moments. "Two songs, I think, maybe three." She looked regretful. "I should have kept track."

Dan smiled reassuringly. "That's okay. It won't matter. What do you remember next?"

"We stopped, and he turned to the right, and that road was a little bumpy like the other. We stayed on that for a while, and then we turned left, and the road was smooth and quiet. We stayed on that for several songs, and then the man on the radio said it was six-thirty."

Dan wrote that down.

"We stayed on the smooth road for a long time before I felt him slow down and stop. I heard other cars, and then we started moving again."

Stop sign or traffic light, thought Dan.

"The man on the radio said it was time for the news, and that was when he turned the radio off."

Seven o'clock news, thought Dan. "What happened then?

"We made several turns and stops before we stopped, and he shut the engine off."

"How long do you think you drove after he shut the radio off?"

She thought for several moments. "Not long. We sat parked for a while, and then I heard the driver's door open and close, and then the back door opened. He told me that if I cried out, I would never see my mother and father again."

"Bastard," said Mrs. Jefferies with welling eyes, then looking embarrassed, said, "Excuse me, Mr. Morgan."

Dan smiled. "That's quite alright, Mrs. Jefferies." Then he looked at Mary. "Go on, Mary, it's important."

She took a breath and continued. "He helped me out of the van, telling me to be quiet, and after he closed the door, we just stood there for a while."

Dan figured he was checking to see if anyone was watching.

"He guided me to a place where he helped me sit down and then told me that you would come to get me in a few minutes. He tied my feet, and then I heard him walk away, and then it got quiet." She looked at Dan. "I was really scared."

He felt sorry for her. "I bet you were."

She began to cry. "I was so happy when you came for me."

Mrs. Jefferies moved closer to her daughter, put an arm around her, and looked at Dan. "Please, Detective Morgan. I think she's done enough for one day."

Dan smiled. "Yes, ma'am, I believe you're right." He closed his pad, put it and the pencil away, and started to get up.

Mary reached out and touched his arm, looking worried as she wiped the tears from her face. "It still scares me."

Dan settled back in his chair, wanting to say something, but the words escaped him.

She looked down at the floor as if ashamed. "Pa had to sleep out here on the sofa last night so that I could sleep with Ma." She wiped her eyes and face with her hands.

Mrs. Jefferies looked at Dan. "She had nightmares all last night."

Dan didn't wonder as he looked at Mary. "They will stop."

Mary looked unsure. "How do you know?"

"I had bad dreams when I returned from Europe after the war. Most of us did." He smiled reassuringly. "They'll stop in time." Then he stood and looked at her mother. "Thanks for the coffee, Mrs. Jefferies."

She stood. "You're most welcome, Detective Morgan."

He looked at Mary standing with her mother's arm around her. "Thanks for talking to me, Mary. I know it was difficult, but everything you told me helps."

Mary looked at Dan. "Will you catch him?"

"We're gonna try like hell." He smiled. "Now, you do as your mother says and get some rest."

They walked Dan to the door, where Mary gave him a big hug.

Dan looked at her and smiled. "One day, this will all seem like a bad dream, and at times you will wonder if it ever really happened. You're going to be just fine, Mary." He said goodbye, and as he stepped off the porch, he looked at his watch, thinking he would hurry home to change clothes before going into the office.

Jack Brolin looked up from the file he was reading as Dan pulled the chair from his desk to sit down. "Did you talk with Mary Jefferies?"

Dan plopped into his chair, looking tired. "Yeah."

"How is she doing?"

"Better than I would be."

"Tough little gal," said Jack.

Agreeing, Dan stood. "Let's go see Foley." Once in the captain's office, Dan told his partner and Captain Foley everything Mary had related about the bedroom, bedposts, and the hook with three pulleys hanging from the ceiling above the bathtub. He continued to describe the bumpy road, the cattle crossing, and everything else she had told him about the trip. "He made a lot of turns toward the end," said Dan. "I think he was trying to throw Mary off, but we still might be able to narrow the distance to where Paul lives." He looked at Foley. "We just need the direction."

Foley thought about that. "Still not much to go on, but it's more than we had yesterday."

Dan looked at Foley. "Has the girl in Washington Park been identified?"

"Not yet."

"I think it'd be a good idea," said Dan. "If Jack and I were to talk to Professor Pappel again. I have a few questions I'd like to ask him about Paul and Mary Jefferies."

Captain Foley stood. "That might be a good idea. Now if you'll excuse me, I have an appointment. Keep me in the loop."

When they got back to their desks, Jack plopped into his chair and watched Dan open his desk, pull out a map of Denver proper and the surrounding vicinity. As Dan unfolded the map, Jack got up from his chair, walked to Dan's desk, and leaned on his hands, looking down at the map. Considering that it was a lot of territory, he said, "If we only knew which direction to search."

Dan nodded in silent agreement, got out his notepad, and turned to the section on Mary. "She said they turned and stopped several times near the end." Dan drew a circle around the downtown area with his finger. "I bet he was driving through downtown to confuse her."

Jack looked at the map. "Yeah, but the important part of the trip is the one we can't retrace."

Dan looked at Jack. "Let's pay a visit to KFXX on East Colfax and see if they have a schedule of the songs played that night."

Jack looked puzzled. "What good will that do?"

"I'm not sure, but I believe disc jockeys have to make a program so the commercials and news can be slotted in by the producers."

Jack looked at Dan. "Well, that'd give us the songs and their length."

Dan looked back down at the map. "It's a little thin, but it's all we have." He paused. "I thought that after we get the list, we'd revisit the Jefferies girl."

Jack looked optimistic. "I'll drive."

Detectives Dan Morgan and Jack Brolin walked through the front door of KFXX Radio Station and immediately noticed a young, buxom, blonde girl who nicely filled a pink cashmere sweater at the receptionist's desk. She looked up as they removed their hats. Smiling, she took the gum out of her mouth and tossed it in the trashcan. "May I help you?"

Dan returned her smile, thinking she looked fresh out of high school, showed her his badge, identified himself and Jack, and then asked for her name.

"Karen," she said while watching Jack as he sat on the edge of her desk and picked up the magazine she had been reading. She glanced from the badge Dan held to Jack and frowned as she took the magazine out of his hand and set it back down on the desk.

Jack smiled. "We'd like to talk to the station manager,"

Still frowning at Jack, she stood. "I'll let Mr. Brooks know you're here and see if he has time to see you." Then she walked down a narrow hall and disappeared through a doorway.

Jack picked the movie magazine up and began flipping through the pages while Dan glanced at the wall filled with pictures of different singers. Hearing a door close, he turned.

Karen walked out of the hall, saw Jack looking at her magazine again, took it from him, and gestured down the hall. "Follow me, please." She turned and started walking down the narrow hall with its walls covered with 45 RPM records encased in glass frames on the left and 78 RPM records on the right. Reaching a door, she knocked, opened it, and stepped aside with her back against the open door so they could pass.

"Come in," said a man looking to be in his late forties and dressed in an expensive-looking suit. He stood and walked around the metal desk with an open hand. "Stan Brooks," he said with a friendly smile. The three shook hands, and then Stan looked at Karen. "Thanks, sweetheart."

She smiled at Mr. Brooks and Dan but gave Jack a different look as she stepped out of the office and closed the door.

Jack grinned with a soft chuckle.

Stan gestured to four metal chairs with black vinyl seats. "Please." Then he sat down and waited until both men were comfortable. "What can I do for the Denver Police?"

Dan shifted, trying to get comfortable. "We are investigating a crime which we can't comment on at present, Mr. Brooks, and we need your help."

Stan Brooks looked puzzled, and then he smiled. "And how can a station manager help solve a crime?"

Dan leaned forward, holding his fedora hat with the fingers of both hands. "I'm not quite sure how to ask this, but are records kept of your previous shows and the music that was played?"

Stan Brooks thought that was certainly a strange request. "Well, yes. All DJ's make a list of recordings they plan on airing so the producers know when to break for commercials and the news. All of the recordings have to fit into a certain time block." He quickly glanced from one face to the other. "Is there something, in particular, you're looking for?"

"Monday night between six and eight," said Jack.

"Shouldn't be a problem," said Stan. He reached for the buzzer on his desk, and moments later, the young girl in the pink cashmere sweater walked in.

"Karen," began Stan Brooks. "Be a dear and get Buster's worksheets for Monday night and bring them in." He looked at Dan and Jack. "Buster is the DJ that works Saturday and Monday nights."

"Could we get a copy?" asked Dan.

"Of course," replied Stan. "We keep several carbon copies on file just in case." Then he looked at Karen. "You know where the worksheets are kept, now be a dear and get them."

"It'll take a few minutes," she said, looking irritated.

Jack smiled at her. "We'll wait."

She chewed her gum, giving Jack another of her looks, stepped out, and closed the door.

Stan looked a little exasperated as he sat back in his chair. "A man should never hire his daughter."

Jack drove west on Colfax Avenue while Dan glanced at the carbon copy of the program sheet provided by the station manager. "Well?" he asked.

"I don't know," replied Dan, sounding disappointed. "I need to talk to the Jefferies girl again." Then he thought about Cathy and looked at his watch. "You hungry?"

Jack looked at the clock on the dashboard, seeing it was one fifteen. "A little. There's a restaurant in the next block that has good food."

Moments later, Jack parked at the curb while Dan looked at the white letters in red trim on the restaurant window across the sidewalk. 'Giuseppe's Ristorante'

Hoping they had a telephone, Dan followed Jack inside to a small crowd of people eating a late lunch, where a man showed them to a table next to a window, giving them a clear view of the sidewalk and Colfax Avenue. As he walked away, a waiter approached, smiled, and handed each of them a menu. "Would you gentleman care for a glass of wine?"

"Iced Tea for me," said Dan.

"Same," replied Jack.

"Yes, sir," replied the waiter. "Would you like to order now?"

"Not just yet," said Dan. "Do you have a pay phone?"

The waiter gestured to the back of the restaurant. "You'll find a pay telephone by the restrooms."

Dan thanked him and looked at Jack as he got up. "I have to make a phone call."

Jack smiled. "Tell Cathy hello." Then Jack glanced around the room of red and white checkered tablecloths and the few patrons eating lunch, took a pack of cigarettes out of his coat pocket, and waited for the tea and Dan to return.

Dan stepped into the small lobby where the restrooms were, finding a pay telephone tucked away in the corner. Glancing back toward the door and half-expecting Jack, he picked up the receiver, dropped a nickel into the slot, and dialed Cathy's work number. While he waited for Cathy to answer, he turned and looked at the doorway leading to the restaurant, concerned that Jack might walk in.

"Sheriff Brumwell's Office."

Dan put his lips close to the mouthpiece and softly said. "Hi."

Cathy smiled. "Hello. Where are you?"

"In some restaurant, Jack picked out for lunch. I would have called sooner, but we were a little busy."

"That's alright. Why are you whispering?"

He glanced around. "The telephone is close to the restrooms."

She thought about that, wondering what difference that made. "Oh."

He thought about last night. "Are you okay?"

She considered his question, smiled, and lowered her voice. "I'm fine."

Dan glanced around for Jack. "Why are you whispering?"

She laughed softly. "I don't know, maybe because you are?"

He thought about that. "If I'm not too late, would you like to get something to eat?"

"I would like that."

Jack suddenly walked into the small lobby and smiled at Dan as he walked past him into the men's restroom.

Feeling embarrassed, Dan waited for the door to close and then told Cathy that he would call her at home around six. They said goodbye, and then he hung up, returned to their table to wait for Jack, took a sip of tea, and wondered what Paul was doing at this very minute.

Jack grinned as he returned from the bathroom. "How is Mrs. Holman?"

Dan glanced around, looking embarrassed, picked up his glass, and said, "It would sound better if you referred to her as Cathy, and yes, she's fine."

Jack chuckled as he leaned his forearms on the table. "Seriously, Dan, how are you two getting along?"

Dan shrugged. "Fine, as far as I know. We're going out to dinner tonight."

Jack was happy for his friend. "Good." As the waiter approached their table to take their order, Jack grinned. "You better order something light if you're going to be taking your lady friend out to dinner."

Twenty-Six

Jack was on the telephone talking to his wife Lori, and Dan was sitting on the edge of his desk studying a map of Denver and the surrounding area that he had pinned to a large bulletin board. Dan had drawn small circles in red ink and written the victims' names on the map to show the places where Paul had dumped each body.

Captain Foley walked up, stood next to Dan, and glanced at the red circles while shrugging into his coat. Without taking his eyes off the map, he said to Jack, "Tell Lori you'll call her back."

Jack told Lori goodbye and quickly hung up.

Foley looked from the map to Dan. "What's your next step?"

"We're going to go see the Jefferies girl once again tomorrow morning and go over the list of songs we got from KFXX to see which ones she remembers."

Not sure what good that would do, Foley asked, "Then what?"

Jack leaned forward with his elbows on his desk. "We'll try and figure out the distance she traveled."

Foley turned and looked at Jack and then returned his gaze to the map. "Humph."

Dan saw the skepticism on the captain's face. "It's slim, I know, but we thought we'd try and trace Paul's route backward from Micky's."

Foley looked at the map. "That's a hell of a lot of ground to cover."

Dan shrugged. "It's the only thing we have at the moment, Captain."

Foley thought about that and then nodded his approval. "I know you two are doing everything you can to catch this bastard. I'll see you both in the morning."

"Anything on the gas stations?" asked Dan.

Foley shook his head. "Not yet. There must be a couple hundred."

As Foley walked away, Dan went back to studying the map while Jack picked up his telephone to call Lori.

Todd Anderson was at Dan's desk, holding out two ten by twelve manila envelopes. He handed one to Dan. "Here's what I have from last night." As Dan took the envelope, Todd handed him the second. "I ran into Pete downstairs. He asked me to give this to you."

Dan took the second envelope. "Did you get any good prints off the telephone at the hotel?"

270

Todd frowned. "Several and more from the men's room and the front door." Having an idea of Dan's next question, Todd said, "We'll be checking them as fast as we can. It's a slow process, Detective, and I'll let you know." Then he turned and walked away.

Knowing it was a tedious job of manually comparing prints, Dan picked up the envelope from Pete and started to open it when his telephone rang. "Detective Morgan."

"Is little Mary home safe and sound?" said a familiar voice.

Dan quickly reached over and switched on the recorder and motioned to Jack. "She is." Dan thought he would play on the good side of Paul if he had one. "Letting her go was a good thing."

Jack told Lori he would call her back, hung up, and hurried around his desk, where he stood next to Dan with his ear close to the telephone.

Paul collapsed into an overstuffed chair, took a sip of cheap wine, and stared across the dim room at the flames in the fireplace. "Consider her a gift, but don't expect another."

Dan's mind turned to the girl in the park. "When did you take the girl we found in Washington Park?"

The telephone line was quiet as Paul put his head back against the overstuffed chair and closed his eyes, remembering the girl and her eyes staring into his as he choked the life out of her before he made love to her. "What does it matter, Detective?"

Dan hesitated. "Let's just say I'm curious."

Paul thought about that. "I took her after you took Mary from me." He took a sip of wine. "You see, I was lonely after Mary Jefferies left with you and that partner of yours."

Stalling to keep Paul on the telephone so his call could be traced, he asked, "Why Mary? Why did you take her in the first place?"

Silence filled the telephone for several moments. "Was she special to you, Dan? Like a daughter, perhaps?"

Dan became angry over the mention of his daughter. "I didn't know her that well."

"But you did visit her a while back, didn't you? I'm going to hang up and call you back. I don't want that trace to find me."

Dan heard a click, disappointed that Paul knew when to end the call, so he hung up the telephone and waited until the telephone rang. "This is Morgan."

"Do you believe in God?" asked Paul.

Thinking that was a strange question for Paul to ask, Dan considered his reply. "Yes, I do. Why?"

"After all that has happened in your life," said Paul, "You still believe in God?"

Dan was well aware that Paul knew a lot about him. "My faith has been shaken. I'll admit to that, but I still believe."

"Do you still go to St. Mathews?"

The image of the big church filled his memory, remembering that he had not been there in a couple of years and wondered how Paul knew about the church. "No, but that doesn't mean I don't believe in God because I do."

The telephone was silent for a few moments as he looked at Jack, who motioned to keep Paul on the line a little longer.

"What do you think happens to us after we die?" asked Paul.

Puzzled by the conversation, Dan glanced at Jack with a bewildered expression. "I'm not sure."

"Do you think that after we are dead, we'll see the people we met here on earth?"

Detective Dan Morgan considered that. "In purgatory, perhaps."

Paul thought about that for a moment and then softly said, "Ah yes, purgatory. It seems I have a lot to atone for."

Dan saw a chance to end this. "Why not atone now, Paul? Stop what you are doing and come in?"

"You know I can't do that, Detective."

Being called Detective, Dan knew their conversation was about over. "And why not?"

Paul chuckled softly. "The game is not over, and no one has won."

"I'm going to stop you, Paul."

"You and all your fellow policemen haven't been able to stop me in all these years. You didn't even know I existed until Sally Ann Crowder, and that is only because I wanted you to know I existed."

Dan stood from his chair and looked at the map. "I'm going to give it my best shot."

Paul looked at his watch and knew the time was getting close for the trace to locate him. "Look at the other pictures, Detective, and when you do, I'm sure you will understand why we talk and how I know so much about you." He paused and then laughed. "I'm certain you're dying to know."

Dan heard a click followed by the dial tone, placed the receiver on his telephone base, switched off the recorder, and stared at the telephone for several moments, thinking about Paul's last comment. He looked at Jack. "He was different tonight."

Jack looked puzzled as he sat on the edge of Dan's desk. "What do you mean different?"

Dan frowned. "He was different. Sad or tired, I'm not sure which."

Jack thought about that. "He's just trying to keep you off balance, Dan. Don't let him outthink you."

Not agreeing with him, Dan stared at the telephone. "Maybe." Then he looked at his wristwatch, seeing it was almost four-thirty, and thought about seeing Cathy when his telephone rang again. "Morgan." He listened, then hung up and looked at Jack. "They weren't able to trace the call."

Not surprised, Jack pointed to the envelopes on Dan's desk. "Those from Washington Park?"

"Yeah, Todd dropped them off while you were on the telephone. One has pictures of the crime scene, and the other one is from Pete." Dan pulled out his billfold and found the card Professor Pappel had given him. "I'm going to call the professor and tell him that we have a couple of recordings from Paul."

Jack stood. "I'm going downstairs to get a cup of coffee. Want one?"

Dan shook his head no, picked up the telephone, and dialed the professor's number.

"Pappel residence," said a female voice.

"Is the Professor in?"

"Who is calling?

"Detective Dan Morgan."

"Just a moment."

While Dan waited, he opened the envelope from Pete Lange, which contained several eight-by-ten black and white photographs of the latest victim. Turning the envelope upside down, he watched as they fell onto his desk. He set the envelope down and then picked up a photo of a young girl lying on one of Pete's metal tables.

"This is Professor Pappel."

Dan stared at the pretty, young face of the girl who had died in place of Mary Jefferies.

"Hello," said Pappel. "Are you there?"

Dan blinked and placed the picture on top of the others. "This is Detective Morgan." He glanced at the picture again and then placed the envelope on top of it. "We have a couple of conversations with Paul recorded, and I thought you might like to hear them."

"Well, yes, of course," said Pappel.

"When could you come in?"

Pappel thought a moment. "Not until Thursday, I'm afraid."

Disappointed, Dan asked the professor what time would be convenient.

The Professor thought for a moment. "I have an afternoon class, but I could be there around three if that's agreeable."

"Three would be fine, Professor," Dan said goodbye, hung up his telephone and thought about the conversation with Paul as Jack set a paper cup of coffee in front of him.

He looked up, recalling that he had said no about coffee, but thanked him anyway. "The professor will stop by Thursday around three."

Jack looked disappointed. "Too bad we have to wait until Thursday." Jack knew that his partner was still troubled about Paul, so he sat down on the edge of Dan's desk. "Paul's getting to you, isn't he?"

Dan took a sip of coffee as he stared across the room. "Remember Professor Pappel telling us that he believes Paul has been doing this for years?"

Jack took the paper lid off his cup and tossed it into the trashcan next to Dan's desk. "Yeah, so?"

"Paul said we haven't been able to stop him in all these years." Dan looked up at Jack. "Paul is right. We never knew he existed."

Jack considered that as he worried about his partner.

Dan picked up his telephone and dialed a number, and after several rings, he looked at the clock and hung up the telephone. "Josephine must have left for the day."

Jack asked what he wanted with Josephine.

Dan looked at Jack. "Tomorrow morning, I'm going to ask her to go back in time and check for open cases of missing persons."

Jack sipped his coffee, knowing where Dan was going. "I'm almost afraid of what she might find."

Dan took a drink of his coffee and thought about that. "We should call other police departments around the state."

"Good idea," said Jack. "We might try Cheyenne while we're at it. It's only a hundred miles up highway 85 and 87."

Dan nodded in agreement, thinking about the place where Paul had held Mary captive. "If the professor is right about Paul, he would need someplace to bury his victims."

Jack pondered that while he took a drink of coffee. "A farm?"

"Maybe." Dan picked up the pictures Lange had sent over and looked at the first picture, feeling sorry for the victim's family.

Jack stood up from the edge of Dan's desk, pulled up a chair, and sat next to Dan so that he could see the pictures.

Dan handed Jack the black and white photograph he had been looking at while talking to the professor, and then he looked through a few more before giving the entire stack to Jack. He was more interested in the coroner's report, and while Jack looked at the photos, he started reading aloud. *Race: Caucasian. Height: 5'2'. Weight: 89 pounds. Hair: Brown. Eyes: Blue.* His eyes scanned the typed document, noting the cause of death, and looked at Jack. "She died from strangulation."

Jack looked up from the photograph in silence, thinking of how terrified she must have been as she fought for her life.

Dan looked up from reading the coroner's report. "Semen was found in her pubic hair. That and her missing panties are the only things consistent with the other girls." He put the report down and quickly sorted through the pictures until he found one of just her face, stood, and walked to the bulletin board set up with one picture of each of the murdered girls, plus one of Howard Trenton. He pinned the picture on the bulletin board next to Marie Phillips, the girl found in the alley behind the Paramount Theater. He stepped back and folded his arms as he looked from the first to the last, silently reading their names written on white pieces of paper tacked under each picture. Then he looked at the large city map with red circles where Paul had dumped each body. "There's no pattern."

Jack sat back in his chair and looked at Dan. "This guy's insane. Did you really expect one?"

Dan stared at the map remembering the words of Professor Pappel: *'He may want you to stop him.'* He looked at Jack. "I just thought we might have missed something Paul was trying to tell us."

Jack took a drink of coffee and looked at Dan. "Well, if he is, he needs to try a little harder."

Dan smiled as he took a drink of coffee, realizing something. "There are no bodies dumped north of Denver."

Jack got up from his chair with his coffee cup, walked to the map, and studied it while taking another drink of coffee. "You're right. Maybe the bastard lives north of Denver."

"That's what I was thinking," said Dan as he stepped closer to the map. "Do you think the son of a bitch is unconsciously trying to point us north?"

Jack stood next to Dan, thinking about that. "Maybe. Who knows what the SOB is doing?" Then he looked at Dan. "But maybe you're right. He could be doing that unconsciously."

Dan stared at the map thinking again of what the Professor had told him: that Paul might want him to be the one to stop him. "Let's concentrate on that area after our talk with the Jefferies girl tomorrow." Then he walked to his desk and picked up the manila envelope from Todd Anderson, remembering Paul telling him to look at the other pictures. He opened the envelope, took out the black and white crime scene photographs, and started looking through them. "I wonder why Paul finished with this girl so quickly." He looked at Jack. "He usually keeps his victim a day or two, but he barely kept this girl a few hours." Dan's phone rang, so he walked to his desk and picked up the receiver. "Morgan." After a brief conversation, he hung up the phone and looked at Jack. "There's a Mr. and Mrs. Allyson downstairs wanting to talk to someone about their missing daughter." While Jack got up from his desk, Dan took the picture down that he had just pinned onto the bulletin board.

Thinking of how the Allysons had reacted to hearing of their daughter's death and then identifying her in the morgue, Jack shrugged into his suit coat in silence. Watching his partner sitting at his desk, staring at the black and white photos of their latest victim, he opened his desk drawer, took out his Thirty-eight, and slid it into his holster.

Dan wished that Paul would go away so that he wouldn't have to talk to another parent about their dead daughter or look into the lifeless eyes of another young girl.

Jack was at the edge of Dan's desk. "Go have dinner with Cathy and try to get this out of your mind for an evening. I'll see you in the morning."

Dan was thinking of the Allysons. "Goodnight, Jack." He watched his partner disappear down the stairs then he picked up the picture of Deborah Allyson. He studied it for a long moment, wondering if she was a good student, a happy young girl, or a young girl in love for the first time. He knew nothing about her, only that a madman had strangled her in place of another young girl he had saved from a similar fate. Standing, he pinned the picture back onto the bulletin board, wrote her name on a piece of paper, and pinned that under the picture.

Stepping back to look at the board, he thought of Mrs. Allyson, trying to be brave but breaking down and weeping when Pete Lange pulled the white sheet away from her daughter's face. Dan thought Mr. Allyson was going to faint, but instead, he buried his face in his hands as he stood over his daughter's body and sobbed like a child.

Dan wrote Deborah Allyson on the file folders Todd had given him and on the coroner's folder after crossing out Jane Doe. He looked at his wristwatch, seeing it was six-thirty, knowing Cathy was waiting for his call, reached for the telephone and started dialing.

"Hello," said Cathy.

"Hi."

Sensing something different in his voice, she asked, "What's wrong?"

"We've identified the girl Paul murdered after we picked up the Jefferies girl." He paused a moment. "Her name was Deborah Allyson."

Cathy tried to think of words that would be a comfort, but none came to her.

"Jack and I watched Mr. and Mrs. Allyson identify their daughter about twenty minutes ago."

"That must have been terrible."

"Yeah, it was. It seems like we're doing a lot of that lately. Look, Cathy, I'm not much for company right now."

"I understand," she said, feeling disappointed.

"You're not mad?"

"Of course not. Disappointed, yes, but I understand."

Dan quickly reconsidered, but in his present frame of mind, he thought it best if he were alone tonight. "Can I call you later?"

"I'll be right here," Cathy said goodbye, hung up her telephone, and, feeling disappointed, walked into the kitchen to fix something to eat. Opening the refrigerator, she looked for something to fix when her eyes settled on a half-bottle of Rose` wine. Picking up the bottle and then taking a glass from the cabinet, Cathy poured a half glass, cut up some cheese, and placed the pieces on a plate with some saltine crackers. With the wine glass in one hand and the plate of cheese and crackers in the other, she walked into the living room and curled up on the sofa to keep the television company.

It was almost dark when Dan drove into his driveway and went into the house, carrying the manila envelopes of Deborah Allyson. Wishing he hadn't canceled dinner with Cathy, he turned the light on in the foyer and closed the door, noticing the pile of mail on the floor. After locking the door, he scooped up the mail, finding another postcard. Turning the card over, he saw no return address and read the scribbled words written in ink, *Doing Fine.'* Disappointed there was not more from his son, he tossed his keys into the glass bowl and placed the two envelopes of Deborah's case on the foyer table with the others. After he hung up his fedora, he walked into the living room and stood over the desk, looking at the postcard from Chicago while setting the rest of the mail on top of it. Wishing his son Robert would come home so they could talk, he opened the desk drawer and put the latest card on top of the others. He closed the drawer and then walked out of the living room into the foyer and down the hall into the kitchen.

Turning on the kitchen light, he walked to the refrigerator, took out a bottle of beer, opened it, and as he took a drink, he decided to call Cathy, hoping she wasn't mad because he had canceled their dinner date. They talked for twenty minutes, and when they said goodnight and hung up, he thought of their lovemaking and regretted his decision canceling their date.

He went into the kitchen and fixed a dinner of eggs, bacon, and toast, which he ate at the kitchen table, listening to soft music on the radio that sat on top of the refrigerator. The conversation he had held with Paul

277

that afternoon kept rolling through his mind like a recording, and he wondered how long Paul had been watching him and why. Finished eating, he cleaned up the kitchen, shut off the radio, got another beer out of the refrigerator, and headed for the living room. Dan kicked off his shoes, sat on the sofa with his stocking feet on the coffee table, and took a drink of beer, hoping they could catch Paul before he grabbed another girl. He looked toward the foyer where the stack of ten by twelve manila envelopes waited, set the bottle on the coffee table, put his shoes on, picked up his beer, walked into the foyer, and picked up the manila envelopes.

Walking to the garage, he unlocked the door, opened it, and as he stepped inside, he was greeted with a small rush of heat the garage was holding from the day. He stepped inside, turned on the light, and placed the two beers he had brought with him on the counter. Then he went about the task of putting everything back up on the east wall, and when he finished, he sat on the wheeled stool and glanced at the pictures. Taking a drink of beer, he slowly made his way from Diane Wagner, the girl in Littleton, to Gail Thomas, Sally Crowder, Marie Phillips, Ruth Spencer, Howard Trenton, and finally to Deborah Allyson. He stopped and thought of Paul's words, *'Have you looked at the other pictures?'* He stared at each picture of Deborah Allyson for several moments, wondering what it was that Paul wanted him to see. As his eyes went back and forth, they settled on one showing the Allyson girl's body lying next to the lake with her right arm in the water. He stared at the picture for a long time before he got up from the stool and stood in front of the wall, looking more closely at the arm in the cold, black lake.

There was something familiar about this picture, and he quietly whispered, "What are you trying to tell me?" He slowly walked back past the other pictures, noticing the similarities he had never noticed before. All five girls had their right hand and arm lying to the side, almost exactly alike. The difference was that Deborah Allyson's hand and arm were in the water. He started to take a drink of beer when his skin began to crawl, and he suddenly felt drawn to his brother's old photographs, now hidden in the basement. Turning, he walked to the side door of the garage, set the beer bottle on the counter, and looked out the garage door window at the rear of the house. Opening the door, he stepped outside, closed, and locked it, and hurried across the dark yard and up the back steps into the house. Turning the light switch at the top of the stairs that lit the basement, he hurried down the stairs to the musty-smelling room of trunks and an assorted menagerie of things no longer used.

Standing in the silence of the dim basement, he looked toward the far corner where he had hidden the box so many years ago so Robert and Nancy would never see it. Hurrying to the corner, he started moving boxes and items away from the wall. He soon came upon an old trunk next to the basement wall and climbed up onto it. Using his penknife, Dan carefully removed a piece of the false ceiling, and in the shadows of the dim light, he saw the tattered wooden box. He folded his small penknife, put it back in his pocket, carefully reached up into the opening, and removed the box from its hiding place. Blowing the dust off, Dan set it down on the trunk, replaced the ceiling, and moved everything back to where it had been. He picked up the box and headed for the stairs brushing the dust off with the other.

Setting the box on the dining room table, he took the lid off and stared down at the stack of faded pictures of his identical twin brother. He hadn't seen the pictures since the day he found them in his father's garage so many years ago. After his father died, he had never looked inside the box but instead had hidden it in the basement. Norma didn't even know they existed.

Pulling a chair away from the table, he sat down and stared at the box for several moments. The top picture, faded and slightly wrinkled, was of Donnie's naked body lying on the snow-covered ground, his legs and arms partially covered in snow. The next picture was also faded and wrinkled. Donnie's right arm and hand were in the cold water of the shallow Sand Creek stream that ran through Englewood City Park. He thought of the Allyson girl's picture and knew without a doubt that Paul had staged it for him. At last, he understood what Paul was telling him. But how had Paul known these pictures existed?

Carefully, Dan placed the first two pictures on the table, thinking it was like looking at himself as a young boy, and that unsettled him. He had never wanted to look at those pictures and still didn't, but something kept pushing at him, and now he had to. The next picture, even more wrinkled and faded than the others, was of Donnie's chest, shoulders, and head partially covered with snow. He put it down and looked at the next slightly creased picture of the entire body and thought about how cold Donnie looked lying in the snow. Suddenly he felt a deep chill himself. He continued looking at the rest of the pictures showing various angles of the body in the snow, some more faded and tattered than others. There were several faded pictures of two sets of shoe prints partially covered by new snow leading from a wooded area to Donnie's body and then back into the woods. Dan couldn't tell from the faded photo if one set of shoe prints was bigger than the other. There was also a photograph of automobile tire tracks in the snow, and he wondered where this photo had been taken.

He set the last picture down on the table and picked up a folded piece of paper, finding another set of pictures with Donnie lying on a metal table in the morgue. Not wanting to look at those just yet, he opened the paper with the handwritten coroner's report. The ink was faded, the paper had turned yellow, and he had a hard time reading the scribbled words. The document carried the date of *January 14, 1918. Sex: Male Age: 8. Weight: 67.5 pounds.* Looking farther down the document, he found the words *'sexually assaulted. The anal canal shows signs of trauma and tearing. Male semen was present.* Dan paused and looked at a picture of his mother sitting on the bookcase a few feet away. Recalling how she cried when she told him that Donnie had been raped before he was murdered, he turned and picked up the document. He kept reading until he found, *'Cause of Death: Exsanguination from a cut on the neck.'*

His heart pounded against his chest. The skin on the back of his neck felt like something was crawling up into his hair. He stared at the words for several moments and then set the report down and picked up an old notepad. Still thinking about the cause of death of his identical twin, he thumbed through the notepad, realizing it contained notes of his father's investigation into Donnie's death. He put the notepad down on the table to look through later and began looking for a picture of Donnie's neck. Finding it, though it was badly faded, he could see the small cut that penetrated the jugular. Suddenly his stomach wrenched, and he felt sick. Dropping the picture, he stood suddenly, knocking over the chair, and hurried into the bathroom across the hall, where he vomited into the toilet bowl. Kneeling on the floor over the toilet, he wrapped his arms around the base of it and vomited again and again until there was nothing left for him to vomit. Coughing and spitting to clear his mouth of the terrible taste, he wiped the sweat from his forehead and face and slowly stood. He reached above his head and pulled the chain of the toilet reservoir attached to the wall, emptying the porcelain bowl. As the water rushed down the pipe on the wall to the toilet bowl, flushing his vomit into the sewer, his eyes welled as he sank back to the floor next to the toilet and cried.

The gentle sound of water refilling the porcelain tank on the wall above him mixed with his quiet sobbing. Lifting his head, he looked past the bathroom door across the hall to the dining room with watery, blurry eyes and thought of the pictures of his brother sitting on the table. When the water stopped and silence returned to the small room, he wiped the tears from his eyes and cheeks, placed his hands on the cold porcelain sink, and helped himself up. Not wanting to look at his image in the mirror for fear he'd see Donnie, he turned the cold water on, splashed it onto his face, and then rinsed out his mouth and spit into the sink.

He dried his face and hands with a towel, walked to the liquor cabinet in the living room, filled a glass with bourbon, and with slightly trembling hands, took a big drink. He closed his eyes and swallowed, feeling the familiar warmth of the bourbon going down. He looked at the dining room table covered with Donnie's pictures next to the overturned chair and thought about his dad believing that Donnie's killer was an adult man. He took another drink, and as tears filled his eyes, he looked at a picture of his dad sitting on a shelf in the bookcase. "How were you to know it was a young boy that killed Donnie?" Dan wiped the tears from his eyes and face as he walked back to the table. Taking another drink, he picked up the coroner's report, knowing now that Donnie was the connection between him and Paul. Still feeling a little sick to his stomach, he walked into the foyer, unlocked the front door, and stepped out onto the front porch, making sure the screen door didn't slam. Moving to the edge of the porch and feeling the cool night air on his clammy skin, he filled his lungs with fresh air. He leaned against the porch post, looking up between the eaves of the roof and the leaves of the elm tree at the black, moonless sky filled with stars. He thought about Heaven and wondered if Donnie was with their mother and father.

A dog barking somewhere in the distance broke the stillness of the midnight hour. Dan looked in the direction of the sound, drank the last of his bourbon, then filled his lungs again with fresh, cool air, thinking of the horror his brother must have gone through. Exhausted, he stepped away from the post, went back inside, locked the screen, then the door, and set the empty glass on the table next to his car keys. He paused at the dining room door to look at the mess of pictures and papers he had left on the table, not wanting to look at them anymore, and went upstairs.

Returning minutes later, dressed in pajama bottoms and a t-shirt, he walked into the living room, carrying Norma's pillow and a blankct.

Twenty-Seven

Dan Morgan opened his tired eyes, reached for the alarm clock sitting on the coffee table, and pushed the button shutting off the alarm. Feeling tired from a restless night and having a headache, he thought about the pictures of Donnie scattered across the dining room table and the notepad he still needed to look through. Sitting up, he adjusted the pillow behind his back and reached for the pack of cigarettes and matches on the coffee table. Lighting his cigarette, he blew out the match and looked out the east window at the sunrise above the trees beyond the Schaffer house next door. He took a drag from the cigarette and thought about his father searching for Donnie's killer for all those years, looking for an adult when all the time he was a boy living in their neighborhood. He took another drag, tapped the ashes into the ashtray he held on his lap, and then exhaled, blowing the smoke into the quiet living room air. Images of the older teenage boys in the old neighborhood and at school marched through his memory, but none stood out. He was only eight back then and had forgotten all but a few. His cigarette almost gone, he thought of Professor Pappel saying people would never suspect anyone of being a psychopath, not even a member of their own family. Crushing the cigarette into the bottom of the ashtray, he felt his father's frustration and wondered how in the hell he was going to catch Paul, much less find out who he was.

The sound of footsteps on the porch and rattling glass bottles told him the milkman was on the porch. Tossing the single cover off, he got up, walked into the foyer, and peered through the lace curtains of the front door window. He watched as the milkman, dressed in his white pants, shirt, and hat, climbed back into the white truck, and drove toward the house next door. Dan opened the door, bent down to get the milk and butter, wondering if he should tell Jack the truth about Donnie. Letting the lid to the milk box drop, he reached out, picked up the morning newspaper, stepped back inside the house, and closed the door.

Putting the milk and butter into the refrigerator, he took Wednesday morning's newspaper from under his left arm and read the headlines: '*H-Bomb detonated on Island in Eniwetok Atoll.*' He tossed the newspaper onto the red Formica table, thinking the United States was poisoning the world with their testing, and then he went about the task of fixing his coffee.

Neither Jack Brolin nor Captain Foley was in when Dan got to his desk, and he was grateful because he wasn't in a very talkative mood. He took off his coat, hung it over the back of his chair, slipped his Thirty-eight pistol out of its holster, put it in the top right-hand drawer of his desk, and sat down. Picking up the telephone to call Josephine Marshal in Missing Persons, Dan quickly changed his mind. He placed the receiver back on the telephone, got up, and walked across the noisy office of typewriters and ringing telephones to the stairs. Stepping onto the first floor, he visited the coffee shop, bought a sweet roll and two coffees, and then walked through the door of Missing Persons. Seeing Mrs. Marshall busy at her desk, he walked across the noisy room past several desks and stopped in front of her desk with a big smile.

Josephine was a thin, older woman with short, curly, gray hair and thick glasses on a small nose. She looked up, saw the two cups of coffee and the sweet roll, and smiled. "Good morning, Detective."

"Good morning, Josephine." Dan set one cup of coffee with the paper plate and sweet roll on top of it on her desk and then sat down in an uncomfortable, wooden, straight-back chair next to it. He smiled. "Aren't we looking nice today?"

Josephine lowered her head and looked at Dan over the top of her glasses, and then she looked at the coffee and sweet roll on her desk. "What is it this time, Dan?"

Dan took the lid off his coffee, took a sip, and then set the cup down. "I need a favor."

"Really!" She went to work on the lid of her coffee. "What kind of favor?"

"Could you have one of your girls check for any open cases involving young missing girls over the past three years?"

She picked up her sweet roll, looked at it, and then at Dan. "Sort of small, isn't it?"

He grinned. "That was the biggest they had."

Sure, it was she asked, "When do you want this favor?"

"Yesterday?"

She took a small bite of the sweet roll, set it down on the paper plate, and glanced around while lowering her voice. "This have anything to do with those dead girls?"

He took a drink of coffee and nodded yes as he said, "Sorry, Josephine, I can't divulge that information."

She sat back with a smile. "You're so full of crap, Dan. I'll see what I can do." Then she gestured with her hand. "Now, get out of here so I can get back to work."

When Dan got back to his desk, there was still no sign of Jack or the captain. Thinking that was strange, he sat down, leaned back in his chair, and took a drink of coffee while looking again at the photographs of Paul's victims tacked to the bulletin board. The pictures of Donnie and what had happened last night flowed through his mind, and Dan hated Paul more than ever for taking his only brother from him. Faces of a few of the older kids in the neighborhood he could remember flashed across his memory, and he wondered if one of them had killed Donnie, but it all seemed so surreal. Drinking the last of his coffee, he tossed the empty cup into the trash, stood, and walked to the side of his desk, sat on its edge, and began studying the red marks on the map indicating where Paul had dumped each body.

"Sorry, I'm late," said Jack as he walked past Dan.

Without looking at Jack, Dan thoughtfully said, "That's alright. I haven't been here all that long." When he turned to sit down, he noticed the white bag from Grandma's Donuts sitting on Jack's desk. Picking it up, he looked inside, finding two glazed donuts, then looked at Jack. "Don't you want any?"

Jack frowned. "One is mine, asshole."

Dan grinned. "Let's head out to Englewood and talk to Mary Jefferies. We can eat these on the way."

"Won't she be in school?"

Dan shook his head. "I called last night to see if we could stop by, and Mrs. Jefferies said Mary was not returning to school for a while."

Jack considered that. "Can't say as I blame her."

"I'll drive," said Dan.

Jack thought Dan seemed exceptionally quiet as he drove south on Broadway toward Englewood. Hoping there was no problem between him and Cathy, he feared again that this Paul thing was getting to him. Jack ate the last of his donut, wishing he had a cup of coffee to wash it down. "You're awfully quiet. Is everything alright with you and Cathy?"

Dan took one hand from the steering wheel, reached into his suit coat, pulled out a pack of cigarettes from his shirt pocket, and handed it to Jack. "Everything's fine. Light us up one."

Jack took the cigarettes, pushed in the cigarette lighter on the dashboard, and while he waited for it to get hot, he took two cigarettes out, wondering what was eating his partner. He glanced out his window, trying to think of something to say, when he heard the lighter pop out. Turning from the window, he lit one cigarette, gave it to Dan, and then lit the second.

Dan took a deep drag, blew the smoke out of the open window, and decided to tell Jack everything about his brother. "Remember me talking about my brother Donnie?"

Jack returned the lighter to the hole in the dashboard, realizing that he and Dan had not met until long after Donnie's death. "Yeah, you had said that he died when you guys were both little."

"Donnie and I were eight."

"Yeah," said Jack wondering what that had to do with anything. "What about it?"

Dan slowed the car for two pedestrians running across the street to catch the streetcar behind their car and, once it was safe, sped up. "I've never told anyone this before, but Donnie was raped and murdered, and his nude body was left next to Sand Creek in Englewood."

This was one of those rare moments when Jack was completely speechless as he stared at Dan.

Dan's eyes were on the street as they drove south. I found out the truth about fifteen years ago."

"Geez, Dan, I don't know what to say."

"You needn't say anything. It's just something I never talked about."

Jack took a deep drag of his cigarette, wondering why Dan was telling him this now. "I can understand why, but why tell me now?"

Dan told him about the time years ago when he had found the pictures hidden in his father's garage and the argument that followed. "I only looked at two of the pictures before I tossed the box into my father's lap, and I never looked at the others until last night."

Jack looked confused. "Why look at them at all?"

Dan took another drag from his cigarette and then tossed it out the window. "Remember Professor Pappel saying that Paul may want something from me?"

"Yeah."

Dan looked at Jack. "A couple of times, Paul had mentioned pictures."

"Yeah, I remember. You said Paul wanted you to look at the pictures."

"Well, yesterday, he kept asking if I had seen the other pictures. I thought he meant the ones of the Allyson girl in Washington Park."

Jack took a drag of his cigarette while Dan continued.

"There is a picture of Deborah Allyson, the last victim, lying on the ground with part of her arm and hand lying in the lake. Last night I was looking at the pictures on the garage wall when I noticed that each of the girls had their right arms in about the same position." He looked briefly at Jack. "I remembered a picture of Donnie posed the same way at Sand Creek." He looked out the window at a girl walking down the sidewalk. "I figure Paul staged the Allyson girl for my benefit because I wasn't getting the message from the others." Then he told him of what he had read in the coroner's report about Donnie's cause of death and of finding the faded picture from the coroner showing a small cut on the side of his brother's neck.

Jack stared out the windshield for several moments in disbelief, tossed his cigarette out the window, and turned to Dan. "Are you telling me that Paul raped and killed your twin brother?"

"That's just what I'm telling you, and for now, I don't want this going any further than this car."

"What about the captain?"

Dan considered that. "I may tell him, but no one else is to know."

"I won't say anything, not even to Lori." Jack paused. "Then that's the reason he's been calling you. He wanted you to figure that out."

Dan nodded. "Exactly."

Jack looked puzzled. "But why? No one would ever have figured it out after all these years." He looked out the window at the passing buildings and pedestrians on the sidewalk. "Makes no sense."

Dan continued staring out through the windshield at the street as he drove. "I've been going over the names and faces of a few of the older kids I remember from back then. From what the professor has said, it could have been any of them."

Jack thought about that. "If he was one of the older kids, you may not have known him, if at all. Children tend to stay within their own age group."

Dan considered that. "I'm sure you're right. There was a small notepad belonging to my dad at the bottom of the box under the pictures of Donnie." Dan paused, remembering how sick he had been last night at finding out the truth.

Looking curious, Jack asked. "What sort of notepad?"

"I haven't had the chance to go through it. My dad started it when he began his own investigation a few years after Donnie's death. I thumbed through it, and it's full of names, addresses, notes, and stuff like that."

"Maybe there's something in there that a fresh set of eyes will see a little more clearly."

Dan considered that. "I'll go through it tonight."

"Wait a minute," said Jack looking at Dan. "How the hell would Paul know about the pictures?"

"I've thought about that myself," said Dan. "He must have been hanging around the crime scene watching while the police took the pictures. Knowing my dad was a policeman, he probably figured I had access to them." He looked at Jack. "Paul's one smart son of a bitch."

286

Mary Jefferies looked carefully over the list of songs on the program from KCXX and told Dan and Jack the title of the first song that she had heard and then the last, giving them a timeline to work with. Dan asked if she would write down the number of turns she felt while sitting in the back of the van, and while she did that, Mrs. Jefferies surprised the two detectives with sandwiches and coffee.

Mary finished and handed the paper to Dan, who read what she had written while finishing his sandwich.

"Will it help?" asked Mary.

Dan smiled at her. "It might. I know this was a difficult thing for you to do."

Mary looked worried. "I just want him caught."

Jack frowned. "So do we."

Dan picked up the papers, folded them, shoved them into the inside pocket of his suit, and smiled at Mrs. Jefferies as he stood. "Thanks for the sandwiches and coffee, Mrs. Jefferies."

Jack stood. "Yes, thank you."

"You're both welcome," smiled Mrs. Jefferies as she stood. "I hope you catch this man soon."

"Yes, ma'am," said Dan. "So do we."

Looking weary, Mary stood.

Dan gently put his hand on her shoulder and looked into her tired soft eyes. "This is a big help, Mary. Thank you so much. When are you returning to school?"

Mrs. Jefferies put her arm around her daughter. "Not for a while. Mary's not quite ready for all the questions and stares."

"I can understand that," said Dan. Then he looked at Mary. "One day, this will all be over."

Mary looked doubtful. "I hope so."

Dan and Jack said their goodbyes and left the Jefferies's' house for Micky's Bar.

Sitting in Dan's car in the parking lot of Micky's Bar, Dan and Jack looked over the timeline of the radio program that listed each song and its length in time and compared it to what Mary had written down. Adding the total minutes from the first song Mary had heard until the last song, they came up with approximately 57 minutes of music until Paul turned off the radio. The only thing they were unable to determine was when he made the turns Mary had alluded to on the paper she had given them.

Dan was studying the papers. "We both agreed yesterday that Paul probably lives to the north since no victims have turned up in that area." He handed Jack the papers and started his car. "Let's go under the premise that Paul's place is to the north." Dan started the car, drove out of the

287

parking lot, and headed down Champa Street to 15th. Turning west, he drove to Santa Fe Drive, then headed north on Highway 85 & 87. Thinking that Paul would have stayed just under the speed limit so he wouldn't get pulled over, Dan also drove carefully to stay at the same speed.

Fifty minutes from the bar, Dan pulled off the asphalt, two-lane highway, shut the engine off, and got out of the car. He walked around the front of the car to the other side, leaned back against the front fender, and as the quiet day began to fill with the buzzing of insects, he stared across the Colorado farmland.

Jack stepped out, feeling a slight warm breeze, left his door open, stood next to Dan, and looked out across the land. "What's on your mind?"

Dan turned, put his hands on top of the fender, looked toward the west and the foothills of the Rocky Mountains, then walked to the open car door, opened the glove box, and took out a map of Colorado. He unfolded it and spread it across the hood of his 1949 Ford, holding it down to keep the slight breeze from blowing it off. "We're about here," he said, pointing to a spot on the map. "The last road was about three miles back, and it looks like the next is about four miles to the north, just short of Adams County."

Jack studied the map. "Either of those could be the road."

"Or neither." Dan looked back toward Denver, remembering Mary saying that the road was noisy. "I noticed the last road was gravel. Let's see if the next road is." He folded the map, walked around the front of the car, waited for another car to pass, got in, and handed it to Jack. While Jack put the map back into the glove box, Dan started the car and drove north along the two-lane highway. Coming to Henderson Road, Dan slowed, turned off the highway, and stopped.

Jack glanced up and down the deserted gravel road. "It has to be this one or the other one."

Dan looked thoughtful. "But which one? Which direction? Which house?"

Jack considered that. "I don't know, Dan, but I have to believe we're a hell of a lot closer to Paul than we were a few days ago."

Dan looked through the windshield along the lonely gravel road. "It's still the proverbial needle in the haystack."

"Yeah," agreed Jack. "But it's a smaller haystack."

Dan looked at his watch. "It's after four." He started the engine, turned the car around, got back on the asphalt highway, and headed toward the tall buildings of Denver in the distance.

It was almost five when Dan and Jack walked up the stairs to Homicide, finding Captain Foley at his desk. Foley looked up. "Where have you two been all day?"

Dan told him about driving out to Englewood, talking to the Jefferies girl, and then leaving Micky's and driving north on Highway 85 & 87. "We believe Paul lives north of Denver."

Captain Foley looked curious as he told them to sit down. "What led the two of you to that conclusion?"

Jack sat down and then leaned forward in his chair. "Paul has never dumped a body on the north side."

Foley considered that. "I guess he could be staying away from the north side for that reason." He looked skeptical. "There's a lot of territory out there. You can't start knocking on doors asking if they know a creep with an alias of Paul."

Dan chuckled. "I know that, Captain. Jack and I were talking on the way back, and tomorrow we'd like to take different cars and spend the day riding around looking for a white van parked in someone's yard." He paused. "Maybe we'll get lucky."

Still looking skeptical, Captain Foley locked his desk, stood, and slipped into his coat. "I have a feeling all you'll do is create a lot of dust on those gravel roads and burn up a couple of tanks of gasoline. But I guess it's all we have at the moment." He paused, looking at Dan while straightening the sleeves of his coat. "Sounds a lot like a dog chasing its tail."

Dan looked disappointed. "Once in a while, the dog catches his tail. Just give us the day, Captain. Maybe we'll get lucky."

"I don't believe in luck." Foley picked up his hat. "Do what you have to do. Just catch this bastard and soon." He started for the door of his office but then stopped. "Isn't Professor Pappel coming in to see us tomorrow?"

"In the afternoon," replied Dan. "Jack and I will check out the two roads first thing in the morning." He and Jack followed the captain out of his office, told him goodnight, and went back to their desks.

"You going home?" asked Jack while picking up what was in his inbox.

Dan reached for his telephone. "As soon as I call Cathy."

Jack started for the stairs with a grin. "Tell Cathy I said hello. I'll see you bright and early in the morning."

Dan ignored Jack and dialed the Littleton Sheriff's Office.

"Sheriff Brumwell's Office," said Cathy.

"It's Dan. I'm glad I caught you."

"I was getting ready to walk out the door. Where are you?"

"At headquarters," said Dan. "Would you like to get something to eat?"

Katherine smiled. "I would love to."

Dan stood and began clearing off his desk. "I'll be there in twenty minutes."

"No, pick me up at my house. Uncle is giving me a ride home. That'll give me a chance to freshen up a bit."

"Okay, how about a movie after dinner?"

"That sounds nice."

Then Dan paused and considered her uncle. "Does Uncle know about us?"

She hesitated. "Is that alright?"

"Yeah, I was just curious. What did he have to say?"

She laughed softly. "Uncle is waiting. We'll talk later."

Dan hung up the telephone, wondering what the sheriff thought about his niece dating a Denver Detective.

All through dinner, Cathy had the feeling that Dan's mind was somewhere else. Figuring it was on the murdered girls, she avoided the topic and noticed that he had barely touched his dinner. Several times she had to ask him if he heard what she had said, and finally, she reached across the table and touched his hand. "What's wrong, Dan?"

He smiled and took her hand. "Can we skip the movie tonight?"

Feeling disappointed, she said, "Sure."

"Can we go to your place after dinner instead? There's something I have to tell you."

Fearing he was about to end their relationship, she suddenly lost her appetite. "It looks as though neither of us is hungry. Maybe we should leave."

It was a long, quiet ride to her house, and once inside, she told Dan to pour himself a drink. Feeling slightly irritated toward him, she went into the kitchen and poured a large glass of wine. Dan was sitting on the end of the sofa staring into his drink when she returned. She glanced at him and then sat in the blue barrel chair across from him, watching as he took a drink of bourbon.

She took a sip of her white wine and waited.

He looked at her. "Jack is the only other person in the world right now that knows what I am about to tell you."

More curious now than afraid, she took another sip of wine.

Dan scooted to the edge of the sofa while holding the bourbon and looked at her. "I told you about my identical twin brother, but I never told you how he died."

Relieved he was not ending their relationship, she settled back and listened.

"When Donnie and I were eight, he was raped and then murdered. Someone found his body in what is now Englewood City Park. Back then, it was just an empty landscape." He looked into the glass of bourbon. "There's a small stream that snakes through it ---"

"Sand Creek," interrupted Cathy.

He looked up from the glass. "That's right. Anyway, for years, my parents told me that he had fallen on some ice, hit his head, and died. One day, just before my daughter's first birthday, I found a small box with pictures of the crime scene hidden in my dad's garage. I only looked at two pictures briefly and became very angry, knowing that my parents had lied to me about Donnie. Dad and I had a terrible argument; I stomped out of the house, and a few days later, Mom came to see me and smoothed things over between dad and me. When Mom and Dad passed away years later, I took the pictures and hid them in the ceiling of my basement so Robert and Nancy wouldn't ever find them."

Curious, Cathy asked, "Did your wife know you had them?"

He shook his head. "I don't believe so. I never told her I had them." Then Dan told her that each of the dead girls had been placed in a position much the same as Donnie. He had never noticed that until the picture of Deborah Allyson with her hand in the water at Smith Lake. It was then that he remembered the picture of his brother Donnie in the same pose lying next to Sand Creek with his hand also in the water. He went on to tell her about retrieving the box from his basement, of reading the coroner's report, and then finding the small puncture in Donnie's neck in one of the pictures, the same sort of puncture in the pictures of the girls Paul had murdered.

Surprise filled her face. "Paul killed Donnie?"

Dan nodded. "I'm sure of it."

"My God," she said with one hand over her heart. "That means he must have lived near you back then." Cathy sat back. "Why, that's almost unbelievable."

"I'm having a hard time believing it myself." Then he took another drink of bourbon.

She got up from the chair and sat down next to him, covering his hand with hers. "This is why he has been calling you, isn't it?"

He nodded. "I believe it is."

She looked worried. "What are you going to do?"

"The only thing I can do. Try and catch the bastard." Then he apologized for his language.

Cathy smiled. "As if I haven't heard my uncle use that word a time or two and much worse. You mentioned a small notepad in the box."

"I glanced through it last night, and it's more of a diary of Dad's investigation into Donnie's death. I'm going to read through it again tonight."

"Do you think your father had any suspicions about Paul?"

He thought for a minute. "I don't know. If he did, he might have written something in that notepad." Feeling a sudden urgency to go home and read his father's notepad more thoroughly, he looked at her. "I have to read that notepad."

With an understanding look, she said, "Go home and read it."

"You wouldn't mind?"

"Of course not. The truth is, I feel a little relieved."

Dan looked confused. "Relieved?"

She laughed softly. "I feel foolish now, but I thought you were going to tell me you weren't going to see me anymore."

Dan laughed. "Why would I do that?"

She shrugged with embarrassment. "I don't know. Foolish girl's thoughts." Then she stood up, feeling flushed. "Call me before you go to bed."

They walked to the door, where he kissed her goodnight. She watched until his car disappeared down the street before she closed the door, leaned against it, and smiled with relief as she took another sip of wine.

The first thing Dan did when he got home was to make a pot of coffee and fill a mug to the brim. Then he walked into the dining roomand stood over the table, drinking his hot coffee while gazing down at the pictures, the box, and the notepad. After setting his mug on the table, Dan pulled out a chair, sat down, and began to read the police reports filled out by the two police officers who had been investigating Donnie's death. Finding nothing of importance in them, he picked up the coroner's report and reread it, then set that down and picked up his father's notepad. Instead of opening it, he looked at it while recalling the day he had become so mad at his father, never realizing how much Donnie's death had consumed him. He slowly opened the notepad to the first page and began reading his father's handwritten notes.

October 23, 1920

Investigation into the murder of Donnie Chandler Morgan

That occurred on January 14, 1918

Dan recognized the significance of the 1920 date as the date the Denver Police Department had officially closed the case, and his father, Charles Morgan, had begun his own investigation. His father's handwriting, at times, was hard to read; the paper had yellowed, and some of the penciled words had faded. On every page, his father had carefully recorded the date, name of the person or persons he had interviewed, and what that person had told him. Dan was quite impressed at the number of people his father had interviewed and re-interviewed during the years after Donnie's case had gone cold. Proud now of his father, he softly said, "You were persistent. I'll give you that."

Two hours passed, as did an entire pot of coffee and a couple of trips to the bathroom. Dan was growing tired and about to quit for the night when he turned a page finding the name Timothy Perkins, followed by *MISSING* in capital letters. Dan read that Timothy Perkins was a seven-year-old boy who went missing on July 16, 1916, two years before Donnie was murdered. There was a written note at the bottom of the page. *'Last checked missing person file on March 25, 1936, and Timothy Perkins is still missing.'* Dan turned the corner edge of the page down for future reference, closed the book, stood, and stretched while looking at the time on his wristwatch. He walked to the desk in the living room, picked up the telephone as he sat down at the desk, and dialed Cathy's number.

"Hello," answered Cathy sounding sleepy.

"Did I wake you?"

Standing in the hallway where the telephone rested on its small mahogany table, Cathy looked at the clock in the living room. "Are you still reading your father's notepad?"

"I sort of lost track of time."

Sounding half-asleep, Cathy asked, "Find anything interesting?"

"A seven-year-old boy by the name of Timothy Perkins went missing from an Aurora neighborhood two years before Donnie was murdered."

Cathy thought about that. "That's interesting. Anything come of it?"

"According to my dad's notes, he was still missing in 1936." He looked at the grandfather clock in the corner of the living room. "Look, it's almost ten-forty, and we both have to get up early. I'll call you tomorrow."

"Would you like to come for dinner?"

"I would but let me see how things are going at work. I'll call you. Want me to bring anything?"

She smiled. "Just you."

293

Dan smiled. "I think I can manage that. Goodnight." He hung up the telephone and went upstairs to change into his pajamas, but instead of going to sleep on the sofa, he dumped his blanket and pillow on it and went back to reading the notepad.

A half-hour into the notepad, he came upon a page where his father had crossed out the names Harold and Martha Schmidt, son Vernon, and wrote: *'Martha died of influenza Dec 1917, Harold Schmidt fell off the roof of his house May 9, 1918, and died two days later.'* Realizing that this date was four months after Donnie's death, Dan looked at the address, seeing it was only three blocks away from where he had lived as a boy, and thinking about it, he vaguely remembered the accident. Unable to place a face with the name Vernon and wondering what had become of him, he turned the page. He read another interview, another, and another until he came to the page about Steve and Ann Taylor's son Paul. The hair on the back of his neck began to slowly stand. Their names were crossed out, and *'Moved February 1918'* was written under them. The date was only a month after the murder of Donnie, and that perked up his interest even more. He stared at the name Paul, thinking that this would be too easy, but still, he didn't rule it out. Then he noticed that the Taylors had lived across the street from the Schmidt family.

Thinking that the two boys were probably friends, he tried to put a face to the name Paul but he couldn't, any more than he could put one to Vernon. Several minutes later, the long day caught up with him, and feeling very tired, he folded down the corner of the page and closed the notebook. Getting up, he headed for the sofa, where he lay down and wrestled with his thoughts about the two families and the missing seven-year-old boy until sleep overtook him.

Twenty-Eight

Dan reached out, pushed the button on top of the alarm clock before it went off, sat up, put his feet on the floor, and looked out the window. His mind filled with thoughts about Paul Taylor, wondering why, if he was so sure of himself, he would give his real name. After a few moments of wondering, Dan stood, shoved his feet into his leather slippers, and paused to look at the picture of his mother and father. Thinking of the countless hours his dad must have spent on the case and the frustration he must have felt, he headed for the kitchen to start the coffee.

Showered, shaved, and dressed in his tan three-piece suit, Dan took a bite of jellied toast, a drink of coffee and considered the relationship between the Schmidt and Taylor families. Putting the last of the toast into his mouth, he knew it would have been difficult in 1920 to follow up on the Schmidt boy or the Taylor family. Drinking the last of his coffee and wishing his father were still alive so he could ask him some questions, he started to clean up his mess in the kitchen. When he finished, he went into the dining room, wrote down the names and addresses of the two families in his dad's notebook into his own notepad, and headed for the front door.

Instead of going into headquarters, Dan drove downtown, parked across the street from Civic Center, and walked toward the architecturally Greek building known as the Carnegie Building that housed the Denver Public Library. Once inside, he walked across the marble floor to the information desk manned by an attractive woman in her forties with light brown hair and dark-rimmed glasses.

She looked up from what she was doing and smiled. "May I help you?"

"I hope so. Where might I find past issues of the newspapers."

"Those would be downstairs in the Archives Room," she said while gesturing toward the stairs. "Just go down those stairs to the basement." She smiled again. "You can't miss it."

He thanked her, walked across the marble floor, and headed down the marble steps of the wide staircase to the basement. Seeing the sign 'Archives' above a door, he opened it and stepped inside, and stepped up to an L-shaped counter. The room seemed busy, with several people busy at their desks. Behind them, the walls were lined with rows of filing cabinets.

A young, heavyset woman of Mexican heritage in her early twenties with long, black hair and big, dark eyes stood up from her desk and walked toward him. She smiled, looking friendly as she approached the counter. "May I help you?"

Dan returned the smile. "I'm interested in looking through the newspapers from May 1918."

"I think we can manage that." She walked to the gate at the end of the counter and pulled it open. "Everything is on microfilm nowadays. We no longer keep paper copies of past issues. I hope that's alright."

"That's fine," said Dan. "Just so I can read them." He followed her to the back of the room and a long table containing several microfilm machines.

She stopped next to a machine. "You can use this one. What date were you looking for again?"

Thinking the machine looked like something out of a science fiction movie, he said, "May 1918. I'm not certain of the exact date."

She turned and started walking. "I think that would be down here."

Dan tossed his fedora on the table next to the big machine and followed her past several filing cabinets until she stopped and pointed to one. "What you're looking for should be in this cabinet. Do you know how to load the film and use the machine?"

Dan smiled, "I'm not sure."

"I'll show you." She showed Dan how to load the film and use the controls to search the documents. He said he understood, and she smiled. "If you should need any help, I'll be at my desk."

"Is there a telephone I could use?"

She gestured at her desk, "You can use mine."

He followed her back to her desk, picked up the telephone, and dialed his partner. "Jack, this is Dan. I'm at the Denver Library."

Curious as to why, Jack asked, "What the hell are you doing there?"

"I'll explain when I get in. All I can say right now is that I ran across something in my dad's notepad, and I have to check out some old newspapers."

"I thought we were going to take a ride north and see if we could get lucky."

Dan remembered what the captain had said yesterday. "Maybe the Captain was right. We would just be chasing our tails. I think I've stumbled onto something, but I have to go right now. I'll tell you about it when I get in." He hung up, thanked the young lady, and headed for the filing cabinets containing several rows of labeled microfilm. He looked through them until he found May 1 to May 14, 1918, and a second labeled May 15 to May 31, 1918. He lifted both out of the drawer, closed it, and returned to the table where his hat and microfilm machine waited. He took his notepad and his stubby pencil out of the inside pocket of his suit coat, placed them on the table, took off his coat, and draped it over the back of his chair.

He loaded the first half of May 1918 into the viewer. With his heart racing, he began turning the small crank on the side of the machine until he saw the first page of the newspaper dated May 1st and then looked at the table of contents on the bottom of the page to see what page Obituaries were on. Finding it, he turned the crank until he had the page in view, and since there was no Harold Schmidt, Dan went on to the following day, the next, and the next until he had finished the entire roll of microfilm.

Disappointed and afraid he might not find anything at all, he rewound the reel, took it off the machine, and inserted the second reel. As he viewed the obituaries of May 15, 1918, he found the entry: *'Mr. Harold Martin Schmidt passed away May 9, 1918, after falling from the roof of his home. Mr. Schmidt was born August 12, 1884, in Chicago, Illinois, and at the time of his death, Mr. Schmidt was employed at the Englewood Iron Works on South Santa Fe Drive. Mr. Schmidt is survived by his fourteen-year-old son, Vernon D. Schmidt, and sister, Mrs. Victoria Schmidt Schultz, who resides with her husband, Joseph, in Denver.'* The article made no further mention of what was to become of Vernon Schmidt, but Dan suspected he had gone to live with his aunt and uncle somewhere in Denver County. He opened his notepad and started writing.

He returned both rolls to the file cabinet, put on his suit coat, picked up his hat, notepad, and pencil, and then walked toward the Mexican woman who had helped him.

She looked up and smiled. "Did you find what you wanted?"

"I did, thank you." Then he gestured to the gate in the counter. "I'll show myself out." Dan climbed the staircase from the basement to the first floor and smiled at the pretty young receptionist as he walked across the marble floor to the exit. Stepping outside, he paused between the tall, gray cement columns and the steps leading down to the sidewalk, thinking about the obituary. Seeing a small food cart on the sidewalk, Dan hurried down the steps, bought a cup of coffee and sweet roll that he carried through the park to Civic Center. Finding an empty bench in the shade of an oak tree, he sat down, placed his sweet roll wrapped in a paper napkin onto the bench next to him, and carefully took the paper lid off the white, paper coffee cup.

While he ate, he pondered the mystery of Vernon Schmidt and Paul Taylor, thinking now that he had names and how that information gave him a couple of options. The first was the County Property Tax Department, and the other was the Department of Motor Vehicles. He took a sip of hot coffee to wash down the sweet roll and looked out across the green grass of Civic Center at the City and County Building, wishing strongly that his dad were still alive. When he finished the last of his sweet roll and coffee, he tossed the empty cup and wrapper into a trashcan next to the bench and headed for the doors of the County Building.

Pushing his way through the big, heavy, glass doors, he stopped at the Information Desk and asked the woman behind it where he might find the Property Tax Department. She directed him to the second floor, and after sprinting up the marble stairs, he found the room he was looking for. Stepping inside, he was greeted by an older, heavyset woman wearing a blue dress with white polka dots. She smiled. May I help you?"

"Good morning." Dan grinned. "I hope so." Then he showed her his badge and introduced himself, leaned toward her, and lowered his voice. "I'm working on a case, and I need to find out where a certain individual who has passed away once lived. Can you help me with that?"

She turned to her desk, picked up a pad and pencil, turned back, and then smiled at him. "May I have the individual's name?"

"A Joseph and or Victoria Schultz. They may have left their property to their nephew, Vernon D. Schmidt. I think it may be a farm north of Denver if that helps."

She smiled. "That may help. What years are you interested in?"

"1929 and later."

The smile left her face. "I'm not sure those are on microfilm."

He considered that with disappointment. "First try looking for a Vernon Schmidt within the last couple of years. That may make it easier. I can help if you want."

She smiled. "I'm afraid no one is allowed to look through them, Detective Morgan. If you give me your card, I'll call as soon as I find anything. I must warn you that it may take a while."

Disappointed once again, Dan gave her one of his cards, and as she took the card, he thanked her. "This is very important. Thank you, Miss..." he let the sentence trail off.

The lady smiled. "Mrs. Gracie Evans."

"Thank you, Mrs. Evans."

"I'll see what I can do, Detective, but I can't promise anything."

"I understand." Dan turned and walked into the hall, thinking the Department of Motor Vehicles was his next stop.

Walking into the DMV, he pulled his badge out and excused himself past several people who were in line waiting to see a clerk. Glancing around for someone who could help him, he saw a woman in her fifties sitting at a desk just beyond the gate of the counter. He walked up to the counter and leaned against it. "Excuse me."

She looked up through black-rimmed glasses, stood, and walked to the counter. "If you're here to renew your license, you'll have to wait in line."

Dan showed her his badge. "I'd like to see your supervisor."

She glanced at the badge and then at Dan. "Just a moment." She turned and walked to a wood and glass-enclosed office, opened the door, and stepped inside. She said something to the man sitting behind a messy desk and gestured toward Dan. The man gave him a quick glance, stood, and then accompanied the woman back to her desk and walked to the counter.

"I'm Frank Jackson. How may I help you, Detective?"

"Is there someplace we can talk, Mr. Jackson?"

He motioned toward the gate at the end of the counter. "We can talk in my office."

"That would be great." Dan followed him to the end of the counter, where Mr. Jackson opened the gate so he could step inside, and then they walked into his office.

Mr. Jackson gestured to a chair and sat down, waiting for Dan to tell him what he wanted.

"I'm in the middle of an investigation, Mr. Jackson, and I need to locate an individual."

"What sort of investigation?"

"I'm not at liberty to say, sir, but I could use your help."

"Of course," replied Mr. Jackson, feeling foolish for asking. "What sort of help?"

Dan reached for the ink pen resting in the inkwell on Mr. Jackson's desk. "May I have a piece of paper?"

Frank Jackson opened his desk, pulled out a pad of paper, and handed it to him.

Dan wrote Vernon Schmidt and Paul Taylor on the pad, put the pen back, and slid the pad toward Mr. Jackson. "I'm particularly interested to see if the first name has a valid driver's license with an address."

Frank Jackson looked at the name on the pad, and as he picked it up, he looked at Dan. "There could be several men with these names."

Dan considered that. "The person would be in his late forties. Would that help?"

Frank smiled. "That would narrow the search down. How soon do you want it?"

Dan grinned. "As soon as you can."

Mr. Jackson looked at the names on the paper and then glanced at the big, white-faced clock on the wall. "I'll take care of this myself, Detective. Leave me a card where I can reach you, and I'll give you a call as soon as I have something."

Feeling hopeful, Dan handed him his card and stood. "Thank you, Mr. Jackson. I appreciate the assistance." They shook hands, and Dan turned to leave but then stopped, thinking he would toss Mr. Jackson a bone. "The truth is, Mr. Jackson, I'm investigating an old murder case involving a young boy."

Mr. Jackson smiled while looking interested. "I'll get right on this."

"Thank you." Having another thought, Dan looked at him. "Can you check for a particular type of car or truck to see who the owner would be?"

"Do you have a license plate number?"

Dan shook his head, "No, just the color, make, and model."

Frank Jackson smiled. "That would be almost impossible. Maybe one day we will have the technology to do so, but I'm afraid that may be a long time in the future."

Dan left DMV, climbed into his 49 Ford, and shoved the key into the ignition, hoping Mr. Jackson would find something. Instead of starting the car, he sat back in the seat and stared out the windshield as the old, faded pictures of Donnie raced through his mind. After several moments, he turned the key, started the engine, shifted into first gear, and drove away from the curb.

Dan parked his car on the grass just off the paved street that curved around the edge of Englewood City Park, shut the car off, and lit a cigarette as he looked out across the grass and shade trees of the empty park to a wooded area of shrubs and weeds. Taking a drag from his cigarette, he blew the smoke out the open car window and looked toward the place where he knew Sand Creek would be, even though he had never been there. Taking a puff from his cigarette, Dan opened the car door, stepped out, closed the door quietly, and stepped onto the soft, green grass. He glanced to neither the right nor the left as he walked with his heart pounding toward the trees and shrubs on the southwest corner of the park. Images of Donnie lying in the snow were as clear in his mind as if he had just looked at the body.

Reaching the shallow stream, he stopped at its edge, finding it shaded by a group of cottonwood trees. He looked down at the clear water where several crawfish just below the surface of the water were living. He took a drag from his cigarette, blew the smoke into the air, then tossed the cigarette into the water, and watched as the slow current carried it downstream and around the bend that disappeared behind the thick underbrush.

His heart was racing as he knelt and touched the ground as flashbacks of Donnie's nude body lying in the snow came at him. Looking up, he saw a path that led through the trees and underbrush and thought about the badly faded pictures of shoe prints and tire marks left in the snow. Standing, he followed the path through the thick underbrush to a long, weed-covered hill about as tall as a two-story house. Reaching the top, he found a maze of narrow bicycle paths where kids raced their bikes up and down the hills after school or on the weekends. Beyond the hills lay a weed-filled vacant lot of some two hundred square yards, and beyond that, across a gravel road, was a white building with the words Swimming Pool in bright red letters spanning the front of the building.

Turning from the swimming pool building, he walked down the hill to the spot where they had found Donnie's body and followed Sand Creek through the park. As he walked, he wondered if the two boys were in this together. And if they were, how did two teenage boys of fourteen manage to get a body from south Denver to Englewood in 1918 without a car? He paused and glanced around the park, trying to picture what it looked like back before it became a park with nothing but trees, weeds, and open land. A perfect spot to dump a body, he thought. As Dan followed Sand Creek, he wondered how a couple of kids living in South Denver would even have known of such an isolated spot. Reaching the bend where his cigarette had earlier disappeared, he stopped to look west toward the mountains. Standing motionless, Dan stared at three tall stacks spewing black smoke into a cloudless blue sky. Remembering Harold Schmidt's obituary mentioning his working at the Englewood Iron Works, he knew the answers to his questions of how and who.

It was after four in the afternoon when Dan climbed the stairs and walked into the office of the Detective Squad. The sounds of busy typewriters, ringing telephones, and inaudible voices followed him through the maze of desks. Seeing Jack on the telephone as he got to his desk, he wondered if his partner had ever talked to anyone but his wife, Lori. He tossed his hat on top of his desk, put his Thirty-eight in the top right drawer, and sat down, feeling tired.

Jack hung the phone up. "You missed the professor."

Dan looked at the clock on the wall above the stairs. "Crap. Did he listen to the tapes?"

Jack nodded. "He didn't have much to say. I think he was a little disappointed that you weren't here."

301

Dan looked at his partner. "You feel alright?"

"Just a little tired," responded Jack.

Dan felt terrible about missing the professor. "I'll call him later and apologize."

Jack sat back in his chair, looking tired. "That was Josephine downstairs I was talking to when you walked in. She said you had asked her to see if there were any open missing person cases."

"And?"

"She found four cases, all involving young teenage girls over the past three years. I asked her to send up what she had."

Dan sat back, looking thoughtful. "If we ever find where Paul lives, I'm sure we'll find their remains and maybe the remains of several others."

Jack thought about that for a moment. "Speaking of your pal, he called about a half-hour ago. I told him you were out, and he hung up." Jack looked curious. "Have you been at the library all this time?"

Dan looked toward the captain's empty office. "Is Foley gone for the day?"

Jack nodded. "Left about twenty minutes ago." Then he repeated, "Have you been at the library all this time?"

"No," replied Dan, and then he told Jack what he had found in his father's notes regarding the two families, the picture of footprints and tire tracks in the snow, and the obituary of Harold Schmidt. Then he told him about visiting the County Tax Department, asking them to look for anything on the Schultz family or Vernon Schmidt, and asking DMV to check for Vernon Schmidt as well.

Jack sat forward. "You believe this Vernon Schmidt is your Paul?"

"I do, Jack." Lastly, he told him about his visit to the park in Englewood.

"Why did you go out there?"

Dan sighed softly. "I had to see the place, and it's a good thing I did. The obituary for Harold Schmidt mentioned him working at the Englewood Iron Works."

Jack looked confused. "So what?"

Dan leaned forward with his forearms on his desk. "The mill is right behind Englewood Park. Vernon or Paul, whatever his name is, would not have known about such an isolated spot back then. But his dad sure as hell would."

Jack considered that for a quick moment and sat forward in his chair. "You think this Schmidt fella helped his son get rid of Donnie's body?"

"How else would they know about that isolated spot? The boys would have been too young to drive. They were only fourteen."

"You said there were two sets of footprints in the picture. Maybe they belonged to the other boy?"

"No," said Dan. "It had to be Harold Schmidt. That's the only explanation that makes sense, Jack. The place is too far away for two boys to know about, especially in 1918. I think Vernon killed Donnie, and his father helped him get rid of the body."

"So, you don't believe the boy that lived across the street from Vernon Schmidt had anything to do with the killing of your brother?"

Dan looked unsure. "Shit, I've thought about that until I'm blue in the face, and at times I wonder, but right now, I don't. I remember Paul hesitating when I said I needed to call him something if he was going to continue to call me." Dan sat back in his chair. "I think Paul Taylor and Vernon Schmidt were friends before the Taylor family moved away. They probably never saw one another again, so it would be a safe thing to use his friend's name rather than his." He looked at his partner. "Are you sure you're okay? You don't look well."

"The truth is, Dan, I don't feel well." Then he stood and slipped into his suit coat. "I think I'll head home a little early." Jack frowned as he pulled his pistol from his desk drawer and holstered it. "I think I'm just tired. I'll see you in the morning." Then he said goodnight and headed for the stairs but stopped after a couple of steps. "A thought just occurred to me."

Dan looked up, interested.

Jack looked thoughtful. "You said that Mr. Schmidt died from falling off the roof."

"That's what the obit said. Why?"

"I was just wondering," said Jack, "if Paul was up there helping him."

Twenty-Nine

Dan fixed himself dinner and ate at the kitchen table while listening to soft music from the radio on top of the refrigerator, and when he finished, he cleaned the kitchen and put the dishes away. After he filled the percolator with water and coffee grounds for the morning, he turned off the radio, sat down at the desk in the living room, and took the professor's card from his wallet.

"Pappel residence," said a woman's voice.

"Is the Professor in?"

"Who is calling?"

"Detective Dan Morgan."

"Just a moment."

Dan could hear the woman's footsteps fade into silence.

"This is Professor Pappel."

"Hello, Professor. This is Detective Dan Morgan."

"Good evening, Detective."

"I hope I'm not interrupting your dinner," said Dan

"Not at all. In fact, your timing is excellent, as we just finished." Curious about the phone call, the professor asked, "What can I do for you, Detective?"

"First, I want to apologize for missing you at Headquarters this afternoon." A thought crossed his mind about party lines. "I wanted to talk to you about my friend, but I'd rather not do it over the telephone."

Sensing some urgency in the detective's voice, the professor invited him over by giving him his street address. Dan wrote it down, said goodbye, shoved it into his shirt pocket, and headed for the front door.

Professor Pappel opened the front door, smiled, and stepped back. "Come in, come in." After Dan stepped inside, Pappel closed the front door, they shook hands, and then the professor showed him into his study. Gesturing to one of two matching overstuffed chairs with a small table between them, the professor asked if he would like a brandy.

A drink of brandy sounded good to Dan as he sat down.

Professor Pappel walked to a small table where a carafe of brandy and several glasses waited and started pouring two drinks. "The tapes were fascinating."

Dan glanced around the room with a dark, cherry wood desk, bookshelves, framed certificates, and two small, floral oil paintings. "I thought you might enjoy them."

Pappel handed Dan a glass of brandy. "Here you are, Detective."

304

Dan took the glass and waited while the Professor sat down in the other chair and took a small sip of brandy.

The Professor looked at Dan. "Now, Detective, what's on your mind?"

"I'm curious whether or not you thought Paul was different in the recent tapes."

The Professor thought about the tapes. "He seemed very sad in the last conversation."

"That's what I thought," agreed Dan. "This may sound funny, but at one point, it was like I was talking to two different people."

Pappel nodded as he took a sip of brandy. "The eternal fight between two personalities. It sounds to me that one hated letting this young girl, what was her name, go?"

"Mary Jefferies."

"Yes, that's right, Mary Jefferies. I'm sure Paul was glad, but I'm sure the beast was not."

Dan took a drink. "He said that he loved her. Is that possible?"

"Oh yes, yes, indeed. Most have a deep affection for their victims. That's why they keep mementos."

Dan thought about that for a moment. "What did you make of his asking if I believed in God?"

Pappel sat back in thought. "I believe that was not the beast talking, and Paul fears death and the accounting afterward." The Professor paused as he looked at Dan. "He seems to know a lot about you, so please be careful." He took a drink of brandy. "Is there anything else?"

Dan nodded and sat forward in his chair. "Paul has told me several times to look at the pictures."

"Yes," said the Professor. "He did so in the last conversation."

Dan Morgan went on to tell him about the pictures on the wall of his garage and how he had just recently realized that they were all posed with the right arm and hand in a certain position.

Professor Pappel carefully listened while Dan told him about his twin brother, the pictures his father had of the crime scene, and his brother's naked body lying in the snow.

"Words are of little value, Detective, but I am sorry to hear about your brother."

Dan sipped his drink. "It was a long time ago, and we were both just eight years old." Dan paused, composing himself. "I looked at those pictures last night for the first time in years, and Donnie's arm was posed the same, with part of it in the cold stream. The coroner's report said Donnie died from exsanguination from a cut on the neck, just like the young girls. I'm positive that Paul killed my twin brother thirty-five years ago."

Shocked by the news, the Professor took a sip of brandy and stared into his glass in thought. "We all suspected there was something between the two of you. However, I could never have imagined this."

Dan told the Professor about his father's notepad with its notes on the Schmidt and Taylor families.

Pappel sipped his brandy while deep in thought and then looked at Dan. "You think this Paul Taylor is your Paul?"

Dan shook his head. "No, sir, I don't. I think Paul is Vernon Schmidt using Paul's name."

"What brought you to that conclusion?"

"I drove out to Englewood and visited the place where Donnie was found. I couldn't understand how two young boys living in south Denver could get a body all the way to Englewood in 1918. Then I remembered the obituary stating that Mr. Schmidt worked at the Englewood Iron Works, which is located just a couple of blocks west of the park. But back in 1918, there was no park, just weeds and trees and a small creek."

Professor Pappel stood up with his glass, picked up Dan's empty, and walked to the liquor cabinet, thinking methodically about everything Dan had told him. As he poured two more drinks, he talked over his shoulder. "You believe this Harold Schmidt helped his son dispose of Donnie's body?"

"I do. At first, I believed the two boys had killed Donnie, and that was why the Taylor family moved during the dead of winter."

The Professor turned from the liquor cabinet. "But not now?"

Dan shook his head. "No, not any longer. I believe just one of them killed Donnie."

Pappel handed Dan his drink and sat down as he smiled. "A father will go to great lengths to protect his son."

"Jack thinks Paul killed his father by pushing him off the roof."

He looked at Dan. "That would not surprise me if he felt threatened by his father." He paused a moment. "The murder of your twin may be the underlying reason that your Paul does not actually have sex with any of his victims."

Dan looked puzzled. "I don't follow."

Professor Pappel took a sip of brandy and sat back in his chair, holding the glass on his lap with both hands. "The psychopath's psyche is difficult to understand. It's 1951, and more research is sorely needed, but if you want my personal opinion, I'll give it."

Dan nodded. "That's why I'm here, Professor."

Professor Pappel thought for a moment while he set his glass on the small table between them. "I think that in addition to Paul's other issues, he has always liked men over women. He probably wanted your brother, and after he had him, the guilt set in, and he blamed your brother for his own sins."

"How could he? I don't understand."

"It's always easier to place the blame than it is to accept it. Paul wanted your brother and had a hard time dealing with those emotions. He undoubtedly fought them fiercely for many years. But, as he grew older, he probably tried young girls but wasn't able to complete the sexual act. One of them probably laughed at him, and he killed her." Pappel picked up his glass, took a drink, and then set it down. "That was the beginning, and over the years, he has perfected what he does. I believe his desire to kill them far exceeds his need for sexual gratification, which only comes by masturbating on them afterward."

Dan took a sip of his drink and stared across the room at the shelves of books. "It all makes sense now." He looked at the professor. "But why call me after all these years?"

Pappel looked at him for a long moment in careful thought. "You are the living reminder of what he wanted and killed after he had it." The Professor paused in thought. "He may believe that in order to resolve the issue of thirty-odd years ago, he has to finish what he started with your brother. I am fairly certain that he feels the need to finish what he began using you and possibly ending it."

That unnerved Dan. "You believe he wants to do the same thing to me as he did to Donnie?"

Professor Pappel thought a moment. "I'm only guessing, Detective. You and you alone are the living reminder of his killing Donnie. You look exactly as your twin brother would if he was still alive, and I believe that haunts him. When he is lucid, part of him may want you to be the one to finish the battle for him."

"What battle?"

"The battle between him and the beast." Pappel looked at his watch and then stood. "I'm sorry, Detective, but I have papers to correct, so I need to cut our visit short. Perhaps we can continue our talk another time?"

Dan stood. "Of course. I appreciate your time, Professor." Then he followed the professor to the front door

The professor opened it and looked at Dan. "Whatever Paul wants with you, Detective, please be careful."

Dan shook the professor's hand, thanked him, and then stepped out onto the dimly lit front porch.

Pappel stepped into the open doorway. "One last thing, Detective."

Dan turned.

"I have been thinking about that prostitute," he paused. "What was her name?"

"Ruth Spencer."

"Would Paul have any reason to believe this Ruth Spencer meant something to you?"

Dan considered that for a moment, recalling how Paul had talked about his daughter Nancy. "He may have."

"I don't mean to worry you, but that may be why he killed her."

Dan remembered the car the night Ruth surprised him in the alley and Paul sitting in the bar across the street from the theater, watching Mary Jefferies through the theater's open doors. Thinking of Cathy, he felt the need to get to a phone, so he could call her. "Thanks, Professor."

Dan drove to the nearest telephone booth and called Cathy.

"Hello,"

"Are you alright?"

Recognizing Dan's voice, Cathy said, "Of course. Why?"

"Nothing," he said, feeling relieved.

Knowing there was more to it, Cathy asked, "You sound worried. What's wrong?"

"It was nothing."

"It wasn't nothing," she persisted. "Now, what is it?"

"Maybe you should stay with your uncle for a few days."

Thinking that was strange, she asked, "Does this have something to do with that Paul character and those young girls?"

Dan hesitated. "I was talking to Professor Pappel tonight, the professor that is helping us with the case, and he asked if Ruth and I were friends --"

Cathy interrupted. "And you think that if Paul finds out about me," she hesitated. "That he may come after me?"

Dan didn't want to scare her, but he had to be honest. "I'm not saying that, but as a precaution, I think you should stay with your aunt and uncle until we catch him."

She thought about that for a moment. "I'll not let this creep run me out of my own home. I have a gun, and I know how to use it."

Dan smiled, knowing this was going to be difficult. "I know, but he could sneak in while you're asleep or break in and be waiting for you when you get home."

Cathy knew that was true, and it frightened her. "I'll borrow my aunt's dog, Butch. He always sleeps with me on the occasions I stay over."

Knowing that barking dogs often ward off intruders, Dan considered her idea while picturing her holding a gun as she and the small dog huddled together on the bed. "I'd still prefer it if you stayed with your aunt and uncle."

"I'm staying in my own home, Dan. I can protect myself."

Realizing how stubborn she was, he said, "I can see there's no arguing with you about it."

She smiled. "Glad you agree. I'll ask Uncle to bring Butch over after work tomorrow."

Dan sighed as he gave in. "Alright, have it your way, but make sure everything is locked up."

"I will, I promise. When will I see you?"

"How about dinner tomorrow night?" offered Dan,

Cathy considered that. "Let's stay in tomorrow night. Call me when you get off work, and I'll have dinner ready by the time you get here."

Dan smiled. "It's a date. Make sure you're locked up good and tight tonight." Dan hung up, looked at his watch, seeing it was ten-fifteen, and headed for his car parked a few feet from the phone booth.

Feeling tired when he got home, Dan went upstairs and returned several minutes later in his pajama bottoms and t-shirt carrying Norma's pillow and his blanket. After spreading the blanket on the sofa, he started to sit down when he thought about his pistol sitting on the desk. Dan picked up the Thirty-eight Smith and Wesson and laid it on the floor next to the sofa within easy reach. Feeling a little foolish about doing that, he turned off the lights and crawled under the blanket. As he lay in the darkroom bathed in the dim light of the streetlamp coming through the leaves of the elm tree, he thought about Cathy and her aunt's dog, wishing she had not been so stubborn.

He heard every sound in the house that he had never bothered with before, and that kept Dan from getting a good night's sleep. If asked, he couldn't tell how many times he got up from the sofa with his Thirty-eight pistol in hand to check a door or window to make sure they were locked. The night slowly passed, and now the warm morning sun coming through the east window made a perfect impression of the lace curtains on his face and pillow. Opening his eyes to the alarm clock, he reached over, pushed the button, and looked out the front window in the early morning. The faces of the murdered teenage girls rushed into his mind, followed by Howard Trenton and then Ruth Spencer. Then his mind settled on what

Professor Pappel had said last night, renewing his fears for Cathy. In the stillness of the morning, the house talked in creaks and moans as the sun warmed up the old boards and shake roof. His eyes found the picture of Norma on the end table, and instead of feeling guilty about Cathy, he feared for her.

He turned from Norma to the elm tree and watched the early morning birds dart from limb to limb or quickly fly away. He thought about his life before he met Cathy, remembering not only how simple it was but also how lonely and meaningless it had become. Hearing the milkman on the porch, he tossed the blanket back, got up, sat down at the desk, and dialed Cathy's number.

"Hello," answered Cathy after several rings, sounding as if she had just woken up.

"Good morning."

Sleepily, Cathy asked what time it was.

Dan looked at the grandfather clock across the room. "It's a quarter after six."

Trying to keep her eyes open, she looked at the clock and yawned as she pushed the button so her alarm would not go off. "Is everything alright?"

"I just wanted to make sure you were okay before I went upstairs to get ready for work."

She smiled, thinking that was thoughtful. "I'm fine."

"How did you sleep last night?"

"Not well," she said. "Every noise woke me."

"I still think it'd be a good idea if you stayed with your uncle for a few days."

"Didn't we settle that last night?"

He searched for a better argument. "You settled it; I didn't."

"And I'm the deciding vote. How did you sleep?"

He lied. "Good."

"Seriously?"

He paused. "No, not really. Every time I dropped off for a few minutes, the house would creak, and I would be wide awake with my hand on my gun."

Cathy laughed softly. "I wasn't too far from mine, either. I'll feel better when I get Butch. He's so cute."

Cute didn't make Dan feel any better about her staying alone. "I better clean up and get dressed."

"Alright. Call me later?"

"I will. Goodbye."

Cathy said goodbye, hung up the telephone, plumped up her pillow, and then snuggled down into the covers to sleep another twenty minutes.

*** Thirty ***

The smell of fresh coffee greeted Dan when he came down the stairs dressed in his navy blue suit, white shirt, and red tie with white stripes, his suit coat draped over one arm. Setting the coat over the arm of a chair holding his brown suit from yesterday, he hurried into the kitchen. Turning off the gas to the burner under the coffee pot to let the grounds settle, he fixed two pieces of toast. Pouring a cup of coffee and picking up a slice of toast, he stood at the kitchen window, watching the cat from the house across the alley sneak through his fence. His mind thought of Mr. Jackson at DMV and Mrs. Grace Evans with the County Property Tax Records, hoping both would find something for him today.

His toast eaten, he poured the rest of his coffee into the sink, washed his cup out, and cleaned up the kitchen, wondering when his housekeeper was going to return from Brooklyn. Retrieving his Thirty-eight from the floor next to the sofa, he put on his fedora, gathered up his suit coat and the suit he would drop off at the cleaners, and walked out the door.

Pretty sure the coffee upstairs would be terrible, Dan stopped at the coffee shop in the lobby of Police Headquarters, bought two cups of coffee, and then headed up the stairs to busy typewriters and ringing telephones. Thinking of the Grandma's donuts his partner would bring to work, he put his gun into the desk drawer. Sitting on the edge of his desk, Dan looked at the map of Denver tacked to the big bulletin board along with the pictures of the victims. He carefully peeled the lid off his coffee, wondering where his partner was with the donuts. While drinking the hot coffee, he studied the map of the country north of the city.

The telephone rang, and hoping it was either the DMV or Property Tax Records, he turned and picked up the telephone. "Detective Morgan."

"Dan, this is Lori."

Surprised at hearing Jack's wife on the telephone, he remembered how bad his partner had looked yesterday. "Hi Lori, is everything alright?"

"I tried to call you at home, but I guess you had already left. Jack's pretty sick. He's been in the bathroom most of the night with it coming out both ends."

"Have you called the doctor?" asked a concerned Dan.

"I have," replied Lori. "He'll stop by later this morning."

Dan told her that he would call her later in the afternoon to check on Jack. They said goodbye, and as he hung up, he saw Captain Foley walk into his office. Deciding he would finish his coffee and let the captain get settled for a few minutes before he went in to talk to him, he turned his attention to the map.

His coffee gone, Dan tossed the empty cup into the trashcan next to this desk, stood and walked to the captain's office, and tapped on the window of the closed door.

Foley looked up and motioned him to come in.

Dan opened the door and stepped inside, closing it behind him. "Lori Brolin called earlier. Jack is sick and won't be in today."

The captain looked concerned. "Did she say what was wrong with him?"

"Apparently, he spent most of the night on the toilet. She's called the doctor, and he's supposed to drop by this morning. I told her I would call later and check on him."

Foley looked concerned. "Hopefully, it's just something he ate."

Dan doubted that, recalling that he was sick when he had left work. "He didn't look all that good when he left yesterday."

Foley considered that for a moment. "I'm sure he'll be alright."

Dan felt that he had to tell the captain about his twin brother. "May I sit down, Captain?"

Foley gestured to the chairs and waited.

Dan sat down and told Foley about Donnie, the photographs, the notepad, and the Schmidt and Taylor families from his old neighborhood. He then told him that he believed Paul was really Vernon Schmidt, who was the one who had killed his twin brother.

Captain Foley thought back on the deaths of Dan's daughter and knew how troubling this latest news about his brother must be. "I had no idea you had a twin brother."

"Few people do, Captain."

The captain sighed as he looked at Dan, sitting in the chair across from him. "Shit, Dan, I don't know what to say. I can't imagine what you're going through right now." He paused. "Well, that certainly explains Paul's interest in you." He leaned forward, looking concerned. "Are you sure that you're okay working this case?"

Dan nodded his head. "Oh, yes, sir. I want to finish what my dad started thirty years ago." Then he told the captain about the obituary of Harold Schmidt he had found on microfilm at the library, which mentioned a sister and his only son Vernon. Then he told of his visit to the property tax department and the DMV in search of Vernon Schmidt.

Captain Foley looked pleased. "Now we have a name. That was good detective work, Dan. It looks like we may be closing in on this bastard."

"I hope so, Captain." Dan thought about his visit to the professor's last night. "I may as well tell you that I went to see the Professor last night after dinner."

Foley looked interested. "Oh, what about?."

"I wanted to apologize for not being here yesterday, and I wanted to hear what he had to say after listening to the tapes."

Foley considered that. "Probably a good idea. What did the professor have to say?"

Dan told him most of what the professor had told him, leaving out the part about Ruth Spencer and his concerns over Cathy, who Foley did not know about. He stood. "I'll be gone for a couple of hours. There are a couple of things I'd like to look into, but I should be back by close of day."

"Alright, Dan," Foley smiled. "Again, good police work, and I'm sorry about your brother."

It was after eleven in the morning when Dan parked in the shade of an oak tree in front of the house where the Schmidt family had lived in 1918. Shutting the car off, he sat back, lit a cigarette, and glanced around the quiet neighborhood of older two-story dark, red brick homes with manicured green lawns. Tall oak trees lined the grass strips between the curbs and sidewalks. He looked through the passenger window at the house beyond the trees with its narrow sidewalk leading to the stairs of a big, covered porch. Across the porch was the dark, ominous front door of the house that had once belonged to the Schmidt family.

Getting out, he walked around the front of the car, took a drag from his cigarette, dropped it into the gutter, and stepped over the curb, feeling the soft, green grass of the parkway underfoot. With eyes focused on the front door, he walked up the narrow walk separating the green lawn and up the four steps of the big, covered porch to the front door. Taking out his badge, he knocked on the door and waited several moments before he knocked again, and when no one answered, he put his badge away, walked across the porch, and stepped onto the driveway. Pausing a moment to glance around the neighborhood, he proceeded toward the dark brick single-car garage with white wooden doors sitting beyond the house in the backyard. Opening the side door, he stepped inside the dim garage filled with garden and yard tools, greeted by the odor of musty cement.

Leaving the door open for light, he walked across the cement floor and stood in the dusty image of the window left by the morning sunlight. In the stillness of the garage, he looked up at the rafters lining the attic, then down at the lightly stained cement floor, and somehow knew that this was where Donnie's life had ended. Kneeling, he touched the slightly stained cement and looked up, imagining Donnie hanging upside down from the rafters over a pool of dark blood. Feeling like he was going to vomit, he stood and rushed to the open doorway, stepped outside, leaned over, and threw up his coffee and toast. Leaning against the doorjamb, he took off his hat, pulled a handkerchief from the back pocket of his trousers, wiped the perspiration from his face, and then the vomit from his mouth. Taking a deep breath, he spit to cleanse his mouth and then put on his hat. Standing upright, he shoved the handkerchief back into his pocket, closed the door, and walked back down the driveway to his car. He slid the keys into the ignition, but instead of starting the car, he turned and looked back up the driveway at the garage doors. Then he sat back with his head against the seat and closed his eyes, wishing this nightmare was over.

It was after one when he walked into Micky's feeling a little out of sorts, sat down at a table in the corner, ordered a glass of bourbon straight up, and a roast beef sandwich. While he waited for the sandwich, he took a sip of bourbon and thought about Professor Pappel telling him, '*A father will go to great lengths to protect his son.*' Dan wondered if he could go to those lengths if Robert were to kill someone. Unable to answer that, he turned his thoughts to Grace Evans at the Property Tax Department. He took out his notepad and flipped through the pages of penciled words until he found her telephone number written above Frank Jackson of the DMV.

Getting up from the table, he walked to one of the telephone booths in the rear of the bar, sat down on the wooden seat, and closed the door turning on the dim light above him. He lifted the earpiece, put a nickel in the slot, and dialed the number.

"City and County."

He put his lips close to the mouthpiece on the front of the black box, "Mrs. Grace Evans in Property Tax, please."

"One moment."

The telephone rang several times before a female voice said, "Property."

"Grace Evans, please."

"This is Mrs. Evans."

"Mrs. Evans, this is Detective Dan Morgan."

"Oh yes, Detective Morgan," Grace sounded excited. "I was just about to call you. I think I found what you are looking for."

Dan's heart raced with anticipation.

"You were right about Vernon Schmidt. He now owns a farm that once belonged to a Joseph and Victoria Schultz."

Dan couldn't believe his good luck, thinking to himself, 'I've got you, you son of a bitch.' then he asked, "Where is the farm?"

"It's located on Rural Route 15 north of Denver. I looked it up on one of our maps, and it's about twenty-five miles north along Highway 85 & 87."

Dan was so excited that he dropped his pencil. "Just a moment, please." After he retrieved his stubby pencil from the floor of the booth, he wrote while he talked. "Rural Route 15, off Highway 85 & 87."

Phyllis corrected him. "RR15 does not meet the highway. You have to take Henderson Road east from the highway to RR15 and then go north. The address is Box 395."

Dan wrote that down, thanked her, said goodbye, and hung the telephone up. He sat there a minute looking at the paper with the address while wild thoughts of killing Paul raced through his mind. Knowing instead that he had to arrest him so he could be put on trial, Dan opened the door, stepped out of the booth, and walked to his table and sandwich. Tossing the notepad and pencil on the table, he sat down, took a bite of the sandwich, and as he chewed, he looked at the address written on his notepad. He picked up the pad and shoved it and the stubby pencil into the inside pocket of his suit. Leaving a half-eaten sandwich and a half glass of bourbon on the table with some money, he stood and walked toward the door.

Forty minutes later, Dan turned off Highway 85 & 87 onto a gravel-covered Henderson Road and drove past the spot where he and Jack had stopped and turned around earlier in the week. Thinking how close they were to Paul that day and didn't know it, he drove on, chased by a small cloud of dust. Approaching an intersection with a small corner store and an old-style gasoline pump on the southeast corner, he slowed. Reading RR15 on a weathered street sign, Dan turned left and headed north, searching the mailboxes for the number 395.

Several minutes passed before he came to a farmhouse off to his right, sitting several hundred yards from the road at the end of a long dirt driveway. Approaching a mailbox resting atop a support built by 2x4's, he slowed and read the big black numbers, then sped up, looking for the next mailbox. Two miles farther down the road, he came to a white, two-story farmhouse on the left, sitting some three hundred yards from the road, nestled among several poplar trees. He slowed as he approached the gated driveway and rusty, dented, black mailbox atop a 4x4 post. His heart pounded when he read the white faded number 395, then continued down the road, looking for somewhere to pull over.

Seeing an oak tree and red berry bushes up ahead out of sight of the farmhouse, he slowed, and as he approached, he saw an opening between the bushes large enough for a car. After glancing in the rearview mirror, he turned off the road and parked beside the oak tree, hidden from the house and the road by the berry bushes. Getting out of the car, he opened the trunk and pulled out a black case containing a pair of German binoculars he had brought home from the war. Taking them out of the black case, he stepped back toward the road to see if any cars were coming. Not seeing any dust from cars on the gravel road in either direction, he stood next to the trunk of the oak tree and looked out across the green haze of new alfalfa sprouts. He adjusted the binoculars, looked at the two-story farmhouse, and whispered, "I said I'd get you."

He looked at the front porch with a single kitchen chair sitting between the screen door and the front window. As he moved the binoculars over the house, pausing at each window, he took particular notice of the narrow windows of the basement. He figured that it was behind those windows the young girls had died, and he wondered where Vernon was at this very moment. He moved the glasses to the garage, which was painted the same white with black trim as the house. The big garage door was closed, and he wondered if he would find the white van parked inside. Dan moved the binoculars to the weathered barn just as a figure stepped out into the sunlight, walking toward the house. Excitement flooded his mind and body at seeing Vernon, wishing he was a little closer so he could get a better look at the face under the wide-brimmed straw hat. After the figure disappeared into the house, Dan lowered his binoculars and stared across the green haze of alfalfa, wondering what Vernon had been doing inside the barn.

Deciding to come back after dark and visit the garage to see if it contained the white van, he hoped the side door had a window he could peek through. Putting the glasses back to his eyes, he looked at the rest of the farm, seeing an old tractor rusting beneath an oak tree several yards from the barn. A chicken coop sat a few yards beyond the house, and a pigsty and corral with two cows were next to the barn. Then he noticed a group of poplar trees beyond the corral and barn filled with weeds, unlike the rest of the land, and he thought that it would probably be the perfect spot for Vernon's victims. Checking the road once again, he saw a moving dust cloud in the distance coming from the direction of Henderson Road. Looking at the cloud through his binoculars, he saw a black pickup truck racing ahead of the dust, slow down, and turn into the driveway of another farm. Concerned about being seen, he put the binoculars into their case, tossed the case in the trunk, backed out of his hiding spot, and drove back along Rural Route 15.

While stopped at the corner of RR15 and Henderson Road, he looked across the dirt road at the single, old-style gas pump with the glass reservoir. A sign atop the building read 'Henderson Corner Grocery.' Then he looked at the gas gauge, and seeing he was getting low on fuel, he glanced up and down Henderson, then drove across the road, parked next to the gas pump, and got out of the car.

317

An elderly man in his seventies wearing a faded red shirt and bib overalls walked out of the store. "You need some gasoline, young fellah?"

"Five gallons should do it." Dan opened the lid to the gas tank and took the cap off while the old man flipped a lever on the side of the pump that began filling the glass reservoir with gasoline.

The stillness of the day was suddenly filled with the noise of the reservoir filling with gas. The old man looked at Dan. "Getting to be a warm one."

"Yes, it is." Dan watched the glass reservoir on top of the pump fill with gasoline, and when it reached the five-gallon level, the old man pulled the lever down, stopping the flow of gas. He took the nozzle from the pump, stuck it into the neck of the gas tank, and squeezed the nozzle handle. As the reservoir emptied and the tank in the car filled, the old man gestured toward the store. "Got cold soda pop inside or a beer if that pleases you."

Dan thought a cold pop sounded good and waited until the gas was in the car.

When the reservoir was empty, the old man hung the nozzle up on the side of the pump and pushed the lever, shutting off the power to the pump. "That'll be 85 cents."

Dan replaced the gas cap, and then he followed the old man inside and stopped at a long blue cooler with a large picture of a happy-looking young boy with yellow hair holding up a bottle of Squirt. He slid one of the lids to one side, reached in, and picked up a bottle of root beer from the icy water.

The old man pointed toward the back of the store. "Beers in the cooler in the corner."

Dan considered a beer briefly but decided on the root beer.

The old man gestured to a towel hanging on a nail next to the window. "You can use that towel to wipe the water off the bottle."

Dan wiped the water off, returned the stained towel to the window ledge, slid the bottle cap under the opener attached to the cooler, and opened his root beer. After tossing the cap into the trashcan, he took a long drink. Glancing around, Dan noticed a metal stand with bags of peanuts on the counter. He pulled a bag off the rack, set it and the bottle on the counter, and smiled at the old man. "What's the damage?"

"85 cents for the five gallons of gas and ten cents for the soda and peanuts."

Dan handed him a dollar bill, put the nickel change into his pocket, and then struggled to open the bag of peanuts.

The old man sat on a tall stool and watched in silence until the battle was won. "Don't believe I've seen you around here before."

318

Dan put the open end of the bag to his mouth filling it with salty peanuts, and then he smiled. "I haven't been this way before."

"Out joy riding?" asked the old man.

Dan chewed the peanuts, took a drink of root beer, knowing the old man wasn't going to let it go and shrugged with a wry smile. "I took the afternoon off work and decided to go for a ride."

The old man studied Dan for a moment. "Life gets a little hectic at times in the big city, I reckon."

Dan grinned. "It does at that."

"Well, that's why I live way out here." He offered his hand. "Names William, but folks around these parts call me Willie."

Dan put the bag of nuts in his left hand with the root beer and shook the hand. Not wanting to give his real name, he told Willie his name was James. "You own this place, Willie?"

He grinned proudly. "Built the place in 1937."

Dan looked out the window across the gravel road at the green haze of alfalfa fields that seemed to go on forever and wondered if he knew Vernon Schmidt. "Nice and quiet out here away from Denver." He looked at Willie and smiled. "If you drive with the windows down and the radio off, you can hear your tires in the gravel and the whippoorwills competing with the insects."

Willie grinned. "Bastards never shut up."

Dan chuckled. "Still, it's nice and peaceful. There are a lot of nice looking places along the road north of here. I like the green haze of new crops across the land."

Willie looked out the window at the fields across the dirt road and nodded. "Yep, that'd be the alfalfa coming up."

"I imagine you know most everyone."

Willie nodded with a smile. "Some folks I know pretty good, others not so much."

Dan glanced around. "I imagine most everyone shops here or gets gas."

"Most do, but a few prefer the Safeway stores toward town and the gas wars of the big city. There's always someplace to get gas a few cents cheaper."

Dan smiled, knowing that was true. "I guess that's progress."

Willie nodded. "But we don't have to like it."

Dan noticed a faded picture of four people standing in front of the store on the wall behind the counter.

Willie turned to see what Dan was looking at and smiled in memory. "That was taken the day we opened. The handsome one on the right is me with my arm around my wife, Mildred."

319

Dan smiled. "Where is Mildred these days?"

"She passed a few years ago."

Dan thought of Norma. "Sorry to hear that."

"We had a good life," smiled Willie. "I still miss her."

Dan knew how that felt. "Who are the others?"

"That would be Harold and Victoria Schultz."

Dan's heart skipped a beat, and he almost choked on the peanuts while Willie gestured out the window in the direction Dan had come. "They used to own a place up the road a piece." He stood and dumped his cold coffee into a small sink behind him and refilled the cup with hot coffee from a pot sitting on a warming plate.

"What became of them?"

Willie took a sip of his coffee and sat back down on the stool, looking thoughtful. "Joseph Schultz died of a heart attack in '43. His wife Victoria followed in '44." He smiled in memory. "She was my Mildred's closest friend."

Dan leaned against the counter with his right hip. "Their children own the place now?"

"Joseph and Victoria never had any children, but they did have a nephew by the name of Vernon they raised. I don't recall where he came from." He thought for a moment. "I think his parents died; I'm not sure. He just showed up one day at the school further up Henderson Road." Willie looked troubled. "My daughter didn't like him very much."

Dan took a drink of root beer, thinking that Paul had an accent, and wondered if the Vernon the old man was talking about did, but didn't know how to ask him. "Why is that?"

"She said he was mean to animals." Willie had a stern look on his face. "A person that mistreats animals will do the same to children. Vernon joined the Marines in 41, became a..." he paused in thought. "What do you call those men that help wounded soldiers?"

"Corpsman?" replied Dan, thinking that was interesting.

"No, that ain't it."

"How about a Medic?"

"That's it. When Joseph Schultz died in '43, the army let Vernon come home. Hardship, I think they called it. He sure took Victoria's death hard when she passed away the next year. She left the place to that young man, lock stock and barrel."

Dan raised his brow. "Wow. He ever get married?"

Willie frowned. "No, he never did."

Dan wanted to ask more questions but didn't want to appear overly interested and wondered what Willie would say if he knew what Vernon was doing in the basement of that farmhouse. He looked at his watch and then gulped down the last of his root beer. "I better head back to Denver." Then he bent over and placed the empty bottle into one of the empty square slots in the wooden soda crate sitting on the floor next to the blue cooler.

Willie grinned. Glad you stopped by."

So was Dan. He told Willie goodbye, walked outside, got into his car, and drove away from the gas pump and store following Henderson Road west to Highway 85 & 87, contemplating all that Willie had told him.

When Dan got back to police headquarters, he was anxious to tell the captain that he had found Paul but was disappointed at finding the captain had already left for the day. He sat down at his desk, wondering how Jack was doing, and reached for the phone to call Lori when he decided to call the DMV first. Frank Jackson at DMV had found two addresses for Vernon Schmidt, including the one on Rural Route 15. He thanked Mr. Jackson and hung up, thinking it was all coming together.

Looking across his desk at his partner's empty chair, Dan picked up the telephone and dialed his number. "Lori, this is Dan. How is Jack feeling?"

"Much better. The doctor was by and said he had a stomach virus. He's resting right now."

"Rest is probably the best thing for him."

Lori spoke with humor, "If I come down with this, you may be attending his funeral."

Dan chuckled. "Well, for Jack's sake, I hope you don't. When he wakes up, tell him I called, and I'll see him Monday."

They said goodbye, and after Dan hung up, he sat back, picked up a pencil, and lightly tapped the eraser on the top of the desk while staring at the big map where the farmhouse was on RR15. He stood holding the pencil and drew a line from Highway 85 & 87 to the corner store and then to Vernon's farm, writing Box 395, the name Paul, and then circled it. His thoughts turned to the corner store and everything that Willie had told him about Vernon. Looking at his watch, he decided that he had just about enough time to go home and change before driving to Cathy's for dinner.

Thirty-One

Dan's headlights filled the driveway between Cathy's house and the house next door where the little girl Carla lived. Stopping next to the white picket fence, he got out and walked through the gate of Cathy's fence to the front door.

Hearing the doorbell, Cathy opened the door, smiled as she unlocked the screen door, and stepped back. "Hi."

She was dressed in a white blouse with short, puffy sleeves, dark red slacks, and a white apron with a big blue flower on the front. Complimenting her on how nice she looked, he stepped inside.

Closing the door, he turned, seeing a very large, black and brown Doberman, and the smile suddenly left his face.

Seeing the expression on his face, Cathy turned to the dog. "Sit, Butch."

Butch did as commanded but never took his dark, piercing eyes off Dan, who whispered to Cathy, "I thought you said he was cute."

She smiled as she closed the door. "But he is, and very sweet." Then she looked at Dan. "By the way, he doesn't like men."

"Thanks for the warning." Then he thought of her uncle. "What about your uncle?"

"Butch is my aunt's dog, so I guess he tolerates Uncle. She got him as a puppy a few years back and had him trained as a watchdog because Uncle works late at times."

"He seems to mind pretty well."

"Yes, he does, and he'll stay put unless you do something silly, like grab me. Then all ninety pounds will be at your throat."

"Ninety pounds?"

She smiled. "Auntie feeds him very well."

"Not men, I hope." Dan looked at the black face with a touch of dark brown under the chin, black pointed ears with brown tips, and brown eyebrows over dark eyes.

She grinned and then called to Butch, who trotted across the floor and sat at her feet, waiting for her next command. She pointed to Dan, "Friend." Cathy handed Dan a piece of dry dog food from the pocket of her apron.

Looking unsure, Dan took the piece of food and offered it to Butch. As the dog took the treat, Dan was surprised at how gently he took it.

"Lay down," commanded Cathy. Butch turned, trotted to a spot where a large towel lay on the floor. As he settled onto it, he kept up a keen interest in Dan.

Dan smiled. "I'd like to give you a small kiss hello but I'm afraid I'd end up in the hospital."

She laughed and kissed Dan on the cheek. "Let's go into the kitchen."

"Who trained him?"

Cathy walked toward the kitchen, talking over her shoulder. "A friend of Uncle's. He trained guard dogs for the military during the war."

Dan followed her toward the kitchen, making a wide berth around the dog. When they got to the kitchen doorway, Dan paused and looked back at the dog still staring at him.

Cathy gestured to the table. "Have a seat while I pour us each a glass of wine."

Dan pulled a yellow padded, chrome chair away from the yellow Formica table and glanced back at the doorway as he slowly sat down, making sure he didn't antagonize Butch.

She held up a bottle of light Rose' wine. "I hope this is okay with dinner."

Dan looked at the bottle, agreed, and then looked back at the kitchen doorway, finding that Butch had moved from the towel. "He moves quietly."

Cathy turned from what she was doing. "That's part of his training."

She handed him a glass of wine, and as he took it, he noticed the lettuce, cucumber, carrots, and tomato sitting on the counter. "Want me to fix the salad?"

She leaned back against the counter and sipped her wine. "Relax and enjoy your wine. I can fix the salad while we talk."

Dan took a drink of wine, looked at Butch, and said jokingly, "I think he likes me."

Cathy laughed softly. "Butch, go to bed."

The Doberman got up and trotted away.

"Where's he going?"

She set her glass on the counter. "Butch sleeps on a bed of lamb's wool in my bedroom."

Dan thought about that. "Of course, he does."

She smiled. "Drink your wine." Then she looked at him. "You seem in a good mood."

Thoughts of the farm, along with Willie and Vernon, occupied Dan's mind as she worked on the salad. Watching her, he wondered if he

323

should tell her about his day and decided to go ahead. "I believe I have found Paul."

She turned from the salad, looking both surprised and excited. "Seriously? You know where he lives?" Then quickly added, "So now you can arrest him!"

Dan frowned. "It's not that easy."

Cathy looked puzzled. "Why not?"

He set his glass of wine on the table. "I need something a little stronger." He stood and walked into the living room, paused to look for Butch, then poured a glass of bourbon, and returned to his chair in the kitchen. As he sat back down, he took a small drink began. "Remember me telling you about my dad's notepad?"

Finished with the salad, she wiped her hands on a towel, picked up her wine, and turned leaning her back against the countertop. "Of course."

Dan sipped his bourbon while telling her about finding the details on the Schmidt family and their son Vernon in the notepad. He told her about the obituary he had found in the Denver Library, of visiting the house where Vernon had lived as a young boy, and about driving out to visit Englewood Park.

Cathy moved from the counter to the table. "You've been busy." She sat down across from Dan and took a drink of wine. "So, you think this Paul is really Vernon?"

"I do." Then he told her where Mr. Schmidt had worked before, he died. "I believe the father helped Vernon with Donnie's body."

Astonished at that, Cathy asked, "Why would anyone do that?"

Dan shrugged while thinking of what Professor Pappel had said about a father's love for his son. He decided not mention that he and Jack believed he had also killed his father. Then he told her about getting an address from the county Tax Office for the farm where Vernon had lived with his aunt and uncle until they passed away, willing him ownership of it. Finally, he told her of his ride out to the farm earlier in the day. "All that I have right now is conjecture on my part. Not even enough good circumstantial evidence to ask for a warrant."

Cathy stared at him with a disappointed look. "What are you going to do?"

Dan considered her question for a moment. "I'll call Captain Foley at home tomorrow and tell him. Maybe he'll have an idea."

She sighed. "I'll be glad when all of this is over." Then she stood, turned the oven broiler on, and got two steaks out of the refrigerator.

After dinner, Dan helped Cathy with the dishes, and when he dried the last plate, he stood with his back against the counter and watched as she prepared Butch's meal. Dan set the dishtowel down, walked up behind her, put his arms around her, and kissed her on the neck. She put the fork down, closed her eyes, and turned to put her arms around his neck as they kissed.

Butch barked impatiently.

Cathy looked down at Butch and then smiled at Dan. "He wants to eat."

Dan chuckled. "He's not much on timing, is he?"

While Butch busied himself with his dinner, they went into the living room to watch television. Cathy kicked off her shoes and curled up next to Dan with her head on his shoulder.

Hearing the sound of a metal dish sliding across the kitchen floor hitting the wall or a cabinet, Dan asked, "What the hell is that?"

Cathy laughed. "That's Butch's way of asking for more." She got up from the sofa. "I better pick it up, or he'll be in here with it." She returned after a few moments and curled up next to Dan while Butch lay on the floor next to the front door. "If you want to leave," she said, "You'll have to move him."

Dan smiled at her. "Guess I'm in for the night." Then he looked at Butch. "Are we all sleeping in the same room?"

Cathy chuckled. "Worried?"

Dan nodded. "A little."

She laughed, turned, and curled up against him. "I think we can leave him out here for a while."

Dan lay on his back, holding Cathy's naked body against his while staring out the bedroom window at the full moon hanging above the trees in the yard across the alley. The light from the moon spread across the bed, changing the lime green bedspread to silver. Listening to Cathy's shallow breathing, his mind turned to the garage next to the farmhouse, and he wondered again if he would find a white van inside. Thinking of a cigarette, he remembered they had been left in the other room. Deciding he needed one, he carefully took his arm from around her and slowly got out of bed. Pausing to look at the lump of covers in the moonlight, he quietly opened the door, backed into the hall, and then softly closed the door. Turning, he came face to face with the dark figure of Butch, looking much larger in the dim light of the hall.

"Shit," he whispered as he reached behind him for the doorknob, opened the door, backed into the bedroom, and quickly but quietly closed it.

Cathy lifted her head and glanced at the clock on the nightstand, and then sat up. "It's midnight. Where are you going?"

Startled, he turned. "I was going to get my cigarettes in the other room, but Butch is guarding the hall."

Looking agitated, she asked, "You want a cigarette now?"

Feeling foolish, he nodded. "I can't sleep and thought I could get them without waking you."

Cathy got out of bed, grabbed a robe from the closet, and slipped it over her naked body as she hastily walked to the door. Opening it, she said, "Butch, come." As the dog hurried past her to his wool bed, Cathy gestured toward the hall with a nod. "It's safe now, Gunga Din. Go get your cigarettes."

Dan opened his eyes later from a restless sleep and looked at the green glowing hands of the alarm clock, seeing it was only a little before two in the morning. In the stillness of the room, Cathy's breathing mixed with the soft snoring of Butch, sprawled out on his bed next to the closet. The moonlight had moved from the bed to the wall, and he wished he could just go back to sleep. He turned and looked out the window at the moon half-hidden behind the trees across the alley, then turning onto his back, he looked up at the ceiling. His mind flooded with thoughts of the farmhouse, garage, and the unworked piece of land amid the trees. Turning back onto his side he thought about the four missing teenage girls that Josephine had found. He was sure their remains would be found in shallow graves in the same area.

Cathy rose up on one elbow and looked at his face in the dim light of the bedroom. "You don't sleep much, do you?"

"Sorry," he said as he sat up against the headboard. "I didn't mean to wake you."

"That's alright." Running her hand through her hair, she looked at the clock and said with humor, "I've had a couple of hours of sleep." She looked at him. "Why can't you sleep?"

Dan reached for his cigarettes and matches. "I was just thinking about the farm and Vernon." The match blazed into a small flame that lit up his face as he lit the cigarette. Taking a drag, he blew the match out, returning the room to darkness filled with silver moonlight and dark shadows.

"What about them?" she asked.

He looked past her at the green glowing face and hands of the alarm clock. "I can't sleep. Would you be mad if I got dressed and left?"

Thinking that she could get some sleep if he did but that she would probably be mad, she plumped her pillow against the headboard and sat back against it. "I guess," she said, sounding irritated. "It would depend on why you want to leave."

He took a drag of the cigarette. "I want to take a drive out to the farm and nose around."

She sat forward and looked at his face in the dim light, wondering if he'd lost his mind. "At this hour, in the dark? What on earth for?"

"I have to see if there is a white van in the garage."

She thought for a moment and then shook her head. "Dan, that's crazy."

He chuckled. "Probably, but it's what I have to do. I'll be alright."

Cathy scoffed. "Out there all alone in the dark? I don't think so. Can't we just go back to sleep and do this in the morning?"

"I can't go sneaking around in the daylight to get a look in that garage. He'd see me."

"So, you want to sneak around in the dark and get shot for breaking and entering."

Dan chuckled softly. I won't get shot."

"How do you know?"

"I'll take a quick look through the window and then get the hell back to my car. The whole thing shouldn't take more than five or ten minutes." He crushed the glowing red tip of the cigarette into the bottom of the ashtray. "I have to do this."

Cathy looked at him. "You don't have to do anything."

"If I find the van, I'll call Foley first thing and get a warrant."

She thought for a moment, watching as he set the ashtray on the nightstand. Then she turned on the lamp, threw the covers back, and got out of bed.

Looking at her body, Dan asked, "What are you doing?"

"Getting dressed," she said while putting on her bra.

Seeing movement out of the corner of his eye, Dan looked at Butch sitting up in his bed, watching them. Then he looked back at Cathy. "For what?"

"I'm going with you."

Dan chuckled without humor. "No, you're not."

She stepped into her panties and pulled them up. "Give me Jack's phone number. I'll stay in the car, and if you're not back within thirty minutes, I'll get to a telephone and call him."

He shook his head. "I'll not leave you alone in the car in the damn darkness."

Cathy opened the drawer of her nightstand, pulled out her small .32 caliber pistol, and looked at him. "This and Butch will keep me company."

Dan considered that while thinking she looked kind of sexy standing there in her bra and panties, holding a gun.

With a look of defiance, she said, "I'm going."

Smiling at how she looked and knowing it was a lost argument, he tossed the covers back and stood. "Alright. But you do just what I tell you." Then he looked at Butch. "That goes for you too."

Cathy looked at Butch and then at Dan. "Fine."

Cathy sat on the passenger side of Dan's 1949 Ford holding her pistol on her lap and glancing out the windows into the black night. A full moon that slowly dipped into the west lit up the tree trunk they were parked next to, as well as the berry bushes, but beyond them, everything was pitch-black. Butch's panting from the back seat seemed loud while Cathy stared out the windshield in the direction Dan had gone. While only minutes had passed, to her, it seemed like at least an hour. An owl high up in the tree next to the car hooted, causing Butch to stop his panting and stick his head over the back of the front seat, staring out the windshield. Glad they had brought him, Cathy checked again to make sure all of the doors were locked and then petted his neck. "It's just an owl, Butch."

Dan made his way across the dark fields of alfalfa sprouts to the corner of the barn, where he paused to look around. He could see the house and garage bathed in the white light of the full moon. As he looked at the door and dark windows of the house, he hoped Vernon was sound asleep inside. An owl somewhere in the night hooted, joining the crickets and other night sounds. Something small, dark, and fast darted across the open space disappearing into the night. Hoping it was a cat but figuring it was a rat, he crouched down and trotted across the yard to the side door of the garage. Standing with his back against the side of the garage, he looked across the yard to the rear of the house for signs of life. Seeing none, he turned, put his flashlight up to the window, looked at the house once again, turned the flashlight on, looked inside, and then quickly turned it off.

Disappointed at finding a dark blue 1948 Chevrolet in the garage and not the white van he had hoped for, he turned and looked at the rear door of the house and thought about the barn. He hurried across the open space to the barn, made his way to a window, and looked inside the barn with the flashlight. Seeing nothing but a late model tractor parked in front of the rear doors, he started across the dark fields of alfalfa sprouts toward Cathy and his car.

Butch's low, soft growl alerted Cathy that someone was coming, and hoping it was Dan, she lifted the pistol from her lap and stared into the darkness. Seeing movement before Cathy did, Butch growled and stuck his head further over the front seat. As the figure got closer to the driver's side, Butch growled and lunged toward the door.

"It's me," said Dan, just above a whisper.

Cathy grabbed Butch by his collar and pulled him away from the door. "It's okay, Butch, down."

Dan opened the car door, slid into his seat, and was greeted by Butch's big wet tongue as he closed his door.

Cathy pulled Butch away and looked at Dan. "You were gone for a long time."

Pushing the dog away, Dan wiped his face and then handed her the flashlight to put it in the glove box. Starting the car without turning on the lights, he backed away from the tree and bushes onto the dirt and gravel road. Shifting into first gear, Dan carefully drove along the gravel road using the bright moonlight to see the road. When they were a safe distance from the farm, he turned the headlights on and drove toward Henderson Road.

"Did you see the white van?" asked Cathy.

"No," replied Dan, sounding disappointed. "Maybe he's out hunting."

Cathy quickly considered that. "I certainly hope not." She put her pistol in her coat pocket and slid across the seat next to him.

"What if I'm wrong about Vernon, and all this is for nothing." He paused. "I was so sure."

Reaching the stop sign at Henderson Road, Dan stopped and put the car into neutral while glancing across the gravel road at the corner store lit up by the headlights of his 1949 Ford. "Willie, the old man that owns the store across the road, has known Vernon most of his life."

"So?"

"The Paul I talk to on the phone has a slight accent."

"And Vernon doesn't?"

"I don't know if he does or not." He shifted into first gear. "I wish I had found a way to ask Willie without sounding overly interested." Disappointed, he stepped on the gas and turned onto Henderson Road. "What if all of this shit was for nothing."

"Maybe not," said Cathy in a consoling tone. "Just because the van was not there doesn't mean anything. Like you said, he may be hunting."

"I was so sure I had found Donnie's killer and the killer of all those young girls, plus Ruth and Trenton. Everything pointed to Vernon."

She touched his arm with her hand. "You're just tired."

Thinking she might just be right, he decided to take her home and then go to his house and get some sleep. "I'd feel better if that damn white van was in either the garage or the barn."

"That still doesn't prove you're wrong, Dan." Feeling tired, Cathy laid her head on his shoulder and closed her eyes.

The eastern horizon was turning lighter when Dan shut off the headlights as he turned into Cathy's driveway. Coming to a stop next to the gate in the picket fence, he shut the engine off and looked at her while she slept. Thinking it had been a long day for everyone, he gently touched her shoulder. "Cathy, you're home."

She slowly opened her eyes, raised her head as she sat up, and glanced out the window at her front door. "What time is it?"

"Almost five."

Stifling a yawn, she turned and looked at the dog, stretched out comfortably in the back seat. "I think we wore poor Butch out."

Dan chuckled. "We better get you inside."

"You staying?"

He opened his car door. "It's almost dawn. I should go so we can both get a little sleep, and I have to mow my lawn later." He slid out of the car, helped her out, and opened the back door. Butch jumped out lazily, and once inside the yard, he rushed to a nearby bush, did his business, and then followed them to the front door. Cathy rummaged in her purse for her keys, and when she opened the door, Butch hurried inside and disappeared into the kitchen for a drink of water. She turned to Dan. "Call me later?"

"I will." Then he kissed her goodnight. "Thanks for the company. I may trade you for Jack."

She smiled. "It was an adventure that I'll remember for years to come." Then she kissed his cheek, said goodnight, and closed the door.

He heard the lock click as he turned and walked to his car.

The sun was still not above the horizon as he got out of his car and looked up at a light blue sky mixed with oranges, pinks, and purples. Locking his car, he walked toward the steps to the front porch just as the paperboy tossed the morning newspaper onto his porch. Dan climbed the steps to the porch and bent down to pick up the newspaper, thinking the boy's aim was getting better.

The empty house seemed chilly as he locked the door and slipped out of his jacket. Feeling tired, he went upstairs to gather his pillow and blanket.

It was almost one o'clock Saturday afternoon when Dan finished mowing his lawn and put the mower and tools away in the garage. After glancing at the pictures on the wall for a few minutes, he locked the side door of the garage and walked across the freshly cut lawn to the back door into the kitchen. He washed his face and hands, opened the refrigerator, took out a cold bottle of beer, and after tossing the cap in the cap in the trash, he took a quick drink. Thinking about last night, he walked down the hall to the desk in the living room. Pulling the chair away, he sat down, set the bottle on the desk, picked up the telephone, and dialed Jack's house.

"Hello?"

"Jack, this is Dan. How are you feeling?"

"Much better."

"You gonna make it to work on Monday?" asked Dan.

"I should. Anything new on Paul?"

Dan sipped his beer, sat back in the chair, and told his partner everything that had happened Friday, including the location of the farm where Vernon lived with the matching number on the mailbox. Then he told him about his conversation with Willie at the corner store and of his and Cathy's adventure to the farm.

"You took Cathy with you?"

"Yeah, along with her .32 and Butch."

"Who the hell is Butch?"

"A ninety-five pound Doberman. I'll explain him later."

Jack thought about that, then asked, "Did you see that white van?"

"No, the only thing parked inside the garage was a dark blue 49 Chevy and a tractor in the barn, but no van." Dan took another drink of beer. "He could have it parked someplace else, I guess."

Jack thought for a moment, "Or he could have had it out last night to grab someone."

"That's a possibility, but I hope not," said Dan, thinking of the last victim and how Paul could have come driving in while he was peering into the garage. I'm in no mood to face any more parents."

Jack quickly considered that. "Too bad we can't get a warrant for thinking the bastard is guilty."

Dan agreed. "If you're up to it, we can take a trip out there later tonight and nose around a bit. We may even find the van in the garage."

Jack thought about that as the phone went silent.

"Jack?" asked Dan.

"I'm thinking." Jack paused for a few moments and then said, "And what if we do find a white van?"

"Dan considered that. "Well, that could serve as probable cause for a warrant."

"We call Foley?" asked Jack.

"One of us stays to keep an eye on Paul. The other drives to the captain's home so he can call a judge and get a warrant."

Jack thought about that. "Let me guess. You stay, and I drive to a phone and call the captain."

Dan grinned. "It amazes me how quick you are. There's a phone booth at the corner store, by the way."

Jack chuckled. "Look, I'm still a little weak, but if I take a long nap, I should be up to it later tonight."

Dan considered that. "I'll pick you up in the parking lot of headquarters around ten-thirty."

"Okay," replied Jack. "Are you seeing Cathy tonight?"

"I don't know. We had dinner last night, but nothing was said about tonight." He paused, thinking that she should be up by now. "If I do, I'll still see you around ten-thirty if you're up to it. For your information, I drew the route to Vernon's farm on the map at work, including the address on his mailbox."

"Sounds like you've been busy without me."

Dan grinned. "I've been doing the work of two detectives, so get your ass back to work." Dan hung up the telephone and dialed Cathy to see if she would like to go out and get something to eat. After several rings, he hung up, picked up his beer, and walked out the front door, letting it close with a bang. He walked to one of the white wooden chairs, sat down, and took a drink, thinking about the absence of the white van in Vernon's garage and barn. As he sat in the warmth of the sun, he went over every bit of information he had gathered over the past several days, feeling sure Vernon was Paul, even without the presence of the white van. As far as the accent Paul spoke with, it could be a ploy, but then again, he could have picked up a slight accent from his parents or aunt and uncle, the Schultze's, who were German.

Getting up from the chair, he walked inside, called Police Headquarters, and asked if anyone had reported their daughter missing. When the desk sergeant told him there had been no reports filed, he hung up the telephone and dialed Cathy. The telephone rang several times, and he wondered where she was, but then remembered that she got her hair done on Saturdays and had mentioned taking Butch to the vet for his rabies shot. He hung up the phone, picked up his empty bottle, and went into the kitchen. After getting another beer, he turned the radio on to a Denver Bears ball game and sat on the sofa smiling while he thought about Cathy with her .32 pistol and Butch waiting in the car last night at the farm.

Dan opened his eyes after falling asleep while listening to the ball game, sat up with a start, and looked at the grandfather clock, seeing it was almost six-forty-five. Getting up from the sofa, he turned off the radio, walked to the desk, and dialed Cathy's number. After it rang several times, he hung up and stared out the window in thought. Getting an uneasy feeling, he picked up the holster containing his Thirty-eight pistol and slipped it over his belt, picked up the telephone, and called Jack, but the line was busy. He hung up and tried again, getting the same busy signal. Cursing the telephone, he slammed the receiver down, rushed into the foyer, opened the closet door, and put on his black as he hurried out the front door.

Thirty-Two

Dan Morgan turned into Cathy's driveway, curious as to why there were no lights on in the house. He left the car running as he climbed out, and without closing the door, he hurried through the gate. Pushing the button on the doorjamb, hearing the doorbell chime inside, but no sound of Butch barking. He stepped off the small cement porch into the flowers under the picture window, cupped his hands around his face, and tried looking through the window. Unable to see anything, he stepped back onto the small cement porch, opened the screen door, and turned the knob of the door. Finding it unlocked, he drew his Thirty-eight Smith and Wesson and pushed the door open. Fearing Paul may be inside, he glanced around the darkness while reaching around the door jamb for the light switch. Turning the lights on, he called out, "Cathy!"

Hearing a dog whining from somewhere in the house, he stepped inside and called to Butch. Moments later, the big dog staggered around the corner of the sofa on wobbly legs and then collapsed onto the floor. Thinking the dog had been poisoned, Dan knew immediately that Paul had taken Cathy and ran toward the bedroom calling her name. Turning the light on in the bedroom, he found the room empty and the bed unmade. Remembering her pistol, he hurried to the nightstand, opened the top drawer, and found the gun was missing.

As Butch lay on the floor whimpering, Dan returned to the living room, bent down, and gently rubbed the dog's shoulder. As Butch looked up at Dan with his black eyes, Dan wondered how the dog had been drugged or poisoned when he had been trained not to take food from strangers or eat food left on the ground. He would not eat from anyone but the family unless told to do so. Thinking of the dog's water bowl, Dan stood, hurried into the kitchen, picked up the bowl, and smelled it, finding a strange odor. He figured it must be something Paul had put into the water that put the dog to sleep quickly, hoping it was hot poison. He poured the water out, recalling all the times he tried to call Cathy during the day and wondered whether Paul had been in the house early that morning when he had brought her home, explaining why the van was not at the farm. Wishing he had come in with her, he filled a new bowl with water, carried it into the living room, and set it down next to Butch, who lapped up the fresh water without getting up. Dan rushed to the telephone, dialed Jack's number, and got another busy signal.

Butch got up and staggered past Dan, heading for the open front door, pushed the screen door open, and stepped outside. Figuring the dog

334

had to go to the bathroom, he hung the phone up and dialed Jack again, getting a busy signal. Hearing Butch scratch at the screen door, he opened the door, and as Butch headed for the bedroom, where he flopped down on his wool bed, Dan hoped he would be alright. Then Dan called Jack again, getting the same busy signal, and hollered into the phone in frustration. "Lori, get off of the damn phone!" Thinking of Captain Foley, he dialed his number, and after it rang several times, he slammed the phone down. Thinking he had wasted enough time on the dog, Foley, and Jack, and headed for the front door. As he passed the blue barrel chair, he saw Cathy's small .32 automatic lying on the floor next to the open drapes. He picked it up and instinctively smelled the barrel, finding it had not been fired. He shoved it under his belt, thinking Cathy must have dropped it during a struggle. Then he hurried out the front door and closed it, leaving the lights on, and rushed across the yard and through the gate. Climbing into the running car, he closed the door, put the car in reverse, backed out of the driveway, shifted to first, and squealed up South Pennsylvania Street, imagining a terrified Cathy with Paul.

As the headlights of Dan's car lit up the lonely gravel road ahead of him, he gripped the steering wheel as he rounded a wide curve, seeing the lighted windows of Vernon's farmhouse in the distance. Knowing Cathy would be in the basement, in the same room that held Mary Jefferies and the others, he pushed a little harder on the gas pedal. As he approached the mailbox, he was afraid Vernon might see the lights of his car, so he drove past the mailbox and closed gate, past the place he had parked earlier with Cathy, to a hill he knew was just a little farther up the gravel road. Starting down the hill, he looked into the rearview mirror, and when the lights of the farm disappeared behind the top of the hill, he slowed to a stop at the bottom and turned the car around.

Turning off the headlights, he used the faint light from the parking lights and the full moon to drive back up the hill and parked next to the familiar oak tree and berry bushes. Turning off the parking lights and then the engine, he took a small flashlight out of the glove box, got out of the car, and quietly closed the door. Glancing around, he moved next to the oak tree and looked across the dark fields at the lighted windows of Vernon's house. Figuring that Vernon couldn't possibly know he had found him, he hoped that would work to his advantage. Then hoping Paul would take his time with Cathy before killing her, he stepped away from the tree and berry bushes, hurrying across the soft soil giving way under his shoes.

Reaching the barn, he stepped around the corner into the shadows, seeing a covered van parked a few feet away under a carport he never noticed last night. Peering around the corner of the barn, he looked at the soft yellow color of the shades covering the windows, wishing Jack's telephone had not been busy. Wondering where the captain was since he had never answered his telephone, he pulled his Thirty-eight from its holster, bent over, and crept across the dark yard to the side of the house. He knelt next to one of the dark basement windows, and as his heart beat against his chest, he glanced around into the darkness, thinking of the night patrols he and Jack had gone on during the war. He touched the window screen, finding it fastened securely, and cursed at it in silence. He crept toward the front of the house, where he checked the next window, finding it also secured, as was the third window.

Kneeling by the last window, he wondered how he would get in and decided that he would enter blasting if he had to. But of course, there was the danger that Cathy would be hurt or killed, or maybe he would be killed. Quietly and carefully, he walked to the front of the house, stood by the waist-high porch, and peered around the corner at the front door that suddenly opened. Stepping back into the shadows, he knelt, pressing himself against the side of the house, trying to be invisible. Hearing the screen door creak as it opened, followed by the meowing of a cat, he peered around the corner of the house. A large cat strolled toward the steps of the front porch, sat down, and began cleaning itself. Afraid the cat would give him away, he quietly stepped back, pressing his back against the side of the house. The screen door creaked as it closed, followed by the front door closing and then the sound of the lock turning. As he peered around the corner of the house, he watched as the cat jumped off the porch disappearing into the darkness toward the gravel road. Glad the damn cat was finally off the porch, he bent down and crept along the ground around the porch to the other side of the house, hoping he'd find an open window.

Reaching the other side, he paused with his back against the wall, looked back across the porch, and then in the direction the cat had gone, hoping it would stay gone. Turning back, he crept to the next basement window, and as he knelt to touch the screen, light suddenly filled the window. Moving back against the side of the house, he slowly leaned toward the window, hoping to see Cathy, but found it covered with brown paper. While his heart raced, Dan wiped his clammy hands on his pants, wishing Jack was with him. The light went out, and as he heard a door close, crickets seemed suddenly loud as Dan took a deep breath to calm his racing heart and heavy breathing. Touching the screen, he found it loose, holstered his gun, set the flashlight down, and took a small penknife out of his pocket. A light came on in the first-floor window above him, followed by muffled voices and music. Standing on his toes, he looked through a narrow opening between the drawn window shade and the windowsill, seeing part of a white, flickering television screen. Hoping that Vernon

336

was going to watch television and leave Cathy alone, he knelt and, using the penknife's blade, quietly managed to take off the screen. To his surprise, the slider portion of the window was slightly ajar. Concerned about the brown paper, he slipped the narrow blade of his penknife between the window and the windowsill and then slowly slid the window to one side.

His heart raced as he looked to the rear of the house and then to the front. He folded his small penknife, shoved it into his pocket, and picked up his flashlight. Getting onto his hands and knees, he glanced toward both ends of the house, then lay down on his stomach and slid feet first through the open window. Once inside, he lowered himself into the room with his feet resting on something he discovered was the back of an old sofa. Turning with his back against the wall, he stood on the sofa for a few moments listening to the muffled voices and music from the television above him. Stepping down, he took the handkerchief from his back pocket, covered the lens of the flashlight, and turned it on. In the dim light filtering through the handkerchief, he saw a wall covered with small wooden bins and knew he was in the trophy room. His hand found the grip of his pistol, and as he pulled it out, it occurred to him that in all the years he had carried it, he had never fired it when on duty.

He looked down to see if any light was coming through the crack under the closed door, and seeing none, he approached the wall of bins. Finding several that were empty, he soon found one that contained a pair of shoes, panties, and a wallet. Glancing back at the bottom of the door for light, he picked up the wallet and fumbled through it until he found a student ID card with the name Deborah Allyson, the Washington Park victim. Taking a quick look over his shoulder at the crack under the door, he put the wallet back and went to the next bin. Shining the covered flashlight into the next bin, he saw a fruit jar which he carefully picked up, and as he held the covered flashlight to it, he saw something move in the dark liquid and knew the jar contained a small finger floating in blood. Putting the jar back, he checked the crack under the door and then picked up the wallet sitting next to a pair of panties. Opening it, he read the name Marie Susan Phillips, the girl from behind the Paramount Theater.

Wishing Jack was with him, he continued to pass along the wall of bins, glancing into several with the dim flashlight and finding panties, wallets, and fruit jars he knew contained the fingers of each of Vernon's victims. Hearing the television upstairs go silent, he turned the flashlight off, turned toward the door with his gun, and waited. Hearing the television again and thinking Vernon must have changed channels, he decided it was time to leave the bins and find Cathy. He turned the small flashlight off and returned it and his handkerchief to his back pocket.

337

With his right hand holding the gun, he reached for the doorknob with his left when he realized there was one more bin to check. If Donnie had been Paul or Vernon's first victim, he thought, surely one of the bins must hold his clothes. It would only take a few seconds to know for sure.

Taking the small flashlight and handkerchief from his back pocket, he stepped toward the first bin.

He looked at it for a long moment before he slowly put his hand into it. Feeling something soft, he pulled it out and, in the dim light, recognized the shirt Donnie had worn the day he disappeared. Filled with a surge of excitement and grief, he stared at the shirt for several remembering they always wore clothes alike. Then he reached up and took out his brother's pants, socks, shoes, and then a coat and hat. Feeling sick while his eyes welled with tears, he stuffed everything back into the bin and turned the flashlight off. He wiped the sweat from his face and the tears from his eyes with his hands. Then, fighting the urge to vomit, he shoved his flashlight and handkerchief into his back pocket and returned to the door. Putting his ear against it and hearing nothing but the television above him, his hand slowly turned the knob. Carefully and quietly, he opened the door enough to peer into the dim outer room of the basement. Light from an open doorway at the top of the stairs lit up the long wall of the stairs to the basement floor filling the room with a dim light. Seeing the dark nook under the stairs, he tightened his grip on the gun, cautiously stepped through the doorway, silently closed the door, and crept across the room.

Standing beneath the staircase, he looked across the dim room at the light coming from under another closed door, suspecting that it could be where Cathy was. His eyes returned to the open door at the top of the stairs, and as his heart pounded, he stepped out of the darkness and crept across the floor. Dan looked through the peephole Mary Jefferies had mentioned and saw Cathy dressed in Levi's and a white blouse lying on the bed, her feet and hands bound. Worried about Paul, Dan turned to look at the top of the stairs and then through the peephole at Cathy. She wasn't moving, and he hoped she was either asleep or drugged. Turning to look up the stairs and open doorway once again, he quietly turned the deadbolt, opened the door, stepped inside, and quietly closed the door behind him.

He knelt to one knee beside the bed, set his gun on it, and gently turned her face toward him. "Cathy," he whispered while gently stroking her face. "It's Dan."

Opening her eyes was a struggle, but she looked at him with drowsy eyes, half smiled, and whispered in a tired voice, "Paul."

Glad she was alright, he whispered, "I know." Then he told her she was safe and to go back to sleep, took his pocketknife, and cut the ropes that bound her hands and feet. Knowing he couldn't carry her up the stairs and fight Vernon at the same time, he knew he had to take care of Vernon first. Easing himself off the bed, he pulled the bedspread over her, picked up his pistol, stepped out of the room, and quietly closed the door leaving it unlocked. Standing in front of the door for a moment, he considered his options and quickly decided that his best advantage would be to wait for Vernon to come down the stairs. He crept back across the floor to the dark nook under the stairs. The minutes slowly passed, and while he waited, he thought he should have left Cathy's small .32 pistol on the bed next to her. Hearing what sounded like scratching at the trophy room door, he stepped to the edge of the alcove just as the door moved, and the cat from the porch scurried across the dim basement floor and up the stairs. Figuring it must have come through the open window and realizing his mistake, he moved back into the darkness listening to the cat upstairs crying. He knew it wouldn't take long before Vernon would figure it out.

Surprised at hearing Kitty, Vernon got up from his leather chair and walked into the kitchen, finding the cat sitting in front of the refrigerator meowing. Wondering how she had gotten back into the house, he walked into the laundry room and checked the back door finding it closed and locked. Upon returning to the kitchen, he looked down at the crying cat. "How did you get in?" As the cat meowed and rubbed against his pant leg, Vernon looked at the open doorway to the basement, thought about the window he had opened a few days ago, and knew that Detective Dan Morgan had found his beloved Cathy. Knowing that his detective was smarter than he realized, he smiled as he reached out and flipped off the lights in the kitchen and hall, giving light to the stairs and basement.

Standing in the darkness under the stairs, Dan knew that Vernon had figured it out. He stepped out of the alcove, looking up the stairs into the darkness listening to the muffled sounds of the television. Wondering where Vernon was and what he was doing, he considered his options. He could try and outwait him, except that he could get tired and fall asleep. Or, Cathy could wake up and stumble out of the room, and Vernon might shoot her by mistake. He could go into the room and protect her until he could figure something out, but that could take days. Deciding to take the fight to Vernon, he crept along the staircase wall leading up to the kitchen. Reaching the bottom of the staircase, it suddenly became quiet. Stepping onto the landing, he looked up at the open doorway filled with soft, flickering, white light from the television with no sound. He looked at his watch, thinking of Jack, and seeing it was almost eleven, imagined him either impatiently waiting in his car in the parking lot of Headquarters or at home, still sick and in bed. Pointing his Thirty-eight Smith and Wesson toward the open doorway at the top of the stairs, he cautiously began his way up, taking one slow step at a time.

Stopping at the second step from the top, he peered through the doorway into the dark kitchen filled with the flickering light from the television in the room across the hall. Movement off to his left caused him to turn, pointing his gun, and then he saw the cat walking across the kitchen floor and disappear into the darkness of another room. The quiet, flickering white light danced eerily across the walls and kitchen floor. Remembering that the networks went off the air at eleven, he glanced around the dim kitchen and edged into it with his back against the wall. His eyes quickly roamed the room, darting from this to that until they settled on the open doorway. Moving closer, he looked across the hall into another room, seeing both the edge of a sofa and leather chair covered in the flickering light. Glancing around the dim room, he saw a glass sitting on the counter, picked it up, and quietly walked across the kitchen floor toward the doorway. With his back against the kitchen wall and his gun pointed at the open door across the hall, he tossed the glass, hitting the open door.

Vernon fired both barrels of his 16-gauge shotgun, blasting the door and doorjamb, and immediately realized that he had been duped into firing. As smoke from the shotgun mixed with debris from the wall, he stepped through the doorway tossing the empty shotgun through the kitchen door and ran for the front door. As the shotgun fell to the floor, Dan stepped into the hall, getting off a quick shot that missed Vernon as he disappeared out the front door. Dan ran down the hall, through the living room, and out the front door to the edge of the porch in time to see Vernon sliding through the same window he had crawled into earlier. Dan got off another quick shot, hitting the top of the window frame and missing Vernon's head. Turning, he ran into the house, down the hall to the basement door, and flipped on the light switch at the top of the stairs filling the basement with light. He raced down the stairs and headed for the room where Cathy was.

Vernon stepped out of the trophy room, holding a .22 caliber pistol he had grabbed from a drawer of the desk inside.

Seeing Vernon, Dan turned and raised his gun to fire, but Vernon was quicker and fired his .22 first, hitting Dan in his left side.

Feeling the burning bullet tear through his skin and muscle, Dan fired his Thirty-eight, hitting Vernon in the left leg.

Vernon got off a second shot, hitting Dan in the right shoulder.

With his collarbone shattered, Dan dropped his Thirty-eight pistol, and as he fell to his knees, he tried desperately to pick it up with his left hand.

Vernon hobbled across the floor, kicked the gun away, and pointed his pistol at Dan's face.

Dan looked at his gun lying several feet away and then into Vernon's cold, dark eyes, knowing he was about to die and there would be no one to help Cathy.

Vernon pressed the barrel of his pistol into Dan's temple. "I underestimated you." He grinned. "Looks like I won the game after all. Tell me, Detective, how the hell did you find me?"

Surprised that Vernon didn't shoot, Dan looked up at him. "What difference does it make? I found you, just as I said I would. I know you killed Donnie."

Vernon pulled the gun away from Dan's temple but kept it pointed at his face while he grinned. "So, you finally figured it all out. I was afraid you never would, but as I said, I misjudged you." He smiled with curiosity. "How did you figure it out?"

Thinking he might live long enough to get Cathy's .32 pistol from his belt with his left hand, he began to explain. "I finally figured out that the pictures you were talking about were those of Donnie posed in the same position as the girls."

Vernon chuckled. "I was beginning to think you would never figure that part out."

Dan told him about his father's notebook, the newspaper article about Vernon's parents'death, and his aunt's married name.

Vernon thought about that, and then he chuckled. "So, it was your old man's police work after all and not yours."

Dan stiffened in pain. "I found Donnie's clothes along with all the girl's belongings in that room, you bastard."

Vernon smiled. "I was going to do the same to you, but my father died, and I had to move away. But I've never stopped thinking about you, and I've watched you grow over the years." He paused. "It was like watching Donnie grow up."

Dan needed more time to get the gun from under his pants belt. "You killed your father, didn't you?"

Vernon frowned. "The man got a conscience and wanted me to turn myself in and confess to the killing. I couldn't allow that, Dan." He smiled as he stepped closer. "I'm going to enjoy you and your little friend in the other room." He paused a moment in thought. "I think you have a rough idea of what I will do to her." Vernon looked at the bloody hole in his pants leg. "You almost got me, Detective." Then he smiled. "Don't you see the irony of it all, Dan? You're going to end up in the same bin as your brother." Then he laughed.

Dan's hand couldn't reach Cathy's gun hidden in his belt.

Vernon looked at Dan's wounds. "If you live from your wounds, you'll be hanging over my tub, watching your own blood flow down the drain while I take your little finger." He paused and then smiled. "Before you die, I'll let you watch while your precious Cathy's life flows down the drain of my bathtub, knowing you can't save her." He leaned closer, put the gun against Dan's cheek, pushed hard, and said in anger, "I'm not done with little Mary Jefferies, either."

Dan tried to get up. "You bastard."

Vernon grabbed Dan by the collar of his jacket and put the .22 pistol under Dan's jaw. "I'd kill you now, but I want to enjoy you and your little friend in the other room."

Dan could feel Vernon's foul breath on his face as his left hand grasped Cathy's .32 pistol, slowly pulled it out, and smiled.

Puzzled, Vernon looked at him. "You won't be smiling for long, Detective."

Dan heard a gun go off, thinking Vernon had shot him.

Vernon had a surprised look on his face as he fell over Dan.

Cathy stood a few feet away, holding Dan's Thirty-eight with both hands. She slowly lowered the gun and dropped to her knees, letting the gun fall to the basement floor, then covered her face with her hands and wept.

Dan struggled to push Vernon off, tossed the .22 across the room, and then crawled the short distance to Cathy and put his left arm around her. As she curled up against him sobbing, Dan turned and looked at the still body of Vernon Schmidt and thought that his father's search for Donnie's killer was finally over.

Jack appeared in the open doorway at the top of the stairs with his gun drawn, and having heard the shots, he yelled, "Dan?"

"We're down here."

Jack hurried down the steps finding Dan and Cathy huddled together on the cement floor. Seeing Vernon's body lying a few feet away, he knelt next to it and felt his neck for a pulse. Finding none, he moved next to Dan and examined his bloody left side and right shoulder, then turned to Cathy, "Are you hurt, Mrs. Hollman?

Dan looked up at Jack. "She's fine." Then he gave him a look. "You were supposed to rescue us, asshole."

Jack grinned. "I'd have been here sooner, but my ride never showed."

"When you never showed, I figured something was wrong, so I went upstairs to the office and called your house. There was no answer, so I looked at the map and knew there would be only one reason you didn't show up. I got here as fast as I could." He nodded toward the stairs. "I'll go upstairs, find a phone, call this in, and get you two an ambulance."

***Thirty-Three ***

An hour later, Vernon Schmidt's farm had turned into a hectic scene of police cars, a coroner's wagon, an ambulance, and several uniformed police officers. Captain Foley stood on the porch next to Jack Brolin as the ambulance carrying Dan and Cathy pulled away from the front porch, siren blasting, chasing its headlights toward the open gate at the end of the long driveway.

Watching the ambulance turn onto Rural Route 15 heading toward Denver, Captain Foley turned to Jack. "Your partner and his lady friend are lucky. They both could have been killed here tonight."

Hearing a sound, Jack and Foley turned, seeing a gray cat run from the open front door of the house across the porch, then disappear into the night. Jack looked back through the empty night toward RR15. "Yes, Captain, I believe they are lucky. Very lucky."

Having read the Chicago Newspaper story about Vernon Schmidt and the Denver Police Detective who was shot while saving a woman held captive, Robert Morgan boarded a Trailways bus for Denver. Three days later, he stood in the doorway of his father's hospital room, set his suitcase on the floor, stood quietly at the door, and watched his father sleeping.

Dan slowly opened his eyes and looked at the blurry figure, and as his vision cleared, he smiled. "I have to get myself shot before you come to visit?"

Robert's face filled with a broad smile. He picked up his suitcase, walked across the room, set it on the floor, and then bent down and gave Dan a small hug. "Are you going to be alright, Dad?"

Dan smiled. "I'm going to be just fine, son."

Robert looked worried. "The Chicago newspaper carried the story about the terrible things this Vernon Schmidt had done over the years." He paused. "When I saw your name…." Robert paused.

"I know, son." Dan gestured to a chair sitting a few feet away. "Pull up a chair. I have a few things to tell you."

Curious about what those things could be, Robert pulled up the chair, sat down, and listened while Dan told him the truth about his uncle Donnie and all the years his grandfather had spent searching for the killer. While he listened, Robert thought about the death of his sister and knew his dad had searched for the driver of the car in the same way as his grandfather had searched for his uncle's killer. When Dan finished, Robert had tears in his eyes. "I'm sorry for the way I've acted, Dad."

Dan reached out and took his hand. "That's all behind us now, son." Then he smiled. "Time for a new start."

Robert wiped his eyes and smiled. "How is the lady you rescued?"

"She's going to be okay. It was a terrible ordeal for her." He looked at Robert. "You should know that she saved my life."

"I didn't know that. What happened?"

Dan told his son all about Cathy, why Vernon took her, and what happened that night at the farmhouse.

Cathy appeared in the doorway dressed in a hospital robe. Seeing the suitcase, she looked at the man sitting in a chair next to Dan's bed and knew right away who he was.

Dan sat up. "Son, this is Cathy Holman."

Robert turned as he stood. "Hello."

Dan smiled proudly. "This is my son, Robert."

Cathy smiled as she walked across the room, held out her hand, and as they shook hands, she said, "Your father has spoken of you often. He's very proud of you."

Looking a little embarrassed, Robert told her to sit in his chair.

Instead, she sat down on the edge of Dan's hospital bed, smiled as she took Dan's hand, then turned to Robert. "How long are you going to be in Denver?"

"I have a week's vacation."

Cathy glanced at Dan, then looked at Robert. "Is there a girl in Chicago?"

Robert put his head down, looking embarrassed, and then smiled at her. "There is a girl."

Dan looked surprised but happy. "Tell us about her. What's her name?"

"Not much to tell. Her name is Barbara, and we're both tellers working at the same bank."

"Do you have a picture?" asked Cathy.

Robert grinned proudly and reached into his back pocket, pulled out his wallet, and opened it to a picture of Barbara.

"She's very pretty," said Cathy.

"Yes, she is," agreed Dan. "You're a lucky man."

The nurse came in to give Dan his medications, so Cathy stood from the bed and squeezed Dan's hand, saying she would be back a little later. She looked at Robert as they shook hands again. "I hope I get to see you before you leave." She turned, smiled at Dan, and then stepped into the hall.

While the nurse attended to Dan, Robert followed Cathy into the hall. "Mrs. Holman."

345

She turned, and half smiled with curiosity. "Call me Cathy."

Robert glanced back at his father's hospital room. "I can tell from the way you two look at one another that you're more than just friends, and I'm glad Dad has someone."

"I'm glad you feel that way, Robert. That means a lot to me, and I'm sure it will to your father. He loves you very much and has missed you terribly."

Robert glanced back at the door to the room and then looked at her. "I know he has been lonely this past couple of years, and I'm to blame for that. I've been a foolish son."

Cathy tenderly put one hand on the side of his face, leaned forward, and kissed his cheek. "Go spend some time with your father. He needs you."

Cathy was released from the hospital a few days before Dan, spending the first few days with her aunt and uncle until she felt that she could go home. When she returned to her house, a healthy Butch accompanied her, and in time, she fully recovered from the ordeal, and the nightmares ended.

A few days after being released from the hospital, Dan hugged his son as he boarded a Trailways bus destined for Chicago and watched the bus until it disappeared around the next corner. Staring at the empty street and feeling a little sad, he turned and walked to his car. In time his wounds healed, and Dan made it a point to visit the graves of his father and mother. Sitting on the grass, he told them that with the help of his father's notebook, he had caught Donnie's killer. Before he left the cemetery, he placed a dozen red roses on Ruth Spencer's grave.

Dan and Cathy married in the spring of 1952, sold both of their homes, and bought a new home in East Denver, not far from where Jack and Lori live. Both Dan and Jack received commendations and promotions for solving the murders, and Dan continues to visit the graves of his wife Norma, their daughter Nancy, and his friend Ruth Spencer every month.

Epilogue

After the death of Donnie Morgan, Vernon Davis Schmidt fought his urges until he could no longer resist the beast that would one day control his life.

Soon after his 20th birthday in 1925 and no longer satisfied with the torture of small animals he had killed and buried on the farm, he abducted his second victim, a young girl from Brighton, Colorado. After hours of torture, he cut her throat and watched her bleed out on the ground next to his uncle's pickup truck. Taking her finger was an afterthought, but one which became part of his ritual. The beast was satisfied for several months, and he killed only occasionally. It was not until his return from the war in 1943 that the beast's appetite began to grow.

Police agencies' inability to communicate easily with one another made it possible for Vernon Davis Schmidt's reign of terror to go unnoticed for over thirty years. Had it not been for his obsession with Dan Morgan, he more than likely would never have been caught.

Over the next several weeks after Vernon's death, the unworked land behind the barn gave up the skeletons of sixty-three teenage girls from southern Wyoming, western Kansas, and various parts of Colorado. With the help of the items in Vernon's trophy room, most of the families of Vernon Schmidt's victims found closure for their losses. Jack had taken Donnie's belongings out of the bin and gave them to Dan after he was released from the hospital. Dan made a small wooden box, put Donnie's belongings into it along with the pictures of Donnie, the coroner's report, and his father's notepad, and buried them next to his father's headstone, hoping he now could rest in peace.

Other books by Richard Greene

Death of Innocence

Befriended by a slave and the captain of a riverboat, a young runaway named Joseph Samuel Greene finds adventure on the river and the love of a young Mary McAlexander. The Civil War will not only test their love for one another but the faith of the McAlexander, Chrisman and Patterson families as each endures the war's death and destruction.

Death rides across the South in the guise of the southern home guard, taking the innocent without hesitation or regret. The sorrow they leave will last forever as each proud family endures while losing their innocence.

The book Death of Innocence is a story about five families of my ancestors who lived during the Civil War. The story is based on fact, along with fiction and family lore. What happened to each of these families, for the most part, is true, but I also added in some fiction to fill in the gaps. Joseph Samuel Greene, the main character, was my great-grandfather. I think you will find the story interesting as well as entertaining.

Wade Garrison's Promise

Wade Garrison is a simple man who, as a young man, came west chasing the stories he had read about in cheap western novels while growing up on a farm in South Carolina. He is not a violent man, and like most men of humble beginnings, he holds his name and promises in high regard.

Watching the pine coffin containing his friend Emmett Spears's lifeless body lowered into the dark grave Wade makes a silent promise of revenge. It is a promise that will take him far from the girl he loves and the Circle T Ranch in eastern Colorado.

As young Wade Garrison trails the four men responsible for his friend's death, he will soon find himself unprepared for the death and violence he will find. He is unaware that in fulfilling his promise to avenge Emmett Spears, he will lose himself in the process.

Wade Garrison

God's Coffin

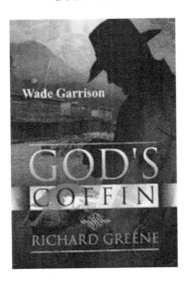

Sequel to Wade Garrison's Promise

Wade Garrison rides out of Harper, Colorado, into the New Mexico Territory in 1872, believing he is riding away from a troubled past.

Now, six years later, his old friend, Sheriff Seth Bowlen, in Sisters, Colorado, is in trouble and needs help. Sheriff Bowlen sends a wire to United States Marshal Billy French in Santa Fe, who, in turn, sends Deputy Marshal Wade Garrison to help their old friend.

Innocently, Wade decides to take his wife, Sarah, and son Emmett, with him so they can visit her family in Harper, a small town northeast of Sisters. As he and his family boarded the train in Santa Fe, he could not have known that a terrible storm of violence was already brewing, and this fateful decision could destroy his wife and child.

Wade Garrison

Atonement

Sequel to God's Coffin

In August 1878, Wade Garrison took his vengeance against the men who took the life of his unborn daughter and tried to kill his wife and son to settle a score. When the last man was dead from Wade's Sharps Rifle, he rode out of Harper, Colorado, a wanted man, and disappeared into the Montana Territory.

Morgan Hunter was a forty-eight-year-old gunman from west Texas `wanted for killing a sheriff and his deputy. Fleeing from those killings and riding away from the sorrow that caused them, he rode into the Montana Territory. Unaware of the other, both men rode toward the same destiny.

Sarah looked toward the top of the hill every day, waiting for Wade and his red sorrel mare to come home. The days turned into weeks and then into months, and still no word of him or from him. The only person she could turn to was the man who was inadvertently responsible for all that had taken place, Sheriff Seth Bowlen.

Wade Garrison

The Last Ride

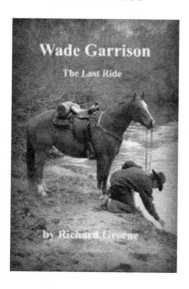

Sequel to Atonement

It has been a year since Wade was shot and nearly died after being found innocent of murder at his trial in Harper, Colorado. Keeping his promise to God and Sarah, his Colt pistol lies tucked away in the bottom drawer of a chest in his bedroom, and the Sharps rifle covered in the rawhide sheath stands in a corner behind the chest. While he misses the life of a United States Deputy Marshal, he is content being with his wife Sarah, son Emmett, and daughter Mary Louise on their ranch.

Unknown to Wade and Sarah, he is about to be thrust into a life of violence once again by events in the small town of Harper, Colorado. When the people of Harper seek his help for justice, the old life pulls at him. Resisting those old ways, he fears the town and his son will think he is a coward. How can he break his promise to not only Sarah but to God?

353

The Last Time I Saw My Dad

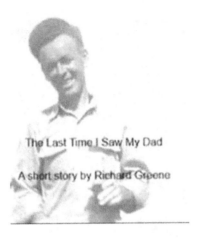

My Dad, Edward Greene, left the family in 1951. This true-to-life short story is about the last time I saw my dad in 1961. The story deals with lots of memories of the summers I spent in Houston, Texas while visiting my dad.

*****

Made in the USA
Monee, IL
28 April 2024

57634065R00203